TREMAINE'S TRUE LOVE

THE TRUE GENTLEMEN—BOOK ONE

GRACE BURROWES

GRACE BURROWES PUBLISHING

DEDICATION

Dedicated to those for whom
the love of animals has become a calling

CHAPTER ONE

"The greatest plague ever to bedevil mortal man, the greatest threat to his peace, the most fiendish source of undeserved humility is *his sister*, and spinster sisters are the worst of a bad lot."

In the corridor outside the formal parlor, Nicholas, Earl of Belle-fonte, sounded very certain of his point.

"Of course, my lord," somebody replied softly, "but, my lord—"

"I tell you, Hanford," the earl went on, "if it wouldn't imperil certain personal masculine attributes which my countess holds dear, I'd turn Lady Nita right over my—"

"My lord, you have a visitor."

Hanford's pronouncement came off a little desperately but had the effect of silencing his lordship's lament. Quiet words were exchanged beyond the door, giving Tremaine St. Michael time to step away from the parlor's cozy fireplace, where he'd been shamelessly warming a personal attribute of his own formerly frozen to the saddle.

Bellefonte's greeting as he strode into the parlor a moment later was as enthusiastic as his ranting had been.

"Our very own Mr. St. Michael! You are early. This is not fashionable. In fact, were I not the soul of congeniality, I'd call it unsporting in the extreme."

"Bellefonte." Tremaine St. Michael bowed, for Bellefonte was his social superior, also one of few men whose height and brawn exceeded Tremaine's.

"Don't suppose you have any sisters?" Bellefonte asked with a rueful smile. "I have four. They're what my grandmother calls *lively*."

So lively, Bellefonte had apparently bellowed at one of these sisters for the entire ten minutes Tremaine had been left to admire the spotless Turkey carpets in Belle Maison's formal parlor. The sister's responses had been inaudible and then an upstairs door had slammed.

"Liveliness is a fine quality in a young lady," Tremaine said, because he was a guest in this house, and sociability was called for if he was to relieve Bellefonte of substantial assets.

His lordship was welcome to keep all four sisters, thank you very much.

"Fat lot you know," Bellefonte retorted, taking a position with his back to the fire. "If every man in the House of Lords had rounded up his *lively* sisters and sent them to France, the Corsican would have been on bended knee, seeking asylum of old George in a week flat. How was your journey?"

Bellefonte had the blond hair and blue eyes of many an English aristocrat. The corners of those eyes crinkled agreeably, and he'd followed up Tremaine's bow with a hearty handshake.

Bellefonte would never be a friend, but he was friendly.

"My journey was uneventful, though cold," Tremaine said. "I apologize for making good time down from Town."

"I apologize for complaining. I am blessed in my family, truly, but Lady Nita, my oldest sister, is particularly strong willed." Bellefonte's hearty bonhomie faded to a soft smile as feminine laughter rang out in the corridor.

"You were saying?" Tremaine prompted. When would his lordship offer a guest a damned drink?

"Nothing of any moment, St. Michael. My countess and my sister Della have taken note of your arrival, though her ladyship has an urgent appointment in the nursery. Shall we to the library, where the best libation and coziest hearth await? Beckman gave me to understand you're not the tea-and-crumpets sort."

When and why had his lordship's brother conveyed that sentiment? Another thought intruded on Tremaine's irritation: Bellefonte knew his womenfolk by their laughter. How odd was that?

"I'm the whisky sort," Tremaine said. "Winter ale wouldn't go amiss either." Not brandy though. Not if Tremaine could help it.

His lordship was too well-bred to raise an eyebrow at tastes refined in drovers' inns the length of the realm.

"Whisky, then. Hanford!"

A little old fellow in formal livery stepped into the parlor. "My lord?"

Bellefonte directed the butler to send some decent sandwiches 'round to the library, to fetch the countess to her husband's side when the fiend in the nursery had turned loose of her, and to inform the housekeeper that Mr. St. Michael was on the premises earlier than planned.

His lordship set a smart pace down carpeted hallways, past bouquets of white hothouse roses, across gleaming parquet floors, to a high-ceilinged, oak-paneled treasury of books. Belle Maison was a well-maintained example of the last century's enthusiasm for the spacious country seat, and whoever had designed the house had had an eye for light.

The library was blessed with tall windows at regular intervals, and the red velvet draperies were caught back, despite the cold. Winter sunshine bounced cheerily off mirrors, brass, and silver, and here, too, the hearth was blazing extravagantly.

The entire impression—genial Lord Bellefonte; his dear, plaguey sisters; roaring fires even in empty rooms; the casual wealth lined up on the library's endless, sunny shelves—left Tremaine feeling out of place. He had been in countless aristocratic family seats and more than a few castles and palaces. The out-of-place feeling he experienced at Belle Maison was the fault of the sisters, whom Bellefonte clearly loved and worried over.

Commerce, Tremaine comprehended, and even gloried in.

Sisters had no part in commerce, but the lively variety could apparently transform an imposing family seat into a home. Bellefonte's sisters inspired slammed doors, fraternal grumbling, and even laughter, and in this, Belle Maison was a departure from Tremaine's usual experience with titled English families.

"I know you intend to stay for only a few days," Bellefonte said, gesturing to a pair of chairs beneath a tall window, "but my countess declares that will not do. You are to visit for at least two weeks, so the neighbors may come by and inspect you. Don't worry. I'll warn you which ones have marriageable daughters—which is most of them—and my brother George will distract the young ladies."

After the winter journey from Town, the cozy library and plush armchair were exquisitely comfortable. To Tremaine, who had vivid memories of Highland winters, comfortable was never a bad thing.

"A few days might be all the time I can spare, my lord," Tremaine said, seating himself in cushioned luxury. "The press of business waits for no man, and wasted time is often wasted money."

"Protest is futile, no matter how sensible your arguments," Bellefonte countered, folding his length into the second chair. "My countess has spoken, and my sisters will abet her. You are an eligible bachelor and therefore a doomed man."

The earl crossed long legs at the ankle, the picture of a fellow to whom *doom* was a merry concept. "Her ladyship will ply you with delicacies at every meal," he went on. "Kirsten will interrogate you about your business ventures, Susannah will discuss that Scottish poet fellow with you, and Della will catch you up on all the Town gossip. George will be glad you're on hand to distract our sisters. The Haddonfield womenfolk are like faeries. A man falls into their clutches and time ceases to have meaning."

Avoid faeries as if your life depends on it. Tremaine's Scottish grandfather had smacked that lesson into his hard little head before Tremaine had been breeched.

"What about your sister Lady Bernita?" Tremaine asked. The sister putting the worry and exasperation in her brother's eyes and inspiring the earl to raise his voice.

Tremaine would never approach an objective without reconnoitering first. Knowing who got on with whom often made the difference between closing a deal or watching the profits waltz into some other fellow's pocket.

"Oh, her." Bellefonte's gaze went to the window, which looked out over terraced gardens in all their winter solemnity. Rosebushes were pruned back to knee height, so that only canes of thorny bracken remained. The shadows of the hedges harbored dirty snow, and not a single bird enlivened the scene.

A tall, blond woman marched off toward the stables along a walk of crushed white shells. She wore a riding habit of dark blue and a man's riding jacket—no clever hat or pheasant feather cocked over her ear—and her briskly swishing hems were muddy.

Bellefonte's gaze followed the woman, his expression forlorn. "Lady Nita is very dear to me. She will be the death of us all."

The baby was small and vigorously alive, two points in her favor—possibly the only two.

"Your mother is resting," Nita said to the infant's oldest sibling, "and this is your new sister. Does she have a name?"

Eleven-year-old Mary took the bundle from Nita's arms. "Ma said a girl would be Annie Elizabeth. Ma wanted a boy though. Boys can do more work."

"Boys also eat more, make more noise, and run off to become soldiers or worse," Nita said. Boys became young wastrels who disported with the local soiled dove, heedless of the innocent life resulting from their pleasures, heedless that the soiled dove was a baronet's granddaughter and a squire's daughter. "Have you had anything to eat today, Mary?"

"Bread."

Thin, freckled, and wearing a dress that likely hadn't been washed in weeks, Mary looked younger than her eleven years—also much, much older.

"Your mother will need more than bread to recover from this birth," Nita said. "I've brought butter, sausage, jam, sugar, boiled eggs, and tea in the sack on the table."

Nita would have milk sent over too. She'd been distracted by her altercation with Nicholas, and in her haste to reach Addy Chalmers's side, she'd neglected the most obvious need.

Mary pressed a kiss to Annie's brow. "She's ever so dear."

Would that the child's mother viewed the baby similarly. Nita went down to her haunches, the better to impress on young Mary what must be said.

"When Annie fusses, you bring her to your mother to nurse. When Annie's had her fill, you burp her and take her back to her blankets. She'll sleep a lot at first, but she needs to sleep where it's quiet, warm, and safe." Though the little cottage wouldn't be warm again until summer.

Mary cradled the newborn closer. "I'll watch out for her, Lady Nita. Ma won't have any custom for weeks, and that means no gin. Wee Annie will grow up strong."

Mary was an astute child, of necessity.

Nita rose, feeling the cold and the lateness of the hour in every joint and muscle. "I'll send the vicar's wife by next week, and she'll have more food for you and your brothers, and maybe even some coal." The vicar's maid of all work would, in any case. "You store the food where nobody can steal it, and here..." Nita withdrew five shillings from a pocket. "Don't tell anybody you have this. Not your mother, not your brothers, not even wee Annie. This is for bread and butter, not for gin."

"Thank you, Lady Nita."

"I'll come back next week to check on your mother," Nita said, shrugging into one of George's cast-off coats. "If she runs a fever or if the baby is doing poorly, come for me or send one of your brothers."

Mary bobbed an awkward curtsy, the baby in her arms. "Yes, Lady Nita."

Then Nita had nothing more to do except climb onto Atlas's broad back and let the horse find his way home through the frigid darkness.'

~

"They are charming, the lot of them," Tremaine said. "I'd forgotten what a big, happy family can do to a man's composure." Particularly a big, happy, healthy family with Saxon good looks and a thriving appreciation for life's finer comforts. "Bellefonte is besotted," Tremaine went on, scratching William's hairy withers. "As is his countess."

"I'm told it works better that way."

William hadn't spoken—William was a gelding and the voice was decidedly feminine.

A tall, blond female, rosy cheeked from the cold, led a saddled specimen of plow stock down the barn aisle. The flame of the stable's single lantern gilded red and gold highlights in her hair, and the hem of her dark blue riding habit was damp.

She brought the beast to a halt outside William's stall. "I don't recognize you, sir."

Tremaine recognized her though. The sculpted cheekbones, defined chin, height, and bearing—and the muddy hem—proclaimed the late-night arrival to be Lady Nita Haddonfield, oldest of the earl's sisters, and the selfsame woman who'd marched across the barren gardens hours ago.

"Tremaine St. Michael, at your service, my lady. I am visiting your brother to discuss common business interests."

Something about his recitation bothered her. She was too tired to hide it, or perhaps she didn't care if she offended him.

"May I take your horse, my lady?" Though why the grooms weren't thundering down from their quarters above the carriage house, Tremaine could not guess.

"Why would you do that?" she asked, stuffing her gloves into a pocket. She wore a man's coat, well made but too big, as if sized for one of her brothers. The cuffs had been turned back to accommodate her shorter arms, the collar turned up.

The great beast at her side let out a gusty sigh, as if to say debate and discussion could wait until he'd been unsaddled.

"I'd see to your horse because you are a lady and I am a gentleman," Tremaine said, which was half-true, "and you should not have to manage your own mount at this late hour." She should not be *allowed* to do a groom's work at any hour.

Her ladyship patted the horse's shaggy neck. "Atlas and I have kept much later hours than this. I'll unsaddle him, but if you'd make sure he has hay and water, I'd appreciate it."

What manner of lady went about unescorted after dark with what looked like bloodstains on the cuff of her sleeve?

Tremaine made short work of the hay and water, and Lady Nita was equally efficient removing the horse's saddle and bridle. Atlas ambled into his stall without being haltered or led, and commenced a friendly sniffing through the bars with William.

"Your gelding is very handsome," Lady Nita said, closing the stall door. "Atlas's charms are more subtle."

Nothing about Atlas was subtle. He had feet the size of tea trays and quarters suitable for displaying an entire service.

"Charms such as?" Tremaine asked.

"Atlas has never been known to buck or spook. Steadiness in a fellow is a fine quality."

Very likely the horse was too lazy to buck or spook, though he applied himself to his fodder with singular diligence.

While Lady Nita's eyes were shadowed with fatigue. "Your absence was remarked at dinner, my lady."

"You know who I am, then. Nobody warned me you were coming, Mr. St. Michael, or I might have sent my regrets to dinner."

Suggesting her ladyship would not have attended, even if she'd known the family was entertaining.

"May I escort you back to the house?" Tremaine asked. "I've assured myself William's not kicking down a wall or dying of thirst, and the day has been wearying." Dinner with the Haddonfields had been every bit as wearying as the trip down from London, though significantly warmer.

"My thanks for your courtesy."

Her ladyship's thanks were tired though sincere. Why had no one come out from the house to see to her well-being? Tremaine took the lantern down from its peg, causing shadows to grow and dance. He did not offer his arm. A woman who could ride the countryside by moonlight was well equipped to negotiate the paths of her own garden.

"Is my presence at Belle Maison an unpleasant surprise?" he asked.

Her younger sisters would have turned Tremaine's question into a joke or a flirtation. The Haddonfields seemed much given to joking and flirtation, with the exception of present company.

"Please do not be offended if I say your presence is a matter of indifference to me now," her ladyship informed him as they left the stable for the chilly air of a winter night. "Not so very long ago, I was the one who would have made sure your room was prepared, a bath waiting for you, refreshment and cut flowers in the chamber I'd selected for you."

Tremaine appreciated honesty more than he did the laughter and banter of the Haddonfield dinner table.

"I do not presume to know you, but arranging flowers and ordering a tea tray could not be much of a challenge for you."

His observation pleased her ladyship enough that a hint of a smile flitted across her features, while somewhere in the distance, a dog commenced barking. In the manner of winter nights, the sound carried, lonely and annoying.

Lady Nita moved along the garden path far more slowly than she had hours earlier. Either she was exhausted, or she wasn't looking forward to returning to her home.

"I'd like to sit for a moment," she said as they approached a gazebo. "Seek your bed, if you wish. I'll be fine alone."

She believed this, despite the cold, despite the hour, despite her obvious fatigue. Tremaine took a seat beside her, ignoring the siren call of his quilts and pillows because, in another sense, she was not fine.

Lady Nita was quite alone, however, and Tremaine knew how that felt. A half-moon hung above the horizon, stars shone in frosty abundance, and the dog had gone silent.

"The child lived," she said. "I want to wake up each and every member of my family and inform them of that. The mother was also resting comfortably when I took my leave of her."

"You attended a birth." The only acceptable reason for blood-stains on a lady's attire.

"The midwife can only attend one birth at a time," Lady Nita said. "The babies are rude though. They do not appear one at a time. I have explained this to my brother repeatedly. In fact, when the weather changes, the babies conspire to arrive all at once, and the midwife, understandably, will go where her services are remuner-ated. The women with the least consequence deliver with the least support, and yet they need the most help."

Despite Lady Nita's calm and euphemistic summary, she was all in a lather. Her emotional fists were raised, and she would make her blows count.

Though she wouldn't rain them down on Tremaine. "You are a reproach to your family, then," he concluded.

The lantern sat on the bench opposite them, casting little light because the wick was low. Even so, Tremaine had the sense his words earned him the first smidgen of genuine regard from the lady beside him.

"I am a reproach, Mr. St. Michael? They've certainly become free with chides and scolds aimed in my direction."

Now they were. Now that she'd been deposed as lady of the manor. Bellefonte probably hadn't the first inkling of the hurt he'd done Lady Nita when he'd acquired a countess.

Tremaine's backside ached from hours in a cold saddle, and yet he remained on the equally cold bench a moment longer. He withdrew the lady's gloves from the oversized pocket in which she'd jammed them and passed them to her.

"A great debate ensued after the fish course, my lady, as to whether country assemblies should permit the waltz when so few know how to dance it properly. While this inanity held the company's entire attention, you helped a new life get a start in the world. Yes, you are a reproach to your family, and to all who think Christian charity is a matter of Sunday finery and Boxing Day benevolence."

A great sigh went out of her ladyship, interrupted by a sneeze. She leaned her head back against a support and closed her eyes. She hadn't put on her gloves.

"You're Scottish," she observed.

What Tremaine was, was cold. He put his handkerchief on the bench between them, in case the sneezing, tired, honest lady had need of it. Despite Lady Nita's willingness to wrestle demons on behalf of the newborn parish poor, she was attractive.

The local beauties would refer to her as "handsome" in an effort to denigrate her features politely, but she was lovely nonetheless. Her brows were the perfect graceful complement to wide, intelligent eyes; her eyes, nose, and mouth were assembled into a face that deserved excellent portraiture and needed no cosmetics.

The beauty of her features was such that even weariness became her.

"I can sound Scottish," Tremaine said, "particularly when in the grip of strong sentiment. My mother was born in Aberdeenshire." He could hold a grudge like a Scot too, and endure cold and handle strong drink.

"And your father?" She had a good ear, did Lady Nita. Also pretty ears.

"French." Tremaine waited for her to put more questions to him, but she instead turned the lamp wick down until the light extinguished.

"We were wasting oil," she said.

"The hour is late and the night cold. We should go in. If you'd like to linger here in solitude, I'll bid you good evening," Tremaine said, rising. To be found alone with him in the dark would cause greater problems for the lady than to be found alone with her discontents.

He bowed over her bare, cold, elegant hand. "A pleasure to have made your acquaintance, my lady."

Tremaine left Lady Nita the unlit lamp and his handkerchief and made his way to the house. Nita Haddonfield was an earl's daughter who understood the practicalities, and she didn't dress her sentiments up in tedious dinner conversation. She was easily Tremaine's favorite Haddonfield of the lot.

What a pity he'd have no time to get to know her.

In Nita's experience, the best intelligence officers in any big family were found among the younger siblings. They began their careers while small, nonthreatening, and unobtrusive. By adolescence, they developed formidable powers of observation and recollection, to say nothing of an ability to lurk at keyholes and befriend the servants.

Thus, Nita started her morning with a visit to Della's room. Her youngest sister liked to sleep late, a habit Della claimed would stand her in good stead when she made her come-out in the spring.

"Wake up, Baby Sister," Nita said, exchanging a look with the chambermaid adding coal to the hearth. "It's a new day and breakfast awaits."

"Spring?" came from the tangle of pillows and blankets.

"Not yet, but Nicholas and George will eat up all the oranges if you tarry abed, and Kirsten will swill every last drop of chocolate."

Nicholas, Kirsten, and George would gobble up every crumb on the breakfast sideboard given the opportunity. Ethan and Beckman were similarly fond of their victuals—as was Nita.

"Tray." A croak that nonetheless sounded imperious.

"Leah permits only tea trays in the bedrooms in the morning," Nita said, climbing onto Della's bed. "She thinks we should join each other for the morning meal." A fine theory, though Nita typically made it a habit to come down earlier or later than her siblings.

"Hate you." Della's dark crown disappeared beneath the covers.

Nita took an orange from her pocket and began to peel it while she waited for the maid to leave.

"I have a few questions, and I'm willing to bargain for the answers," Nita said when privacy was assured and the peel stripped from the orange.

"Go away, Nita."

"I'll bargain with fresh sections of a sweet, juicy orange."

Della flipped the covers down to peer at her sister. "Fiend. What do you want to know?"

Nita held out a bite of fresh fruit, which was like dangling a bit of haddock before a barn cat. "Tell me about Mr. St. Michael."

Della took the piece of orange. "He's here to transact business with Nicholas, at least nominally. Something about the woolly sheep Papa bought from the King all those years ago. This is a divine orange."

Nita helped herself to a bite. "It's quite good. You're sure Nicholas isn't matchmaking?"

"He might be, or maybe Leah is," Della said, pushing to a sitting position and accepting the rest of the orange. "Kirsten was convivial at dinner, and Mr. St. Michael made Susannah blush."

"Kirsten was convivial in a pleasant way or a Kirsten way?" For Kirsten was beset with a restlessness that could make her a difficult conversation partner for the average, unsuspecting gentleman.

Della munched philosophically on another section of orange. "Kirsten behaved, which was interesting. Mr. St. Michael spouted some poem about a mouse, and Susannah was impressed."

Nita was impressed with Mr. St. Michael as well. For starts, he hadn't had a fit of the vapors when she'd put up her own horse last night. Men, particularly gentlemen, were prone to the vapors, in Nita's experience. Mr. St. Michael had instead helped when Nita had asked it of him.

How lovely, to meet a man who *helped* rather than fussed and scolded.

Nita had also been impressed with Mr. St. Michael's voice, which had blended beguilingly with night shadows and winter-brilliant stars. His burr hinted of far-off hills and the canny competence of a man who'd bested life on his own terms, rather than through hereditary advantages. He spoke slowly, though Nita had no doubt his mind was as nimble as a baby goat.

Despite his canniness, Mr. St. Michael's company in the frigid little gazebo had been restful. He didn't presume or put on airs. He smelled good, and he was of a size with Nita's brothers while being far less inclined to share his opinions uninvited.

His features were not refined, having already acquired a weathered quality about his eyes, and yet his looks would change little as he aged. He'd become distinguished, and he already managed to be formidable, for all his unassuming ways.

Nita could not see Mr. St. Michael spouting poetry though, much less about a mouse. Shrewd of him, to realize literary matters were dear to Susannah's heart.

"I'm glad Mr. St. Michael trotted out his poetry for Susannah," Nita said. "He'll remind Suze that the list of eligibles does not begin and end with Edward Nash." Though the present list of suitors for Susannah's hand did.

"Mr. Nash is kind to Susannah," Della said, tearing apart the last two sections of orange. "What's more, she likes him. Where did you get this orange?"

"I still have my set of keys to the larders," Nita said, taking the second succulent portion for herself. "Edward Nash is not a suitable husband for any of you, and that's an end to it."

Della drew her knees up, her dark braid falling in a ratty rope over one shoulder. She was out of the schoolroom but could still look achingly young.

"It's not like you to be a snob, Nita. Edward is old-fashioned about some things, but Susannah is too. Help me dress, and we'll further inspect Mr. St. Michael over breakfast."

The offer was generous and would assure at least one other sibling joined Nita at the table. Having rested and considered the previous evening's encounter with Mr. St. Michael, Nita was not proud of her behavior. Fatigue and delivering another baby doomed to poverty or worse had soured her manners, and a guest at Belle Maison deserved better than that.

"I'm in a green mood today," Della said, slogging out of the bed. "Green and warm, not in that order. You were out quite late."

That Della would notice was reassuring. "Addy Chalmers had a girl. Mother and child were doing well enough when I left."

Della stretched luxuriously, like a small, sleek cat upon rising from a cozy hearth. "I don't know how you stand it, Nita. Let's hope this child fares better than the last. Velvet for today, I think, and my paisley shawl."

Nita helped Della dress and arrange her hair, but that small comment, about hoping the child fared better than Addy Chalmers's last baby, stung.

Della was as kindhearted as the next young woman of means and good birth, but a child's life and death should be worth more than a passing sentiment expressed between the wardrobe and the vanity.

～

Tremaine endured as much conviviality from the Haddonfields over breakfast as he had at dinner the previous evening, though the informality of the morning meal meant Bellefonte could bill and coo at his countess even more openly.

Tremaine's tolerance for billing and cooing had improved in recent months, with the reintroduction into his life of his late brother's wife, child, and the wife's sister, but Bellefonte's besottedness would strain anybody's digestion.

The earl lifted a pink Sevres teapot in his countess's direction. "More tea, lovey?"

The countess patted his hand. "I'm having chocolate, Nicholas."

His lordship took a sip of the countess's beverage. "So you are. Cold mornings call for the fortification of chocolate. Ah, Nita, and who is that with you? Given the hour, that cannot possibly be our dearest little Della."

Two Haddonfield sisters stood in the door, one petite and dark, the other tall, fair, and not as sure of herself as she had been the previous evening.

"Ladies, good morning." Tremaine rose and held out the chair next to him, letting the invitation stand or fall on its own merit. Lady Nita obliged him by taking the seat he offered, which put her directly in the path of a sharp beam of winter sunshine.

The morning light revealed fatigue around her eyes and mouth, and confirmed that she was not in the first blush of youth. A relief, that, for reasons Tremaine did not examine when his eggs were growing cold.

"Nita reports that Addy Chalmers had a daughter," Della said, appropriating the teapot. "Nicholas, did you leave me any cream or sugar?"

A wince was exchanged at the table, between the earl and his countess, and between Lady Kirsten and Lady Susannah. George Haddonfield, who'd been the soul of good cheer the previous evening, aimed a flat stare at Lady Della.

In the space of a moment, Tremaine gained a clear sense of Lady

Nita's situation. He resisted the temptation to squeeze her hand beneath the table.

"The cream is in short supply, Lady Della," Tremaine said, passing the pitcher down the table, "but sugar remains abundant. I can also recommend the eggs, and I've seldom had bacon so delectable."

George left off glowering while Bellefonte's relief was written on his handsome features.

"Eat up, St. Michael," the earl said, "If we're to inspect the sheep, we'll have a chilly morning."

The earl's observation was a little too hearty, a little too pointless. Tremaine had already been out to check on William, and the morning's weather made "chilly" the mother of all delicate understatements.

"Nicholas, you promised me you wouldn't leave me to Vicar's tender mercies again," Lady Bellefonte said. "Twice now I've had to brave his calls on my own, and he's incapable of leaving while a cake remains on the tea tray."

While Bellefonte, of course, would excel at denuding the tray of cakes, such were the accomplishments of the typical peer.

"I would never abandon you, lovey," Bellefonte said. "At what time is His Holiness—?"

The countess clearly was not fooled by this display of guilelessness.

"I'll take Mr. St. Michael to see the sheep," Lady Nita said, when Tremaine had been hoping to see an earl scolded at his own breakfast table. "It's not that cold out if the wind remains calm. Perhaps we might make a riding party of it?"

Lady Nita aimed her question at her sisters, who'd thus far been busy demolishing their breakfasts.

"Kirsten, Della, and I are off to pay a call on Mrs. Nash," Lady Susannah replied. "We'll take the coach in this weather."

"That leaves me," George Haddonfield said, "to shepherd the

inspection of the sheep, so to speak. Shall we say in three-quarters of an hour?"

George was a spectacularly handsome young man, in the same blond, blue-eyed mold as most of his siblings. Though tall by comparison to most men, he was shorter than his older brother by several inches.

George made a more subtle job of exuding jovial harmlessness than the earl did, and he was quieter about it. Tremaine's instincts suggested George would be slow to anger, formidable when roused, loyal as hell, and attractive even when roaring drunk or in the grip of an ague.

"Your outing to see the sheep can wait for an hour," Bellefonte said. "Nita just sat down to her breakfast."

Beside Tremaine, the lady silently bristled at her brother's solicitude, as if she would rather have spoken for herself.

"Jam, my lady?" Tremaine held out the jar of preserves, and another of those familial awkwardnesses passed in silence.

"Thank you, Mr. St. Michael." Her ladyship spread raspberry jam on her toast, her movements relaxed, even graceful, while Tremaine resigned himself to cold eggs. In his thirty-odd years on earth, he'd often been grateful for far worse fare and far worse company.

Though the Haddonfields were not at peace with each other, or at least not with Lady Nita. All families endured such tensions, which was part of the reason Tremaine remained largely outside the ambit of what family he had.

He took another bite of cold eggs and vowed to pin Bellefonte down regarding the herd of merino sheep before the sun had set. The sooner Tremaine transacted his business with Bellefonte and was on his way, the better.

CHAPTER TWO

"What do you hear from my brother Beckman?" George Haddonfield asked as the horses ambled down the frozen lane.

"I hear that he's disgustingly happy with his bride." Tremaine also endured a lot of epistolary ruminating from Beckman Haddonfield about the raptures of married life. In the spirit of furthering mutual interests, Tremaine had proposed marriage to Polonaise Hunt, Beckman's sister-in-law, and been turned down flat—no great loss.

But a small loss. Tremaine would admit that much. He and Polonaise would have rubbed along together adequately.

"How is it you came to be interested in sheep?" George asked.

Nobody in his right mind admitted to an *interest* in sheep, and Tremaine enjoyed excellent mental faculties. He was, however, interested in money.

"My mother's people are Scottish, though my father was French. When France became unsafe, Mama took her sons home to Scotland. My grandfather's wealth rested on the wool trade, and I learned by his example."

A few prosaic sentences that glossed over a small boy's heartbreak and a Scottish curmudgeon's prescription for dealing with it.

"Do you *like* sheep?" Lady Nita asked.

George Haddonfield maintained a diplomatic interest in the winter-drab countryside rather than comment on an arguably peculiar—or insightful—inquiry.

"Whether I like sheep is of no moment, my lady, though I *respect* them. They have neither fangs nor claws, nor great speed or size, and yet we rely on them for a fabric without which life would lose much of its comfort. Sheep know to stick together when trouble comes calling, and they aren't too proud to bolt when imperiled."

Then too, sheep had made Tremaine wealthy.

"Perhaps your Mr. Burns should have written his poem to a sheep rather than a mouse," George quipped.

Burns had had any number of kind words for sheep—also for women and whisky.

"Soldiers owe a debt to sheep," Tremaine replied, "as does anybody seeking to keep warm in winter. Sheep ask little and give much, they look to their own, and are, in their way, stoic. To my eye, a herd of sheep is an attractive addition to any bucolic scene."

Tremaine had spoken too fiercely. Lady Nita was smiling while George Haddonfield looked vaguely puzzled. What would George think if he knew Tremaine, like any self-respecting shepherd, preferred the company of sheep to that of most people?

"I like sheep too." Lady Nita petted her shaggy beast, and she was still smiling a sweet, feminine, interesting sort of smile that shifted her countenance from pretty to... alluring.

"Not much farther," George Haddonfield said, as if they'd completed several days' forced march. "The shepherd bides in that cottage up the hill. I'll alert him to our presence."

George snugged his top hat down and cantered off, his horse's hooves beating a hard tattoo against the frozen ground.

"So tell me, my lady," Tremaine said, "does it really take you an hour to gobble up some eggs and pop into your habit?" Because, for

all Bellefonte's hospitality over tea and toast, some current had under-
lain the earl's words at breakfast.

"Nicholas needed to scold me," Lady Nita said, her tone
perfectly amiable. "He worries, and now that he's a papa, his worry
goes in all directions, like so many chickens when a hound gets loose
among them."

"He scolded you for helping a neighbor in childbed?" Tremaine
hadn't taken Bellefonte for a man to insist on class distinctions in the
midst of the dire and delicate matter of childbirth.

"My mother attended many births," Lady Nita said, "and I
accompanied her when I grew older. Nicholas understands, as Papa
did, that childbirth is not a time to stand on ceremony, but I sent my
groom home when darkness fell."

Tremaine prided himself on a complement of common sense
from both his French and his Scottish antecedents, so he parsed the
rest of the situation out for himself.

"Your neighbor lives in a humble dwelling," he guessed, "a single
room, likely, and the groom's choices were to be present at a birth or
brave the elements for hours on end. You apprised your brother of
your reasoning?"

"I did not. I was too angry."

And her brother was too besotted with his countess. "When I was
too angry," Tremaine mused, "my grandfather sent me to the Highlands, though my problem was, in truth, grief and fear rather than
temper. Mama and Papa had both perished in the bloody glory of
France's transition from one sort of despotism to another, and I could
not comprehend why they'd been taken from me."

Nor could Tremaine comprehend why he'd confide so old and
useless a facet of his childhood to this woman.

"Then you're truly interested in buying these sheep?" she asked.

"What else would I be interested in?" As Tremaine posed the
question, a glimmer of insight befell him. "Or should that be 'who
else'?"

Off in the distance, George swung down from his horse and

knocked on the door of a stone cottage that had a plume of white smoke drifting from its sole chimney. The breeze was faintly scented with that smoke and with the familiar aroma of sheep in winter plumage.

"My three oldest brothers have all recently wed," Lady Nita said, "and thus matrimony is on their minds. Kirsten and Susannah have had their come-outs, and I sense they've given up waiting for me to choose a spouse."

Had Lady Nita given up?

"Am I being inspected?" Tremaine asked. "Should I be flattered?" What had Beckman said to his siblings, and how should Tremaine exact retribution for it?

Lady Nita brought her horse to a halt near a wooden stile set into the undulating stone fence.

"You should be careful, Mr. St. Michael, and honest. I will not tolerate any man trifling with my sisters' affections. Your sheep, sir, are in this pasture."

Tremaine was always careful, and as honest as circumstances allowed. As for the sheep, their plush, woolly coats gave them away. The merino breed was native to Spain, but for years, their export had been illegal. The King of Spain occasionally made gifts of herds to other monarchs, including a gift to George III in the last century. His Majesty had dispersed his herd by sale some years ago.

When Beckman Haddonfield had mentioned that Bellefonte owned the largest intact herd of pure merinos in Kent, Tremaine's commercial instincts had gone on full alert. Merinos grew soft, strong, abundant wool of a far higher grade than the Highland breeds could produce.

To Tremaine's highly educated eye, the specimens in Bellefonte's pasture were of good size, possessed excellent coats of wool, and were in good health.

In other words, Bellefonte's sheep were nothing short of beautiful.

Tremaine St. Michael was different from Nita's brothers, all of whom were tall, blond, and blue-eyed. They had fair complexions and came in varying degrees of too handsome. To a man, they danced well, had abundant charm, and knew beyond doubt exactly how their sisters' lives ought to unfold.

Even George, who had reason to be more tolerant than most, envisioned only a husband and babies for his sisters.

Mr. St. Michael, by contrast, was dark and direct rather than charming. Moreover, he seemed to notice what Nita's brothers did not: that she had a brain and a few ideas of her own about how her life should go on.

"I'd like to walk among the herd," Mr. St. Michael said, dismounting from his bay gelding. "Shall you come with me?"

"I'd like that."

Nita would also like a moment to slip away and check on Addy Chalmers and her baby, but that call could wait until George wasn't underfoot. The rest of Nita's current cases—Alton Horst's persistent cough, Mary Eckhardt's sore throat, Mr. Clackengeld's gout—would have to content themselves with notes and medicinals conveyed by a groom, at least until Nicholas's temper calmed.

Mr. St. Michael assisted Nita off her horse, revealing a strength commensurate with the gentleman's size. Atlas stood more than eighteen hands, meaning Nita rode a good six feet above the ground. Her descent was controlled by Mr. St. Michael's guidance, which was fortunate.

"I hate how the cold makes landing so painful," Nita said, gripping his coat sleeves for balance. "It's worse on the foot one keeps in the stirrup." If her clinging annoyed Mr. St. Michael, he didn't show it.

"Which means for men, the landing is painful for both feet. At least we're not getting more snow to go with the cold."

"Hannibal Thistlewaite says more snow is on the way." Though what would Mr. St. Michael care for an old man's arthritic predictions? Della claimed Mr. St. Michael would be gone soon anyway.

Nita's escort was tall enough that she could honestly use him to establish her balance, and even in the bitter cold, he bore a pleasant floral scent. That scent alone suggested Continental connections.

She turned loose of him and wished she'd worn a proper cloak instead of George's old coat.

"Shall we use the gate," Mr. St. Michael asked, "or can you manage the stile?"

"I've been climbing stiles since I was half my present height, sir. What are you looking for among these sheep?"

Mr. St. Michael was happy to talk about sheep—as happy as Nita had seen him. His gait was not the mincing indulgence of a gentleman escorting a lady, but rather, the stride of a man of the land inspecting his acres. He vaulted the stile in one graceful, powerful movement—he knew his way around a stile too, apparently—then assisted Nita, whose clambering about in a riding habit was ungainly indeed.

"You seek clear eyes, clear nasal passages, dense wool, healthy hooves," Nita summarized some moments later. "What else?"

Mr. St. Michael surveyed the flock, which was regarding him as well. The more cautious sheep had retreated to the far stone wall, while the nearer ones peered at their visitors curiously.

"I listen to their voices," he said, "which can indicate unwellness. I watch how they move, look for the smallest and the most stout, and about the back end, one can observe indications of ill health."

"Much like people."

Oh, drat. Oh, damn. Oh, blushes. Nita should not have said that, not when Mr. St. Michael's reference had likely been to lameness rather than digestive upset. He continued to visually inspect the sheep, his dark brows knitted, as if he had heard those three unladylike words but could not credit that they'd come from her.

"An excellent point, Lady Nita."

Heat, incongruous in the cold, crept up Nita's cheeks.

And now, Mr. St. Michael studied *her*. "A bit of color becomes you—not that your ladyship needs becoming."

Mr. St. Michael was *in trade*, he lacked genteel English good looks, and his antecedents were all wrong, and yet when he smiled...

When he smiled at Nita, spring arrived early in Kent. Tremaine St. Michael's eyes crinkled, his mouth curved up, and a conspiratorial good humor beamed from him that took Nita's breath.

His smile also made Nita foolish, for she wanted badly to smile back. "What do I need, Mr. St. Michael, if not becoming?"

Off by the stone fence, a sheep bleated plaintively.

"Perhaps your ladyship needs befriending?"

Marvelous response. How long had it been since Nita had had a friend? She stood among the sheep, who were milling ever closer, and wished Mr. St. Michael were not merely one of Nicholas's business acquaintances who'd be gone from Belle Maison by this time next week.

"A friend is a precious treasure," Nita said, though Susannah or Kirsten would have had some handy quote to serve up instead.

A moment developed, with Mr. St. Michael's nearness protecting Nita from the bitter breeze and Nita wishing she'd had that handy quote, or that George would come whistling down the lane, or that Nicholas had not been dragooned into meeting with the vicar.

The wind blew a strand of Nita's hair across her mouth— Susannah and Kirsten would also have pinned their coiffures more securely. Mr. St. Michael tucked the lock behind Nita's ear. The sensation of heat in the midst of cold assailed her again, while her insides blossomed with more of that early spring.

Whatever Mr. St. Michael might have said on the subject of friendship was interrupted by the same sheep, bleating more loudly. Mr. St. Michael swung about, toward the far fence, and cocked his head.

"Something's amiss." He marched off in the direction of the unhappy creature, the other ewes scampering from his path.

Had that particular bleating not conveyed distress, Mr. St.

Michael's brisk pace across the hard ground would have. Nita followed, though dread trickled into her belly as the bleating ewe came into view.

A small, dark, woolly lump lay steaming on the frozen earth before her.

"You've an early arrival," St. Michael said, kneeling by the ewe. "A wee tup-lamb."

The little beast wasn't moving, and what manner of God allowed an animal to be born wet and tiny in this cold? Nita cut that thought off—she and the Almighty were not in charity with each other.

"Is he dead?" she asked.

"Not yet," Mr. St. Michael replied, unbuttoning his greatcoat and untying his cravat. "But the mother can do little for him once she's given him a good licking over. At least this ewe didn't abandon him. Hard to save the ones orphaned at birth."

He continued to unbutton—his coat, his jacket, his waistcoat, his shirt even—while Nita endured a familiar blend of helplessness and anger.

"Why did it come so early?" So lethally, stupidly early.

"Some of them just do," Mr. St. Michael replied, "and some come late, and a good shepherd knows which ewes are close to delivering, which are yeld, and which will have late lambs. Had winter been mild and spring early, this fellow would have had advantages over his younger cousins. Take my gloves."

Nita scooped them up, a fine pair of riding gloves lined with some kind of fur.

Mr. St. Michael stroked a bare hand over the lamb, who was breathing in shallow, shivery pants. The ewe stamped a hoof and came closer.

Maybe, like Nita, she dreaded to see the little one suffer and dreaded more to see Mr. St. Michael end its misery. But what could a mother do, when she had neither claws nor a full complement of teeth and her newborn was threatened by the elements and by a creature at least twice her size?

"You won't kill him, will you?" Nita was enough of a country-woman to know that death was sometimes a mercy, and yet she regarded death as an enemy.

"Of course not. This little fellow is valuable livestock." Mr. St. Michael passed Nita the lamb, who weighed less than some of Susannah's books. "If you would tuck him against my belly?"

Mr. St. Michael had undone his clothing right down to his skin, and held it all open so Nita could put the wet, frigid lamb into his shirt, against his bare abdomen.

"Now do up the first few buttons," he directed. "Enough to hold the lamb against me, not enough to smother him."

Nita had to remove her gloves to comply, and while she applauded Mr. St. Michael's quick thinking, the notion of a half-frozen lamb cuddling against his bare skin nearly had her shivering.

The ewe stamped her hoof again and let go a bleat that surely held indignation and dismay. She advanced a few steps, as if to charge her offspring's captor, but stopped short and stamped again.

"I've got him," Mr. St. Michael said to the mother sheep. He moved closer, so the ewe could sniff at his shirt. "Your little lad will be safe, as long as he keeps breathing, and now I've got you too."

Like a predator striking, Mr. St. Michael scooped the ewe onto his shoulders. After some halfhearted flailing, the ewe allowed it, which was wise of her when Mr. St. Michael had all four legs in a firm grip.

He had the entire situation in a firm grip for that matter, and Nita was abruptly glad she'd volunteered to show Mr. St. Michael this herd.

"Now what, sir?"

"To the gate, which you will have to open for us." Their progress was businesslike, Mr. St. Michael slowed not one bit by seven stone of mother sheep across his shoulders. By the time Nita led him through the gate, George had emerged from the cottage and was hurrying down the path.

"Are you reaving sheep, St. Michael, or have you tired of that fine coat you're wearing?" George asked.

"The coat can be cleaned easily enough," Mr. St. Michael said. "We found an early lamb, and he needs shelter from the elements."

George was, in some ways, Nita's favorite brother. He often grasped matters his older siblings had to have explained to them, but the whereabouts of the lamb eluded him.

"The lamb is inside Mr. St. Michael's shirt, to keep warm," Nita said. "Where is Mr. Kinser?"

"He's snug by his fire and complaining of a chest cold," George said. "The lambing pens are in the byre behind the cottage."

Nita mentally added Mr. Kinser to her week's list of patients to treat by correspondence. A chest cold was simple enough—mustard plaster for the chest, a toddy for comfort—but if ignored, could rapidly become lung fever.

Nita followed George and Mr. St. Michael up the hill to a low stone building set into the slope of the land. While the granite walls provided shelter from the wind, the cold within was still considerable.

"Can a lamb possibly thrive in here?" Nita asked.

"Lambs are tough, though he needs to nurse," Mr. St. Michael said, which blunt reply inspired George to inspect the whitewashed stonework. "He'll also need a thick bed of straw."

Mr. St. Michael set the ewe down inside a wooden pen tucked against the back wall. She started up a repetitive baaing that ripped at Nita's nerves.

"She wants her baby," Nita said. Was desperate for him.

"She shall have him," Mr. St. Michael replied, "just as soon as the chambermaids have tended to the linens." He took up a pitch fork and piled a quantity of straw into the pen, his movements practiced and easy. "Mr. Haddonfield, if you could tell your shepherd it's time to move his earliest ewes in here, their presence will add to the warmth and safety of the first lambs."

George scowled at the ewe, whose racket had escalated. "I'll let him know."

"*Now* would suit, Mr. Haddonfield. Lady Nita tells me snow is on the way, and moving sheep doesn't get easier for being done in a blizzard. A dozen ewes at least. Two dozen would be better. They'll need hay, of course, and fresh water too."

None of which Mr. Kinser had yet seen to. "I doubt Difty Kinser is under the weather," Nita said when George had marched off. "Shall I unbutton you?"

"Please." Mr. St. Michael stood before her, the top of his head nearly touching the byre's rafters, while Nita undid his coat, jacket, waistcoat, and shirt. Out of medical necessity, she'd undressed grown men before—old men, ailing men, insensate men—but those experiences did not prepare her for the task she'd taken on.

Tremaine St. Michael was fit, healthy, muscular, and willing to lend his very warmth to a helpless creature. His coat was dirty as a result of the ewe's muddy underbelly across his shoulders, and yet, amid the scent of dirt and straw, Nita could still catch a whiff of flowers.

She stopped short of reaching into Mr. St. Michael's very shirt. "Is he alive?"

The ewe fell silent as Mr. St. Michael extracted the lamb from his clothing. "He is, but he wants his mama. She seems a sensible sort, which always helps."

Mr. St. Michael stepped over the board siding of the pen and held the lamb up to the ewe's nose. She licked her baby twice, and when Mr. St. Michael put the lamb down in the straw, she continued to sniff at her newborn.

"What now?" If the lamb died, Nita's list of disenchantments with the Almighty would gain another item.

"Now comes sustenance," Mr. St. Michael said, positioning the lamb near the ewe's back legs. "If he can nurse, he has a good chance. If he can't, then the ewe's first milk should be saved in case more early arrivals show up in the next day or two."

A gentleman would not have explained that much. A gentleman would not have supported the lamb as it braced on tottery legs and poked its nose about in the general direction of its first meal. A gentleman would surely not have assisted the lamb to find that first meal, but Tremaine St. Michael did.

The ewe held still—all that was required of her—and as Nita looked on, the lamb's tail twitched.

The sight of that vigorous twitch of a dark tail eased a constriction about Nita's heart.

"He's nursing?"

"Going at it like a drover at his favorite alehouse."

"Good." *Wonderful.*

Mr. St. Michael graced Nita with another one of those early-spring smiles as the lamb switched its tail again and Nita tried not to cry.

George interrupted this special, awkward moment. "Kinser says he'll have two dozen ewes up here within the hour. He was planning to move them by week's end, but this one caught him by surprise."

Mr. St. Michael climbed out of the pen. "And the hay and water?"

"I'll send some fellows over to see that it's taken care of," George said. "How's the new arrival?"

"He'll soon be sleeping, snug up against his mama, but now that the first one is on the ground, more will follow. Your shepherd will need assistance, because in this weather, somebody should check the herd for lambs regularly, even through the night. The first-time mothers and some of the older ewes will cheerfully ignore their own offspring unless reminded of their maternal obligations."

Mr. St. Michael plucked his gloves from Nita's grasp and met her gaze for an instant. His eyes held understanding, as if he knew that females of the human species could also misplace their maternal instincts, and no kindly shepherd would address their lapse.

"If we're done here," George said, "I'm for a toddy and a warm fire."

"A fine notion," Mr. St. Michael replied, pulling on his gloves. "Lady Nita, my thanks for your assistance." She'd done nothing except blink back tears and handle a few buttons, and yet, after Mr. St. Michael had boosted her onto her horse, he lingered a moment arranging the drape of her skirts over her boots.

"Not every titled lady would have tarried in the cold for a mere lamb," he said. "I should have left the matter to Kinser's good offices. This is his flock."

"Kinser is likely the worse for drink." Nita had complained to Nicholas of this tendency the last time she'd had to make up headache powders for Mr. Kinser.

"An occupational hazard among shepherds, particularly in cold weather. My thanks for your assistance though. That is a fine little tup, and he'll be worth a pretty penny."

Mr. St. Michael looked like he wanted to say more. Nita plucked a bit of straw from his hair and barely resisted the urge to brush at the shoulders of his coat.

"Ready to go?" George asked, climbing into the saddle.

Mr. St. Michael swung up and nudged William forward. "I believe you mentioned a toddy, sir. I'm sure the lady would enjoy one sooner rather than later."

They rode home in silence, the wind at their backs.

Nita would enjoy a toddy, and then she'd excuse herself from whatever domestic diversions were thrown at her and bring a few extra blankets and provisions to Addy Chalmers and wee Annie Elizabeth.

"I cannot fathom why Elsie Nash has not remarried," Kirsten remarked when she, Susannah, and Della were tooling home, hot bricks at their feet, scarves wound round their necks. "She is the dearest woman."

"Perhaps she's content to be a member of Edward's household,"

Susannah said. "He has no lady of his own, and a widowed sister-in-law makes a fine hostess."

Susannah, in her sweet, determined way, aspired to become Edward Nash's lady, and Mr. Nash seemed keen on the idea too.

"Elsie can waltz," Kirsten said. "Do you suppose Edward can? You might offer to teach him, Suze, if he hasn't acquired the knack." Because for all his memorized couplets of Shakespeare, Edward Nash was in line for a mere baronetcy when some great-uncle or second cousin died. He was rural gentry until that distant day, and likely ignorant of the waltz.

"How would one offer such lessons to a gentleman?" Susannah asked.

In a lifetime of trying, Kirsten would never be as innocent or good as Susannah. "One asks him, in a private moment, if he might assist one to brush up *her* waltzing skills before the assembly," Kirsten explained. "One stumbles at judicious moments in opportune directions when such assistance is rendered, apologizing all the while. One is befuddled by the complexity of the steps."

Susannah's consternation was both amusing and worrisome. In the absence of any legal authority over her own person, a woman benefited from mastering a bit of guile.

"Nita doesn't care for Mr. Nash," Della said from the backward-facing seat. Little more than her face showed from a swaddling of blankets and lap robes. "I can't say I do either."

"Have you a reason for your dislike of Edward?" Susannah asked.

"Elsie Nash is unhappy in her brother-in-law's household," Della said.

Kirsten didn't particularly like Edward Nash either—he had too high an opinion of himself for a man who'd inherited his holdings and done little to make them prosper. He was handsome, though, and he doted on Susannah. Edward and Susannah would have lovely, blond, handsome, poetry-spouting children together.

A dozen at least.

"Widowhood is not generally a cheerful state," Susannah said.

"Elsie's husband died more than two years ago," Della countered. "She has a child to love, and yet she's not—"

"She's not at peace," Kirsten ventured. "Maybe she's lonely. Pity Adolphus is too young for her." Because George, despite his grand good looks and abundant charm, would likely never marry.

"She moves like an older woman and has silences like an older woman," Della said, "as if her heart ached."

"All the more reason to cheer her with some waltzes," Susannah replied. "Might we persuade Mr. St. Michael to stay a few extra days? He has the look of a man who knows what he's about on the dance floor, and our gatherings never have enough nimble bachelors."

Kirsten and Della exchanged a glance that had nothing to do with planning the local assembly, for Susannah had done it again: arrived for innocent reasons at a suggestion that had not-so-innocent possibilities.

"Nita volunteered to ride to the sheep pastures with him in this weather," Della said quite casually, "and she was out late last night with Addy Chalmers."

"Which you had to mention at breakfast," Kirsten reminded her.

"I like Mr. St. Michael," Susannah said. "He doesn't put on airs."

The gentleman had an odd accent—mostly Scottish with the occasional French elision, a combination that would not endear him to Polite Society's loftiest hostesses. He was in trade, and he had a brusque quality that made Kirsten leery, though Nita could also be quite brusque—as could Kirsten, all too often.

"You ask him to prolong his stay, Suze," Della said. "Tell Mr. St. Michael we're shy a few handsome, dancing bachelors, then have Mr. Nash give you some waltzing lessons."

Susannah's brows drew down, and as the coach clattered from rut to bump to rocky turn, her gaze became sweetly, prettily thoughtful.

Also determined.

"Lovey, if you put fewer cakes on the tray, then the Bishop of Haddondale might not stay as long." Nick punctuated this observation with a kiss to his wife's temple. "Not that I'd encourage my dearest lady to anything approaching ungraciousness."

Though, of course, his wife was *incapable* of ungraciousness. Leah was also incapable of idleness, which was why Nick had had to track her down to his woodworking shop, to which she alone had a spare key.

"I do wonder how Nita put up with Vicar," Leah said, glowering at a stack of foolscap on the workbench. "If he didn't feel compelled to add a line of Scripture to his every observation, he might also be on his way sooner. I fear he aspires to match his son up with our Della, which ridiculousness you will *not* approve, Nicholas."

Nick added coal to the brazier, because his shop was at the back of the stable, where warmth was at a premium. Leah worked with fingerless gloves, the same as any shopgirl might have when totting up the day's custom.

She sat on a high stool, but Nick was tall enough to peer over her shoulder. "As my countess wishes, but lovey-lamb, why are you hiding here?" Nick certainly hid in the wood shop from time to time, and only Leah would disturb him when he did.

She tossed down a pencil and leaned against him. "You are so marvelously warm. Where is your coat, Nicholas?"

"My countess will keep me warm. You're working on menus."

The Countess of Bellefonte nuzzled her husband's chest. "I hate menus. I hate mutton, I hate soup, I hate fish, I hate that Cook expects me to remember which we ate Tuesday last and in what order, and I hate most of all that, for some reason, one must never serve trifle at the same meal as lobster."

This was old business, this jockeying between Leah and the staff she'd inherited upon becoming Nick's wife. She'd won over the maids and footmen, and Hanford was devoted, but Cook was temperamental and contrary.

"Shall I have a word with Cook?" Nick dreaded the prospect, though Leah had taken Cook on more than once.

The countess straightened and tidied her stack of papers. "You shall not. Household matters are my domain, Nicholas, though I appreciate your willingness to entertain Vicar when he comes snuffling around."

His Holiness had a prosperous figure for a man of the cloth, because Nick supported the living generously. Nick put Leah's menus aside, turned, and hiked himself up onto the bench, so he faced his wife.

"What was Vicar going on about," Nick asked, "with all that 'the Lord will provide for the less fortunate according to their deserts,' and 'the laborer is worthy of his wage'?"

Leah rested her head on Nick's knee, a rare gesture of weariness.

"He was referring to Addy Chalmers," she said. "Nita likely prevailed upon the vicarage for some charity. Addy has a number of children and her family turned their backs on her years ago."

"Five children now. Five living." Nita had reminded Nick of the total rather pointedly. According to Nita's clipped recitation, the oldest was eleven, an age at which Nick had been haring all over the shire on his pony, his half-brother Ethan at his side, and nothing more pressing on his mind than whether to put a toad in the tutor's boot or in his bed.

"Five children," Leah said, "and winter only half over. I'll send a basket. I should have sent one by now. Children must eat, despite the sins of the mother or the father. I, of all people, know this."

More old business. Prior to marrying Nick, Leah had endured her share of scandal and heartbreak. Nick had his spies in the stables though, and knew Nita had already seen to the basket.

"Addy Chalmers doesn't sin in solitude," he said. "My most enthusiastic sinning was ever undertaken in company. To the extent that Nita's charitable, she has my admiration, but she has no regard for her station."

Leah patted his thigh, then straightened, which was prudent of her. A man married less than a year was prone to certain thoughts when private with his wife, particularly when that dear lady was in need of comfort, the door was locked, and the brazier giving off a cozy warmth.

Alas, Leah had also recently become a mother, and restraint was still the marital order of the day.

And the night.

"I have endless admiration for Nita," Leah said. "She's been very helpful acquainting me with the household matters, but, Nicholas, I doubt that galloping off at all hours to tend to the sick and the dying is making Nita happy."

"It's not making her married, you mean. Perhaps she can find a younger son who's turned up medical." Though where Nick would find one of those for Nita, he did not know. This medical younger son would have to be a forward-thinking chap with some means.

Nita needed somebody with a light heart too, not full of death or Scripture, and it wouldn't hurt if the fellow were inclined to have a large family.

Nicholas's father had maintained that women with large families were too busy managing their own broods to wander into mischief. Nita didn't wander into mischief, she charged at it headlong.

"Come spring, we'll open a campaign to see Nita settled," Leah said. "Kirsten, Susannah, and Della will abet us. I think Della has taken an interest in Mr. St. Michael."

Of all the burdens Nick shared with his dear wife, the burden of being head of his family was the one he most appreciated her counsel about—even when she was wrong.

"Della isn't out yet, lovey. She shouldn't be noticing any gentlemen." Besides, Nick had St. Michael in mind for Kirsten, who, like St. Michael, suffered no fools and didn't put on airs. "Why do you think Della is considering St. Michael?"

Leah hopped off her stool and took her stack of papers to the brazier. One at a time, she fed her menus to the flames.

"When was the last time Della stirred from her rooms before late morning, Nicholas?"

Well, damn. "When your handsome, desirable, and ever-so-widowed brother Trenton came to call over the summer."

"Your strategy to have the family breakfast together isn't working, you know."

Denying the Haddonfield siblings breakfast trays in the hope they'd at least start their day from the same table had been Nick's strategy, and Leah had been against it. She'd given the staff the appropriate orders, however, and thus she bore the brunt of the family's disgruntlement.

"Then deny them even tea trays," Nick said, because the situation was vexing his countess and stern measures were in order.

Leah balled up half a sheet of paper and tossed it into the fire. Probably lobster and trifle on Tuesday night.

"Will you forgo your morning chocolate too, Nicholas? Will you make me give up mine? Your siblings are not sheep, to be herded together for the convenience of their shepherd."

The only full-time shepherd Nick employed had a fondness for the bottle.

"Damned sheep," Nick grumbled. "My sympathy for the challenges Papa faced grows daily. I ran into Edward Nash at the apothecary yesterday. He hinted strongly that the very herds St. Michael wants to buy would make a lovely dowry for Susannah."

Another half sheet went hurtling into the conflagration. "Mr. Nash is presuming."

Mr. Nash was hinting and dithering, while poor Susannah likely went to bed each night praying for a ring from the man. Nick could not afford a large cash settlement for each sister, and Nash's hints hadn't been entirely unwelcome.

"We own an embarrassment of sheep, lovey mine, maybe even enough to entice two handsome bachelors to the altar, but what aren't you telling me?"

Two pieces of paper remained. These Leah folded and stuffed

into a pocket of her cape. "The moon was bright last night, Nicholas."

Nick hopped down and wrapped his arms around his wife, because he could hear voices beyond the door and what Leah had to say was for Nick's ears only. Her shape had changed since she'd become a mother, and she fit against him more comfortably than ever, though her logic eluded him.

He nuzzled her ear. "The moon was bright and...?"

"And when Nita came in from her errand last night, she must have come upon Mr. St. Michael in the stables."

"I threatened to fire Jacobs for leaving Nita at that woman's cottage, but hurling lordly thunderbolts is pointless. The staff is in the habit of doing as Nita tells them."

Fortunately, Nita had told them to heed the countess's direction in all things, or a delicate situation would have grown impossible. In her way, Leah was as stubborn as Nita.

"You're all in the habit of doing as Nita tells you," Leah said, "and that is not her fault. She and Mr. St. Michael tarried in the gazebo."

Nick left off kissing his wife's chin. A gazebo on a midwinter night was nowhere to tarry for mere conversation.

"Last night was colder than the ninth circle of hell," Nick muttered. Complete with a ring around the moon portending snow.

Leah rested her cheek against his chest while, beyond the door, somebody called for Atlas and the Scottish gent's gelding to be saddled.

"Exactly, Nicholas. Despite the cold and darkness, despite having no prior acquaintance with the man, Nita tarried in the gazebo with Mr. St. Michael, and, Nicholas?"

He was becoming aroused, and his dear lady was happily tucking herself closer to him. Whenever Nick held his wife for more than a moment, desire flared, and he wondered why, in the name of all that was sweet, did young men avoid holy matrimony.

To bargain over sheep, for God's sake? "Lovey?"

"Nita blew out the lamp, and still, Mr. St. Michael remained in the gazebo with her."

CHAPTER THREE

"Mr. St. Michael, I assure you, you need not accompany me."

Lady Nita headed for the stables at a pace the King's mail would have envied, though Tremaine's longer legs allowed him to keep up easily.

"You'll ride across frozen ground alone, then?" he asked pleasantly. "Risk your mount slipping on a patch of ice? End up in a ditch, there to freeze while hoping for an early spring?"

Her ladyship came to an abrupt halt beside the gazebo where they'd spent a few chilly moments the previous evening. Lady Nita's skirts swished about her boots in a susurration any grown man would hear as indignant.

"My plans are not your affair, sir."

She doubtless wished they were nobody's affair save her own. Alas, Tremaine could not indulge her ladyship's wishes.

"If I remain in that house," he said, leaning closer, "Lady Kirsten will discuss the financial pages with me, Lady Della will want gossip from Town she's too innocent to comprehend, and Lady Susannah will ask for more poetry recited in my *charming accent.*"

While George's interest likely careened toward territory

Tremaine would not discuss with the man's sister. In the midst of Tremaine's tirade, Lady Nita smoothed a gloved hand over his shoulder though his coat had been thoroughly brushed since their morning outing.

"You do have a charming accent, particularly when in the grip of strong emotion."

"You are laughing at me."

Lady Nita had the decency not to smile, but her blue eyes danced an entire set of waltzes at the expense of his dignity.

"Is it really such an imposition, Mr. St. Michael, to prose on for a few verses about a mouse?"

Two thoughts collided in Tremaine's awareness and tangled with Lady Nita's sweet, lemony fragrance.

First, she had not been present when he'd trotted out his meager store of Mr. Burns's verse for the delectation of the ladies. She'd apparently collected a report about his recitation, which was intriguing. Second, for the space of this small discussion—skirmish, altercation, or argument—Lady Nita had forgotten whatever mission propelled her back out into the elements on a cold winter day.

"The poem is not simply about a plowman overturning a mouse's nest," Tremaine said. "Burns was writing about the tenuousness of life, the ease with which we can inadvertently cause mortal peril to one another, and how the same peril can find us despite our best-laid plans and our innocence of any wrongdoing."

Tremaine might have launched into an explanation of Burns's precarious existence as a Scottish farmer, the poet's tender regard for nature, or some other blather, but the lady was once again about her business.

"Exactly, Mr. St. Michael," she said, striding off. "Innocents among us are not responsible for the harm befalling them. You may spend your afternoon aiding my sister Della in her efforts to master the waltz, so that no missteps befall her in the ballrooms of London this spring. The gossips can be unmercifully critical, and Della is too tenderhearted for her own good."

So tenderhearted that Lady Della was closeted with *Debrett's*, doubtless making a list of eligible dukes, while Lady Nita risked lung fever in her haste to ensure the well-being of a newborn.

Did none of the Haddonfield menfolk regard themselves as responsible for her welfare? Had she turned them all into bleating sheep with her brisk pronouncements and swishing hems?

"Spend the afternoon waltzing?" Tremaine said, resuming his place beside her. "Not on your life, my lady. I'll start off twirling about with Lady Della, all in the name of gentlemanly charity. While the countess smiles at us from the piano, Lady Susannah will come next, and then, when I'm winded from my exertions and all unsuspecting, Lady Kirsten will take a turn with me, until they've counted my very teeth and reported my prospects to Bellefonte in detail."

"They already know you're wealthy," Lady Nita said, her tone... pitying? "Nicholas need not have invited you to his home purely for business purposes, though. He transacts most of his business in the City, or at least sees to it when he's in Town."

Her ladyship's honesty was not so endearing in the cold light of day.

"You confirm my darkest suspicions, Lady Nita, and thus you owe it to me to tolerate my company when you call on that baby. You will take either me or a groom, and the groom will report your activities to your brother."

She stopped outside the stables, the embodiment of feminine frustration. "I am merely after a refreshing hack, Mr. St. Michael."

From which she might well return with more bloodstains on her cuffs, or worse. Based on her brothers' mutterings, Tremaine suspected Lady Nita planned other medical calls, perhaps even to households afflicted with contagion.

Such behavior for an earl's unmarried daughter was insupportable in an age blessed with trained medical men in nearly every shire.

"I'll be gone in another few days," Tremaine said. "Surely you can endure my company until then? 'Wee, sleekit, cow'rin, timorous beastie' that I am."

Her ladyship's sense of humor plagued her again. Tremaine divined this by how severely she glowered at his boots.

"You are not a mouse, Mr. St. Michael."

"I'm not an overbearing older brother either," he said gently, for the grooms were hollering to each other in the barn and some conversations were private. "Somebody should ensure the child still lives and the mother isn't feverish. I understand that."

Lady Nita's gaze shifted to the gray clouds brooding over the Downs to the southwest. "If she's feverish, there's little enough I can do, except try to keep her comfortable and hope a wet nurse will take the child."

"We are agreed then. You will spare me waltzes, and I will spare you awkward questions from your well-meaning family."

The grooms led the horses out, Atlas sporting bulging sacks slung over his withers. *A refreshing hack, indeed.*

"I'll be gone in three days' time," Tremaine said, for Bellefonte would either part with his sheep for a reasonable price or he wouldn't. "'Nae man can tether time nor tide,'" Tremaine quoted. "And no ten men can stop the press of business for one such as I. If your brother won't sell me his sheep, then I'm off to the German states in search of other herds. Humor me this once, madam, and I'll not trouble you again."

Lady Nita accepted Atlas's reins from the groom, and gave the boy a look such that he hustled back into the barn with a muttered, "G'day, yer ladyship."

Tremaine bid William to stand, which the beast would do until spring if need be.

"You may accompany me," Lady Nita said, "but I want to hear that poem about the mouse and life's precariousness. Susannah was quite taken with it."

Tremaine boosted Lady Nita onto her unprepossessing gelding, surprised at her request.

Also pleased.

Nita approached the Chalmers cottage purposefully, though dread dragged at her heels, given what she'd found on other visits here. Did Mr. St. Michael oblige her by remaining on his horse, looking handsome and substantial in his winter finery?

No, he did not.

He swung down and tethered their mounts to the porch railing, then clomped up the sagging steps right behind her.

"This is unnecessary, Mr. St. Michael. You will embarrass the mother and make my errand here more awkward."

He rapped on the door with a gloved fist. "This mother will not embarrass so easily as that."

The cottage stank, as Nita had known it would, of boiled cabbage, unwashed bodies, dirty linen, and despair.

"Lady Nita!" Mary's greeting was enthusiastic but quiet, and her younger brothers said nothing at all.

"Good day, Mary. Mr. St. Michael and I thought to see how you're getting on." The cheer in Nita's voice was mostly sincere. Mary held a small bundle in her arms, and the baby's blanket was still clean.

"Mama's resting," Mary said, the baby tucked securely against her middle. "Wee Annie is thriving."

"You lot," Mr. St. Michael said to Mary's younger brothers. "Outside with me now. Two horses need walking and somebody must show me where the woodpile is." His tone of voice was positively glacial, and the boys dove for their coats and scarves.

"Evan, you stay inside," Nita said. The smallest of the three boys had weak lungs and likely no shoes.

"He can gather up the soiled linens," Mr. St. Michael said. "There's laundry aplenty in need of boiling."

Well, yes. Any household with a new baby boasted a deal of laundry. Within minutes, Nita heard the rhythmic sound of an ax falling, and Evan was scurrying about, making a great heap of dirty clothing, bedding, and linen by the cottage door.

Nita used the relative privacy to fold back the curtain over the sleeping alcove, where Addy slumbered on as if she were the worse for drink.

"She hasn't had any gin," Mary whispered. "Not since wee Annie was born. Mama has slept and slept. I bring her the baby, like you told me to."

The back of Nita's hand to Addy's forehead verified the absence of fever.

"Having a baby can be tiring," Nita said softly. Childbirth could also be fatal, and then what would these children do? Nick allowed them to forage in the home wood for deadfall, and Nita had her suspicions about where the occasional hare in the stew pot came from.

"Annie's awake," Mary said, peering at her sister. "She's hardly ever awake."

The very old and the very young often drifted in a benevolent twilight. When Nita's father had dwelled in that twilight continuously, she'd known his end approached.

"Let's have a look at her," Nita said, closing the curtain and taking the baby from Mary. Annie Elizabeth felt solid, reassuringly so, and Mary had kept the baby clean. A clout had been tied about the infant's small form, one of many Nita had made from old shifts and sheets.

The door opened and fresh, chilly air gusted through the cottage. Tremaine St. Michael dumped a load of split wood into the empty wood box.

"So that's the new arrival?" he asked, peering at the baby in Nita's arms. "Pretty little thing. Ladies of that size always look so innocent."

In this household, the child's innocence was doomed.

"Her name's Annie," Mary volunteered.

Behind the curtained alcove, Addy stirred in her sleep, then fell silent.

"And you're Mary," Mr. St. Michael said, dropping to his haunches. "Your brothers are quite in awe of you. They say you can cook and clean, and should go for a maid in a fancy lord's house because you work ever so hard the livelong day."

Mary's brows drew down at this flattery, though Mr. St. Michael's words were true enough. The cottage was tidy—the dirt floor swept, the baby's linens folded in a short stack on the table, the hearth free of excess ashes. Half of the sausage Nita had brought last time hung from the crossbeam between sheaves of herbs and a rope of onions.

"I couldn't leave our Annie," Mary said. "The boys want me earning coin. They wouldn't know how to help with Annie, though."

Mr. St. Michael rose, his expression displeased. "Give me that baby, my lady," he said, plucking Annie from Nita's arms. "Mary needs a spot of fresh air, you're dying to fill that stew pot, and the water for the laundry will take some time to heat."

"Ma said we weren't to do laundry," Mary murmured, passing Mr. St. Michael the baby's blanket. "We need the wood for heat."

"Get your coat on," Tremaine told the girl as he wrapped Annie snugly in the blanket and put the baby to his shoulder. "One of your brothers is gathering more wood as we speak, to keep the fire under the laundry tub going. The other is walking the horses one at a time. If you can figure out how to climb onto my gelding, you're welcome to walk him out for me."

Mary sent Nita one glance, the merest brush of elated disbelief, then dashed for her cloak and was out the door.

"You're spoiled here in the south," Mr. St. Michael said, stroking the baby's back gently. "You have hours and hours of sunshine, regardless of the season. If the sun's out, those children should be catching a glimpse of it."

He wasn't exactly wrong, and he moved around the cottage with that child affixed to his shoulder as if...

"You *like* babies?" Nita asked as Mr. St. Michael took down the length of sausage.

"Who wouldn't like a baby, for God's sake?" Next he took down the onions, and from a basket near the hearth, he selected a fat turnip, all one-handed. "This will be sharper than anything you can find here," he said, passing Nita a folding knife.

He could have put the child down, of course, but Nita didn't suggest this. Tremaine St. Michael had offered his warmth to a mere lamb. Surely Annie would know she was safe in his arms?

"I liked your poem," Nita said, starting on the sausage. Small pieces, because the children would bolt their stew rather than chew it, and of course, the meat had to last as long as possible.

"Mr. Burns's poem," Mr. St. Michael retorted. Outside, some child shrieked with laughter. "Mary will come to grief if she tries to trot, and then her brothers will take a turn. Every child should know how to sit a horse, and William loves children."

William loved children?

"My new friend remains fast asleep," he went on, "a testament to my limitless charms. Shall I tuck her in with the mother?"

Nita's knife came down decisively, beheading a turnip. "Absolutely not. That box by the hearth is for the baby."

Mr. St. Michael laid the child in the box and arranged her blankets around her. "I thought this box was for kindling."

Likely it had been, but such was the poverty of the household that the simple wooden box was Annie's bed for now. Mr. St. Michael set the box up on the table beside Nita and the pile of winter vegetables.

"She'll be out of the drafts if she's off the floor," he said. "Damned dirt holds the cold and damp, excuse my language. I'm off to check on the laundry and prevent horse thievery. You'll want to add a quantity of potatoes to that stew and a dash of salt."

Mr. St. Michael scooped up the entire lot of dirty clothes, and out the door he went, leaving Evan and Nita to exchange a look.

"He talks funny," Evan said.

"He's from far away. That was a mountain of laundry, Evan. I don't think a single stocking escaped your notice. Would you like a bite of sausage?"

Evan's nod was heart-wrenchingly solemn. Outside, more laughter pealed, interrupted by Mr. St. Michael's stern tones.

"I'll bet he was a hard worker when he was a lad, even if he is a fine gent," Evan said around a mouthful of sausage. "I'll never be as tall as him."

"You'll never be as rich as him," said a voice from the back of the cottage. Addy stood beside the lone bed, the alcove's curtain pushed back. "Lady Nita, greetings. You will excuse me for not greeting you properly."

Addy had been pretty once, and raised in a proper squire's household, though her parents were dead now. As a girl, she'd played hide-and-seek among the gravestones in the churchyard along with all the other children of the parish. She was three years older than Nita, considerably smaller, and already looking careworn.

"Good day, Mama." Evan had finished his bite of sausage, and he kept his gaze on his mother's feet, which were encased in a pair of Nita's much-darned cast-off stockings. An old, blue woolen shawl of Susannah's was wrapped about Addy's shoulders. "The man is from far away, and he can chop wood. He's boiling laundry too."

"Not a Haddonfield, then," Addy said, wrinkling her nose. "I smell meat."

Addy's observation about Nita's brothers was merely honest, for an earl and his brothers did not boil laundry, and the town strumpet didn't expect them to.

"Sausage," Nita said, slicing off an inch-long section and passing it to Addy. "How are you feeling?"

Addy's smile was so sad, Nita regretted the question.

"Not bad," Addy replied, taking a nibble of sausage. "Mary was the worst. I nearly bled to death after she was born, and then her father's family wanted nothing to do with her. This is good, spicy sausage. Evan, you may put my boots on to go out for a moment, but don't you take a chill, and mind Lady Nita's gentleman friend."

Addy's boots were too large for him, of course, and the coat he tied around his waist with twine was too large as well, but a too-large coat could be a blessing when the wind was sharp and a little boy's trousers ended several inches above his ankles.

"Is your fellow good-looking?" Addy asked when Evan had gone.

Nita hacked a potato to bits—a potato she would have forgotten to add to the pot, but for Mr. St. Michael's reminder. Addy had long ago lost the knack of standing on ceremony, probably as much an occupational hazard for soiled doves as it was for those who attended birthings.

"Mr. St. Michael's looks are not excessively refined, and he's not my fellow," Nita said, going after a second potato. "But he recites poetry, loves children, and once upon a time, he was very, very poor."

Which Nita's family likely would not have guessed in a thousand years.

Tremaine had spent years forgetting how dirty poverty was, though the state of his fingernails brought the reality back quickly. He'd also forgotten that boiling laundry was an art, which the child Mary had apparently studied.

Stale bread rubbed on the linen would have taken out the grease stain on her pinafore she'd assured him, though of course no bread survived long enough in her household to become stale. Hot milk should have been applied to the jam Evan had smeared on his sleeve —though no milk could be spared for such a vanity.

Most of the items they'd boiled had been small, stained, and threadbare, a metaphor for life as those children knew it.

"You're very quiet, Mr. St. Michael," Lady Nita observed.

"Thinking about Mr. Burns's mouse," Tremaine replied as the horses clopped along in the direction of Belle Maison. Laundry was a tedious undertaking, thus much of the afternoon had been wasted at the malodorous cottage. At least the laundry had allowed Tremaine to remain outside in the fresh air, while Lady Nita had been indoors, cooking, mending, and cleaning.

And likely breathing through her mouth. "Nobody will believe we spent the past three hours trotting about the shire," Tremaine pointed out. "Not in this weather."

"They won't ask."

Lady Nita had trained them not to ask, in other words. On this refreshing hack through the nearer reaches of destitution, Tremaine had picked up two splinters, a twinge in his left shoulder—a dull ax was an abomination against God and Nature—and dirty fingernails.

Lady Nita was still tidy, serene, and unruffled by their visit to the cottage.

"Your brother won't have to ask *us* what we've got up to," Tremaine said. "He'll interrogate the grooms about how long we were gone and in which direction we rode. He'll inquire in the kitchen about bread, milk, sausage, tea, salt, sugar, and other necessities. He'll inspect your hems and my boots as we pass him in the corridor."

Even the Earl of Bellefonte would recognize the stink of boiled cabbage clinging to their clothing.

Tremaine's recitation did not please her ladyship. She turned her face up to a frigid breeze, as if seeking fortification from the cold.

"Nicholas might ask," she said, "but he won't interfere, though he probably wishes all the infirm and indigent would simply leave the realm, or his little corner of it."

No, Bellefonte wished his sisters would leave—for the dubious comforts of holy matrimony. In this, his lordship was simply a conscientious patriarch.

"Then why not marry?" Tremaine asked. "You'd be out from under your brother's roof." Though Bellefonte appeared to dote on his sisters—on most of his sisters.

Lady Nita glanced back in the direction of the cottage, which now boasted a cheery plume of smoke from the chimney, cubic yards of chopped wood stacked on the porch, and a deal of laundry laid over the bushes and porch railings in hopes it would dry rather than freeze.

"I have no use for marriage," Lady Nita said. "If I hadn't attended Annie's birth, she'd likely have died. Addy was decent once, and she does not cope well with her fall from grace. Women in such circumstances can give up—" She fell silent as the wind gusted, the breeze rewrapping the tail of her ladyship's scarf so the wool covered her mouth.

The horses plodded along the frozen lane while Tremaine considered Lady Nita's point: an evening she might have spent embroidering by a cozy fire was instead spent seeing that a baby arrived safely into the world. She was justifiably proud of that, and yet she was also troubled.

"You hope," Tremaine said, "that by attending the birth, you did the child a service, rather than a disservice, for life in that cottage is precarious indeed."

Lady Nita's plow horse shuffled onward, head down, gait weary. The horse, too, had been out at all hours in bad weather. As the wind continued to whip through the bare branches of the hedgerows, tiny flakes of snow came with it.

Any shepherd boy knew the smaller the snowflakes the more likely the weather would turn nasty in earnest.

"Here is the rest of the syllogism," Tremaine said, because Lady Nita's family had apparently neglected to say these words to her. "Babies will be born and babies will die, and it's the duty of those amply blessed to aid those in precarious circumstances. However, because babies *do* die, we all occasionally need a pretty waltz and a pleasant evening in good company. Martyrs have many admirers but few friends, Lady Nita, and worst of all, they never have any fun."

On the Continent, where decades of war had laid waste to much that was good, sweet, and dear, people seemed to grasp this. Life was for living, for rejoicing in, not for suffering through. In the Highlands, where thrift had become a cultural fixture, the same rejoicing was

brewed into the very whisky and song that punctuated every cele-
bration.

Lady Nita swiped at her cheek, as if a stray snowflake might have
smacked her, then she did it again on the other cheek.

"I love to waltz," she said, gaze on the horse's coarse mane. "I love
to sing, and I like nothing better than to join my sisters for great silliness over cards, until we're laughing so hard we're in tears. Nicholas
would take even that from me to see me married to some viscount or
lordling." On that pronouncement, she sent her horse into a businesslike canter.

Tremaine followed several yards behind and grappled with a
realization. His objective was no longer strictly a profitable transaction with Lord Bellefonte. Where Lady Nita was concerned, a point
had to be made about life and her entitlement to some of its joy.

Then too, a woman constantly in the company of the ill and
impoverished was a woman at risk for illness herself, of the body or of
the spirit. Lady Nita's brothers were remiss in not protecting her from
those harms, though Tremaine lacked any authority to correct their
oversights.

And yet he could not stand idly by while Nita Haddonfield
martyred herself on an altar of guilt and obligation. He was bound for
Germany at week's end if Bellefonte would not offer terms for the
sheep, but in the remaining two days, the choice of weapon belonged
to Tremaine:

Waltzing, singing, or cards. Or perhaps all three.

"Damn fookin' cranky besom yowe! Git ye doon the noo!"

Kinser's affectionate profanity seemed to impress the wayward
ewe—"yowe"—not one bit. She'd leaped up onto the stone wall
marking the boundaries of the pasture, and considered freedom with
what George took for ovine glee.

"Perhaps we should leave her to find her own way off the wall,"

George suggested. "She won't jump back into the pasture if we're glowering at her."

"She'll nae leave her own kind," Kinser said. "Unless she takes a notion to ramble aboot the shire. That un's piss-all contrary."

Every damned denizen of the pasture struck George as contrary —much like the Haddonfield womenfolk—but he hadn't trusted Kinser to get the ewes moved before worse weather arrived. *Kinser* was contrary and, more to the point, plagued with a fondness for both whisky and warmth.

A small boy came trundling down the lane on the far side of the stone wall. He moved with the trudging gait of a child bundled up against the elements and stopped when the ewe baa'd at him.

"Tell her to get down," George called. "Wave your arms and chase her back toward us."

"That be the Nash lad," Kinser said. "On his way home from Vicar's."

The boy apparently grasped the situation, for he rushed the sheep, waving his arms and making a racket. She bounded down from her perch and scampered back to the herd bunched at the far end of the pasture.

"That's it, then," Kinser said, taking another pull from his flask. "My thanks, Master George. Best get ye to a warm hearth soonest."

Kinser waved at the boy, blew a kiss to the sheep, and left George in the middle of the pasture, his toes freezing, his nose freezing, and his arse none too cozy either.

"Digby!" George called to the boy. "I'll take you up on my horse if you're bound for home."

The child did not have to be asked twice. He scrambled onto a stile and waited for George to mount up and trot over to the fence.

"My thanks, Mr. Haddonfield," Digby said, climbing up before George. "B-beastly cold, isn't it?"

"Wretched beastly *damned* cold," George said, for a boy ought to know that colorful language in the company of other fellows was quite acceptable. "You were at your Latin with Vicar?"

"I was keeping warm," Digby said, wiggling in the saddle, which was cold as hell against George's fundament. "Uncle thinks I'm slow, but Vicar has a fire in the study, and the schoolroom at home is freezing."

The child's words were nearly unintelligible, so badly were his teeth chattering.

"Ask Vicar about the Second Punic Wars," George suggested. "The Battle of Cannae is good for at least an hour's diversion."

Digby twisted around to peer up at George. The boy had his mother's lovely blue eyes, bright red hair, and pale complexion. "*You* know about the Second Punic Wars, Mr. Haddonfield?"

"Every Latin scholar worth his salt knows about Cannae. Hannibal won with a smaller force because he used his wits. The Romans charged at him headlong, but he fell back with his main army while sending columns around the enemy's flanks. The Romans thought they were charging to victory until they realized they were surrounded. Have you considered asking your mama to order a fire in the schoolroom?"

A frigid third-floor schoolroom was no place for a solitary boy to learn anything.

"Mama won't allow it if Uncle has said no. I hate winter." Digby drew himself up in the saddle. "I hate Uncle too."

Most little boys hated discipline and structure—George certainly had. He wasn't particularly keen on Edward Nash either, come to that.

"I'll tell you a secret, Digby Nash, just between us Latin scholars. The schoolroom is exactly where you want to spend your time. Nobody will bother you there if it's kept that cold."

"You can see your breath in the schoolroom, Mr. Haddonfield. Uncle says that builds character. I think it saves on the coal bill and gives a lad the sniffles."

Digby had his mother's common sense too. "Maybe a cold school-room does both," George temporized as they approached the Stone-bridge lane. "Make friends with the scullery maid. She'll bring up chocolate with your nooning. As long as you're at your studies, you'll have all the peace and quiet you can wish for—enough to play with your soldiers, draw, read, or take a nap. I'll send you over a few books with lots of battles in them." Though the boy apparently had a few battles of his own brewing. "Does your mama even know how cold the schoolroom is?"

Digby's little shoulders heaved up and down with puerile long-suffering.

"Mama knows," he said darkly. "She argued with Uncle about it, but nobody ever wins an argument with him. He shouts and hits and says mean things. He thinks money is more important than anything."

Digby had his mother's slight size in addition to her blue eyes and red hair, and the notion of anybody striking the child sat very ill indeed.

"Don't provoke your uncle," George advised as the horse negotiated the frozen ruts. "In a few years, you'll be off to public school, having jolly good fun and growing brilliant with the other scholars. They'll envy you for how much Roman history you know, and all because you managed a chilly schoolroom for a few winters."

Even the great general Hannibal had grasped the value of a strategic retreat. Edward Nash was Digby's guardian, and thus Nash's authority over the boy—and likely the boy's mother—was absolute.

"I'll be cold forever," Digby retorted. "Uncle says I'm not to go to Harrow, even though my papa wished it. We haven't the money. Mama says Papa set the money aside, but then Uncle starts shouting. I hate it when he shouts."

George's parents hadn't been exactly quiet, but they'd had the decency to air most of their differences out of the hearing of their children. Perhaps Edward Nash had set the funds aside for university instead of public school.

"Give it time, lad. Things have a way of working themselves out, even when you think you're beyond hope."

For little boys, in any case. For grown men, harsher truths usually applied.

"Like you gave me a ride today," Digby said, patting the horse's shoulder. "I was sure I'd freeze to death on my way home. I can't feel my toes, you know. Vicar gave me a baked potato for each pocket, but I need potatoes for my boots."

What the boy needed was a pony to trot him back and forth to Vicar's house for these weekly Latin lessons, or brothers to tease and fight with, or a damned brazier in his schoolroom.

Or a different uncle.

"Let's warm up a bit, shall we?" George asked. "Grab some mane, and we'll canter." The horse was only too happy to pick up its pace, and soon the Stonebridge stables came into view.

"Mama's waiting for me," Digby said with the air of a boy enduring the entire weight of a widowed mother's anxieties. "She frets, you see."

George brought his mount to the walk and ruffled a gloved hand over Digby's crown, feeling a pang for the father who'd never see this boy reach adulthood.

"Mind you don't hop down," George warned. "Nothing is worse for frozen toes than a quick dismount."

Elsie Nash did indeed look fretful, also half-frozen in her black wool cape.

"Digby, into the kitchen with you," she said, marching up to the horse. "Cook has made biscuits, and you will have at least two. Mr. Haddonfield, my thanks. Will you come in to warm up for a moment?"

George swung down, though the last thing he wanted was to tarry in Elsie Nash's company.

"Afraid I can't stay," he said, lifting the child from the saddle and setting him down gently. "Enjoy the biscuits, Digby, and my thanks for helping out with that ewe."

"Thank you, Mr. Haddonfield!" The boy scampered off, having no notion of the awkwardness he left in his wake.

"Very kind of you to bring him home," Elsie said as Digby skipped up the drive. "Edward says the fresh air is good for him, but the vicarage is two miles of fresh air each way, and Digby hasn't Edward's size."

"Yet," George said. "Give the boy time. I'm the runt in my family, and I struggle along adequately, despite that burden."

Elsie ran an appraising eye over him, though her inspection was dispassionate rather than an assessment of his masculine charms.

Because Elsie Nash knew better.

"Digby's father wasn't particularly tall," she said, "but I wouldn't change a thing about my son. How are you getting along, George? Your sisters natter on about the assembly and some visiting Scottish fellow with a French title, but they seldom mention you. You've been traveling, haven't you?"

George stood beside his horse, trapped by manners and a nagging concern for the boy. "Elsie, you needn't pretend."

"Pretend?"

"I travel on the Continent because my family finds my taste in kissing partners inconvenient." *Dangerous*, Nicholas had said, for certain sexual behaviors, regardless of how casually undertaken or commonplace, were yet considered hanging offenses.

"George Haddonfield, if I were dismayed by every person I found kissing an inconvenient party in the garden, I should never have lasted a single Season as the colonel's wife. You were kind to my son, and that is all that matters to me."

Elsie glowered up at him, five entire feet—and possibly one inch —of mother love ready to trounce George if he contradicted her.

"Your son needs a brazier in his schoolroom," George said, and Elsie's glower disappeared like snow on hot coals.

"Digby exaggerates. You mustn't mind him."

"Digby is a good lad, and he's lucky to have you for a mother." While George was lucky Elsie had never breathed a word about what she'd seen in a certain earl's moonlit garden. God help him, it hadn't even been much of a kiss.

"You won't come in for a biscuit and a cup of tea in the kitchen?" Elsie asked.

Her invitation was genuine, and the day *was* beastly cold. Then, too, George had enjoyed the time spent with Digby—who wouldn't like such a lad?—so he pulled off a glove and gave a piercing whistle.

"If you could please walk my horse," George said to the groom who jogged out of the stable. "Up and down the barn aisle will do, and I won't be long."

Elsie beamed at George as if he'd announced a sighting of blooming roses.

"Perfect," she said, slipping her arm through his. "You must tell me about this Mr. St. Michael. Your sisters seemed to think he might do for Lady Nita, and he's rumored to be quite wealthy."

CHAPTER FOUR

"There you are!" Bellefonte advanced into the library, his tone suggesting Tremaine had been hiding for days, rather than drafting correspondence in plain sight for the past hour.

"I'm writing to your brother Beckman, who will want a full accounting of my sojourn among his siblings. Have you anything you'd like to include with my epistle?"

Bellefonte took a position with his backside to the roaring fire in the hearth. "I like the smell of a wood fire," he said. "Though I'd be better off selling the wood, I'm sure. You may warn Beckman I'm sending Lady Nita to him in the spring, so he'd best ensure all in his ambit are in excellent health. From there, she can visit our brother Ethan, and I've any number of friends who'd be delighted to host her over the summer. My grandmother, Lady Warne, loves showing my sisters off at house parties."

Tremaine sprinkled sand over the page. He and the Earl of Bellefonte had a few matters to clear up of a more pressing nature than social correspondence.

"Are you scolding me, Bellefonte, for accompanying your sister on an outing that you, a team of elephants, and a host of archangels could not have dissuaded her from?"

Women rallied around babies, and Tremaine had no quarrel with that. None at all. Women were supposed to be protective of the little ones—as were men.

"You are a guest in my home, a friend to my younger brother— who has few enough friends—and you mean well," Bellefonte said. His tone implied a list of charges recited at the local magistrate's parlor session. "I'm not scolding you."

Bellefonte made a quarter turn, so he faced Tremaine without giving up proximity to the fire's heat.

"Relieved to hear it," Tremaine replied. "Shall we discuss your sheep, then? I might be a guest, though I'm a guest who would not be under your roof but for a desire to purchase that herd." Lest any thoroughly domesticated earls develop aspirations in other directions.

Bellefonte rubbed a hand over the hip closest to the fire. "Right, my sheep. We'll get to those. Why aren't you married, St. Michael? Beckman said you proposed to Miss Polonaise Hunt earlier this winter."

The list of reasons to thrash Beckman Haddonfield was growing by the hour.

"Miss Hunt turned me down." Polly was now the Marchioness of Hesketh—also head over ears in love with her grouchy, taciturn, tender-hearted marquess. "A near miss, from my perspective." And from the lady's, no doubt. Tremaine hadn't dared solicit Lord Hesketh's opinion, lest the marquess's sentiments be conveyed at twenty paces.

"You're amenable to marriage in the general case?" Bellefonte asked.

"We were discussing your merino sheep, my lord. The herd appears in good condition, but if you continue inbreeding, you'll soon have a greater incidence of ill health, smaller specimens, and stillbirths."

Bellefonte rested an elbow on the mantel, which he could do

easily because of his excessive height.

"So you'll use my sheep for outcrosses, then? Improve the wool in the local strains, improve the health of the merino offspring?"

"That would make sense." As would selling some of the pure individuals in France, the United States, or other countries. Sheep were hardy enough to tolerate sea voyages well, under decent conditions.

"And yet you do not commit to that course," Bellefonte mused. "Others are interested in these sheep, though I've only recently become aware of it."

Tremaine remained seated at the desk and busied himself pouring the sand off his letter, capping the ink, and tossing the parings from the quill pen into the dustbin. Bellefonte was a good negotiator, but if he was as cash poor as most of the aristocracy, he was in a bad bargaining position.

"Others might be interested in your sheep, my lord, but others are not here. Others probably lack the coin I can bring to bear on the situation, and others won't maximize the value of those sheep as I can."

"Others will marry my sisters."

Or maybe Bellefonte was a brilliant negotiator. "My lord, allow me to instruct you about sheep," Tremaine said, "for I blush to inform you I am an expert on the species. Sheep move about on four legs. They grow wool, they bleat. They tend to dwell in herds, and according to some, the breeding rams have an objectionable aroma.

"Sisters, by contrast, typically move about on two legs," Tremaine continued, approaching the hearth. "They may laugh, speak, or whine. They ordinarily do not bleat. They take great pride in their hair—which has little resemblance to wool—tend to pleasant scents, and go exactly where they please, when they please. They do not dwell in placid herds, chewing their cud until the shepherd directs them to another pasture. I am interested in the sheep, and only the sheep."

"You want the sheep; I want my sisters happily and safely married. Beckman has spoken highly of you."

For which Tremaine really must pummel dear Beckman when next they met. Perhaps Hesketh was due a few blows as well, because the aristocracy kept close tabs on each other, and the marquess might have had a hand in any scheme that saw Tremaine marched up the church aisle.

"The issue is not what you want, Bellefonte," Tremaine said, "but rather what your womenfolk want. I have not detected matrimonial interest from them." Interest, yes, the same interest with which the ewes looked over a new collie or watched a horseman canter by, but not *matrimonial* interest.

Nobody was in marital rut in this household, excepting perhaps Bellefonte himself.

"Edward Nash is heir to a baronet," Bellefonte said. "His papa and mine rode to hounds together, and our pews are situated across the church aisle from each other. He owns a tidy holding not two miles distant—Stonebridge—and he quotes poetry to Susannah."

Tremaine had ridden by that tidy holding and recalled the property because the sign naming it was anything but discreet.

"Nash offers to relieve you of a sister, while I offer you only money. What a credit to your priorities, Bellefonte."

Bellefonte's reputation was one of unfailing good cheer, though his blue eyes had abruptly turned colder than the winter skies over Kent.

"Nash offers to *make my sister happy.* Susannah is retiring in the extreme. She didn't *take,* and she loves her books. I love—"

Pity for the earl required that Tremaine make a study of the library's red, blue, and cream carpets, which were wool, probably Scottish wool. The sheep suited to northern climes grew a coarse, durable product that could withstand years of trampling.

"You love your sisters, my lord, and the prospect of seeing Lady Susannah across the church aisle every Sunday is less daunting than the notion that she might catch the eye of some Italian count."

Or, heaven defend the lady, a Scottish wool nabob?

"Nash's sister-in-law dwells with him too," Bellefonte said,

turning another quarter, so he faced the fire. "Susannah wouldn't be
the sole female in his household. She'd have children in due course,
and what woman doesn't want children?"

Addy Chalmers, for one. Tremaine's own mother, possibly,
though in Bellefonte's world, women sought husbands as a necessary
predicate to having children.

"My lord, you must do as you see fit with your sheep. I am
prepared to buy the entire herd, but *only* the entire herd. Their value
decreases significantly if you send one-third down the lane as Lady
Susannah's bridal attendants and another third to sale in London.
The remaining third will be in far less demand for breeding purposes
if you disperse your herd, and I'll have fewer specimens with which
to improve my own stock, which is vast."

Bellefonte wandered to the desk, where he lifted the lid off a blue
ceramic bowl and brought the dish to Tremaine.

"Have a ginger biscuit," the earl said. "Haggling on an empty
stomach isn't well advised."

Tremaine took one. Bellefonte helped himself to three, put the
dish back on the desk, and moved to the shelves lining the inside wall
of the library.

"My countess likes you," the earl said. "My brothers like you. I
think Nita might like you too."

Ah, so all that dodging about the sheep, and shy, bookish Lady
Susannah had been so much diversion. Tremaine took a nibble of a
spicy biscuit lest he admit that *he* liked Lady Nita.

Respected her too. "Lady Nita was simply looking in on a woman
recently brought to bed with child," Tremaine said. "I wanted to see
some of your property and accomplished that aim."

Bellefonte left off perusing a small volume bound in red leather,
and considered one of his two remaining biscuits.

"You were spying on my acres?"

"Gathering information about a possible business associate. Have
you broached the matter of Lady Nita's upcoming travel with the
woman herself?"

Not that Tremaine would raise the topic with her or mention it to Beckman. He hoped to be gone before Bellefonte undertook that folly.

"Nita will never forgive me if I send her away," the earl said, "but spring can bring influenza and worse, and she has no care for what contagion could do to this household."

Thank the celestial powers, Bellefonte at least understood the need to curb his sister's more dangerous charitable impulses.

"You do not mention the risk that Lady Nita herself might fall ill," Tremaine said.

English physicians interviewed patients. They did not touch them in the usual course and often didn't even visit the sickroom. If contagion was a significant issue, then a family member might relay symptoms to the doctor, who'd prescribe nostrums from the safety of his cozy study.

Lady Nita apparently observed no such precautions.

Bellefonte snapped his book closed. "There's no point mentioning the risk of contagion to Lady Nita, such is my sister's disdain for common sense. Nita's healthy as a tinker's donkey, and nothing I say, promise, threaten, or shout makes any difference to her."

An image sprang up in Tremaine's mind of Lady Nita crouching by the shivering lamb, ready to do battle for its life if Tremaine had intended the little beast harm.

"Have you tried *asking* the lady to comply with your wishes, my lord?" Sooner or later, she'd fall ill, if not die, as a consequence of her kindheartedness.

Bellefonte consumed his third biscuit thoughtfully. "I haven't tried asking. I should, though Nita can drive me to shouting more quickly than the rest of my siblings put together."

Well, of course. Demure, sensible Lady Nita left her brother no choice but to rant and carry on like a squalling infant.

"With your sisters, as with your sheep, I'm sure you'll do as you see fit, my lord. I'm off at week's end to arrange travel to Germany if we can't come to terms on your herd of merinos."

"Talk to George, then, if you're bound for the Continent. He's recently returned and has good recall for which inns are clean, which of the packet captains sober. Beckman was our vagabond, but George might take up the post."

Beckman had traveled to escape bad memories, while George Haddonfield appeared to be the soul of sunny charm.

Interesting. "If we cannot come to terms, I will certainly confer with George. And, Bellefonte?"

The earl dusted biscuit crumbs from his hands.

"Lady Susannah might be happy with this poetical baronet-in-waiting," Tremaine said, "but I suggest you make a thorough study of the man's finances before you send her into his arms. Near his manor house, all is in good repair. The surrounding tenant farms, however, have sagging fences, tumbling stone walls, weedy cornfields, and overgrown hedges. Those sheep wouldn't be on Nash's property for a day before they'd be loose about the shire, wreaking havoc in your neighbors' gardens, and comporting themselves like strumpets with the local flocks."

Tremaine ate the last bite of his ginger biscuit, retrieved his letter, and left Nicholas, Lord Many Sisters, contemplating the remaining supply of biscuits.

~

Nita sought the warmth of the kitchen, because worse than being bone tired was being bone tired *and* hungry—which Addy Chalmers likely had been for years.

As Nita fetched the butter from the window box and unwrapped a loaf of bread, she recalled Addy mentioning Mary's father's family. Perhaps the unwritten etiquette of vice prohibited such a topic. Addy had certainly never before referred in Nita's hearing to the fathers of her children.

If she even knew who they were.

Nita poured cider into a pot and swung it over the coals of the cooking fire. Cinnamon would have made a nice addition, also an expensive one.

"Lady Nita, I'm surprised to find you awake at such a late hour."

Tremaine St. Michael leaned a shoulder against the doorjamb, his cravat missing, his shirtsleeves turned back, and his shirt open at the throat. Nita liked the look of him, his bustling energy and fine tailoring made more approachable by a touch of weariness and informality.

"Mr. St. Michael, good evening. Have you wandered belowstairs in search of a posset?"

How long had he been lounging there, watching Nita putter around in her dressing gown and slippers like a scullery maid?

"I'm peckish," he said, prowling into the room. Hungry men walked differently from the well-fed variety, as if they switched imaginary tails and twitched imaginary whiskers. "Too much time in the elements, trotting about the frozen lanes and swinging an ax." He peered into Nita's pot of cider. "What have you there?"

"Cider. You're welcome to join me." She made that offer partly out of hospitality and partly out of wistfulness. Mr. St. Michael would be leaving soon, and his company was oddly agreeable.

"You're content with bread and butter?" he asked. "Your brother has a fondness for ginger biscuits."

"Nicholas does. George can't abide them. What are you looking for?" Mr. St. Michael was peering into cupboards much as Nita's brothers did, holding up the table lamp to illuminate his plundering.

"I'm looking for spices. Cider wants—there it is." He set the lamp down and brought a small jar to the hearth, sprinkling something into the cider. The scent of cinnamon rose as he returned the jar to the cupboard. "I suspect if I looked long enough, I could find the ginger biscuits too."

Ginger biscuits dipped in mulled cider turned a late-night snack into something altogether more delectable.

"Biscuits are in that crock near the window."

Mr. St. Michael brought the entire crock to the raised hearth and pulled up a low stool before the fire. "Does Lady Susannah truly fancy that literary squire?" he asked.

Nita swung the steaming cider off the coals. "I hope not." She prayed not. "Why do you ask?"

"The earl would have me believe that yonder squire will pluck up his courage to make an offer for Lady Susannah, provided her dowry includes a lot of valuable sheep. If true, the squire is stupid and your brother not much brighter."

Nita liked that Mr. St. Michael was blunt, because that allowed her to be blunt too. "The squire is arrogant, Mr. St. Michael, and Nicholas has too much on his mind. Why do you insult them?" She poured cider into mugs, set those on the hearth, then fetched the bread and butter and a cold, red apple. A feast, by the lights of many.

By her lights too. She settled in on the hearth, where heat lingered in the stones from the day's cooking.

"Sheep are generally regarded as simple animals," Mr. St. Michael said, "easily panicked, without much sense. They are deemed thus by the man who curses them when they find the single weakness in any fence or wall, when they do as they jolly well please despite the collie barking and racing about, or when they're solving a problem—such as a lack of fodder—their owner has ignored."

He took a sip of cider while the scents of cinnamon and apples filled the kitchen. The hearth was warm, the cider delicious, and Mr. St. Michael's odd accent—at once rough and plush—absolutely appropriate for his chosen topic.

"The squire's fences are a disgrace," he went on. "I doubt he has a decent sheep dog, and his fields are all in want of marling, from what I could see. He cannot possibly provide adequate care for one of the most valuable herds in England. These biscuits are excellent."

Nita dipped a ginger biscuit in cider and took a bite. Spicy, sweet, warm, and as comforting as the company of a man who didn't mince words and who did care about his sheep.

"Quite lovely," Nita murmured.

"You could sort out the squire in short order, Nita Haddonfield, and yet you disdain marriage. I wonder why."

Nita liked this about Mr. St. Michael too. Liked that his mind was restless and curious, that he tackled real questions and had little patience for platitudes and weather reports.

"You've apparently disdained marriage yourself," she said.

He cradled his mug in both hands, as if warmth—any warmth—must not be squandered. "I'm skeptical of the institution's virtues," he said, "and well aware of its limitations. My parents' union was not cordial, particularly for my mother, and yet she didn't even try to extricate herself when she had the opportunity. Your brother seems happy with his countess."

A tactful, if enormous, understatement.

"Nicholas and Leah are besotted. For them, marriage makes sense. I've already been the lady of the manor and did not have to submit to a husband's dominion to obtain that status. My mother died, my brothers went off on various quests, and my father grew to rely on me. The staff answered to me, the tenants looked to me for guidance, and I developed a taste for independence."

Rather like Nita was developing a taste for ginger biscuits and cider.

Mr. St. Michael dipped his biscuit too, his third. "Independence appeals to many of us. Have you a strategy for maintaining this happy state?"

No, Nita did not, other than sheer determination. "Have you?"

He passed her a slice of buttered bread. "I am in trade, my dear. Notably lacking in address, and in possession of both Scottish and French ancestry. For the nonce, I'm safe."

No, Mr. St. Michael was not *safe*. He dealt easily with children, had a well-hidden streak of practical charity, and looked altogether too appealing over a crock of ginger biscuits. He wasn't precisely handsome, though. Nita liked that too.

"Have a care, Mr. St. Michael. You're wealthy, well traveled, and you can spout poetry. Best not relax your guard. Will you share this apple?"

He produced a knife, the folding knife with the sharp, sharp edge, and set about quartering and coring the apple. Nita was about to ask him why marriage—an arrangement that heavily favored the male of the species—had earned his skepticism when the back door opened on a gust of frigid air.

Her first thought was that Addy or her baby was in distress, followed by a fear that Elsie Nash might have summoned her. Twice before, Nita had silently hurried up the servants' stairs at Stonebridge to attend Elsie when the rest of the household had been abed.

Belle Maison's head groom, a venerable Welshman named Alfrydd, stomped snow from his boots.

"Evening, Lady Nita, guv'nor. Rider out from Town has brought the gentleman a letter." Alfrydd withdrew a sealed note from his pocket, and only now, when a trusted retainer of longstanding studied the bunches of herbs and onions hanging from the rafters, did Nita worry about her appearance.

About *the* appearances, and she should be beyond that in her own—in *her brother's*—kitchen.

Mr. St. Michael tore open the note, scanned it, and cursed in what sounded like Gaelic. "My tups are sickening. Can somebody saddle my horse?"

Alfrydd abruptly left off inspecting the rafters. "It be damned midnight, begging my lady's pardon. Aye, there's a moon, but there's clouds too, and the wind is murderous."

Nita's sentiments weren't half so polite. "You won't do your sheep any good if you end up freezing to death in a ditch, Mr. St. Michael, or if you come down with lung fever. Alfrydd, have you room for this rider in the grooms' quarters?"

"Aye, and a pot of tea to offer the fellow."

Nita wrapped up the remains of the bread loaf in a towel and handed Alfrydd a crock of butter as well.

"Thank the rider for his heroic efforts," she said, "and be ready for Mr. St. Michael to leave at first light."

"But my tups are the most valuable—" Mr. St. Michael began, speaking in the loudest—and most Scottish—tones Nita had heard from him.

"Alfrydd, our thanks," Nita said.

Alfrydd swept Nita with a look that encompassed her slippers, her upset guest, and her hair, hanging over her shoulder in a single braid.

"G'night, my lady. Sir."

Nita planted herself directly before Mr. St. Michael, between him and the door. "What did the note say?"

"The damned weather is to blame," he muttered, his gaze on the door Alfrydd had pulled stoutly closed. "Winter hasn't been bad until these past few weeks, and then we had two snowstorms back-to-back, and some truly bitter temperatures. The water freezes, or is so cold the silly sheep won't drink it, and if they—my lady, I must go."

So he could risk his neck for some adolescent rams? "Mr. St. Michael, tell me what the note said." Nita used the same tone on patients who hadn't yet realized the seriousness of an injury.

Also on her siblings.

He took the paper from his pocket and shoved it at her. "They're sick, some of them are down, and that's a very bad sign. These are my best lads, the ones I had in mind for breeding to your merinos. These fellows don't get sick, they're great, strapping youngsters in excellent health, and I *must* go."

His accent had traveled farther north the longer he spoke, his r's strewn along the Great North Road, his t's sharpening into verbal weaponry as they crossed the River Tweed.

As Nita read the note her mind was pulled in two directions at once. First, Mr. St. Michael took the welfare of his flock seriously, and not out of simple duty or commercial concern. He cared for these smelly, woolly, bleating creatures. Their suffering mattered to him.

That insight was at variance with the gruff, businesslike

demeanor Mr. St. Michael showed the world.

Nita's second thought was an unwelcome question: Was this how she herself reacted to word that some child had fallen ill or some grandmother was at her last prayers with no one to sit with her? St. Michael's sheep had shepherds as well as the sheep's equivalent of stable boys, and yet he trusted no one to deal with the situation but himself.

Grandmothers had grandchildren. Children had mothers and fathers, and yet, never once had Nita questioned that she must hare off to attend any who summoned her.

In this weather, at this hour, she'd permit no haring off. "Mr. St. Michael, please sit."

"I don't want to blasted *sit*. When I've taken every precaution, fed them extra rations, added hot water to their icy buckets at considerable effort on the part of—"

Nita took Mr. St. Michael by the shoulders and turned him toward the hearth, which was rather like persuading Atlas away from his hay.

"Listen to me," she said, when he'd finally acquiesced to her prodding and resumed his seat. "My brother has pigeons. Your sheep are in Oxfordshire?"

"This herd is."

She put a biscuit in Mr. St. Michael's hand. "We have pigeons in the dovecote from Mr. Belmont's estate in Oxfordshire. Are these extra rations from the same hay you normally feed?"

Mr. St. Michael stared at the biscuit. Nita could see him trying to make himself focus, the way she had to focus when deciding what supplies to grab when somebody was badly injured. Catgut, scissors, poultices mostly, and a prayer that Dr. Horton hadn't already been consulted regarding the course of treatment.

"I had the steward buy some particularly good hay," Mr. St. Michael informed his biscuit. "We've saved it back to feed on the coldest nights. That hay is beautiful, soft, green... Quite dear, but worth the expense." '

"Send a pigeon in the morning," Nita said. "Tell your men to switch back to your usual hay."

Mr. St. Michael half rose, then sat back down heavily, as if an excess of strong spirits had caught up with him.

"Pretty hay isn't always the best quality," he murmured. "Noxious weeds can spring up in any field."

In other words, Nita's theory had merit, and she hadn't even had to raise her voice or slam a door. Reason had joined them in the kitchen, a far more agreeable companion than panic. Mr. St. Michael broke the biscuit in half and offered Nita the larger portion.'

"Unless you've moved your herd or recently added to it," she said, "a sudden illness affecting many of the flock isn't likely. If it's not contagion, then a problem with their fodder is the next most likely culprit."

Mr. St. Michael dispatched his sweet in silence, though as Nita took a place beside him before the fire, she sent up a prayer the problem was as simple as a noxious weed in the hay. Diagnosis was equal parts science and instinct, with common sense mediating between the two.

"May we send the pigeon tonight, Lady Nita?" Worry and the Aberdeenshire hills still laced Mr. St. Michael's voice.

"Certainly. A good bird will be in Oxfordshire before your shepherds are at their morning chores. Alfrydd manages the dovecote."

The apple went next, in a few crunchy bites, while Mr. St. Michael remained quiet, and Nita's feet grew chilly.

"The grooms sleep above the carriage house?" Mr. St. Michael asked.

"Alfrydd among them. You might take them some biscuits." Apparently nobody would get any rest until Mr. St. Michael had done something to ensure the welfare of his sheep.

While Nicholas thought to send the merinos *and Susannah* to Edward Nash?

"You truly think it's the hay?" Mr. St. Michael asked, rising. He took his mug to the sink, tossed the apple core into the slop bucket, and wiped his hands on the towel kept for that purpose near the bread box.

"I'm nearly sure of it," Nita said, though no medical situation was ever certain. "You'll also want to scrub out the water buckets. If all you're doing is adding hot water to icy buckets, then the buckets haven't been truly cleaned for some time. Start fresh, and see if the sheep aren't more interested."

"Excellent advice," he said, draping the towel over its hook exactly as he'd found it. "I might have come to the same conclusions by the time I reached London—provided I hadn't landed on my arse in the ditch at the foot of your lane."

Mr. St. Michael offered Nita his hand, and without thinking, Nita let him draw her to her feet. They were in the kitchen, she was wearing two thicknesses of wool stockings, and front parlor manners were the farthest thing from her—

Tremaine St. Michael hugged her. The sensation was rather like being enveloped in a blanket left to warm on a brass fender, all comfort and ease, a hint of heather and lavender, and an irresistible temptation to relax.

To relax *everything*. Nita's mind, her body, her worries, her *heart*, yielded to the pleasure of Tremaine St. Michael's embrace.

"I worry over those young fellows," he murmured. "I am in your debt, my lady."

Tremaine St. Michael's debts were patiently repaid. He made no move to march off to the stable. Nita rested her head on his shoulder —so few men were tall enough to afford her that comfort.

She offered him the words nobody offered her. "You're good to worry for them, Mr. St. Michael.

They count on you to look after them, to keep them healthy, and your shepherds were right to bring this problem to you. A few days of proper rations, a nap in the sun, and your tups will recover. Keep them in your prayers, and this time next week, they'll be good as new."

He stroked her hair, another invitation to relax, to be safe and warm. "One doesn't admit to praying for sheep."

One just had, perhaps even two.

Nita stepped back and Mr. St. Michael let her go. "Take the biscuits to the stable lads," she said.

"William will benefit. You'll probably have word back from Oxfordshire by sunset tomorrow."

Mr. St. Michael picked up the entire crock of biscuits, kissed Nita's cheek, then lingered for a moment, so he spoke very near her ear.

"I am grateful to have been spared a frigid, dangerous, crack-brained midnight ride, Lady Nita. I meant what I said: I am in your debt. Collect your boon at the time and place of your choosing."

He marched off to the rack of capes and coats hanging in the back hallway. Nita spared the dirty dishes a thought, grabbed a carrying candle, and took herself up the servants' stairs, rather than linger in the kitchen.

The stairwell was cold and dark, but she paused on the landing to watch through the oriel window as Mr. St. Michael made his way across the snowy gardens. In the depths of a winter night, he would have hopped on his trusty steed and charged to the rescue of a lot of smelly sheep twenty leagues beyond London.

A gust of chilly air doused the candle. Nita found her way to her room through the familiar darkness, said a prayer for Mr. St. Michael's sheep, and went to bed. Her last thought was that she should be a little ashamed of herself.

Her mother had taught her that a person in possession of the ability to help, especially a person well-placed in Society, was both privileged and obligated to render aid to those in need.

Nita hadn't offered her opinion on the ailing sheep out of a sense of privilege or obligation. She'd tendered her diagnosis simply because she hadn't wanted Mr. St. Michael to leave.

She wasn't ashamed of that at all.

CHAPTER FIVE

Nita Haddonfield possessed keen medical insight, long blond hair, *and curves*. Tremaine had guessed at the first two, but the third...

The third revelation was a problem. His body had awoken with that problem in mind, a puzzle and an inconvenience. A few minutes of self-gratification did nothing to solve the puzzle.

Why her?

She'd made a fetching picture in a faded velvet dressing gown the same shade of blue as her eyes, and she'd brought a cozy elegance to the business of nibbling biscuits. Tremaine's imagination—ever as unruly as a healthy tup—had latched on to the idea that Lady Nita would be cozy and *fun* in bed. How he'd leaped to that conclusion about a woman who lacked romantic sentiments, had no use for marriage, and little use for men—

A knock sounded on Tremaine's door, too decisive to be a footman with more coal or a maid with a tea tray.

"Come in."

George Haddonfield sauntered through the door, showing a country gentleman's attire to excellent advantage.

"Ready to go down to breakfast, St. Michael?"

"I am, in fact," Tremaine replied, whipping his cravat into a mathematical. "The earl says I'm to quiz you about coaching inns, packet captains, and French highwaymen."

George lifted the dish that held Tremaine's shaving soap and took a whiff. "Beastly time of year to travel. This is quite pleasant. Is it French?"

"Scottish, and no time of year is good for travel. Mud, flies, storms, rain, coaching accidents, pestilence, blistering sun, every season has some blight to offer the weary traveler." Tremaine could, that very minute, have been racketing about the snowy lanes of London in a headlong dash for Oxford.

What had he been thinking?

"So don't travel," George said. "Linger here for another week or so. The ladies would love to show you off at the assembly."

"A temptation, to be sure." To be shown off like a prize ram? "I might be leaving today, despite the lure of the assembly. One of my most valuable flocks has taken ill, and I'm awaiting word of their prognosis."

Tremaine's wardrobe stood open, and George surveyed its contents.

"You'd be a perishing idiot to ride any distance with that sky promising snow," George graciously opined. "You've traveled on the Continent before. Your waistcoat whispers of Italian silk, and that's Flemish lace on your shirt cuffs."

A touch of lace only. French blood would tell. "I've traveled at length, though less so in recent years. Why aren't you married, Haddonfield? You're comely, well placed, and overly endowed with charm."

George touched the sleeve of one of Tremaine's fancier shirts, fingers lingering on the frothy cuff. "I ought to marry. Travel in quantity doesn't agree with me."

Whatever that had to do with anything. Some married men traveled a great deal.

Tremaine dragged a brush through his hair, which was overdue for a shearing. "Lady Nita has also apparently eschewed holy matrimony," he observed, "while the earl wants nothing more than to see his sisters well settled."

Now George examined the embroidery on a paisley waistcoat. "I suspect Nicholas made some promise last year to our dying father about finding husbands for the ladies. Nicholas promised Papa he'd marry, and he kept that promise.'"

The ladies were doomed then, all but Lady Nita. Tremaine's money was on her to thwart her brother, and yet she needed marrying. Needed somebody to share biscuits with her late at night, appreciate her curves, and give her children of her own, lest she waste her days wiping the noses of other people's offspring and brewing tisanes for other people's uncles.

Tremaine tucked a sleeve button through the buttonhole on his cuff. "If Bellefonte won't sell me his merinos, then I'm for Germany. The earl has some notion that he can lead Mr. Nash to the altar by parading the sheep before him."

The sleeve button wasn't cooperating, or perhaps Tremaine was in a hurry to get down to breakfast.

"Let me do that." George captured Tremaine's wrist and tended to each sleeve button, left then right, with the practiced efficiency of a valet. "I'd not like to see those sheep go to Nash."

"Neither would I," Tremaine said, "but my interest is mercantile, while yours is—what?"

George Haddonfield was a pattern card of male beauty, and yet what made his appearance interesting was a quality of self-containment, a guardedness his older brother Nicholas lacked. George had spent time on the Continent too, a sad and weary place in the wake of the Corsican's republican violence.

"Nash is guardian to his nephew," George said, straightening a fold of Tremaine's cravat. "I don't think the boy is happy. I know he's not, in fact. Neither is his mother. How a man treats his dependents says a lot about him. No one is more dependent than a wife, and

Susannah has no wickedness, no instinct for self-preservation. Managing Nash will take sharp wits and nimble self-interest."

Business instincts, in other words.

"Have you shared your sentiments with your titled brother?" Tremaine asked. He wanted those sheep, wanted them badly, but his question had more to do with keeping them from the wrong hands than putting them into his own. As for Lady Susannah...

Lady Nita didn't think much of this Nash fellow.

George held the bedroom door open. "Bellefonte wouldn't be interested in my opinion regarding a possible match for Susannah. He and I manage the civilities, but we're not close."

As Beckman hadn't been close with his brothers, and a fourth brother, Ethan Grey, had apparently been estranged from them all until recently. Another brother bided at Cambridge in some scientific capacity.

No wonder Bellefonte fretted over his siblings. A scattered flock was at the greatest risk for predation.

"I had only the one brother," Tremaine said as he and George traveled the carpeted corridor. In memory of that late brother, a lazy scoundrel with too much charm, no honor, and little sense, Tremaine would meddle, just a bit.

"I didn't always like my brother," he went on, "and I often didn't respect him, but he's dead, and even the civilities are lost to us. Talk to the earl, Mr. Haddonfield. Bellefonte is a reasonable man. If Lady Susannah must marry, the union should have at least a chance of happiness."

Though if Susannah Haddonfield was determined to wed her poetical squire, Tremaine suspected little anybody could say, do, or threaten would stop her. She had Lady Nita's firm and misguided example to follow, after all.

∾

Nita managed breakfast without falling asleep at the table, though she hadn't rested well through the night.

"What have you planned for today, Nita?" Nicholas's expression was mere brotherly interest, but if Nita said she wanted to check on wee Annie, he'd set aside his teacup and cast a look down the table to his countess that boded ill for the King's peace.

And Nita didn't dare mention persistent coughs, sore throats, or head colds, though they were on her mind. "I'm inclined to practice the pianoforte today," she replied. "Some pieces that might allow the musicians a break at the assembly." *Then* she'd check on Annie.

"Thoughtful of you," Leah said, and to Nita's surprise, a look went the opposite direction, up the table, from countess to earl.

"Mr. St. Michael," Nita said, "have you plans for today?"

He would say nothing of their shared biscuits and cider, of that Nita was certain. Did he know she'd nearly kissed him, nearly turned a sweet, friendly embrace into something sweet, friendly, and improper?

Why hadn't she? Mr. St. Michael had an even dimmer view of marriage than Nita did. He wouldn't have followed a stolen kiss with awkward declarations or lewd presumptions.

"As it turns out, I'm off for London later today," he said. "Word came last night that one of my flocks has taken sick. Bellefonte, your man Alfrydd was good enough to send a pigeon for me to Oxfordshire, but in the absence of encouraging news this morning, I must go."

Another look went winging around the table, this time from Kirsten to Susannah to Della—and what was Della doing at the breakfast table twice in one week?

"A pity that anybody should have to attempt the King's Highway at this time of year," the countess said. "Nicholas, please pass the teapot to our guest."

Nita ate something—eggs, possibly bacon, buttered toast—then excused herself. As Mr. St. Michael had recited his plans for the day, he'd done Nita the courtesy of keeping his gaze elsewhere, and yet, would a hint of regret have been so inappropriate?

Rather than seek him out and ask such a brazen question, Nita applied herself for the next hour to country-dances at the pianoforte.

"If you hit those keys any harder, the poor instrument will lose its tuning."

Tremaine St. Michael had ventured into the music room, a pair of worn saddlebags over his shoulder. Nita brought the music to a cadence and folded the lid over the keys.

"Mr. St. Michael. I gather you're leaving us." Leaving her.

He took a seat on the piano bench, which left little room for Nita. "I honestly don't want to, my lady. I looked forward to turning down the room with you, learning how you cheat at cards, or singing a few duets with you. 'Green Grow the Rashes, O,' comes to mind."

"Mr. Burns again?"

"At his philosophical best. Will you walk with me to the stables, my dear?"

The door to the music room was open, which preserved Nita from an impulse to kiss Mr. St. Michael. She'd refrained the previous night—good manners, common sense, some inconvenient virtue or other had denied her a single instant of shared pleasure.

"I'll need my cloak."

Mr. St. Michael stayed right where he was, which meant Nita was more or less penned onto the piano bench.

"I told the earl the Chalmers boys would be useful in any effort to harvest timber from the home wood," Mr. St. Michael said. "They'll know where the deadfall is, where the saplings haven't enough light. The girl, Mary, is plenty old enough to start in the scullery."

Nita hadn't dared make that suggestion, though many apprentices began work at age six. "Mary is needed at home, especially now that the new baby is here."

"The baby has a mother." Mr. St. Michael rose, his tone quite severe. "An infant that young ought to be in her mother's care."

Nita came to her feet before he could assist her. "Addy tries, but she can't find honest work, and that leaves only what vice the *men* in the shire will indulge in, and she drinks."

Such was the fate of women who did not preserve their virtue for marriage. Mr. St. Michael spared Nita that sermon, though Nicholas had alluded to it enough to disappoint Nita more than a little.

As if any of her brothers had preserved *their* virtue for holy matrimony? As if they knew for a fact that Addy had cast her good name heedlessly aside, that it hadn't been wheedled from her grasp by a predatory scoundrel—or worse?

Mr. St. Michael held Nita's cloak for her when they reached the kitchen door, and when Nita would have closed the frogs herself, his hands were already at her throat, competent and brisk. He did up the fastenings exactly right—snug enough to be warm, loose enough to allow movement and breathing.

"Have you a bonnet, Lady Nita?"

So formal. If Nita had had a bonnet, she might have smacked him with it, surely the most childish impulse she'd felt in years.

"We're only walking to the stable, Mr. St. Michael, and the sun has hardly graced the shire in days." What would freckles on Nita's nose matter, anyway? "I take it you couldn't sleep?" she asked by way of small talk.

His eyes looked weary to her, like the gaze of a mother who'd been up through the night with a colicky infant.

"I did not sleep well; you're right, my lady. I'm accustomed to waking up in strange beds, but I do worry for those sheep."

Nita let him hold the door for her, though his observation was odd.

Mr. St. Michael bent near. "I meant I travel a great deal, and spend many nights in inns, lodging houses, and the homes of acquaintances. You have a naughty imagination, Lady Nita."

She took his arm, though she was entirely capable of walking the gardens without a man's escort. Nita did have a naughty imagination, about which she'd nearly forgotten.

"Will you send word when you reach Oxfordshire, Mr. St. Michael?"

"I'll have your Mr. Belmont send a pigeon, but you mustn't worry. I'm a seasoned traveler, William is an excellent fellow under saddle, and the distance isn't that great."

The distance was endless, because Mr. St. Michael, having failed to wrangle Nicholas's sheep free, would never cross paths with Nita again.

"I wish you had taught me a few verses of that song, the one about Mr. Burns's philosophy." Nita wished this more dearly than she wished to study German medical treatises on surgical procedures.

"The song is a bit naughty too," Mr. St. Michael replied. "The lyrics are at once profound and frivolous." He paused among the shorn hedges and dead roses and offered Nita a mellow baritone serenade:

The sweetest hours that e'er I spend, Are spent among the lasses, O!
But gie me a cannie hour at e'en, My arms about my dearie,
O, An' warl'y cares an' war'ly men May a' gae tapsalteerie, O!

"Burns goes on in that vein," Mr. St. Michael said. "About how lovely and dear the ladies are, nature's best work. Men are simply the practice model, while women have the greatest wisdom and so forth."

"Those are frivolous sentiments?" To be sung to was precious, not frivolous at all. Maybe this was why Susannah was so susceptible to Mr. Nash's recitations, because when a man offered exquisite verse, his gaze full of sincerity and sentiment, a lady was helpless not to listen.

Mr. St. Michael took Nita's hand and resumed walking. They hadn't bothered with gloves, and his grip was warm.

"Mr. Burns had rather a lot of dearies," he said, his burr once again more in evidence.

While Nita had no one dear, other than her family. A gust of bitter wind blew down from the north, snowflakes slanting along it.

"Must you go, Mr. St. Michael?"

"I don't like the look of those clouds either," he said as they approached the stable, "but I'll probably make London before the weather does anything serious. Will you grant me a favor, my lady?"

"Yes." Nobody asked Nita for favors. They asked her to set bones, deliver babies, listen to their coughs, poultice their wounds, or—in the case of Nicholas—they ordered her to sit at home and stitch samplers.

"You don't know what I'm about to ask."

"I know you. You wouldn't ask if it weren't important." Nita also knew she'd miss Mr. St. Michael. He was not friendly, but he had somehow become her friend.

"Please see that this gets to the Chalmers household." He passed Nita coins, a good ten pounds, a fortune to Addy and her children. "I'm not sure whether the best approach is to give it to the mother, so she knows she need not immediately return to her trade, or to give it to the child, Mary, so it won't be wasted on gin. I'm delegating that decision to you."

Nita slipped the coins into the pocket of her cape. "Some would say you're condoning sin." While Nita wanted to hug him.

"If feeding children and preventing them from freezing to death is sin, then I condemned myself to eternal hellfire ages ago, simply through the number of youths I employ to tend my flocks. My parents were quite wealthy, but they chose to guard their wealth rather than remain with their sons. Addy has not abandoned her offspring, though her children are one storm away from either death or the poorhouse, and I know not which is worse."

"Thank you, regardless of the theology or your motivations." Mr. St. Michael was kind, though he would not want that put into words.

He dropped Nita's hand and signaled the groom to bring William out. "May I make a farewell to your Atlas, my lady?"

"Of course." Despite her heavy cloak, Nita was chilled, and the barn would be relatively warm.

They walked into the stable, out of the wind but into near dark-ness. In warmer months, the hay port doors, windows, and cupola would be opened to let in light and air, but in winter, warmth was more important than light.

Atlas lifted his head over the half door, a mouthful of hay munched to oblivion as Nita and Mr. St. Michael approached.

"You need a more elegant mount," Mr. St. Michael said. "Just as you need a silly evening of cards, a waltz or two, and more poetry. I had hoped to give you that."

Nita *needed* to kiss him. Tremaine St. Michael had offered her a rare glimpse of how male understanding could comfort and please, he'd offered her poetry, and he was leaving.

"Good-bye, Mr. St. Michael."

Nita didn't have to go up on her toes to kiss him, but she did have to stand tall. Despite the bitter wind outside, despite his lack of hat, scarf, or gloves, Mr. St. Michael's lips were warm. He tasted of peppermint with a hint of ginger biscuit. Nita hadn't planned more than to press her lips to his, but Mr. St. Michael was apparently willing to indulge her beyond those essentials.

His hands landed on her shoulders, gently but firmly, as he tucked her between himself and the wall of Atlas's stall. He slid a hand into her hair, cradling the back of her head against his palm. Soon, he'd gallop off to Oxford, but the way he held Nita said, for the moment, *she* wasn't going anywhere.

Well, neither would he. Nita wrapped an arm around Mr. St. Michael's waist—blast all winter clothing to perdition—and sank a hand into his dark locks.

"I'll miss—" she managed before his mouth settled over hers, and Nita's worldly cares, her disgruntlement with her family, her concern for the Chalmers children, all went quite...tapsalteerie-o.

Kissing Tremaine St. Michael bore a resemblance to the onset of a fever. Weakness assailed Nita, from her middle outward, through her limbs, and then heat welled in its wake. He held her snugly—she would not fall—but she felt as if she were falling.

His kiss was a marvel of contradictions: solid male strength all around Nita and feather-soft caresses to her lips; dark frustration to be limited to a kiss and soaring satisfaction to have a kiss that transcended mere friendliness; utter glee to find that her advances were enthusiastically returned and plummeting sorrow because Mr. St. Michael's horse awaited him in the stable yard.

He cupped Nita's jaw as he traced kisses over her eyebrows, nose, and cheeks.

"You deserve more than a stolen kiss in the stable," he whispered. "But if a stolen kiss is what you'll take, then I hope this one was memorable."

This one kiss, this one series of kisses, had banished winter from Nita's little corner of Kent in less than a minute.

She rested against him, as she had for a moment in the kitchen late at night. "You'll let us know when you've arrived safely to Oxford." She was repeating herself.

"I'll let *you* know, and, Nita?"

Not Lady Nita, but plain Nita. How that warmed her too. "Tremaine?"

She felt the pleasure of her familiar address reverberate through him, because he kissed her ear as he held her in the gloom of the stable.

"Please be careful. Your brother is right to worry about you. Tending to the sick is noble but perilous. I would not want harm to befall you."

Nita added two more feelings to the bittersweet confusion in her heart. Tremaine St. Michael cared for her, and yet he sounded as if he nearly agreed with Nicholas: the Earl of Bellefonte's oldest sister ought to spend her afternoons stitching samplers, indifferent to the suffering of others.

"I'll be careful," Nita said. "You avoid the ditches."

"I generally do, though I wish—" Mr. St. Michael stayed where he was a moment longer, peering down at Nita as a heathery fragrance sneaked beneath the stable scents to tease at Nita's nose.

She was hemmed in by the wall, the horse, and Mr. St. Michael, so she turned her face away, from him, and from his wishes.

"Safe journey, Mr. St. Michael."

He stepped back, and as he tugged his gloves on, Nita could see his focus withdraw from her and affix itself to his sheep, to the journey he undertook to ensure their safety.

Nobody had *ever* tormented him with orders to stitch samplers while a child suffered influenza or a maiden aunt endured a female complaint in mortified silence. Nita was the first to move toward the stable yard, lest Mr. St. Michael ruin a delightful kiss with parting sermons and scolds.

William waited outside, a groom leading him in a plodding circle. Snowflakes graced a brisk breeze beneath a leaden sky, and Nita's resentment receded to its taproot: worry, for Mr. St. Michael, for the infirm whom she tended.

And a little worry for herself, too.

"I have enjoyed my stay at Belle Maison," Mr. St. Michael said, taking the reins from the groom. "Every bit of it."

He led William to the mounting block, the first few steps of a distance that must widen and widen between him and Nita. She wanted to throw herself into his embrace just once more, but instead spared the sullen sky a glance.

Mr. St. Michael swung up as a flutter of white caught Nita's eye, followed by a thin, tinkling peal from the bell in the dovecote.

Elsinore Mayhew Nash was a furious woman, also a mother devoted to her son. When her brother-by-marriage summoned her to his library, she took off her apron, slapped a vapid smile on her face, and hastened to Edward's side.

"You wanted to see me?" Elsie's tone imparted eager, if timid, good cheer. The only eagerness she'd felt in the past year had been to wallop Edward with a poker in locations chosen to ensure he never became a father.

"Elsie, a moment."

So, of course, she must remain standing while Edward pretended to pore over a column of figures. Elsie could relax, though, because his complexion assured her he'd not yet begun to drink. The Stonebridge "library" had once been the housekeeper's sitting room. Now that Edward had appropriated it, the library was the warmest room in the house.

Also home to fewer than a hundred books, the rest having been sold.

Little did Edward know, but Elsie's ball gowns had been sold too. She'd taken care of that before leaving London to join Edward's household, a brilliant precaution quietly suggested by another lady who'd buried not one but three husbands.

"Please have a seat, my dear," Edward said, returning his pen to its stand. "You're looking well."

Elsie's guard went up. Not only was Edward sober, but he was also on his good behavior—for now.

"Thank you," she said, perching on the edge of a straight-backed chair. "We're making pies, which I enjoy. Apple is your favorite, isn't it?"

More eager good cheer. Elsie had considered poisoning Edward, but how would Digby manage if his mother swung for murder? What little money she had hidden wouldn't last long. Edward's aging greatuncle, the baronet, was the sole relation left to provide for the boy in Edward's absence, and the baronet might be worse than Edward.

"I do favor an apple pie," Edward said. "I do not, however, favor George Haddonfield in any proximity to my nephew."

Eager good cheer gave way to feminine confusion. Elsie had mastered the transition by her second week under Edward's roof.

"George Haddonfield? Surely we'd remain on friendly terms with Lady Susannah's brother? He brought Digby home from his tutoring session merely as a kindness on a frigid day."

Edward retrieved his quill pen and brushed it over his fingertips. "The situation is delicate. Friendly terms with Susannah's siblings for now is a prudent course, but George Haddonfield in particular is to be avoided."

Susannah, not *Lady* Susannah, because Edward already appropriated the privileges of a fiancé. He had systematically decided that most of the ladies with whom Elsie corresponded were not quite the thing, a less-than-ideal association, or better suited to friendship with a woman not bereaved.

In other words, he was choking off Elsie's friendships, one after the other, lest somebody get wind that Edward Nash was rolled up, a sot, and desperate to marry well.

If only those were the worst of Edward's shortcomings. "Does George have excessive debts?" Elsie asked.

He did not, of course. The Haddonfields as a family were free of the vices Edward assiduously failed to acknowledge in himself.

"He well might be in dun territory," Edward said, stroking the feather against his chin. "The Haddonfields have been known to put their unsavory family members on remittance, and George looks to be taking Beckman's place in that regard."

"Don't many gentlemen live in hock to their tailors?" Questions were risky, but Edward was not yet imbibing, so Elsie could venture a few inquiries in the interests of understanding his latest queer start.

More twiddling of the feather while Elsie remained on the edge of her chair and resisted the urge to crack a window, so stuffy did Edward keep this one room

"George's situation is not as innocent as a few overdue bills among the merchants, Elsie. He has tastes I would not expect a woman of your refinement to comprehend, but they place him among the least appropriate associations you or my nephew could form."

In a family of large, loud, dramatic men and headstrong, outspoken sisters, George Haddonfield had a quiet independence that appealed strongly to a widow under the thumb of an abhorrent in-law.

So what if George wasn't a Puritan? Elsie had followed the drum for two years and had become difficult to shock.

"I'll tell Digby to avoid Mr. Haddonfield's company," Elsie said. "Do I maintain a distance from him at the assembly?"

Edward thrived on instructing Elsie, the maids, Digby, and their man of all work, whom Edward insisted on referring to as a footman. Edward probably instructed his horses and hounds, who were at least free to bite and kick him.

Though they'd regret such displays sorely.

"In public, you will show Mr. Haddonfield every courtesy," Edward said, twiddling the feather between his palms. "Dance with him, make small talk, inquire after his health. Bellefonte is protective of his siblings, and I cannot have it said we were less than gracious to any of Susannah's family. Other than the civilities, though, you will avoid him. I offer you this guidance, because I know Pendleton would expect it of me."

Elsie blinked a few times in rapid succession, as if mention of her late husband still had the power to move her to tears. She had Penny to thank for landing her in this hell, and for handing over Digby's funds to a mean, intemperate wastrel. Penny had been a dear in most regards, but also old-fashioned and something of a pedant.

"I owe you so much, Edward," Elsie said, rising. "I am very grateful for your guidance. Was there more you wanted to say, or shall I get back to those pies?"

Because making pies was doubtless the acme of every gentlewoman's ambitions, in Edward's view.

"Don't let me keep you, but please have the kitchen send up a tray. These endless figures make a man peckish. A toddy or two as well. Something to ward off the chill, and some comestibles to fortify me until my next meal."

He came around the desk and held the door for Elsie, doing his impersonation of a blond, handsome exponent of good manners and faultless breeding. Edward would have been better served by fewer manners, more common sense, and a dash of self-restraint. When the door had closed behind her, Elsie paused in the corridor long enough to let the chilly air wash over her.

Of the three Nash offspring, Penny had been the sensible middle brother, not as pretty as Edward, but willing to work to earn his bread, less concerned with appearances, and genuinely devoted to his son. He'd not been the brightest of officers, but he'd worked hard and had had a streak of gruff kindness that had made his sternness bearable.

Norton had been the brash, ginger-haired youngest son, happy to gallop off and buy his colors rather than molder away in rural Kent as an unpaid steward or extra at whist. Elsie suspected Edward had been happy to see Norton go, because younger sons without means could author much mischief.

While Edward was a trial without end. Elsie honestly wanted to warn Lady Susannah to look past the same three tiresome Shakespeare sonnets and a pair of soulful blue eyes. To look at the empty shelves in the so-called library, at how short Digby's trousers were, at how cold the house was but for the rooms Edward occupied.

Elsie could not afford to warn Lady Susannah, because if Edward did not soon marry wealth, Elsie and Digby might both find themselves on the charity of the parish.

CHAPTER SIX

Tremaine knew he was in trouble—serious, interesting trouble—when he heard the little bell tinkling in the dovecote as the sound of reprieve. He wanted to remain here in Kent, haggling with Bellefonte over his sheep, preventing Lady Nita from attending to her most rebellious errands.

And kissing her.

"Was that a pigeon?" Her ladyship sounded annoyed. "I couldn't tell."

"Whatever it was, it flew straight to your dovecote," Tremaine said, stepping off his horse. "Perhaps I won't be journeying to Oxford just yet."

For the first time, his obligations to his livestock, his employees, and their families felt not like an anchor, not like the enviable result of commercial success, but like a burden.

"I'll hold William," Lady Nita said, lifting the reins over the horse's head. "Alfrydd was in the saddle room. You'd best fetch him."

A ladylike version of an order, with which Tremaine complied. Alfrydd tottered up the ladder to the mow, leaving Tremaine in the gloom of the stable, surrounded by horses munching hay and shifting in their stalls.

He was worried for his sheep, of course he was. He was worried for Lady Nita too.

He *ought* to worry for himself. Nita Haddonfield was decent, a lady to the bone, and an innocent, despite her ill-advised medical adventuring. Tremaine's dealings with her should be either polite, gentlemanly distance or matrimonial overtures.

Lady Nita wouldn't understand the first, and she'd laugh at the second.

"From Mr. Belmont," Alfrydd said, advancing down the ladder by lowering his left leg, pausing, then the right. Left, pause, right. Tremaine's grandfather had moved in the same fashion when his hip had been predicting a winter storm.

"I expect it's for you, sir," Alfrydd said, passing over a tiny rolled cylinder of paper. Outside, under the sullen winter sky, Lady Nita stood waiting beside William, while in the shadows of the stable, Tremaine wrestled with a choice.

He could tell her ladyship, regardless of what the note truly said, that he was needed in Oxford. Leave the sheep, the sisters, *and the kisses* behind, climb onto his horse, and tend to business.

Atlas hung his head over his stall door, as if to inquire of any news.

"Thank you, Alfrydd." Tremaine took the note out into the light.

Tups coming right. Will feed only regular fodder. No news is good news. MacNeill

The writing was tiny; Tremaine's relief was enormous, while Lady Nita patted his horse and asked nothing of him save that he travel safely. She was so calm, so alone.

She was also a delight to challenge over a hot, spicy, late-night mug of cider.

And to kiss.

"You were right, my lady," Tremaine said. "You were exactly, absolutely, one hundred percent right. My boys are rallying."

He expected one of her ladyship's sweet, beaming smiles. He was certainly smiling, smiling like a shepherd boy smitten with the goose girl. What greater gift could any shepherd have than his flock returned to well-being?

Lady Nita peered at the sky, she fiddled with William's reins, she stroked the horse's hairy shoulder.

"I'm glad." Another lingering pat, this one to the beast's neck. "Will you be staying then, Mr. St. Michael?" Nita Haddonfield was the least presuming woman Tremaine had met, or perhaps the most disappointed.

"I will tarry another few days," Tremaine said. "Isn't there an assembly next week?"

Now Lady Nita smiled—at the cold, hard ground, true, but a happy smile nonetheless, one that whispered of mulled cider and midnight ginger biscuits.

"We do have an assembly in the offing," she said. "Leah will be in alt to present you to the neighbors. You must practice your dancing and flirting."

Tremaine and Lady Nita could practice dancing and flirting with each other, though flirting had ever been beyond him. Strategy, however, was in his gift. He took the reins from her ladyship and passed them to Alfrydd.

"Lady Nita, might you accompany me on a call to Mr. Nash?"

Her bashful, endearing smile winked out like a star fallen from a December night sky. "I think not, Mr. St. Michael. Susannah is on better terms with Mr. Nash than I am. She, Della, or Kirsten would happily accompany you. All of them together, in fact, and likely the countess as well."

She named a flock of curious ewes, climbing all over Tremaine's attempts to gather information—and not only information about Nash.

"Your company will be the more discerning," Tremaine said. "Nash is competing with my attempts to acquire your brother's sheep. My call will not be entirely social, and I think you might have planned an errand or two for this afternoon."

Alfrydd hovered in the doorway to the barn with William, out of the wind but within earshot. He was very much the earl's man, of course, while Tremaine was...

In trouble.

"An errand or two, Mr. St. Michael?"

"We could stop for a pint at your local posting inn," Tremaine suggested. "Enjoy a cottage pie, ensure the vicar has sent some charity to those in need."

He would not abet her ladyship's attempts to visit any sickrooms, but for a chance to spend more time with her, he'd endure a call upon the new mother. Lady Nita was as guileless as her sister Susannah was reported to be, because Tremaine saw the moment understanding dawned.

"I'll need to change into my habit."

"I'll accompany you to the house," Tremaine replied, "and warn Bellefonte his hospitality is not yet at an end."

Nor was the fate of the merino sheep settled. Bellefonte had agreed to name a price by correspondence for which Tremaine could purchase the sheep. The sum likely depended upon a blunt discussion with Mr. Nash about the cost of the repairs needed to put Stonebridge to rights and an equally blunt discussion with Lady Susannah.

Complicated business, tending to marriageable sisters, particularly when the earl's ready capital appeared to be limited and unavailable to dower those sisters. The aristocracy was often caught between the stability of centuries-old agrarian wealth and the need for cold, hard coin that would allow commercial diversification.

"Alfrydd, if you'd have Atlas saddled?" Lady Nita asked, another polite command. "He'll need his saddlebags. No telling what Mr. St. Michael and I might come across in the shops."

"I'll see to it, my lady."

Alfrydd led William back into the barn, while Tremaine rehearsed his announcement to Bellefonte. *I'm back, your lordship, and more intent on taking possession of those sheep than ever.*

In a friendly, temporary, adult sort of way, might Lady Nita consider taking a little possession of Tremaine, as well?

You were exactly, absolutely, one hundred percent right.

Nita was often right. She'd been right that Daryl Bletching's hand could be saved with poultices, stitching, good care, and liberal doses of willow bark tea. She'd been right that Norma Byler had been carrying twins. She'd been right that Darinda Hampton's youngest could not tolerate strawberry jam. She'd been right that Winnifred Hess's ague was the onset of chicken pox.

Nobody rejoiced when Nita was right, Dr. Horton least of all.

Tremaine St. Michael had rejoiced and accorded Nita full victory honors.

How handsome he was when he smiled like that, openly, exuberantly, lips, eyes, cheeks alit with joy, and half of rural Aberdeenshire in his accent—because of her.

Because of what Nita had done for his best lads.

She finished buttoning up the skirt of her riding habit and surveyed her reflection in the mirror. The garment was several years out of fashion, had been mended in two places around the hem, and was looser than when Nita had made it.

She'd never cared about any of that before, nor had she ever hurried to pay a social call on the Nash household, but she did today. Mr. St. Michael boosted her into the saddle, waved off Alfrydd's offer to send a groom along, and then swung up on William.

"Lead on, my lady. I expect it to start snowing at any minute."

"A handy excuse for not tarrying at Nash's. What will your motivation be for calling on Edward socially?" Nita asked, though country households visited back and forth routinely.

"Nash is a fellow appreciator of good poetry." Said with an amusement that should have made wolves nervous.

"You're up to something." Men were frequently up to something, but Tremaine St. Michael would confide his plans in Nita, not shout his orders at her.

"Does Squire Nash want the sheep more, or the lady?" Mr. St. Michael mused as the horses ambled out of the stable yard. "By asking to include the sheep in Lady Susannah's dowry, maybe Nash is so intent on winning the lady that he's proposed a bargain easy for the earl to agree to. The sheep are overgrazing their pasture, they require a dedicated shepherd, and they're becoming inbred."

Nita applied her diagnostic abilities to Susannah's situation, something she'd yet to do.

"Or does he want the sheep," she replied, "and asking for Susannah's hand ensures he'll get them, because Nicholas dreads to see his sisters growing old, haunting Belle Maison in their endless spinsterhood. Then too, Edward appears to dote on Susannah, and she is a lady upon whom any husband ought to dote."

They turned out of the drive, onto the lane that led into the village, and directly into the wind.

"All wives ought to be doted on, at least a little," Mr. St. Michael observed. "Or where's the benefit in accepting a fellow's suit?"

Most girls were raised with an eleventh commandment their brothers were spared: *A bad match is better than no match at all.* The benefit was in avoiding the shame of spinsterhood. Nita was not interested in marriage—ten commandments were enough for her—but when she'd stood in the stable yard, holding William's reins and hoping, hoping, *hoping* that Mr. St. Michael didn't have to leave, she'd been honest with herself.

She was interested in *him.* In letting him dote on her, in doting on him.

"Nicholas and his countess are devoted," Nita said. "Their mutual doting is sweet."

"It's nearly nauseating," Mr. St. Michael countered. "Lovey this, lambie that, darling Nicholas the other. Five years from now, they'll barely speak to each other over their morning tea."

Mr. St. Michael was wrong. Whatever else was true about Nicholas, he loved ferociously and unrelentingly, and his countess reciprocated his sentiments.

"What will you call your wife, Mr. St. Michael, when you're doting on her a little?" Nita regretted the question immediately, because any answer would make her sad. Mr. St. Michael wouldn't ever be doting on *her*, would he?

"I'll call my wife Mrs. St. Michael," he replied. "Tell me about Edward Nash's situation."

Mr. St. Michael was shy about this doting business, and yet Nita had the sense he'd make a thorough job of it, nonetheless.

"Edward Nash is the oldest of three brothers," Nita said, "two of whom are deceased. He's always known a baronetcy was coming his way, and thus he deals from a sense of entitlement. His vanity has been indulged too, by his parents and the local mamas, and that didn't help."

"Vain, selfish, and handsome. He ought to be a viscount, at least. What are his weaknesses?" A fox reconnoitering a henhouse would ask such a question.

"A want of coin." Nita had been up the back stairs at Stonebridge, seen the barren corridors, uncurtained windows, and unlit sconces. "Perhaps it's more that Edward suffers an inability to properly manage coin. He's parsimonious with his sister-in-law and nephew, and he has trouble keeping help. Even at the holidays, the Nash household doesn't entertain to speak of."

Nita could share that much, because those were facts rather than medical confidences.

"Despite that," Mr. St. Michael said, "Mr. Nash himself is doubtless always dressed in the height of rural fashion, he rides a handsome young piece of bloodstock, and he's considered quite the catch by the ladies of the parish."

"Some of the ladies." Perhaps other ladies were warned by their fathers and brothers that Edward Nash was pockets to let and an embarrassment to his gender when in his cups. Nita allowed the conversation to wander to other topics, but all too soon the horses were cantering into the Stonebridge stable yard.

"Your expression is not congenial," Mr. St. Michael observed as he assisted Nita to dismount.

The groom led the horses away, allowing Nita to speak freely.

"I usually approach this household with dread, fearing my sister might end her days in misery here. I do enjoy the company of Mr. Nash's widowed sister-in-law, and Elsie Nash has a delightful son, Digby."

Mr. St. Michael shifted, so his sheer bulk stood between Nita and the bitter wind. She had the sense his movement was instinctive, because he'd taken the same position when they'd inspected the sheep.

"Shall I buy the merinos simply to make it less likely your sister will wed Nash?"

Was he offering to buy the sheep because of Nita's fears regarding Susannah, or was he speaking hypothetically?

"I am for anything that makes a union between Susannah and Edward Nash less likely, Mr. St. Michael, but at the same time, I want you to have those sheep because you'll care for them properly. You appreciate their value. Susannah is a grown woman, though. Who am I to override her choices?"

He winged his arm at Nita, abruptly the gentleman escorting a lady, but his expression had been fleetingly puzzled, as if his conscientious regard for livestock ought to have escaped Nita's notice.

Shy and bashful both, and in the space of a few minutes' conversation. Oh, yes, Nita was interested in this man. Dangerously interested.

Edward was on his best, gratingly gracious behavior, inquiring earnestly after Nita's family, most especially after *dear* Susannah, and hoping that Mr. St. Michael could join in the rustic merriment at the assembly.

"Will Mrs. Nash attend?" Nita asked, and where was Elsie, the closest thing Edward had to a hostess? Nita had served the tea at Edward's request, but the one cake she'd attempted had been stale.

"You may depend upon it," Edward said with a smile Nita could barely endure. "Our diversions are few enough here in the country, we must enjoy them when we may. Mr. St. Michael, a pleasure to make the acquaintance of a friend of the Haddonfields."

Edward showed them to the door, cautioning them to take care against the cold, entreating them to give his regards to the earl and his countess, also to our *dear* Susannah—of course, *of course!*—and assuring them he looked forward to seeing them at the assembly.

The soul of earnest charm. Nita wanted to retch.

"Interesting exercise," Mr. St. Michael said, whipping the tail of his scarf over his shoulder as they took the path toward the stable. "You're right again. Nash is either suffering financially or he pinches what pennies he has. The carpets are dusty and bare, the house smells of tallow, and the andirons haven't been blacked in a week. Where are your gloves, my dear?"

"Drat. I left them inside." How quickly he'd noticed too.

"I'll let the groom know we're ready for the horses while you retrieve your gloves."

Nita headed back to the house but took the path around to the kitchen door, rapped on the glass, then let herself in. Elsie kneaded bread at a sturdy wooden table, her red hair under a plain white cap, a long apron over her dress.

"Lady Nita, greetings," Elsie said, giving the dough a smack. "I thought you were in the library with Edward."

The maid of all work shot Nita a glance and hurried off toward the pantries.

"Mr. St. Michael wanted to make Edward's acquaintance," Nita said. "Are you well, Elsie? I expected you to join us for tea." Elsie wasn't taking off her apron. She appeared to find the potted violets struggling on the windowsill fascinating, and she wasn't inviting Nita to have a seat.

"One can't drop everything to take tea," Elsie said, her humor forced. "Bread dough must rise when it's ready and bake when it's ready."

Conversation faltered, along with Nita's spirits. She advanced into the kitchen and came around the table. "The maid could punch down that dough, Elsie Nash. What's amiss?"

Beneath carefully applied cosmetics, Elsie's right eye was bruised, the flesh around it slightly swollen.

"I fell down the stairs."

"In the middle of a discussion with Edward," Nita guessed. "What was it this time? You needed a dress for the assembly? No, you'd never bother asking for something so frivolous. The argument had to do with Digby."

Something heavy shifted on the pantry shelves down the hallway.

"Digby needs heat in the schoolroom," Elsie said tiredly. "He has a constant sniffle, and I fear he'll develop lung fever."

Digby was his mother's world. Nothing less could tempt Elsie to take the risks she did. Nita gently tilted Elsie's chin up, so what light the window afforded fell on her face.

"You used arnica and ice?"

"I did. It doesn't hurt, my lady."

"It hurt terribly, at first. Your vision hasn't suffered?" Elsie shook her head, but as far as Nita was concerned, Elsie was gradually losing her ability to see truth when it smacked her across the face.

"Elsie, one of these days Edward will do something you can't hide, ignore, or have me treat. Then where will Digby be?"

"Digby will be grown and safely away from this place. Edward always apologizes for his little tempers, and he's dealing with a lot. Digby and I are added expenses, and I should know better than to mention my petty complaints when Edward has been drinking."

Nita hugged her, gently, carefully. Elsie was petite and could all too easily suffer serious injury during one of Edward's little tempers.

"Avoid staircases, my friend," Nita said when she wanted to have a little temper of her own, or a very great temper. "Send for me anytime. Bundle Digby up, and don't fret too much about a sniffle. Keep him in clean handkerchiefs and hot soup."

Elsie went back to studying the plants, which at this time of year bore not a single bloom. "My thanks, Lady Nita." Booted footsteps sounded above them. "You'd better go."

Nita unwrapped her scarf—woven of merino wool—and passed it to Elsie. "For Digby."

As footsteps sounded on the stairs, Nita scurried from the kitchen. She paused outside the door to withdraw her gloves from the pocket of her habit. Edward would complain about the stale cakes, but he'd been sober, so Elsie was not at risk of immediate further harm.

As for the scullery maid, she likely knew enough to remain out of sight if Edward came below stairs.

When Nita had quelled the rage roiling inside her and assembled a calm expression, she returned to the stable. She found Mr. St. Michael checking Atlas's girth and looking impervious to the elements. Nita wanted to simply watch her escort for a moment, to let the sight of Tremaine St. Michael, self-possessed and honorable, shy and tenderhearted toward beasts and children, wash away the despair that besieged her.

"Shall we be off?" he asked. "I see you've found your gloves, and I could use a pint and a plate."

Nita stepped into his cupped hands. "Hot food sounds tempting. Do you consider our visit to have been successful?"

Nita considered this call an abject failure. Elsie did not yet condone Edward's behaviors, but she already made excuses for them, and in another year, she'd believe she deserved his violence.

"The visit was all that was congenial," Mr. St. Michael said, flipping a coin to the groom. A few moments passed in relative silence, wind soughing forlornly through a stand of nearby pines as the horses walked down the Stonebridge drive.

"Nash might care for your sister," Mr. St. Michael said as they turned into the lane, "though he cares for himself far more. But tell me, Lady Nita, how is it you sought your gloves not in the foyer, where our host greeted us and took our wraps, but 'round back at the kitchen? I also notice that while you've found your gloves, you've lost your pretty scarf. Merino and angora would be my guess, a lovely article."

He nudged William closer to Atlas. Nita was concocting some prevarication when Mr. St. Michael's scarf settled around her neck, soft, warm, and bearing his heathery scent.

"You hate Edward Nash," he said quietly. "I'd like to know why."

Tremaine suspected that just as shepherds passed songs, remedies, flasks, and sheep lore around the campfire, schoolgirls traded insights about all manner of feminine wiles and artifices. One trick girls were apparently taught was that men were fascinated by women who fluttered.

Ladies fluttered their eyelashes, their painted fans, their graceful hands, their embroidered handkerchiefs, much like birds displayed their plumage when trying to attract a mate. Women fluttered their dower portions before the eligibles, and when they'd bagged their man, they fluttered *him* like a prize before all the other mamas and young women.

Lady Nita must have skipped this chapter of the young ladies' manual of marriageable deportment. Sitting atop her inelegant horse, she was still, calm, and all the more interesting because of it.

"Hatred is a strong emotion, Mr. St. Michael, also unchristian."

"Hatred is a human emotion. I hated my parents for years, my mother in particular."

Tremaine had dented Lady Nita's monumental calm with that disclosure and disconcerted himself more than a little.

"I could never hate my family," she said as the village came into view. Haddondale was a snug collection of shops and a tavern around a green, and it also boasted a handsome steeple on its house of worship. Lady Nita affixed her gaze to that distant spire.

"I might resent my siblings," she went on. "I might be vexed with them, but never hate them. I suspect their sentiments toward me are similar."

She provoked their admiration and bewilderment, not their vexation. "They worry about you," Tremaine said, "whereas my parents shuffled my brother and me off to my grandfather in Scotland, where we knew nobody, struggled with the languages, and were consigned to considerably reduced circumstances without any explanation."

Lady Nita gave him the same look she'd worn when diagnosing his Oxfordshire sheep. Considering, interested, determined to get to the bottom of a puzzle.

"Tell me more, Mr. St. Michael. Scotland is reported to be beautiful, and surely your grandparents loved you?"

What had that to do with deciphering Gaelic or subsisting on endless servings of mutton? Tremaine had refused to eat mutton or lamb since leaving Scotland, and he now spoke Gaelic mostly to communicate with his shepherds.

"Grandmama died before I was born," Tremaine said, "and, yes, in his way, Grandpapa loved us, but his way is stern. My father was titled and obscenely wealthy and very much a proponent of the status quo in France. This, of course, did not sit well with the people starving on his lands while he dressed in silks and grew stout on endless delicacies."

Or so Grandpapa had explained, but what did a homesick boy care for politics?

"France has been troubled for some time," Lady Nita said. "Your parents sent you to safety, from which one could conclude they cared for you."

A memory rose, Tremaine's last image of his mother as she scampered up the gangplank of the ship that would take her back to her husband and his wealth, her wide skirts dancing in the wind. She'd been fluttering her silk handkerchief in the direction of the sons she'd never see again.

Maybe that memory explained Tremaine's intolerance for fluttering.

"My father cared for the title," Tremaine said, turning his collar up against the cold, "and he cared for appearances. We were to visit Grandpapa for only a summer, but Grandpapa refused to send us boys back to France. He demanded that Mama also remain in Scotland, and the comte refused Grandpapa's invitation on Mama's behalf."

"Did that invitation include your father?"

"Of course." Grandpapa had been at pains to explain as much to the comte's bereaved young sons. Tremaine's ire had only increased, to think Papa might also have been saved by accepting a little familial hospitality. Rage at his mother's desertion had taken years to fade.

"I gather your parents did not survive the Revolution?" her ladyship delicately inquired.

"They didn't see most of the Revolution." For which Tremaine had learned to be grateful. "They were victims of their own discontented peasantry and arrogance. They fell ill—lung fever, typhus, measles, I'm not sure which—the harvest was poor, and the physician did not dare treat them in the midst of ongoing riots."

"Arrogance befalls many of us, but I gather you begrudge your parents their portion."

No matter which way the lane turned, the wind seemed always to be coming straight at them. Now, Tremaine resented Lady Nita's calm, wanted to push her off her horse and then gallop away, like the furious boy he'd been so many years ago.

"Scottish doctors are among the finest in the world," he said. "They don't distinguish between the intellectual and practical aspects of medicine, as the English still do. In Scotland, there's no genteel separation between the physician, who literally doesn't get his hands dirty, and the barber-surgeon, who deals in ignorance, blood, and death, often in that order. Had my mother remained with us, she might yet be alive. I have long wondered how my grandfather could allow his daughter, a woman whom he dearly loved, to return to a country in chaos, much less abandon her own sons."

Grandpapa was alive and enjoying his wee dram morning and night. Also still quite stern, though Tremaine no longer found fault with sternness.

"Have you ever fallen down the stairs, Mr. St. Michael?" Lady Nita put the question mildly.

"I have not. Why do you ask, my lady?"

"Perhaps you've seen others fall, inebriates, the naturally clumsy, small children. When we fall, our instinct is to put out our hands to break the fall, though that way, we often injure a wrist, a thumb, or forearm. Even if we can manage to break a fall, we'll usually also suffer injury to a hip, the knees, even the shoulders when we land."

Her ladyship was waltzing around some female point, though Tremaine had seen others lose their footing often enough to know she also recounted simple facts.

"Did Mrs. Nash suffer a fall?" he asked.

"Well, of course," Lady Nita said, combing gloved fingers through Atlas's dark mane. "They all say they've suffered a fall, but when we fall, we do not land on our eyes, do we? A blow that leaves bruises around the eyes is generally of a different nature."

What was she going on about?

"If somebody delivers that sort of blow to me, my lady, I'll return it with interest or call the fool out." Though few took on a man of Tremaine's dimensions when sober.

"Elsie Nash dare not return the blow, Mr. St. Michael, and your mother might have been legally unable to remain with you in Scotland. A married woman ceases to exist as a legal person, she has no more rights than your horse, no more rights than Susannah will have should she marry Edward. Think of your sheep, Mr. St. Michael, in the hands of a careless shepherd. That might well have been your mother's fate."

What had the law to do with a man's moral obligation to keep the members of his household safe? To keep the mother of his children safe?

They'd reached the edge of the village. Tremaine suspected they were also nearing the limits of Lady Nita's self-restraint, and if the topic didn't shift, she'd turn her destrier about and go tilting back to Stonebridge.

"I had a violent temper as a boy," Tremaine said, though he hadn't exactly planned that admission. "After my parents died, I was in scrape after scrape, until I hit a cousin two years older than me. She was also bigger, taller, faster, and by far the more scientific pugilist. Grandpapa threw me to the sheep after that."

Tremaine could still recall the startling, fascinating pain of being clobbered stoutly on both ears in the same instant. He'd sunk to the dirt like a rock tossed into a well, and thanked God his cousin hadn't gone after him with her booted feet.

Lady Nita combed out a braid she'd plaited into the horse's mane. "Your grandfather threw you to the sheep? Not to the wolves?"

No wolves, but all manner of demons.

"When the shepherds drove the flock up to the higher pastures that spring, I was sent with them. They were a rough lot, but good people. Between the shepherds, the sheep, and the fresh air, I was at least able to attend my studies come autumn. I spent much of seven years in those summer pastures."

Tremaine had had his first whisky there, his first adolescent heartbreak, his first serious brawls, all among the high hills and lush pastures of the Scottish summer. Those memories defined him in a way he wasn't comfortable sharing, even with Lady Nita.

This was her village, so Tremaine let her lead him around the right side of the barren green.

"Were you angry at the sheep?" she asked.

"I was angry at everything, at everyone, at God himself. I was the angriest boy who'd ever flung rocks at trees or broken off sapling after sapling out of sheer fury. I regret that destructiveness now."

This time of year, the center of the village was an acre of dead grass with a bank of dirty snow along one side. Two huge oaks stretched bare branches to the pewter sky; a pair of enormous ravens hunched amid them.

"You regret a boy's displays of grief?"

That terrible temper had been grief. Grandpapa had seen that as easily as Lady Nita had.

"Much of the Highlands used to be oak forest," Tremaine said, "but that far north, trees grow very slowly. The forests were decimated to build ships for the Royal Navy—replacing them would take centuries, if anyone were of a mind to do so. I should not have killed trees in an effort to blanket the very hillside with my orphaned rage."

Her ladyship halted her horse before a tidy Tudor establishment, the Queen's Harebell, according to the signboard luffing in the chilly breeze.

"We can grow more trees, sir, but we cannot grow another Tremaine St. Michael or another Digby Nash. I'm sorry you lost your parents, sorry you had only the company of sheep and nature to ease your loss. Your mother loved you, or you would not have mourned her death so passionately."

More female logic, and more truth. Tremaine had also mourned his father and, more recently, his brother. He was bloody sick of what few people he cared for going to their eternal rewards.

Abruptly, he wished he and Lady Nita were not perched atop their horses in the middle of the village street, where all and sundry might see them, because an urge plagued him to kiss the woman who understood small, violent boys and raged against small, violent men.

He swung out of the saddle and came around to assist the lady from her horse. Lady Nita unhooked her knee from the horn and slid down the side of her gelding, right into Tremaine's waiting arms.

"I had the shepherds too," he said. Inanely. "They're a philosophical lot, unless somebody threatens their flocks. They lent me their books, answered my questions as best they could, taught me their songs and how to hold my drink."

"They taught you how to live despite your anger," Lady Nita said, her hands braced on Tremaine's arms. She stepped back, and he let her go, both relieved and reluctant to put this topic behind them. "I gather you never struck another female?"

The question allowed Tremaine a smile. "I'd got the worst of the encounter, which I suspect was why Grandpapa let me confront Agnes. She had a reputation Gentleman Jackson would envy. Grandpapa sent me away thereafter, in part for my own safety, lest my opponent's five sisters finish what I had so foolishly started. I dowered Agnes with a tidy farm eight years ago, and she's raising a brood of sturdy girls with her equally sturdy husband."

Some cloud in Lady Nita's gaze cleared, and she turned a sunny smile on Tremaine. An hour ago, he would have described the scarf he'd lent her as blue lamb's wool. Now, his scarf was the same blue as Lady Nita Haddonfield's eyes, halfway between a Scottish summer sky and periwinkle, with a beguiling hint of lilac.

Those eyes narrowed, and her smile disappeared. "That is Dr. Harold Horton," she said, glowering at an ungainly rider on an elegant gray trit-trotting around the far side of the green. "I might as well tell you, I do not hate Dr. Horton, though he has cause to hate me."

CHAPTER SEVEN

Patience Goodenough, a gentle Quaker lady, had cursed like a drover when delivering her firstborn.

Daryl Bletching had cried and begged Nita to try to save his hand when Dr. Horton had sent the surgeon to fetch a saw.

Old Mr. Clackengeld claimed he saw the devil when drunk and swore Nita to secrecy, lest the parson catch wind of such wickedness.

Winnifred Hess believed the angel of death had sat upon her chest counting her chicken pox.

The ill and the injured inflicted their confidences on Nita when she'd far rather they did not.

By contrast, she *craved* Tremaine St. Michael's confidences, even as she was puzzled that he'd offer them from atop his horse. Worse, she wanted to share her innermost thoughts with him, which might explain her remark about Horrible Horton.

"The physician looks like Father Christmas out of his seasonal robes," Mr. St. Michael said. "He hates you?"

"Not quite," Nita replied, adjusting a scarf that bore the scent of the faraway Highlands. "I'm not worthy of his hatred. I merit his condescension, his amusement even. Shall we go inside?"

Dr. Horton gossiped, and if he saw Nita escorted by a strange fellow without benefit of a groom or a sibling, he would surely mention it over a consultation with the vicar regarding his gout.

"I'm famished," Mr. St. Michael said. "Even so, I'd rather not let the horses stand for half the day."

While Nita was loath to linger in the village at all if Dr. Horton was about. "We'll be quick."

Mr. St. Michael tucked her hand onto his arm, even to travel the short distance to the door of the Queen's Harebell.

"You don't want to pay a call on the vicar, my lady? I'd assumed you had charitable tasks to assign him."

The vicar likely hated Nita most of all. He frequently preached that God alone—abetted by Dr. Horton—should determine who succumbed to illness and who thrived. The pious among the flock were to meekly endure ill health as a sign of God's disfavor and pray for God's mercy.

"Perhaps we'll call on Vicar another day," Nita said.

Mr. St. Michael's pace suggested he was a stranger to hurry, or maybe the cold didn't affect him, their progress across the street was that leisurely. He studied the shop fronts, the bleak village green, the ravens huddled in the barren oak, the ruts frozen into the street.

While Nita's heart sank.

"Lady Nita!" Dr. Horton called, clambering off his gray. "Why, it is you, but I don't believe I know this gentleman. A female of your delicate constitution ought not to be out in such weather, if you'll take the word of an old physician. How does your family go on, my lady, and will you introduce me to your friend?"

Dr. Horton was friendly, Edward had been gracious, and Nita was abruptly exhausted.

"Mr. St. Michael, may I make known to you Dr. Horton, our local physician and a family friend. Dr. Horton, Mr. Tremaine St. Michael, a guest of the earl's and connection through my brother Beckman."

Nita had lied. Dr. Horton was no friend to her family. Even

Nicholas had little use for a physician who gossiped. Dr. Horton did look like Father Christmas, though, all combed white beard, friendly blue eyes, and prosperous country gentleman's attire.

"Dr. Horton." Mr. St. Michael bowed, though he outranked Horton. "Lady Nita and I were making a quick stop for sustenance."

"Then you must join me," Dr. Horton said. "Winter ale fortifies the blood, I always say. Do I detect a bit of the North in your accent, sir?"

Nita let the small talk wash around her, content to be ignored as her joy in the day ebbed. Perhaps she should throw rocks at the oaks on the green or find some saplings to tear down.

The Harebell's kitchen was serving cottage pie and winter ale along with a plate of cinnamon biscuits, though Nita had little appetite. Dr. Horton chattered on about the approaching assembly being a dare to the gods of weather, though it did a man a power of good to see all the local ladies attired in their finest.

"You're not eating much, Lady Nita," Mr. St. Michael remarked.

Dr. Horton patted her hand, and because they were at table, nobody wore gloves.

"Lady Nita has refined sensibilities," Dr. Horton said. "Beef and potatoes do not appeal to a sophisticated palate. I heard that you assisted the Chalmers woman in childbed, my dear. Was that wise?"

Dr. Horton did this, bustled along in conversation, a merry old fellow of great good cheer, then, without warning, he attacked—with even greater good cheer.

"Childbed is not something any woman should face alone," Nita said, "and the birth went well."

The doctor tucked a bite of potato dripping with gravy into his mouth. "The birth went well last time too, I'm told," he said, chewing energetically, "and look how that turned out. What's she up to now? Five? Six? Six more mouths for the parish to feed sooner or later. Best not abet such folly. Bellefonte would agree with me, as would, I'm sure, the late earl."

Papa would never have agreed with this pontifical, judgmental buffoon. Mama had been barely civil to Horton. Nita set her lady's pint down carefully, while beneath the table Mr. St. Michael seized her free hand in a warm grasp.

"You will pardon my lack of fortitude," Mr. St. Michael said, squeezing Nita's fingers gently, "but a bachelor does not find talk of childbirth at all conducive to good digestion. You ride a handsome gelding, Dr. Horton. Did you purchase him locally?"

Nita shook her hand free of her escort's and rose. Mr. St. Michael rose as well, while Dr. Horton shoveled in another bite of potatoes.

"If you gentlemen will excuse me," Nita said, "I'll be back in a moment."

Dr. Horton waved his fork in dismissal, while Mr. St. Michael remained on his feet until Nita had quit the premises. She strode directly across the street, kicked a hole in the ice of the horse trough, and plunged the hand Dr. Horton had patted into the frigid water.

"Nita has taken Mr. St. Michael to call on Edward," Kirsten announced, tossing herself onto Susannah's bed. "All this fresh air must be in aid of something."

Susannah set aside *Macbeth* and drew her afghan around her shoulders, because Kirsten on a tear was impossible to deflect. Then too, reading by the window was a chilly proposition.

"If Mr. St. Michael affords Nita an opportunity to socialize with the healthy rather than the ill, surely that's a good thing?" Nita's sisters had certainly had little success broadening her social life.

"Why didn't she take you?" Kirsten asked, kicking off her house mules and scooting back against the headboard. "Why not take me, Leah, anybody else?"

Susannah knew why not, so did Kirsten. "Because Nita will look in on Addy Chalmers, which doesn't matter." Nita's visit probably mattered a great deal to Addy and her new baby.

"Why does she do this?" Kirsten asked, rearranging Susannah's pillows. "Why does Nita stick her nose into the cottage of every ailing tenant? She's worse than Mama ever was."

Susannah was fifteen months older than Kirsten, which meant she'd had fifteen months more to observe their mother and to ask the same question.

"Mama's people were not wealthy when she was younger," Susannah said. "Her Christian duty weighed on her, and she had a knack for dealing with illness and injury, though in these modern times, we're supposed to leave all that to the medical fellows. Are you jealous that Nita has attached the interest of a potential suitor?"

Kirsten smoothed a hand over the quilt Susannah had pieced together with their mother's help. Mama really hadn't been much for countess-ing when she could instead be a mother or a neighbor.

"Nicholas says Mr. St. Michael is very shrewd," Kirsten replied, "and he trades in far more than sheep. He has connections all over the Continent and is, in truth, a French comte." Kirsten hugged a pink brocade pillow to her chest, looking deceptively girlish. "He's handsome, if you don't mind his accent. He puts me in mind of a wolf, all sleek and quiet, but mind you don't turn your back on him or he'll gobble up your best biddy."

Nita probably didn't even hear that accent, though it did wonderful things for Mr. Burns's verse. Made for interesting Shakespeare too.

"What are you thinking, Kirsten Haddonfield?" And where was Della, who, for all her tender years, was an excellent strategist?

"I overheard Nicholas and Mr. St. Michael discussing those dratted sheep," Kirsten said, setting the pillow aside. "St. Michael wants them, but Edward wants them too."

While Susannah wanted Edward. Not very ladylike of her, but a woman had to marry somebody. Edward did not shout and create noise wherever he went. He did not bring up difficult topics with family when guests were at the table. His command of Shakespeare was limited, but his recitation of it competent.

Edward had made a home for his brother's widow and child, and

—most significant of all—he lived not two miles from Susannah's family. Susannah could recite the list of Edward's virtues in her sleep, because she repeated them to herself nightly.

"I'm not surprised both men are interested in the merino sheep," Susannah said. "Papa did not leave the earldom plump in the pocket, and Nicholas must sell assets where he can."

Susannah emerged from her afghan to poke at the fire in the grate. The footmen would come around with fresh coal soon—Nita had put them on a schedule several winters ago—but Kirsten had left the door open a few inches, and an eddy of cold air slithered across the carpets.

"You are more valuable than a herd of bleating sheep, Suze. Edward wants the sheep to be included in your dowry. All of them, every ewe, ram, tup, and lamb."

Susannah closed the door and took up a chair near the fire.

"Sheep are hard on the land." While Kirsten was hard on her siblings, but she meant well.

"Stonebridge isn't the best patch of ground in the shire to start with," Kirsten observed, which anybody riding past its somewhat ramshackle home farm might conclude. "I'd think Edward's land better suited to cattle, cabbages, or potatoes. Potatoes grow anywhere."

Papa had never expected to inherit an earldom, nor Mama to become a countess. They had been gentry at heart, and Susannah was her parents' daughter.

She had ideas for Stonebridge, ideas she'd discussed casually with George and Nicholas.

Stonebridge was close enough to London that vegetable crops could be profitable, laying hens were always in demand, and even certain breeds of dog could be raised as pets for aristocratic families.

"You have that distracted look." Kirsten tossed the pink pillow across the room to land gently in Susannah's lap. "Are you composing a sonnet to your sheep farmer before he's even acquired a herd?"

"Edward would not like to be called a sheep farmer." Nor was he

Susannah's, not yet, which was a problem. Would he like to be called her husband?

Kirsten folded her hands behind her head, looking much like Nicholas or George at their leisure. "Edward would *like* to be called Baronet, though he hasn't acquired that title yet either."

Kirsten's judgment of her fellow man was severe, but her loyalty to family unwavering. If Susannah married Edward, she need not abandon Kirsten entirely to spinsterhood, nor George to perpetual bachelorhood.

"I know you don't particularly care for Edward." Nita cared for him even less, though Susannah wasn't certain why. Edward wasn't awful. "He's not as loud as our brothers, not as outspoken or direct. I like that about him. His company is restful and he sings well."

Kirsten sat up, one lithe, restless, feline movement. "You are too sweet. Edward rides out with his hounds but doesn't see to his own acres. George says the pond near the Bletchings' farm is silting up, and it's the only water on the west side of Edward's property. How will he irrigate if he doesn't dredge that pond?"

Dredging the pond went on Susannah's list of improvements her dowry would make possible at Stonebridge. Even Papa had muttered about only a bad farmer neglecting to manage his water, and the Stonebridge home farm was on the west side of the property.

"You don't care about a silted up pond, Kirsten. This is England and we've water aplenty. What is it you came here to say?"

To bother Susannah about, because Kirsten lived to bother and agitate, which was her way of showing familial concern.

Kirsten shoved off the bed, leaving the quilt wrinkled. "It's cold in here," she said, joining Susannah by the fire. "Suze, have you noticed that Stonebridge is always cold?"

Yes, Susannah had. That was on her list too, because any household that included a small child needed a modicum of warmth throughout. Elsie Nash was Digby's mother, and she ought to see to something as simple as keeping the boy warm. Elsie had been married to a military man, though, and probably took economies seriously.

"Kirsten, you are an astute woman. Winter is upon us, winter is cold."

When Kirsten was stomping about, casting dark looks at all and sundry, arguing radical Whig politics simply to bait Nicholas, then a certain element of Haddonfield family functioning was as it should be.

When Kirsten's gaze became pitying, Susannah worried.

"Do you *love* Edward?" Kirsten asked, oddly serious. "Do you even know Edward well enough to say if you love him, or have you fallen for a few sonnets and melting glances? We're not that old, and Nita certainly seems to manage well enough without a man."

Nita was dying of loneliness, and many women considered twenty too old to be single.

Susannah rose and faced the fire so she did not have to meet Kirsten's gaze. "I esteem Edward greatly," she recited, for this too was part of her nightly fretting. "I've known him all my life, and I see his strengths as well as those areas where the right wife would be a help to him and his family. While I appreciate your concern, I do not share it."

Any other sister, any normal sister, would have flounced out of the room, nose in the air. Kirsten patted Susannah's shoulder.

"I love it when you're fierce. One forgets you can be fierce. Nothing for it, then. If you want Edward Nash, then we must see that you have him. That leaves us with a puzzle regarding Nita and Mr. St. Michael though, doesn't it? Both men want all those sheep, and Nicholas seems to be telling them they need to marry one of his sisters to get them."

This amused Kirsten, and Susannah manufactured a smile as well—one of her few confirmed skills.

And yet, as Kirsten blathered on about plots and schemes and conjectures regarding the upcoming assembly, Susannah became increasingly discontent.

She was vexed that Edward would attempt to negotiate settlements before securing her explicit consent to a properly tendered offer of marriage.

Exceedingly vexed.

Why would a competent physician, established in his profession and cordial with his neighbors, hate Nita Haddonfield? For Dr. Horton's gaze on Nita's retreating figure had been far from friendly.

Tremaine took a contemplative sip of rich winter ale while the good, if hateful, doctor put away a prodigious quantity of cottage pie. Horton kept an eye on the cinnamon biscuits as well, as if they might skip off to another table when he wasn't looking.

When Tremaine had been a boy in the hills of western Aberdeenshire, nothing could have shaken his focus from a plate of meat and vegetables topped with mashed potatoes. Now, investigating the doctor's antipathy toward Lady Nita eclipsed any interest Tremaine had in the fare.

"That Lady Nita," Horton said. "She's not long for this earth, mark me, Mr. St. Michael. Women haven't the constitution for medicine. They take ill, they blunder, they disregard the learned truths of modern science. Shall we order another ale?"

Such delicate creatures, women, and yet the endless, thankless, wearying burden of nursing invariably fell to the females of the household, particularly in England, where a physician's calling was plied mostly in the parlor and between the pages of Latin tomes.

"Is Lady Nita frail?" Tremaine asked. Her brother had likened her constitution to that of a donkey, and thank the Almighty that was so.

"She's skinny," Horton said, the term an insult. "Don't have to be a physician to see she needs more meat on her bones. Bellefonte should take her in hand, but the old earl was indulgent of his womenfolk. Never a good idea to allow the females a loose rein."

"Is Lady Nita medically competent?" Tremaine knew she was,

Tremaine's *sheep* knew she was, Addy Chalmers's youngest child knew it best of all.

What Nita Haddonfield lacked was a sense of her own value.

"She reads books," Horton said, scraping his remaining potatoes into a heap. "I'll give her that, and she was her mother's right hand. I don't begrudge women the company of their own kind at a lying-in, provided a physician is consulted regarding any complicated matters. The better families increasingly expect physicians to serve as accoucheurs as well. Lady Nita would have it otherwise."

In other words, Nita provided poorer families an alternative to paying for Horton's services at birthings.

"Then you would have attended Addy Chalmers had she asked for you?" Tremaine asked.

A forkful of carrot hovered before the doctor's mouth. "Mr. St. Michael, you will think me devoid of Christian charity when I say I would have made no haste whatsoever to attend that birth had the Chalmers woman had the temerity to engage my services. She cannot provide for her young and refuses to abide by the rules of decent society. To bring another child into that household is to perpetuate a problem that has no happy solution. Lady Nita insists on prolonging the misery of all concerned."

Her ladyship prolonged the children's *lives* too. "Many would agree with you," Tremaine said, finishing his ale. Perhaps even the Earl of Bellefonte agreed with the physician.

Addy Chalmers's children were not the results of immaculate conceptions, though. If Addy and the children were to be condemned out of hand, the fathers ought to bear some shame as well.

The carrots met the same fate as the rest of the doctor's cottage pie.

"You'd best be on your way, Mr. St. Michael. Lady Nita has no doubt been accosted by old Clackengeld, who complains of bilious digestion when what he needs is a good purge and a bleeding or three. He's usually lurking at the livery and knows better than to trouble me with his ailments."

Tremaine dropped a few coins on the table, snatched a cinnamon biscuit before the doctor could inhale them all, and picked up the scarf Lady Nita had left draped over the back of her chair.

"I'll heed your suggestion," Tremaine said, "and be about my business. A pleasure to make your acquaintance, Dr. Horton."

Horton saluted with his pint, and as Tremaine departed from the common, the physician was helping himself to the food remaining on Lady Nita's plate.

Tremaine spotted her ladyship with the horses, across the street from the inn. She looked chilly, and she'd managed to get one side of her hem wet.

"You have a habit of leaving necessary items of apparel where they'll do you no good," Tremaine said, wrapping the scarf about Lady Nita's ears and neck. "Did Horton upset your digestion?"

Her ladyship's expression was serene, as smooth as the inn's windows, which reflected the gray winter sky and gave away nothing of the roaring hearths and bustling custom within.

Insight struck, like the cold gust of wind that sent a dusting of snow swirling across the barren green: the more composed Lady Nita appeared, the greater her upset.

"Dr. Horton is much respected," she said. "Shall we go?"

"You don't respect him," Tremaine replied, tugging on Atlas's girth, then taking it up one hole. "I don't particularly like him."

Lady Nita relaxed fractionally at Tremaine's observation. "He's old-fashioned to a fault," she said, "and refuses to consider any medical advance that didn't originate in England, preferably with some colleague he studied beside when German George was on the throne."

Tremaine had traveled enough on the Continent to understand Nita's frustration. English medicine was considered backward by Continental physicians, and yet men like Horton toiled away in every shire in the realm, doing the best they could with a science that was far from exact.

"Up you go, my lady. What's in the sacks?" Two sacks were tied over Atlas's withers.

"I went around to the kitchen and bought a few things for the Chalmers household." Lady Nita stepped into Tremaine's hands and was up on her horse without Tremaine having to exert himself.

Her ladyship wasn't skinny—Tremaine had reason to know this—but she was fit, and she didn't lace herself too tightly to draw breath. He rather liked that about her, though he did not look forward to this call upon the wretched of the parish.

He swung into a cold saddle and let the shock reverberate through his system for a moment. To combat that unpleasantness, he summoned the memory of Lady Nita's soft warmth pressed against him in her nightclothes.

"Is Horton capable?" Tremaine asked as the horses shuffled away from the square.

"In some matters," Lady Nita conceded. "He insists on bleeding a woman when she's expecting, though if you talk to women who've carried a number of times or to midwives, they'll tell you they don't favor it. Many physicians on the Continent refuse to bleed a pregnant woman, saying it weakens her when she's most in need of her strength. The diet Horton prescribes for an expectant mother wouldn't sustain a rambunctious elf."

In this, Lady Nita's sentiments echoed Grandpapa's, who'd favored hearty fare for children and expectant mothers, contrary to prevailing English medical wisdom.

About which Tremaine did not particularly care.

Though Lady Nita had spared a thought for Tremaine's sheep, about whom he *did* care, because healthy sheep were profitable sheep.

Tremaine also cared about the Chalmers family— inconvenient though the sentiment was—as evidenced by his relief that a plume of smoke rose from the chimney, and the wood piled on the porch remained abundant.

"I can stay with the horses," he said when he'd assisted Lady Nita to dismount. Her hem, formerly damp, was now frozen stiff, and yet

Tremaine could not recall a puddle into which she might have stepped.

"Nonsense. The horses will stand obediently enough." She handed Tremaine the sacks she'd brought from the inn. "The children will want to see you."

Tremaine did not want to see them. "We ought not to stay for long, lest your brother worry."

Lady Nita turned toward the cottage, shoulders square. "Nicholas has greater concerns than whether I tarry for five minutes on my way home from a social call."

Like whether to consign his sister Susannah to a lifetime in a household where women fell down steps. On that rankling notion, Tremaine followed Lady Nita up the rickety porch stairs and wondered what fool had implied he'd be willing to accompany her ladyship on this outing.

She rapped on the door and waited, while Tremaine stood behind her, holding sacks of provisions and pondering the doctor's philosophy. Was it kinder to let this family starve or freeze today? Kinder to see the children into the poorhouse, where their lives would shortly end?

Addy Chalmers opened the door, the baby at her shoulder swaddled in a clean shawl, a tiny knitted cap on the infant's head.

"Lady Nita, Mr. St. Michael, welcome." Addy looked tired but sober, and the cottage was as neat as such a space could be, also not too cold, though Tremaine kept his coat on. Nothing short of the Second Coming would relieve the place of the stench of boiled cabbage.

"Addy, children, greetings," Lady Nita said, sounding genuinely glad to see them. "I think the baby has grown already."

The ladies were off, rhapsodizing about the infant, disappearing into the sleeping alcove while Tremaine was left to investigate the sacks.

"I can hold your horse again," said the girl...Mary? "Or ride him for you."

"Thank you, but I must decline that kind offer," Tremaine replied. "Lady Nita and I can stay only a moment. I do believe there's cottage pie in this sack, still warm, and bread and butter, along with cold milk and a few butter biscuits. What shall we do with it?"

"Eat it," said the youngest boy, whose nose ran ever so copiously.

Tremaine passed Mary a handkerchief. "Please see to your brother. Why don't we start with bread and butter, and save the cottage pie for your supper?"

Keen disappointment registered on four little faces, replaced by eager anticipation when Tremaine cut thick hunks of warm bread and slathered each one with butter.

And still, the ladies remained talking softly behind the curtain.

"Who can show me some letters?" Tremaine asked, because no toys were in evidence, and the only book looked to be a Book of Common Prayer perched on the mantel.

"We haven't paper," Mary said. "I can write my name, though. On paper. We have a pencil. Mama knows where it is."

Tremaine fell back on strategies he'd learned around the shepherds' campfires. "Paper is an extravagance—a luxury," he said. "We need only our minds and a fire in the hearth."

He took a seat, cross-legged, on a floor even colder than his saddle had been and was soon ringed with children. While they watched, he spread a layer of ash over the hearthstones and used a stick of kindling to draw a large letter *M* in the ashes.

"Look familiar?" he asked the girl.

"*M*, for Mary!" she said, her expression suggesting Tremaine had put the entire French language into her keeping. "Do another!"

They had worked nearly through the alphabet—*A* is for apple, *B* is for butter, *C* is for cockles—when the ladies rejoined them. Nita's expression was quietly pleased, the baby was drowsing on the mother's shoulder, and Addy looked...in need of a long nap.

As new mothers generally tended to appear.

"I hadn't thought to use the ashes," Addy said. "We certainly have enough of those, and the boys want to learn their letters." She kissed the baby's cheek, expression puzzled. "Thank you. For the food as well."

"You are welcome," Tremaine said, coming to his feet and resisting the urge to dust off his backside. "I'd never realized one can learn the alphabet by visiting an imaginary pantry. Lady Nita, shall we be on our way?"

The youngest boy was again in need of the handkerchief, while Tremaine needed to be anywhere else. He'd wanted Lady Nita's company for the trip to Stonebridge, but he hadn't anticipated that she'd tarry long here at the cottage.

"It is time we were leaving," she said, readjusting the scarf around her neck. She paused, her gaze on the little fellow docilely tolerating his sister's ministrations with the handkerchief.

The child had weak lungs. Evan was his name. He'd outgrown his trousers a year ago, and the coat he wore like a night robe was fastened with twine.

Lady Nita's eyes held a question, about little boys and scarves, about kindness and the poorhouse. Tremaine nodded slightly, and her ladyship wrapped a beautiful blue lamb's wool scarf about the neck of a wretched boy.

"I'll want to hear letters should I visit again," Tremaine said very sternly, though he'd paid his last voluntary call on this household. "And I'll expect that baby to have doubled in size."

He bolted for the door with as much dignity as he could muster—precious little—and Lady Nita caught him by the hand before they were down the porch steps.

"Mr. St. Michael." She drew him closer, until her arms were around Tremaine's middle, and his had somehow found their way around her too. "You are so very dear."

The words melted an old anxiety in Tremaine. He could tolerate being dear, to Lady Nita anyway, better than he could tolerate the stench of cabbage, dirt, and despair. He rested his chin on her crown, fortifying himself for trotting about in the cold without benefit of his favorite scarf.

"You looked after my sheep," he said.

"You looked after mine. Teaching the children their letters that way was brilliant. Those are bright children. They'll be reading their Book of Common Prayer by Beltane."

Ironic that the only book in that house should be from the Church. Tremaine stepped back, because a chilly ride yet awaited them.

"The mother can read?"

"Addy had a genteel upbringing. Some local fellow got her in trouble, her family turned their backs on her, and the rest is a cautionary tale. I've told her about vinegar and sponges, but they don't work for everybody."

Lady Nita pulled on her gloves, as if such a topic were unremarkable for the proper daughter of a peer. Would Horton have bothered to tell a soiled dove about vinegar and sponges? Did he even know of them? Had Lady Nita's mother been the one to pass along knowledge decent women weren't supposed to have?

And was Tremaine the only soul in Christendom affronted that Lady Nita should be burdened with these concerns?

"Do you ever think the Chalmers family would be better off in the poorhouse?" Tremaine asked.

Her ladyship fairly bounced down the steps, the visit having apparently restored her energy as cottage pie and ale could not.

"Tell me, Mr. St. Michael, would the merino sheep be better off with Edward Nash? Would you leave your tups in his care?"

Tremaine boosted her into the saddle for the fourth time that day and did not dignify her question with a reply.

Lady Nita looked after this family and after others. She did not question the responsibility or attempt to shirk it, even when she ought to.

Who looked after her? Somebody clearly needed to, lest illness or nervous exhaustion carry her off. If Tremaine offered to take up that post, would she make a habit of tucking herself close to him and finding him *very dear*?

CHAPTER EIGHT

"Lovey, I don't trust Mr. St. Michael." Nicholas Haddonfield snuggled up to his countess and pillowed his cheek on her breast. Nick's siblings knew better than to comment if they thought it unusual that the earl and his countess retired to their rooms after the midday meal.

How did women always manage to smell so good? Leah's scent was lily of the valley with other notes. Sweet, kind, lovely notes that Nicholas would die to protect.

"You are not in the habit of allowing men you distrust to gallivant about with your sisters," Leah said. Sweet, kind, lovely—also practical, that was Nick's countess, even before she'd become the mother of his heir.

"I trust Nita," Nick replied, "and I know the effect frigid air can have on a man's base urges. St. Michael lurks in the social undergrowth, like a wolf studying a henhouse from downwind. I wish I knew what he was truly about."

Leah traced Nick's eyebrows with her fingertips, which made Nick want to groan like a horse being groomed in that one particular spot that rolling on the ground and acting like a horse never quite attended to.

"Are you falling asleep, Nicholas?"

"I am composing a letter in my head to Beckman. Nita and George should pay Beckman a visit, if the weather ever breaks."

"If the flu season starts, you mean. Why not send your entire horde of siblings?"

The idea was tempting, which was no credit to Nick's familial loyalty. "I love my brothers and sisters," he said, "but since the baby showed up..." Since the baby had arrived, Nick never had time alone with his wife.

"You worry more," Leah said. "You worry in a whole new way, and you were a prodigiously talented worrier before his lordship arrived."

The little Viscount Reston was healthy as a shoat, with a full complement of Haddonfield blond hair and marvelously merry blue eyes—most of the time. The boy enjoyed marvelously healthy lungs too.

"Am I too heavy?" Nick asked.

"You are too anxious. What aren't you telling me, Nicholas?"

Nick mentally rummaged around among his cares and woes, put aside his curiosity about Tremaine St. Michael, and lit upon his most recently acquired problem.

"Edward Nash mentioned Addy Chalmers when last I spoke with him."

Leah's fingertip paused on the bridge of Nick's nose. "When he attempted to wheedle coin and sheep from you, under the guise of asking permission to pay his addresses to Susannah?"

"I don't like it any more than you do," Nick said, shifting to crouch over his countess. "But Susannah fancies him and she hasn't fancied any other fellow, so what's to be done? When Nash assured me the baronetcy came with a tidy income, I thought he was acknowledging that Susannah's dowry was of no moment. Then he turns around and hints about the sheep, between broader hints about Addy Chalmers."

Leah kissed Nick's nose, a now-see-here sort of kiss. "What did Edward say about Addy? He's caused you to frown, and I prefer my earl smiling."

"Nash asked me how long I intend to tolerate a fallen woman raising up her brood of bastards under my very nose."

"Oh, dear."

Bastards were a sensitive topic among the Haddonfields, and not only because Nick's older half-brother Ethan bore that dubious distinction.

Nick brushed Leah's dark hair back off her forehead. Since having the baby, her hair had become different—thicker, softer, more kissable.

"What sort of 'oh, dear' was that?" he asked, kissing her brow.

"Oh, dear, Edward has appointed himself the moral magistrate of the shire. What business is it of his if you've reduced Addy's rent?"

Reduced it to nothing, while allowing her boys to poach game and firewood from the Belle Maison home wood.

"You'd have me tolerate sin among our tenants, lovey?"

Leah turned her face away, presenting Nick with an ear to kiss instead, but it wasn't an ear-kissing moment. "You've never been a hypocrite, Nicholas. I love that about you."

Such were the Countess of Bellefonte's charms that she could scold while murmuring endearments.

Nick flopped to his back, because his sweet, kind, lovely, practical countess was also the lodestar of his honor. Around them the house was quiet, as if waiting for spring and weary of winter.

"I used to tease little Addy Chalmers in the churchyard. I helped carry her mother's casket. Now, she's no longer decent, but is that the fault of her children? Am I to burn her out and put those children on the parish when their sustenance costs me nothing but a few skinny hares and rotting tree limbs?"

Prostitution was legal—the great men of England who made the laws had been careful about that. Living entirely on the proceeds of immoral commerce was, however, against the law, and Addy had no other reliable means of earning coin.

"Nicholas, do you ever wonder whose children those are?"

Nick did kiss Leah's ear. "All the time. The oldest one, the little redhead, reminds me of somebody. Addy would know who her father is too."

"But Addy has never said. Do we have work here for her?"

A family the size of the Haddonfields could employ a small army, assuming the staff didn't make Addy's life hell.

"Nita has asked the same thing," Nick admitted, "but then who would watch those children? The oldest girl can't watch a newborn. The infant needs its mother." *Her* mother. Addy had born another girl, may God have mercy on the little mite.

"Let me think about it," Leah said, drawing Nick's head down to her shoulder. "Nita says the oldest girl is a bright child, and I'm sure she's a comfort to her mother. Her name is Mary."

Nick allowed himself to be comforted, but the problem of Addy Chalmers was complicated and tangled up in the problem that was Nita. Also, in light of Nash's meddling, the problem that was Susannah.

Given that list, the problem that was Tremaine St. Michael, and a bunch of bleating, stinking sheep, didn't even intrude into Nick's awareness as he fell asleep in the arms of his countess.

What could be more dear than a gentleman decked out in London tailoring, sitting on the floor before the hearth of a simple cottage, teaching children their letters in the ashes?

That sight had upset Nita, had put a lump in her throat where no lump should have been, and filled her heart with an aching joy. Somebody else saw the Chalmers children as worthy, as innocent.

Somebody besides Nita and their own mother, and that was every bit as enthralling to Nita as Mr. St. Michael's kisses.

"Will you stay for the assembly?" she asked as the horses trudged along the deserted lane.

"I'd like to, but perhaps not. Bellefonte has promised to set a price for the sheep, and it shouldn't take him days to do that, if he's willing to part with them at all. I'm needed in Oxford, I have business to tend to in London, and a trip to Germany is still a strong possibility."

"You'd travel now, when winter is at its worst?" Beckman had traveled for years, George had just returned from travel, and Nita had worried for both of her brothers.

She worried for Mr. St. Michael more. He'd said he'd wished he could see her turning down the room. Had that wish meant anything?

"I am known to be a shrewd businessman. I travel when others are snug in their homes. I do business with any with whom I can turn a reasonable profit. I am often accused of sharp practice when, in truth, I'm guilty of working harder, taking more risks, and seizing more opportunity than most. When it suits me, I travel on the Continent as a Frenchman. When it suits me, I'm a canny Scot. When it suits me, I'm an Englishman with substantial holdings in Northumbria and the Midlands."

Quite a speech from him—and a warning too. "You won't cheat Nicholas out of his sheep."

Mr. St. Michael said nothing for a good distance of frozen ruts, bitter breezes, and sheep, who regarded the passersby curiously from behind stone walls.

"Your Nicholas is tempted to send the sheep to Squire Nash. I had the sense that were I to offer for you, the sheep might more easily fall into my hands."

Atlas came to a shuffling halt in the middle of the lane without Nita having asked it of him. "Nicholas said *that*?"

All manner of emotions lay behind her question. Indignation that Nicholas would see any of his sisters as part of a livestock transaction; compassion for Susannah, who would likely be married—and to

Edward—as a result of such a bargain; and relief that Mr. St. Michael would warn Nita regarding Nicholas's nonsense.

These reactions ricocheted through her in the time it took Atlas to stomp one big hoof and swish his tail.

And then... an emotion Nita did not want to name, somewhere between curiosity and hope. "I have never considered marriage very appealing," she said. "Were you tempted?"

Mr. St. Michael sent William forward and Atlas moved off as well. "Tempted? Yes, I am tempted, but not by the sheep."

In the middle of a gray, bitter winter afternoon, as Nita rode home in anticipation of scolds and censuring looks from family, as she worried for Addy Chalmers and her offspring, sunshine, pure, sweet, and warm, flooded her soul.

She hugged that sunshine to her heart until she and Mr. St. Michael had handed their horses off to the grooms and were crossing the winter-dead gardens behind Belle Maison.

"You were tempted by the prospect of marriage to me?" she asked.

Mr. St. Michael marched along beside her until they reached the gazebo, a lonely sentinel guarding the flower beds until spring returned. "You needn't sound so pleased. I'm no sort of bargain as a husband. I have wealth, of course. Many men have wealth, but I travel a great deal. I'm firmly in trade. My disposition is not genial, and I eschew tender sentiments. I frequently come home at the end of the day smelling of sheep or commerce, or preoccupied with how to get 'round some solicitor's clever wording. I lack charm and have all the wrong accents."

Nita took Mr. St. Michael's arm and fairly danced down the garden path with him when he would have stood in the wind reciting his shortcomings all afternoon.

"You were tempted," she said, beaming at the dead roses rather than allow Mr. St. Michael to see her smile. "By marriage to me." A niggling, inconvenient, tender part of her heart pointed out that he'd resisted the temptation—so far.

Nita led the way into the back hall, where warmth and the scent of fresh bread blended with the odors of damp wool and mud.

Mr. St. Michael pulled the door closed, rendering the hallway gloomy—or cozy.

"You are intelligent, attractive, kindhearted, *mostly* sensible, energetic, well connected, and reasonably dowered," he muttered, his fingers at the fastenings to Nita's cloak. "A shrewd businessman rejects no offers out of hand unless the terms are outright illegal or dishonorable. Marriage is an honorable institution, and illegality is not a concern in this case. You are free of prior obligations and of age."

Nita was on the shelf. She started on the pewter buttons to Mr. St. Michael's greatcoat. "You make a list of my faults, sir, not my positive attributes. Hold still."

Holding still for more than an instant was not in Tremaine St. Michael's nature, and yet he'd tarried long enough on the floor with the Chalmers children to get them to the letter *W*.

W was for Welsh rarebit.

Nita undid the last of his buttons and pushed the heavy garment from his shoulders. She hung it on a hook and found her own cloak whisked from her shoulders.

"I tell you things I ought to keep to myself," he said, another shortcoming apparently. "I abet your insubordination of the earl's very reasonable dictates. I consult you on matters a gently bred lady ought not to hear of."

Mr. St. Michael's tone was gruff and Scottish—gruffness was very much in his nature—and yet Nita suspected he was more bewildered than annoyed. She was bewildered too, also damned if she'd fail to seize an opportunity, no matter how unlikely.

"The earl knows better than to aspire to dictates around his family," Nita said, remaining right where she was, before a man soon to depart for damned Germany.

"You're also magnificent." Mr. St. Michael remained right where *he* was, in a gloomy back hallway surrounded by cloaks and boots and two hanging hams.

The last of Nita's common sense evaporated at that accusation. Tremaine St. Michael was magnificent, in his willingness to confront Edward, his dislike for Dr. Horton, his *W* is for Welsh rarebit. Nita wrapped her arms around him and kissed him full on the mouth.

He remained unmoving, as if his brain hadn't quite heard what his lips were telling him, and then his arms settled around her, and his entire posture shifted. He enveloped Nita in warmth and strength, in maleness, and in his embrace. A hint of cinnamon biscuit flavored his kiss, and a hint of tenderness.

He cherished, he tasted, he invited.

While Nita accepted. No winter apparel came between them, no misconceptions, no immediately impending departures. He knew Nita for who and what she was—of age and all that—and he was honest about himself.

Shrewd, capable, literate—and endlessly kind.

The kindness attracted Nita as broad shoulders, poetry, wealth, and even bold, tender kisses could not. Tremaine St. Michael understood her. Nita felt that understanding in his palm cradling the back of her head and his fingers tracing the angle of her jaw.

She wanted to know more than his kisses though, wanted to know the planes and geometry of his muscled chest, the turn of his flanks, the exact texture of—

His tongue traced her lips as delicately as a warm breeze, then again. Nita returned the overture, and the kiss went skittering off into an entire assembly of dances and flirtations Nita had had *no idea* could transpire between a man and a woman.

When Mr. St. Michael lifted his mouth from hers, Nita's back was to the wall, amid her sisters' everyday cloaks, while one of the hams swung gently, as if somebody had bumped it with a shoulder.

"You started it," he said, kissing her brow. "I'll not apologize."

"You ended it." Nita kissed his chin, which was like kissing a bristly rock. "Apologize for that."

He laughed, a hitch of his chest, while Nita tried to draw a steady breath and ended up smiling like Susannah in the presence of an original Shakespeare folio.

"You lack charm and have all the wrong accents," Nita said, sneaking another kiss, this one to his cool cheek, "except for rendering Mr. Burns. You do his verse exceedingly well. For that and many other reasons, I'm tempted too, Mr. St. Michael."

Nita bolted out of his embrace, into the light and warmth of the kitchen, straight up the servants' stairs. She kept on going until she fell, laughing—laughing!—onto her bed.

"Digby should see Dr. Horton," Elsie said when the boy had been excused from the breakfast table to learn his day's portion of frosty Latin.

No other creature on the face of the earth goaded Edward as Elsie did. What could Penny have seen in her? Elsie was pretty, if a man could abide red hair, Edward conceded that much. But then, what did hair color matter in the dark?

"Pass the teapot," Edward said, taking another bite of eggs that the kitchen could never seem to serve hot. Elsie passed him the teapot along with a fulminating look.

"A head cold can turn into lung fever, Edward, and that child is your sole heir. I'd think his health would matter to you."

"I will overlook that remark because you are a concerned mother and your nerves are delicate. Finish your meal, Elsie."

Her next nasty look went to the plate still sitting before Digby's place, upon which the boy had left not a crumb of toast nor a morsel of eggs.

"I am a concerned mother. You should be a concerned uncle."

Elsie could not help herself. Edward had come to this conclusion in the early months of her tenure at Stonebridge. Some women had no means of calling attention to themselves except by being contentious.

Morning sunlight illuminated Elsie's pale cheek and the bruise fading around her eye. That bruise shamed them both, though she might have used a bit more powder to cover it up.

"Send for Horton if you must," Edward said, topping up his cup of tea. "He'll bleed the boy, prescribe a mustard plaster for his chest and feet, and send a prodigious bill after drinking some of my best brandy."

"Thank you."

Elsie's thank-yous were as cold as Edward's eggs. "In future, madam, you will no longer pester me with your importuning. I intend to propose to Susannah on the occasion of the assembly, and as the lady of my household, she will tend to matters of health among the children and servants."

Edward wouldn't propose *at* the assembly, of course, but just before, so the announcement could be made to all their neighbors in traditional country fashion.

"I wish you luck, Edward. Lady Susannah is a lovely woman."

That tone of voice, that mocking, superior tone of voice...Edward would *not* gratify such insubordination with a display of temper.

"What do you mean, Elsie? Of course Susannah is a lovely woman. Do you imply I should plight my troth with a troll?"

Elsie toyed with her eggs, her fork scraping across the plate. "I meant nothing, Edward, except a sincere wish that your proposal be accepted. Lady Susannah will be good company for me. She's well connected and seems to suit you."

In a manner Edward would never understand, Elsie's demure, practical words implied something else entirely. Susannah wouldn't speak to him thus— nobody else spoke to him thus.

"Madam, let me remind you that you and the boy are here on my charity, which I can ill afford. I must marry responsibly, as befits the succession of the baronetcy, and Susannah is my choice."

Edward polished off the last of his eggs, determined to leave the table without shouting. Then the dratted woman muttered something behind her teacup.

"I beg your pardon, Elsie."

Elsie closed her eyes, as if assaulted by a sudden megrim. "*Lady* Susannah. She will always be *Lady* Susannah. You show her disrespect by assuming familiar address prior to an engagement."

The urge to strike the fool woman coursed through him. Edward's arm actually lifted, then fell. A display of temper gratified Elsie somehow, and—the insight nearly had him smiling—this entire round of disrespect from Elsie was merely a symptom of jealousy, because she was to be displaced as the lady of the Stonebridge household.

"I've changed my mind," Edward said, rising. "Digby isn't running a fever, his throat isn't sore. A mere cold does not necessitate a call from Dr. Horton. You may treat Digby as you please, but we'll not incur an unnecessary bill to humor your overprotectiveness. In future, please ensure the kitchen serves only hot eggs and toast."

"Yes, Edward." Elsie could put a wealth of rebellion in two words.

Edward nearly admired that about her. "Something for you to consider, Elsie Nash. This household might not have room for two ladies, particularly once the nursery includes a proper heir to the baronetcy. While I would never disrespect my brother's memory, you're long past first mourning. Perhaps you should consider attaching yourself to another establishment. Digby would of course remain in my care, for I owe the boy nothing less than my personal supervision in his formative years."

That spiked Elsie's guns neatly. She stared at the remains of her meal, her grip on her teacup turning her knuckles white.

Edward enjoyed the moment, with Elsie in a silent temper as he stood over her. This was progress for them. Nobody had shouted, nobody had been forced to a display of violence to settle the matter. His patience with her was paying off, finally.

"Have a pleasant day, my dear."

"You as well, Edward."

He paused outside the door of the breakfast parlor, half hoping to hear the sound of a teacup smashing—which was very bad of him. When several moments of silence had passed, he went off to the comfortable warmth of his library, to do battle once again with a ledger that would not balance.

"I may have proposed to your sister," Tremaine St. Michael said when he'd closed the door to the Belle Maison library.

George liked listening to St. Michael talk. All manner of ancestry presented itself in his vowels and consonants, in what was dropped, elided, or rolled. George also liked looking at Mr. St. Michael, particularly when the man removed his jacket and undid his cuffs, as if in anticipation of some manual task.

Though George had recently discovered he liked looking at Elsie Nash too—a puzzle, albeit a pretty one. He'd enjoyed the company of women in the past, the same as any other fellow at university, some women, anyway.

And a few men.

"I gather Nita did not accept this matrimonial overture, or you'd know for sure whether you proposed," George replied, replacing his volume of Mrs. Radcliffe on the library shelf where it belonged. Nita had established a system for organizing the library books, and one thwarted that system at one's peril.

"Lady Nita neither accepted nor rejected my offer," St. Michael said, "but then, I didn't exactly propose."

"Nita is formidable." George liked St. Michael, but he loved his sister. "Nonetheless, she can't abide a suffering creature. Her rejection would be as kind as possible."

"Also firm." St. Michael draped his jacket over the chair behind the estate desk, sat, and took out writing implements. "My proposal was oblique at best. A lady deserves a sincere, direct proposal."

St. Michael was unhappy with himself for his oblique proposal, or perhaps—George knew of no male who endured the emotion easily—he was bewildered.

"A gentleman deserves to know his suit will at least receive fair consideration," George offered by way of commiseration. "I proposed to a lady once, long ago. The experience was not enjoyable."

He'd never told his siblings this, lest they get that speculative gleam in their eyes.

St. Michael produced a penknife and went to work on a goose quill. "She turned you down?"

"She laughed in my face, and I was as much in earnest as I could be at that age. I enjoyed her conversation, had no need of her dowry, and had pegged her for a practical, good-natured sort." Who wouldn't have minded a marriage where both partners were free to roam, provided appearances were maintained.

The notion struck George as vaguely distasteful now, sad even.

A small pile of shavings accumulated on the desk blotter. "Your expectations of the institution are modest, Mr. Haddonfield. I think your sister's are too—as were mine."

Past tense in any accent was worth noting. Somebody needed to take the library in hand again, because they now had no less than three copies of *The Monk*.

"Your estimation of marriage has changed?" George asked. St. Michael had lovely hands—big, competent, elegant. Nita had probably had the same thought.

"Lady Nita is not a woman of modest accomplishments or modest sentiments. Have you never resumed your search for a bride, Mr. Haddonfield?"

The question was casual, while the goose feather had been pared to a perfect point. St. Michael swept the orts and leavings into the dust bin beside the desk and dusted those big palms together.

"I keep an eye out," George said, which was true. Marriage to the right woman would solve a few problems and stop his siblings from fretting over him. Would it be fair to the lady, though? George liked women, and even desired them on occasion, the way a fellow might desire a hot cup of tea or chocolate with a dash of cinnamon on a cold morning.

Not the way he longed for the fiery pleasure of a good brandy—stupidly, passionately, without any dignity or care for his own well-being.

"Shall we have a drink?" George asked, crossing to the sideboard.

St. Michael uncapped the ink, laid out a piece of foolscap, and began writing. He made a lovely picture at the vast desk, the white feather moving across the page with an assurance George envied.

"A bit early for me," he said, the pen never breaking rhythm, "but don't let that stop you. When I've completed this epistle, could you spare me time for a discussion of your latest German travels?"

"You're proposing to my sister, then decamping for the Pumpernickel Courts? That will impress Nita not at all. She'll go right back to her midwifery and tisanes, and forget you ever existed unless you turn up sick or injured."

St. Michael dipped his pen again, let a drop of ink gather on the tip, and waited, hand immobile, until that droplet had fallen back into the bottle.

"She well might," he said as a second drop followed the first. "Perhaps that's for the best. Do you fancy sheep, Mr. Haddonfield?"

In a different, half-drunken context, George might have misconstrued the question. "I like them well enough. Harmless creatures, pretty, and not given to violence." Rather like himself.

"I'm passionate about sheep," St. Michael said. "Your brother-the-earl would do well to recall this."

George took a steadying sip of excellent brandy and tormented himself by sitting on the edge of the desk, close enough to catch St. Michael's scent. "Are you passionate about my sister?"

"Interesting question." St. Michael did not stop writing, and abruptly, weariness pressed down on George.

St. Michael didn't even *see* him, and if he did—if he somehow divined that George regarded him as potentially desirable—he'd be disgusted or, worse, amused. He would never reciprocate George's interest, and as to that, what did George know of Tremaine St. Michael?

He was attractive, wealthy, and interested in Nita. So George must pant after him in silent frustration?

Must comport himself with all the emotional delicacy of a tomcat?

Such stirrings flattered nobody. They were for strutting, impulsive boys who had one foot planted in rebellion and the other in boredom.

"Nita is lonely," George said, setting his glass down near the ink. "She was born immediately after her older brothers, and it's almost as if Mama and Papa didn't realize there'd been a change in gender. Nita tagged after us boys, rode like a demon, and tried very hard to keep up with us."

"And you humored her," St. Michael muttered, "which she hated."

"Drove her nigh barmy, to be so little and dear. I don't think it much bothers her lately."

St. Michael glanced up from his epistle. "She's very dear, also brave, maybe too brave." He might have asked George to name his seconds in the same tone, so fierce was Nita's newly acquired shepherd boy and champion.

"You did propose," George said, feeling pity for the handsome St. Michael, which was an odd relief from indiscriminate desire. "Maybe you're lonely too, St. Michael."

George certainly was.

Now where had that notion come from?

St. Michael appended a signature to his letter, legible but with a slight flourish to the initial capitals. Beckman had said that St. Michael dealt in fine art in addition to wool.

"The question is, Mr. Haddonfield, does the lady see any advantage in my suit. One must think practically in any negotiation."

St. Michael would think at least in part with his breeding organs,

like any other male. In this, he and George were no different. And yet
loneliness was a problem the breeding organs could not solve.

A day for insights, apparently. George took another sip of his
drink and recalled Elsie Nash's invitation to share a fresh biscuit and
cup of tea on a cold day.

"What does Nicholas say about your proposing to Nita?" George
asked, for any Haddonfield must be mindful of the earl's position on
matters of significance. Nicholas was tolerant, patient, and practical,
but also trying to step into the old earl's shoes, a delicate and difficult
task.

"Bellefonte is attempting to lure two men to the altar with the
same flock of sheep," St. Michael said, casting sand over his letter.
"He's neglected to consider how we're to lure the ladies to the altar. A
man cannot be married to a lot of bleating livestock."

"How to lure the object of one's tender emotions is always a
fraught question," George allowed. "How will you answer it?"

St. Michael sat back. "I want those sheep, but if I acquire them as
part of your sister's dowry, Lady Nita will not be well pleased. Lady
Nita doesn't want Squire Nash to have Lady Susannah *or* the sheep,
but then, what does Lady Susannah want, and what does the earl
want?"

"Do you come from a large family?"

"I own enormous quantities of sheep, but come from barely any
family at all."

"One would not have guessed as much." George passed St.
Michael his glass. "You'll need this more than I do, but when it comes
to my sisters, I've been plagued by a thought."

St. Michael poured the sand off his letter. "Don't be coy. If I'm
not engaged soon, we might be traveling to Germany together."

Interesting prospect, about which St. Michael seemed to feel no
hesitation.

"My sisters each need what the other has." George would never
have aired this notion before Nicholas. "Nita needs more poetry and
rest, Susannah needs a purpose beyond verse and endless sedentary

hours of embroidery. Della needs to be taken more seriously and patted on the head less, and Kirsten needs to laugh more and be cosseted."

St. Michael waved the letter gently over the dust bin, then laid it exactly in the middle of the blotter.

"Nash represents a purpose for Lady Susannah, then," he said. "A household she can take in hand, an estate she can help run. Interesting."

He took the last sip of George's drink, managing to make even that mundane activity attractive. George noted it, probably the way Nita noted that an infant in the churchyard was healthy or St. Michael would note that a herd of sheep was in good weight.

A passing observation, not a passionate preoccupation —thank God.

George took the empty glass over to the sideboard. "So you want Nita, but she'll turn you down if she thinks you're marrying her to get the sheep, and yet, Nash shouldn't have the sheep either. Complicated."

"She might turn me down because I'm no sort of marital bargain, and because I haven't proposed."

St. Michael would propose though. He might not get the prescribed words out in the prescribed order, but he'd convey his intentions well enough.

Lucky Nita. St. Michael would give her babies and a household to run while putting a stop to the endless progression of sore throats, influenza, and rheumatism that now filled her days.

"I would not want to see Lady Susannah attached to Nash's household," St. Michael said, "though my hesitance is unrelated to the fate of the sheep."

George had pleasant associations with Stonebridge. Warm ginger biscuits, the Second Punic War, and Elsie Nash's surprising tolerance.

"Suze wants Edward Nash," George said. "The man's fate is sealed. Nicholas will like that she's close by, and so will I."

"Lady Nita fears for the safety of the women in Nash's home, though I very nearly violate a confidence when I tell you that. If Lady Nita is to be believed, then Mrs. Nash at this moment is sporting a black eye courtesy of the head of her household."

St. Michael's voice was as cold as the wind moaning around the corner of the house.

"Lady Nita is to be believed," George said slowly, while consternation warred with outrage inside him. "Nita does not indulge in falsehoods. Nash struck Elsie?"

Elsie was petite, kindhearted, fair-minded, *a mother*.

"Lady Nita came to that conclusion, and if you're about to tell me I must disclose this situation to the earl, I cannot. I gather Lady Nita is in Mrs. Nash's confidence, and were her ladyship not enraged beyond endurance, she would never have spoken to me so honestly. I apologize for burdening you with this information but will prevail on your gentlemanly honor to keep it between us."

St. Michael was upset about Elsie's situation, upset enough to disclose it when he hadn't meant to. No wonder Nita saw potential in him.

"Nita holds herself to the standards of a physician when it comes to people's privacy," George said—though George did not, and perhaps St. Michael perceived as much. Something would have to be done, and Susannah could not marry a man who lacked control of his own temper. "Shall I have Nicholas frank your letter?"

St. Michael capped the ink and tucked it into a drawer. "Thank you, no. The matter requires some discretion. I'll post it myself."

George set his mind to the problem that was Elsie Nash's safety— Digby had also said Nash had a sour temper—but St. Michael's comment nagged at him too. What could require such very great discretion that Nicholas mustn't even be allowed to *see* the epistle St. Michael had penned with such dispatch?

CHAPTER NINE

The Haddonfields were an incorrigibly merry bunch when the ladies were at their cordials, and Tremaine had thus had an opportunity to give Lady Nita her evening of cards and silliness.

They'd put him in mind of a bunch of shepherds, gathered around the fire and the flasks. Somebody would get out a fiddle, somebody else would tell a tale or start on a rendition of "Willie Brew'd a Peck o' Maut," and the laughter would crest higher and higher until Tremaine's sides ached.

He'd forgotten about those nights, though he hadn't forgotten the hard ground or the cold mornings.

He rapped on Lady Nita's door, quietly, despite a light shining from beneath it. Somebody murmured something which he took for permission to enter.

"Mr. St. Michael?"

Tremaine stepped into her ladyship's room, closed the door behind him, and locked it, which brought the total of his impossibly forward behaviors to several thousand.

"Your ladyship expected a sister or a maid with a pail of coal?"

"I wasn't expecting *you*." Lady Nita sat near the hearth in a blue velvet dressing gown. The wool stockings on her feet were thick enough to make a drover covetous. "Are you unwell, Mr. St. Michael?"

"You are not pleased to see me." Did she think illness the only reason somebody would seek her out?

She set aside some pamphlet, a medical treatise, no doubt. No vapid novels for Lady Nita. "I was not expecting you, sir."

"You were not expecting me to discuss marriage with you earlier. I wasn't expecting the topic to come up in a casual fashion either. May I sit?" Tremaine was egregiously presuming, but he had earned significant coin by seizing opportunities, and Lady Nita had very much the feel of an opportunity.

She waved an elegant hand at the other chair flanking the hearth.

Tremaine settled in, trying to gather his thoughts while the firelight turned Lady Nita's braid into a rope of burnished gold.

"You are pretty." Brilliant place to start. The words had come out, heavily burred, something of an ongoing revelation.

"I am tall and blond," she retorted, twitching at the folds of her robe. "I have the usual assortment of parts. What did you come here to discuss?"

Lady Nita was right in a sense. Her beauty was not of the ballroom variety but rather an illumination of her features by characteristics unseen. She fretted over new babies, cut up potatoes like any crofter's wife, and worried for her sisters. These attributes interested Tremaine.

Her Madonna-with-a-secret smile, keen intellect, and longing for laughter *attracted* him. Even her medical preoccupation, in its place, had utility as well.

"Will you marry me?"

More brilliance. Where had his wits gone? George Haddonfield had graciously pointed out that Nita needed repose and laughter, and Tremaine was offering her the hand of the most restless and un-silly man in the realm.

The lady somehow contained her incredulity, staring at her stockings. "You seek to discuss marriage?"

"I believe I did just open that topic. Allow me to elaborate on my thesis: Lady Bernita Haddonfield, will you do me the honor of becoming my wife? I believe we would suit, and I can promise you would know no want in my care."

A proper swain would have been on his damn bended knee, the lady's hand in his. Lady Nita would probably laugh herself to tears if Tremaine attempted that nonsense. He'd seen her laugh that hard earlier in the evening, over Lady Kirsten's rendition of the parson's sermon on women keeping silent in the church.

Lady Nita picked up her pamphlet, which Tremaine could now see was written in German. "Why, Mr. St. Michael?"

"I beg your pardon?" Tremaine was about to pitch the damned pamphlet into the fire, until he recalled that Nita Haddonfield excelled at obscuring her stronger emotions.

"Why should you marry me, Tremaine St. Michael? Why should I marry you? I've had other offers; you've made other offers. You haven't known me long enough to form an opinion of my character beyond the superficial."

This ability to take a situation apart, into causes, effects, symptoms, and prognosis, was part of why she was successful as a healer. Tremaine applied the same tendencies to commercial situations, and thus he didn't dismiss her questions as dithering or manipulation.

Neither was she rejecting him.

"My appraisal of your character goes beyond the superficial, my dear. You can be shy, but you haven't a coy bone in your body," he said, propping his feet beside hers on the brass fender. "Your heart is inconveniently tender, but you are so fierce and so disciplined, few suspect this about you. I do not pretend my offer is that of a passionate young swain for a lady he has long loved, but I will guard your heart with my life."

She folded the pamphlet but didn't set it aside. "Will you entrust your heart into my keeping?"

Did Tremaine even have a heart to entrust? His parents had shown him the folly of allowing that organ to overstep its biological functions, and yet he liked Nita Haddonfield, he desired her, and her regard for him mattered very much.

"I will entrust my heart to no other." Tremaine could give her that assurance. He sealed his promise with a kiss to her knuckles and kept her hand in his.

"Interesting reply, Mr. St. Michael. I'm happy with my life as it is, though. Marriage has always struck me as a poor bargain for the lady. She ceases to enjoy any sort of independence and must endure her husband's pawings and beatings without recourse to the church or the law. She risks her life in childbirth, repeatedly, and should her husband die, she's best advised to get another as soon as possible."

Lady Nita's objection was to marriage in theory, not to Tremaine personally. He took courage from that.

"You are slow to trust," he said. "I'm not exactly atremble with confidence in the institution myself. Marriage means my wife's entire health, happiness, and safety lie exclusively in my hands, and all my wit, my meager store of charm, my plowman's poetry, and my coin may be inadequate to keep her safe from the foxes and wolves."

Tremaine should probably not have likened a husband's responsibilities to those of a shepherd, but the sentiments were similar. Nita would be his exclusive responsibility.

"I like kissing you," she said, regarding their joined hands. "Will you come to bed with me?"

Tremaine's breeding organs offered an immediate, unequivocal yes. The stakes were too high to indulge in such folly, however.

"Why, my lady? Are you anticipating vows with me?"

"I'm making up my mind," she said. "I like you, Mr. St. Michael, but I would not be a biddable or easy wife any more than you'll be a biddable or doting husband. We both must be very sure of this decision."

Lady Nita would be a loyal wife, one who never compromised Tremaine's interests or countermanded his decisions—not the important ones. As for the doting, a man could learn new skills when suffi-ciently motivated. Tremaine had ever enjoyed a worthy challenge, after all.

"Would it help to know I'll happily purchase a house here in Kent?" he asked, a bid in the direction of doting such as he under-stood it. "There are several possibilities in this vicinity—I've inquired —and I'd happily make our Kent property an addition to your dowry portion."

Some part of Tremaine—the prudent businessman or possibly the awkward suitor—did not want to join Lady Nita in bed unless and until she'd accepted him as a spouse.

"You are thorough about your campaign, Mr. St. Michael, but I cannot take a house to bed. I cannot, with any hope of enjoyment, kiss a house or hold its hand. I cannot fall asleep with the arms of a house about me, and a house cannot recite Scottish poetry about a shepherd boy's heart breaking because he's been banished for loving his shepherd girl."

The "Broom O' the Cowdenknowes." Earlier in the evening, Tremaine had offered up a simple lament as an antidote to the indeci-pherable subtlety of old Shakespeare.

Tremaine's heart would not break were he banished from Lady Nita's boudoir, and that pragmatism was part of why he could offer the lady marriage.

And yet...what she wanted was understandable. "I can be those things you ask for, Lady Nita. I can be the man who holds you as you sleep, who gives you all the kisses you want, who indulges your appreciation for poetry, and whose hand is always yours to hold."

He had her attention now. The pamphlet lay forgotten in her lap, so Tremaine gathered his courage and leaped. "I can be the man who takes you to bed and indulges your every intimate passion as often and as wantonly as you please."

~

Tremaine St. Michael had traveled the Continent in times of war, he moved nimbly between cultures, rattled off poetry in broad Scots *and* French, taught letters to children among the ashes, and turned pages for Kirsten as she raced through Scarlatti at the pianoforte.

Such a man commanded hordes and warehouses of aplomb—Nita's bold proposition had failed utterly to scare him away—and yet something was off.

Nita considered the translation of Paracelsus sitting in her lap and made another grab for logic, reason, common sense, for anything that would keep her from dragging her visitor to her bed.

"How do you know I'm capable of wantonness?" Nita certainly suffered doubts about that quality in herself.

Mr. St. Michael slid from his chair with the ease of a cat hopping to the carpet. He arranged himself before Nita, his arms loosely about her hips.

"Anybody who defies her family as easily as you do, who takes on the worst of winter's weather, who challenges death itself, has a capacity for considerable passion. Stop diagnosing a simple case of attraction between healthy adults and kiss me."

He moved closer, close enough that Nita caught a whiff of mint on his breath. She cupped his cheek, finding it shaved smooth. He'd prepared for his campaign while she'd read medical wisdom written hundreds of years ago.

She was tempted. Tempted by the flesh-and-blood man before her, tempted by his assurance that passion and pleasure could be hers. She set her pamphlet aside, leaned forward, and touched her lips to Mr. St. Michael's. His shoulders relaxed, but he did not assume control of the kiss, a point in his favor.

Nita would allow no man to assume control of *her*, marriage be damned, attraction be double damned.

"More," he whispered. "Again."

As she leaned forward and anchored her hands in his hair, Nita shifted, so Mr. St. Michael knelt between her legs. His arms snugged around her waist, and tension seemed to drain from him.

"I'm not saying yes," she muttered against his mouth. His reply was rendered with more kisses, delicate, entreating, fascinating kisses to which Nita most assuredly assented.

And then she wasn't saying anything. She was kissing him back like a woman who might never have another kiss, who might die, all of her passion spent on other people's colicky babies and gouty grandparents.

Mr. St. Michael shifted up so he embraced Nita as she sat before the fire. The contours of his body were more evident than in any of their previous encounters, because Nita wore only her nightgown and robe while he wore only his shirt and waistcoat above his breeches.

Nita knew the names of the muscles—*pectoralis, subclavius, serratus*—but she was frantic to learn the feel of them, of *him*. Without breaking the kiss, Nita went after the buttons of his waistcoat.

"You will take me to bed," she said as a button went flying.

"You like giving orders." He smiled against her mouth and brushed her hands away. "Like being in charge. Maybe this is part of the appeal of the sickroom."

Nita hated sickrooms. "How can you think of such matters at a time—?"

He rose away from her and she wanted to roar at him to get back to their kissing, except he yanked his shirttails out of his waistband and hauled his shirt over his head, waistcoat and all. Firelight turned his skin golden, and the dratted man must have had some sense of the picture he made, half-naked and all gloriously healthy male, dark hair whorling down the midline of his flat belly.

"I think to please you," he said, extending a hand to Nita.

She regarded that callused, masculine hand, stretched across the marital equivalent of the Sistine Chapel's ceiling.

"I would not be a biddable wife. I would be head-strong and difficult. I am not very sociable. I do not hold my opinions lightly."

"You will not hold your vows lightly either," he said, his hand steady. "You would protect our children with your life, and you'd manage easily when I'm traveling for extended periods. You'd enjoy your independence, in fact, and be neither impressed with our wealth nor heedless of it."

Our wealth. *Her* independence. Nita loved the sound of that, though as for Mr. St. Michael's extended travel... Nita's brothers had traveled. She'd tolerated their absence with an abundance of prayer and activity. People would still fall ill, suffer injuries, and have babies, regardless of Mr. St. Michael's traveling. She'd stay busy. Nita put her hand in his and let him draw her to her feet.

"You will give me time to consider your proposal, sir."

He scooped her up against his chest. "You are magnificently stubborn, which only attracts me more. I will give you something to think about then, besides a few tame kisses."

Tame kisses?

He settled Nita on the bed, and while she tried to decide if she liked being handled like a sack of flour—albeit a precious sack of flour—Mr. St. Michael toed off his boots and peeled away stockings and breeches.

"We didn't bank the fire," Nita said, gaze glued to the middle of his chest. *Sternum, rectus abdominis. Do-not-look-down-imus.*

Wearing nothing but a smile the likes of which would set every female heart in the shire pounding, Mr. St. Michael crossed the room and took up the poker.

Trapezius, latissimus dorsi, gluteus...

Gluteus God-help-me-us. A giggle threatened, a very pleased giggle as Nita's suitor returned to the bed.

"Do you typically wear your robe and stockings under the covers?" His voice was different in the lower light, maybe more French or more Scottish, but definitely less English.

And certainly more naughty. Nita shifted back, swinging her legs onto the mattress. "I do not. Aren't you cold?"

Mr. St. Michael took Nita's foot in his hands and drew her stocking off slowly, so the soft wool caressed her calf, ankle, and arch.

She gave him her other foot, assailed by the certainty that anatomical labels and stubbornness would not see her through what came next.

"Your robe, my lady?" He folded her stockings on the night table casually, as if women's clothing were familiar to him—though they were *wool* stockings.

Nita shrugged out of her robe, an awkward undertaking that involved scooting her hips and rocking from side to side. He waited patiently, his nudity a visual lure immediately to Nita's left.

"My guess is you've seen the male body before," he said, folding the robe across the foot of the bed. "Are these maidenly vapors for my benefit?" He sauntered around to the other side of the bed, the meager light of the banked fire revealing only outlines and shadows.

"I'm not a maiden," Nita said, flipping the covers back so he could join her between the sheets.

He stopped, one knee on the mattress. "Do I have a rival for your hand?"

His tone was merely curious, as if a rival might be an interesting twist to a complicated negotiation, though Nita also had the sense a wrong answer might send him right back into his boots and breeches.

"No rival. You're not disappointed?" Had she hoped he would be?

He settled on the bed. "We have a word in English to describe a woman without sexual experience—she is a maiden. We have no word for a man in a similar untried state. The general term—*virgin*—sits awkwardly on the male, and he has no specific term of his own. I've found this curious."

Mr. St. Michael was comfortable sharing a bed, lounging on his side as if he and Nita shared a blanket in a meadow.

"You're curious about the terminology?" Nita was curious about his anatomy, but also about the passion he'd seen in her—and she sensed in him.

"That too. Come here, please. Some discussions are better undertaken in close quarters."

Nita scooted under the covers—the room would soon grow

chilled—and wished she'd kept a candle lit. "What are we to discuss?"

He arranged himself around her, so Nita was on her back, Tremaine St. Michael draped along her side.

"Were *you* disappointed, my lady?"

A lump rose in Nita's throat, inappropriate, inconvenient, and unwelcome. The question was insightful and quietly tendered.

"I was young. He was a dashing fellow in his regimentals, handsome, charming, and newly down from university. I'd known him most of my life, but he'd gone away a boy and come back a man."

Or so she'd thought. He'd gone away a boy and come back a scoundrel, in truth.

Mr. St. Michael pulled Nita closer and kissed her cheek. "Did your handsome cavalier have the bad grace to die in service to King and Country?"

"He did, of dysentery. Disease carried off nearly as many soldiers as enemy fire on the Peninsula, and he was one of the casualties."

How cozy and comforting to drop her forehead to Mr. St. Michael's sturdy shoulder and share a regret with somebody who would not judge her for her indiscretion.

"Did his death inspire your campaign against illness and injury?" A warm hand settled on Nita's nape, fingers massaging away tension, regret, and even self-consciousness.

"My mother trained me regarding herbs and nursing. That feels good." Nita's mother had also trained her to carry an unrelenting sense of responsibility. Would marriage offer a cure for that affliction or make it worse?

Silence stretched for a long, sweet moment, while the sheets warmed, and Nita relaxed into the novel comfort of sharing a bed with a man who knew his way around the female body.

"Are you still in love with your young soldier?" Such was Mr. St. Michael's sophistication that he wouldn't have begrudged Nita a sprig of willow for a young man long dead.

"You are not as pragmatic and unsentimental as you want the

world to think," Nita said, kissing his shoulder. "I've since realized I was not in love with Norton. I was in love with romance, with the notion of having my own household, of a place where my brothers weren't always leaving and my mother's ill health wasn't increasingly obvious."

Norton Nash would have made a very indifferent spouse. Nita had long since admitted that. He'd been shallow, vain, and without higher principles that might have inspired him to make something of himself. Part of her antipathy toward Edward was a result of the same attributes, allowed to flourish in expectation of a baronetcy.

"Gloomy talk," Mr. St. Michael said, kissing Nita's temple. "What say we relieve you of this shroud you're wearing? Conversation will grow more cheerful as a result, I promise."

This was how he teased, with a bit of a dare in his silliness. Nita hiked up on her elbows and reached beneath the bedclothes for the hem of her nightgown.

"A moment, please, my lady." He sat up, cross-legged, beside her, and untied the three bows holding the nightgown closed at Nita's throat.

"You are very competent with ladies' attire, Mr. St. Michael."

"Do you know, when you scold me like that," he replied, easing Nita's nightgown over her head, "all vinegar and starch, it makes my cock twitch?"

However he might have ended his sentence, Nita could not have anticipated *that*. She ducked back under the covers, which had become agreeably toasty.

"You have a hidden streak of naughtiness," she said. "I like that about you. As for the twitching, a tisane of valerian taken regularly might provide some relief."

"More starch and vinegar," he said. "You're not helping. 'First do no harm,' isn't that the highest canon of a physician? You're dealing mortal blows to my self-restraint."

"I'm not a—" Gracious saints. Without clothing, the business of cuddling beneath the blankets was an altogether less innocent undertaking. "You're very warm, Mr. St. Michael."

"If you don't start calling me by my name, I'll spend before I've so much as kissed you."

"But you've already kissed—"

He kissed Nita again, silencing her retort, pushing the warm, hair-dusted expanse of his chest against Nita's breast and arm.

"My name is Tremaine. When I had more family, some of them referred to me as Maine. In spoken English, this likens me to a part of a horse. In French, I'm part of the human anatomy."

La main, a feminine noun for the hand.

Nita ran *her* hand over the wondrous texture of his chest. "Are you babbling? I'd like it if you babbled a little."

"I will sing 'God Save the King' in any one of five languages, if you'll just keep touching me."

A heavily burred growl more than a babble. She liked that even better. "I'll enjoy your serenades some other time. My brothers would kill you did they find you here, and my sisters would never allow me to live down my disgrace."

"Dammit, Nita, if we're to be married—"

She drew her fingertip around his nipple lightly, clockwise, counterclockwise. "Interesting."

"Heaven defend me from an anatomist in siren's clothing—or lack thereof."

Tremaine had the ability to make Nita smile with his complaining, also to inspire her. She licked that same nipple and inhaled a hint of heather and flowers.

"Do that again at your peril," he hissed, making no move to dodge out of licking range.

"Are you threatening me in my own bed, Mr. St—?"

He pinned Nita's hands above her head, his grip loose but implacable. "You like my naughty streak, may God help you. I didn't even know I possessed one, sober man of commerce that I am, but I hope you come to adore it."

His mouth descended on Nita's breast, a hot, delicate onslaught of sensations that made her want to both squirm and hold very, very still.

"She desists," he muttered, his tongue moving in a slow circle. "And she tastes of lemon."

He drew on Nita gently, but that single overture had her back arching and her hands fisting in his hair.

"I like that."

Assuming Tremaine did not slay Nita utterly with his attentions in the next five minutes, she'd thank Kirsten for the soap. He moved to the second breast, and Nita did squirm.

"Shall I dose you with valerian?" he muttered, lips against her heart.

"Dose me with your kisses, or I'll scold you for the next hour straight. I have five brothers and three younger sisters. I am a prodigious scold when inspired."

He left off tormenting Nita's breasts and loomed over her, his dark hair in considerable disarray.

'For an hour *straight*?"

Straight, as in the hard column of flesh pressing against Nita's hip. She wiggled a hand free of his grip and shifted, so she had room enough to grasp him. His shaft was surprisingly warm and, from what she could recall, of considerably more generous proportions than what Norton had been so proud of.

"You are the boldest lady I've ever met." His tone said he approved of her boldness.

Nita traced the contours of his arousal, from the thatch of down at the base, along the shaft, to the peculiar configuration of the business end.

"Why are you holding your breath, sir?"

He spoke through his teeth. "I'm trying not to spend, you lemon-scented witch."

"I thought spending was the part men liked best." Norton certainly had. All three times, he'd assured Nita he wouldn't, and then... Had he thought she'd not grasped why her handkerchief had been needed while he'd done up his falls?

Mr. St—Tremaine nuzzled Nita's throat. "I'll show you the part this man likes best—with your permission." Nita let him go, because the time for teasing and giggling had passed. Maybe it had passed years ago, and she'd been too busy delivering babies and brewing tisanes to notice.

"Show me, then," she said, giving him permission to become her lover.

But not her husband—not yet

Tremaine enthusiastically immersed himself in the pleasures of trading in art, Holland bulbs, Italian wines, wool, and livestock. The pleasures of the flesh—when they intruded upon his immediate notice—usually struck him as a needlessly complicated road to comparable satisfaction.

He'd traveled that road many a time nonetheless.

Wooing Lady Nita was complicated indeed, involving pursuit of her intimate favors, appreciation for her tireless mind, and enticement of her trust.

What perplexed Tremaine, as he arranged himself over his intended, was how all that effort added up to *fun*. "How long has it been since anybody tickled you, my lady?"

"Your chest hair might be said to be tickling me at this very moment."

Or Nita's nipples *might be said* to be tickling Tremaine's sanity. He kissed her, because his conversational gambit had led straight to folly. She was a fine kisser, having the ability to make a discussion out of what some turned into an excuse for oral aggression.

"You taste sweet," he said. "One wonders..." How would Nita's intimate parts taste? She'd probably allow him to find out, eventually. Maybe on their wedding night.

"You taste like mint and male." She framed his face with soft hands and kissed his brow. "Your hair bears the scent of heather."

Tremaine hoped he tasted like a husband. Nita hadn't capitulated yet though, not entirely, and that was only fair. When a woman surrendered control of her entire future, a man ought to work for the privilege of becoming her spouse.

"Nita, love, we cannot risk a child."

Her hands went still, and the minute undulations of her hips—when had she started that torment?—ceased.

"I haven't vinegar and sponges," she said. "Had not known I might ever need them."

While Tremaine's nearest sheath was in Oxfordshire. He cursed in Gaelic, a language Nita was unlikely to know.

"Do you trust me?" he asked. Her answer mattered, and not simply because the urge to mate had ambushed Tremaine with a ferocity that characterized healthy animals in spring. "The Latin term is *coitus interruptus*, and while it's a distant second to the pleasure you're owed, it will minimize the prospect of a child."

And this approach might allow Tremaine to survive the next hour.

Nita brushed his hair back from his forehead. "You put a choice before me: an assured moment's pleasure, but at the risk of a lifetime of obligation to you."

At least Nita trusted him to provide that moment's pleasure. To give himself time to think, Tremaine indulged in another spree of kissing, which plan backfired horrendously.

When Nita let him up for air, he was crouched over his lady, though his wits had also decamped for Oxfordshire.

"If you understand that marriage is a partnership," Nita said, tracing his eyebrows with her thumb, "if you accept that you have no dominion over me save what I yield willingly, and that my dominion over you is on the same terms"—she traced his lips with that same thumb—"if *you* can trust *me*, Mr. St. Michael, then I am willing to take this risk with you—but only this risk."

Still not an acceptance of his proposal, but progress. "I can honor those terms," Tremaine said, for he'd never intrude on Nita's domestic territory, never overrule her common sense as she applied it to the nursery or household matters, never question her social instincts when moving in circles where she was welcomed and Tremaine merely tolerated.

She traced his ear, a peculiarly arousing touch, when Tremaine was already painfully aroused. "You promise to withdraw?"

"On my honor, I promise to withdraw." Tremaine had enough practice at it that he could make that vow, though he had no experience with Nita, and thus he resisted the screaming imperative from his cock to plunge into her willing heat.

"Doesn't one need to"—her caresses slowed—"that is, in order to withdraw from a location, oughtn't one to *be* in that location in the first place?" Nita sounded curious and worried, as if trusting Tremaine were the most difficult boon he could have asked of her.

"You have the right of it," he said, nudging forward. She would frequently have the right of a situation, and he'd learn to rely on her judgment in the years to come.

The thought of those years steadied Tremaine, gave him some purchase against lust, and allowed him to love Nita with honest affection, with a cherishing respect that was no less passionate for being of the mind as well as the body.

"I like this," she whispered as he progressed languidly toward a complete joining. "This is better."

Better than her soldier boy? Tremaine gathered Nita closer, hoping he could soon make their union better than her wildest imaginings.

"Am I pleasing you?" Was he making her see him as her husband?

"If you could move just a shade more—mmf." Nita bit his earlobe as he added a hint of power to his thrusting. "Like that."

She locked her heels at the small of his back, adding her undula-

tions to his own, and Tremaine was forced to think of... sheep
succumbing to coe, foot rot, scours...

"*Tremaine...*"

His name, full of wonder and maybe a bit of terror, as Nita
Haddonfield's passion found its gratification. He drove her through it,
though she hardly needed herding. Nita went after her pleasure at a
pounding gallop, bucking into him, clutching at his backside with a
ferocious, delightful strength.

"Gracious, merciful, never-ending..." She unhooked her ankles
and purely hugged Tremaine as he went still above her. "I had no
idea."

That she'd had no idea clearly bewildered her, while her befud-
dlement delighted him.

He kissed her shoulder. "Then you'd best have another go, don't
you think? You can confirm your first impression, investigate the
matter further." Make a thorough study of what was on offer, because
irrespective of any marriage proposals, she was owed that.

Damn her soldier boy for a selfish bumbler anyway.

"We can do that again?" she asked. "I thought you said you'd
withdraw?"

"I will withdraw before I spend, but I needn't spend just yet."
Much to Tremaine's surprise.

He pleasured Nita again, and just when he thought she'd had her
fill, she got to experimenting with angle and speed, and had a jolly
good time without Tremaine having to do much besides mentally
attempt the Lord's Prayer in Latin backward.

When his lady lay panting and pleased with herself—and with
him—Tremaine gently slid from her body, knowing she would be a
trifle sore come morning.

Also engaged to be married, he hoped.

He braced himself on one arm and used his free hand to stroke
himself exactly three times, before his self-control joined other valuable assets somewhere in the wilds of Oxfordshire. The pleasure was

glorious, while the mess went all over Nita's belly, for which Tremaine would apologize, just as soon as he could speak.

"You withdrew," Nita said, petting his hair. "You said you would."

She was relieved and pleased and capable of speech. Marriage to this woman would require great reserves of sexual stamina, God be thanked.

"Flannel?" he managed.

While Tremaine hung over Nita, breathing like a spent steeplechaser, she fished on the night table and then passed him a cloth. He tended to her, then tended to himself and tossed the cloth toward the hearth.

"Let me hold you," Tremaine said. Nita would soon learn what he really meant was, "Would you please hold me?" He needed her embrace, needed her sweet kisses and surprisingly affectionate nature. Tremaine pitched onto his back and tucked Nita against his side. "You should take a soaking bath in the morning, madam."

"Will you need a soaking bath too?" Nita was either genuinely curious, or his lovemaking had put her very much on her mettle.

"I shall. You've worn me to flinders." He kissed her temple and tucked her leg across his thighs. "I will need the assistance of at least two stout footmen to get down to breakfast, I'm sure."

Nita's damnably inquisitive fingers toyed with his nipple, and so thoroughly had Tremaine spent his passion that her touch was only eleven times more distracting than a tickle and only fourteen times harder to ignore than a stampeding herd of cattle.

"How does one manage that breakfast table encounter?" Nita asked. "I'm accustomed to dealing with patients in extremis—you'd be surprised the curses a Quaker lady knows when delivering her first child—but this is..."

Mercifully, her fingers went still.

"This is different," Tremaine said, as close as he could come to describing an intimacy entirely without precedent in his experience.

What fool would hare off to Germany to buy sheep in the dead of winter when travel would mean leaving Nita Haddonfield's side for weeks? Tremaine could take her with him, of course, but why spoil a wedding journey with commerce?

Commerce, his faithful mistress since he'd sold his first crop of wool nearly twenty years ago.

Nita patted his nipple. "We shall contrive. Nicholas and his countess manage, and they're shamelessly besotted, not merely investigating possibilities with each other."

If Nita had investigated Tremaine's possibilities any more thoroughly, he'd be—

We shall contrive. Together, they would in the future, *as a couple,* contrive. The sense of her words penetrated the lingering haze of erotic pleasure.

"What conclusion have you come to after all this dedicated inquiry, Lady Nita?"

She snuggled closer. "About?"

"About marrying me. About becoming my wife, or my countess. The title hasn't been an asset on the Continent, so I've not used it, but I'm a French *comte,* a circumstance my grandfather delights in. I have holdings in Provence, Portugal, Wales—sheep do quite well there—Scotland, Ireland, and I'm thinking of buying land in Germany. I have residences in Edinburgh, Aberdeenshire, Paris, London, Oxfordshire, Avignon, Florence, Venice—I like art; have I mentioned that?—and York."

Tremaine liked *her,* liked her exceedingly, and she apparently liked him rather a lot too. The pleasure of that happy coincidence warmed him from the inside out.

"Some of my properties are modest," he went on, "mere town houses, but my holdings in the Midlands are considerable, and I'm more than happy to purchase you a dower property in the vicinity of Haddondale."

He probably didn't need to remind her of that.

Tremaine paused to kiss Nita's temple, wondering what else he had to offer his intended. Her hand on his chest was a slack weight over his heart, her breathing even.

"We'll live wherever you please," he said. "The Oxford estate is commodious, a good place to bring up children, and not that far from your family. Summers there are wonderful." Tremaine fell asleep amid a vision of Nita organizing a family picnic for their brood of children. Sheep would dot the nearby meadow, the children would enjoy the chance to gambol out of doors.

Tremaine's wife would love him and their family, and forget she'd ever been reduced to dealing with the unfortunate, the unwell, and the injured.

CHAPTER TEN

"Nita, wake up." A determined hand shook Nita from dreams of minty kisses. "I'll dash you with water if you don't rouse yourself this instant."

"Kirsten?"

"You were expecting somebody else?" Kirsten dove under the covers on the far side of Nita's bed. "I hate winter. I hate being cold. I hate pretending frigid air is invigorating. Addy Chalmers's daughter is in the kitchen asking for you. I had the child fed, but I fear she wants you to accompany her home."

The last warm, dreamy cobwebs of memory were scoured away by a cold blast of dread. "Mary came for me?"

"She's well enough. I didn't inquire about the baby. If you want to send Horton to them, I'll pay for it out of my pin money." Kirsten drew the covers up to her chin, bouncing the bed all about.

"Horton won't show up until the day's half-gone," Nita said, "if he bothers at all, and then he'll merely look at the child, mutter about weak lungs, and suggest the surgeon should bleed her."

"I thought you weren't supposed to bleed the little ones."

Nita swung the covers aside. "In more enlightened environs, the practice is held in low esteem. Thank you for fetching me."

"You're going, aren't you?" Kirsten groused from the depths of the bed. "The sun isn't even properly up, it's cold as Lucifer's backside out there, and away you must go. I'd admire you if you didn't make me feel so guilty."

Nita opened the wardrobe, where her much worn habit was always kept in readiness. Guilt was not in evidence this morning, not about resenting Mary's summons, not about time shared with Mr. St. —with Tremaine.

"You could come with me," Nita said, taking out her habit. "At some point you will be the lady of a household, and you might want to know basic care for the ill and injured."

Kirsten's honesty about her own shortcomings should not have surprised Nita—Kirsten was relentlessly honest—but Nita had made the suggestion as a dare. Sisters who interrupted dreams of Mr. St. Michael's kisses were not entitled to a cordial reception.

"Very well," Kirsten said, slogging out of the bed. "I had the boot boy alert the stable that you'll need Atlas. I can go along with you and spare myself Della's attempts to flirt with Mr. St. Michael at breakfast."

Kirsten flounced out, muttering about daft sisters and tiresome winter weather, and Nita used the reprieve to send up a prayer. Addy's last child had not lived past the first few weeks. The weather was miserable, and the mother fond of gin. Mary would not have come at such an hour for anything less than an emergency.

Nita did not want to go, did not want to find another small, lifeless body cradled in Addy's thin arms, did not want to face the other children, solemn beyond their years and more afraid than any child should be.

Nita did not want to go, but she must go, as always.

By the time Nita and Kirsten arrived at the cottage, the sun had made a grudging appearance just above the horizon, though a low overcast meant a narrow slice of dawn illumination soon disappeared as the sun rose into the clouds.

"How do you do this?" Kirsten asked as they clomped onto the porch. "These people can't pay you, they're all likely to die of consumption anyway, and you risk your own health every time you heed their summons."

The woodpile was diminished, and from inside the cottage, Nita heard not a sound. Not a crying baby, which would have been the case if colic were the problem, not the children stirring about.

Nothing.

Nita stood facing the door when what she wanted to do was leap onto her horse and never return.

"When Papa was dying," Nita said, "should I have left him alone in his bed for weeks, no one but the servants to change his linens and cajole him into taking some beef tea? He was not long for the world. Nothing I did changed that, nor would he have wanted me to alter matters if I could. Should I have turned my back on him? Addy has no one, these children have no one."

"I'm sorry," Kirsten said, pacing away from the door. "I haven't your moral fortitude, Nita. Sometimes I wonder if I have a single virtue worthy of note. Maybe you'd best leave me out here to freeze."

Honesty was a virtue, and Kirsten had that in abundance.

"You're with me now," Nita said, "and you remembered to raid the larder too." While Nita had brought only her herbs and medicinals, which wouldn't feed hungry children, nor had she brought Mr. St. Michael's gift of coin. "Breathe through your mouth for the first few minutes, and you'll manage."

This, oddly, provoked Kirsten to smiling. "Onward, dear Sister. Sooner begun is sooner done."

Nita knocked softly and opened the door, the familiar stench of soiled nappies, boiled cabbage, and unwashed bodies hitting her harder than usual.

Mr. St. Michael had told her to take a soaking bath this morning, and she'd intended to use Kirsten's soap on every inch of her skin and her hair too.

"Addy, what's amiss?" Nita asked.

Addy sat before the hearth, where a meager fire smoldered. The boys were nowhere to be seen, probably tucked up in the sleeping alcove trying to stay warm, while the baby was cradled against Addy's shoulder.

"She's got the croup," Addy said, despair in every syllable. "Poor wee girl has about coughed herself to death."

Two impressions registered, one positive, one ominous: Addy was sober, and the baby was wheezing with each inhalation. The wheezing was a weak rattle, barely audible.

"How long has she been like this?" Nita asked, setting down her bag and unfastening her cloak.

"Since right after you left yesterday. I didn't want to bother you. She worsened in the night."

When Nita might have howled with frustration—what mattered bothering when dying was the alternative?

Kirsten touched her arm. "What can I do?"

If Mr. St. Michael were with her, Nita would have him chopping a batch of kindling, because a roaring fire was necessary and sooner rather than later.

"Bring in the driest of the firewood, then we'll need water. The cistern is out back, though you'll have to break the ice. When that's done, the children need breakfast."

Somebody should do another batch of laundry, sweep out the ashes spilling from the hearth, start a pot of soup, and otherwise set the place to rights.

"Has the baby taken any sustenance?" Nita asked.

"She's fussy," Addy said, tucking the blanket around the child. "I can't tell if she's hungry or hurting or miserable or all three."

"Offer her the breast," Nita said. "Repeatedly. Her throat is uncomfortable from coughing, and she's tired, so she can't take as much at once, but she needs to keep up her strength."

I hate this, I hate this, I hate this. Babies died so easily, healthy one day, gone the next, sometimes without even a sign of illness. Nita was swamped with a longing for Mr. St. Michael's brisk competence with a splitting ax—and with a hug.

I hate this. Hated the stink, the despair, the weariness, the uncertainty, the death, and the death, and the death.

Addy took the only rocker and put the baby to her breast. The poor little child latched on with desperate greed, though she was soon fussing, her breathing interrupted by an odd, barking cough.

"Is she supposed to sound like that?" Kirsten asked, putting a load of kindling down before the hearth.

"She is not," Nita said. "That's the primary symptom of croup, though she's very young to be so afflicted." And very small, and the birth had not been easy.

What birth was?

"She won't take any more," Addy said a few minutes later. "She didn't even finish on one side."

"You must offer more frequently," Nita said. "And keep your consumption of fluids copious, lest the supply be lacking when the demand resumes."

Nita filled the kettle on the pot-swing with water, dribbled in some peppermint oil, and added the dry wood to the fire.

"We try not to waste wood," Addy muttered, putting the baby to her shoulder.

"We need to create steam," Nita retorted, "to ease the child's breathing."

"That smells good," Addy said, patting the child's back gently. "We have half a field of peppermint behind the garden."

"Have the children pick it, and you can sell it. Peppermint has many uses."

Tooth powders often featured peppermint, for example. When the kettle was bubbling and the scent of peppermint thick in the air, Nita set the steaming pot on the table and used her cloak to fashion a tent over it.

She took the baby from Addy, draping the cloak over her own head and the baby's.

"My mother did that once for my sister," Addy said. "I'd forgotten."

Outside the dark cocoon of the steam tent, Nita heard quiet voices asking about the baby. Not Mary. She would remain at Belle Maison until the grooms brought her back in the dogcart. The boys were stirring, and they were worried about their small sister.

The baby's breathing eased somewhat, while Nita's eyes watered and her nose threatened to run. She lifted her cloak, swaddled the baby in it, and headed for the door.

"Reheat that water. Lady Kirsten brought bread, butter, and eggs for breakfast, also a flask of milk and a jar of preserves."

Nita opened the door and took the well-wrapped infant out to the frigid air of the porch.

"Lady Nita!" Addy was on her heels. "Whatever are you about?"

"Cold air helps," Nita said. "You're fortunate the illness has occurred in winter, because it's just as likely to hit in summer."

"But the child will catch her death! I'll not lose another baby, not as long as I have breath in my body. I can't lose her! You're not a physician, to be subjecting her to the bitter wind like this. Dr. Horton—"

I hate him too. "Horton would not come unless you sent payment when you summoned him, and then he'd bleed Annie to death and tell you it was God's will."

That slowed Addy down for the space of exactly one indrawn breath. "Give me back my baby!"

Hysteria laced the demand. Addy reached for the child, while Nita turned away, the baby cradled against her shoulder.

Kirsten came stomping around the corner of the cottage, a wooden bucket in her hand.

"Will shouting help the child?" Kirsten asked, her tone merely curious. "If so, I'm happy to add to the din."

Addy stopped trying to snatch the baby from Nita's arms. "Lady

Nita means well," Addy said, "but every mother knows a baby should not be subjected to the winter weather. It's madness, and I will not allow daft practices to cost me another child."

"If Lady Nita is daft, then why did you send for her?" Kirsten asked, climbing the porch stairs and setting the bucket down. "Her ladyship was warm and cozy in her bed when I woke her to tell her Mary was shivering in the kitchen. Even if you paid Horton, he'd not likely show up before noon. Besides, the baby—which Lady Nita delivered you of safely enough—sounds much better."

Kirsten's matter-of-fact recitation had ended on the only observation that mattered: Annie's breathing was back to normal, and the child was drowsing contentedly on Nita's shoulder.

"I'll slice the children some bread," Kirsten said, taking up her bucket. "You should both be wearing your cloaks or Annie won't be the only one falling ill."

Silence descended, the impenetrable quiet of an early morning in winter. The baby let out a sigh—a normal, quiet baby sigh.

"I'm sorry," Addy said. "I haven't slept, we've barely any food. I hate to send the boys out for wood again so soon, and if we're not to starve, I should go back to—"

To the tavern, where she plied her trade, unless the proprietor was in a righteous mood, in which case Addy hung about the livery, given the occasional coin for tending the horses but mostly keeping warm between customers.

"Go inside," Nita said. "Kirsten is right. We can't have you falling ill too."

Not the most comforting reply, but Addy's tirade had torn at Nita's composure. A baby's life was more important than a soaking bath, but had Addy no respect for Nita? Would Addy rather Horton killed her child with his condescension and ignorance?

The door scraped open, and Addy went inside while Kirsten came back out to the porch.

"A plague of locusts could not devour that bread any more

quickly than those children. I saved some for Mary and Addy and started a pot of tea brewing."

"My thanks."

"Here." Kirsten took off her own cloak and draped it around Nita's shoulders. "If you must brave the elements, at least do so properly clothed."

Having delivered her scold, Kirsten went inside while Nita remained on the porch, the baby sleeping against her shoulder.

How would Tremaine St. Michael react when his wife was roused from slumber to tend a sick baby? Considering that he intended to travel for weeks or even months at a time, his husbandly patience ought not to be tried very far if Nita heeded the occasional summons from a neighbor.

He'd promised they could bide in the area, Nita recalled that much of their discussion the previous night.

She'd fallen asleep, exhausted, enlightened, enthralled, and also curiously unsatisfied.

Tremaine St. Michael had assessed Nita's strengths and shortcomings with dispassionate accuracy and presented himself without airs or graces. As a lover, he possessed magnificent stores of consideration, unplumbed reserves of humor, and all the manly competence a lady could hope for.

But as he'd prosed on about his properties and his enjoyment of art, Nita hadn't been able to connect the handsome suitor in her bed with the man who'd taught the children their letters among the ashes. She was attracted to the wealthy sheep trader, but she *liked* the other fellow.

Liked him exceedingly.

"Come along, miss," she said to the baby. "Enough fresh air for the nonce. I am in need of a soaking bath, and you must finish breaking your fast before joining your mama in a much-needed nap."

~

Tremaine dawdled over his eggs, lingered over his toast, and swilled enough tea to float a man-o'-war. He was about to inquire of his hostess if he might escort the ladies to the sheep byre to visit the latest additions to the herd—a newborn lamb or three would surely draw his intended out of hiding—when he realized that Nita wasn't coming down to breakfast.

Her family was exchanging the same fleeting glances, the same half put-upon asides, the same overly cheerful conversational sallies as they had during his first meal with them.

Nita had gone off on a call her family disapproved of, and for her to miss the first meal of the day, the call had to be urgent. Lady Kirsten's absence didn't seem to merit any notice, suggesting she, like Lady Della, enjoyed mornings abed.

Which left...the bluestocking, Lady Susannah, settling in on Tremaine's left with a rustle of skirts and a whiff of roses.

"My lady, good morning. Tea?"

"Please. Are you ready for the assembly, Mr. St. Michael? I'm sure word of your visit has spread more quickly than news of Wellington's victory at Waterloo, and probably with an equal amount of rejoicing."

"Are amiable gentlemen in such short supply?" Though "amiable" in Tremaine's case was a stretch. He danced well enough.

From the head of the table, Bellefonte paused in his visual worship of his countess.

"*Eligible*, amiable gentlemen are more precious than rubies in this shire." The earl glowered at George for a moment, then went back to peeling an orange for his lady.

"When Nicholas wed, the young ladies of the parish went into collective decline," George observed placidly. "Then Beckman fell into parson's mousetrap, and I became the sole, unworthy consolation of at least two dozen women. You will cause a riot, Mr. St. Michael, like Gulliver among the Lilliputians. Despite their party dresses and pretty manners, the ladies will take you captive and soon be counting your figurative teeth. I hope your affairs are in order."

"They usually are," Tremaine said, passing Lady Susannah the teapot.

Because he did not want to spend the next twenty minutes discussing which dances he enjoyed the most—he was partial to the Scottish sword dances, come to that—Tremaine embarked on a minor riot of his own.

"Will Lady Nita join us soon? I'm of a mind to see if any more lambs have arrived among the merino herd. One lively young fellow in particular might like to renew his acquaintance with her."

The lively fellow in Tremaine's breeches certainly would.

Lady Susannah tapped her spoon three times on the rim of the teacup, a feminine judge of the breakfast parlor bringing her court to order.

"Disagreeable weather for such an outing," she pronounced. "Today's a day for reading."

George's comment, about Susannah needing to get off her backside, came to mind. She was pretty in a blond, blue-eyed, unremarkable way. Not as tall as Nita, nor as dramatic as Kirsten, she looked suited to—and apparently craved—a life of quiet, peaceful domesticity.

"You should come with me," Tremaine said. "We'll think up names for the new arrivals. Lady Nita might enjoy an outing with her sisters."

Another glance went ricocheting around the table. The countess broke the silence when it appeared none of the Haddonfield siblings would.

"Nita was summoned to a neighbor's early this morning on a medical matter. Kirsten apparently accompanied her. More tea, Mr. St. Michael?"

The earl stood abruptly. "If he drinks any more tea, he'll float away to France. Why didn't anybody tell me Nita had gone haring off again? Now she's inveigling Kirsten into her daft behaviors? Famous."

Bellefonte was legendarily indulgent where his womenfolk were concerned, and when Tremaine wanted to chide his lordship for high-handedness—Lady Nita was not a ewe who'd wandered from her herd—he instead felt sympathy for the earl.

"If your lordship could spare me a moment in the library?" Tremaine said, rising as well. "I'd like to discuss a matter of business."

Bellefonte kissed his countess on the cheek, cast a censorious glance at his siblings, and stalked from the room, tossing an, "I am at your service, St. Michael," over his shoulder.

"Be patient with him, Mr. St. Michael," the countess said. "Nicholas means well."

Tremaine bowed to the ladies. "Lady Nita means well too."

For that matter, so did Tremaine.

"I'm not in the mood to discuss a lot of damned woolly sheep, St. Michael," Nick said as soon as the door to the library was closed. He stomped to the window, assessing a leaden sky that mirrored his mood exactly.

"My two most stubborn sisters have gone off to contract measles, dysentery, or God knows what evil," he went on. "Bad enough I can't contain Nita's excesses of Christian charity, now Kirsten must thwart my authority as well."

Leah claimed Nita was sensible, Nita would take precautions, Nita would not knowingly put herself at risk for contagion.

"Do you know where she's gone?" St. Michael asked, joining him at the window.

Frigid air radiated from the panes of glass, though that did nothing to cool Nick's temper. "My own countess did not see fit to confide that information in me."

"That bothers you?"

St. Michael was an innocent. He was free to get and spend, to lark about the known world, to blithely amass wealth because he had neither wife nor sisters nor mother nor daughters.

For now.

"Will you take a lady to wife, expecting to indulge a penchant for falsehood on her part, Mr. St. Michael?"

"I will marry, if I marry, expecting that domestic matters will fall to my wife's supervision, while dealing with business and greater affairs will remain my responsibility."

"*Greater affairs?*" Nick nearly laughed. "What *affair* is greater than maintaining harmony with the woman you love? Will you keep your wife all buttoned up in the family parlor, studying menus and reading improving tracts?"

St. Michael was a handsome devil, in a tall, dark-haired, broody sort of way. He was bright too, if Beckman's letters were to be believed. Coin and valuable works of art accumulated at St. Michael's bidding as if he were a financial alchemist. He controlled a substantial portion of the wool trade, and yet Nick's question puzzled him.

"I expect my wife will study menus, as your countess does," St. Michael replied evenly. "She'll read whatever she pleases to read."

Leah occasionally read an improving tract for entertainment, though in fairness to St. Michael, the countess was bedeviled by the menus.

"You're barmy, St. Michael, or perhaps trying not to give offense. What did you want to discuss?" No man could explain to another the complexities of sharing a meaningful life with a woman who was her own person, her own soul. St. Michael's wife would have to educate him in that regard.

Nick wished her the joy of such a project.

St. Michael sauntered off, propping an elbow on the mantel over the fireplace. Nick stayed by the windows, where he might catch a glimpse of his errant sisters returning to the fold.

"When last we discussed the purpose for my visit," St. Michael said, "I gained the impression that you regard your merinos as a suitable addition to Lady Susannah's dowry."

"Edward Nash regards them thus." While Nick had increasing reservations about Susannah's choice. George had expressed doubts about Edward Nash, and George's judgment—in *most* regards—was sound.

"I am investigating the possibility that Lady Nita might be receptive to an offer of marriage from me," St. Michael said. "I want those sheep too, and will put them to far better use than Nash could."

Investigating the *possibility* that Lady Nita *might*... St. Michael had probably asked Nita to save him a dance at the assembly. Nita would allow him that much out of sheer pity for a lamb sent to slaughter at the hands of the marriage-mad mamas of Haddondale.

Of which there was a sizable herd.

"I'm *investigating* the *possibility* of splitting the herd," Nick said. "Nash needs those sheep more than you do. You simply want them."

"I want them badly, and I do not want a half or a third of the herd, Bellefonte."

"Nash wants them very badly."

While Nick wanted them not at all. Sheep required land and were hard on their pastures. The merinos were good breeders, which meant Nick owned too damned many of them. St. Michael knew better than to reveal his emotions in the midst of a business discussion, but something—distaste, exasperation, Nick couldn't tell exactly what—crossed his features.

"Then think of it this way, Bellefonte. Which sister is more urgently in need of a husband? Lady Susannah is sweet, biddable, pretty, and content to spend time in the company of the Bard. Lady Nita could at this very minute be dealing with a deadly illness, and now Lady Kirsten is accompanying her."

Well, thank the heavenly powers St. Michael had the sense to be alarmed at that prospect.

"Do you think I don't know that?" Nick wanted to put his fist through the windowpane. "Papa told me to look after the girls. He said the boys would sort themselves out, but for the girls, my influence and support would be needed."

Nick hadn't meant to say that, hadn't meant to allow exasperation and bewilderment to see the cold light of day.

"Bellefonte, I'll give her babies, God willing. What in all of creation can compete with a woman's own children for her attention? Married to me, Lady Nita will have no more need to haunt sickrooms or antagonize the local physician."

Had St. Michael reached that understanding with Nita, or was he simply presuming that his household would run exactly as he envisioned it? Or was Nita so besotted with her sheep count that she'd set aside her medical activities in favor of making lambs with him?

Nick prayed it was so.

"Your proposal to Nita stands or falls on its own merit," Nick said. "You cannot marry a woman you merely tolerate because she's brought you financial gain. Nita deserves better than that."

"Then I have your permission to court Lady Nita?" St. Michael lounged against the mantel, all elegant grace in a country gentleman's attire. Beckman had said not to underestimate him, and not to entirely trust him either.

"You have my permission," Nick said. "I thought we'd established that much." Beyond the window, Nita and Kirsten came marching up from the stable yard. They were arguing or discussing something with great animation in typical Haddonfield fashion.

Nick's relief at the simple sight of them was... troubling.

"Nita loves babies," he said, half to himself. "Kirsten's affections are by no means as tender, but Nita...she loves all the children." She'd been more mother to her younger siblings than sister, *once the countess had fallen ill.*

Why hadn't Nick seen that sooner?

St. Michael appeared at Nick's elbow. "And you love her. You admire her, you respect her, but you don't know what to do with her. She's run this household for years, and now you've taken that from her, and you rail against the only thing she has left that feels meaningful to her."

All true, damn it. "What if the babies don't arrive, St. Michael? Children appear or not as God wills, no matter how badly we want them or dread them." Addy Chalmers probably dreaded them, for all she seemed to do her meager best by the ones in her care.

"I have, at last count, eight separate households," St. Michael said. "I have a niece who must see some of the world and the great capitals. I can take Lady Nita traveling all over the Continent in fine style. I have business associates who must be entertained, connections at various royal courts. Lady Nita would be my countess when it suited her, and that position will keep her well occupied even if we are not blessed with children."

St. Michael was not merely ignorant, he was so uninformed regarding the realities of marriage as to be *innocent*.

When a woman ached to hold a child in her arms, all the royal courts in the world meant nothing. And yet, married to St. Michael, Nita would be well cared for. She'd want for nothing, and she'd probably be transplanted to some other shire, where her mother's legacy of medical meddling wouldn't open the door for Nita to engage in the same folly.

"I wish you luck, then," Nick said as the ladies stopped by the gazebo. Whatever disagreement they were having, they'd at least not brought it into the house.

"One concern yet troubles me, Bellefonte."

The damned sheep could disappear to the land of the fairies, for all Nick cared. "You're doubtless about to inflict it on me."

"Lady Nita deserves more than a husband who tolerates her merely because she brings a herd of valuable sheep to the union. We are agreed on that, though I do want those sheep."

"So you've said." Though apparently, St. Michael could buy all the merinos he wanted elsewhere, and probably buy his own county to stash them in too.

"Doesn't Lady Susannah deserve the same consideration? If you made it clear to Nash that Lady Susannah comes without a substantial settlement, would he still seek her hand, or is he merely tolerating the lady because she arrives in his arms with a fortune in tow? I suggest you test his resolve at least."

"Take your suggestions and go count lambs with them, St. Michael. My sisters have returned, and I must greet them."

Nick would have made his exit, but that troubled, exasperated expression had crossed St. Michael's features again.

"If I'm to marry Lady Nita, and these excesses of Christian charity, as you call them, will soon be curtailed, why bother castigating her for them?"

Innocent and ignorant, but not devoid of all chivalry. Nick took encouragement where he could find it.

"You are willing to marry her, St. Michael, with or without the sheep. I comprehend this and commend you for your great magnanimity or shrewdness or whatever—though I notice you've not mentioned true love. Despite what you might think of my dunderheaded attempts at being the earl, I am also Nita's brother, *and I love her*. You are a fine, well-bred ram, and will turn all the heads at the assembly, et cetera and so forth. Nothing in our discussion, however, allows me to conclude that *Lady Nita* will have *you*."

Nick bowed and left, lest the consternation on St. Michael's face inspire hearty, and not exactly hospitable, laughter.

CHAPTER ELEVEN

"What aren't you telling me, Nita?" Kirsten Haddonfield was plagued with an unladylike curiosity about life in general. When it came to her older sister though, her inquisitiveness was increasingly motivated by concern.

All the way from the malodorous little cottage, Nita had kept maddeningly silent. She swished along through the winter-dead garden, exuding competence and un-spilled confidences.

"I do not gossip, Kirsten."

"And I do? I sit among the good dames of the shire and spread rumor and innuendo over a pot of scandal broth? I'm not asking you to gossip. I'm asking you to talk to me."

Nita slowed as they approached the gazebo. "I haven't thanked you yet for coming with me."

Kirsten drew Nita into the little structure, because privacy inside the Belle Maison manor house was nonexistent. Della lurked at keyholes, Nicholas loomed around corners, George had the knack of being everywhere at once, Leah reported everything to her dear earl, and Susannah—dissembler at large—half the time only pretended to read.

"You should thank me," Kirsten said, taking a seat on the hard wooden bench. "I'll never get the stench out of my habit. Hell ought to include a place of honor for the first woman who realized that boiled cabbage is nominally edible."

"When the alternative is starvation, such a woman should be canonized."

Nita's habit had long since passed the status of a disgrace. The hems were muddy and mended, the blue fading, rather like Nita herself.

"Nita, you are turning into a scold and a drudge, but you will please have a seat and bear me a little more company anyway. Before Mr. St. Michael started cheating at cards the other evening, I thought you'd forgotten how to laugh. It was unfair of Papa to require you at his bedside and to send the rest of us away."

Papa had been gone for more than six months. In accordance with his wishes, the family no longer observed first mourning, but the loss of him lingered in family jokes, stray pieces of music, and his favorite quotes from Alexander Pope. In Papa's final decline, he'd found someplace far from home for every one of his children to be except Nita, the de facto lady of the manor.

A privilege and, apparently, a bitter penance. "Papa didn't want anybody to see him grow so feeble." Nita's reply had the ring of an oft-repeated and unsuccessful attempt at self-comfort.

"Papa was an arrogant old boot," Kirsten said, "and not above taking advantage of your kind heart. Belle Maison would have fallen apart without you these last years. You might remind Nicholas of that."

Perhaps Kirsten would take on that task herself. Nicholas, like every Haddonfield, could be an idiot.

"We should go in," Nita said, popping to her feet and clutching her bag of herbs and medicinals.

"Sit down, Nita Haddonfield. I've been wanting to ask you about Mr. St. Michael. Are you trifling with him?"

Nita did sit, setting her bag aside. "I would not know how or why to trifle with any man. Lest you forget, Norton Nash attempted to trifle with me. Are you interested in Mr. St. Michael?"

On the topic of Mr. St. Michael, Nita was apparently willing to converse, though her question had been carefully tendered.

"Thank you, no," Kirsten said, though if she hadn't given up on marriage entirely, he might have been worth a look. "He's not biddable. He's been allowed to racket about without the guiding hand of a sensible woman for too long. He fancies you, though."

Nita, like Susannah, was blessed with all the dishonesty Kirsten needed and didn't have. Nita could appear calm when she was enraged or intrigued. She could be polite when she was furious, and she could also apparently pretend disinterest when she'd lost her heart—an enviable talent.

"Mr. St. Michael fancies Nicholas's herd of Spanish sheep," Nita said.

Though sometimes, Nita used that talent to deceive herself.

"I've corresponded not only with Beckman," Kirsten said, "but with his Sara, to whom Mr. St. Michael was a brother-in-law for a time. Your Mr. St. Michael is wallowing in filthy lucre, Nita. He'd do." The highest praise Kirsten could offer, because only the best would serve for her siblings.

Edward Nash fell far short of her standards, a situation she'd yet to find a solution for.

Across the garden, the grooms had led the horses into the stable. Not another human soul was in sight, though a furry black cat trotted along the top of a stone wall bordering the knot garden.

"Mr. St. Michael has offered for me," Nita said oh-so calmly.

"You *are* trifling with him. Nita, I am proud of you." A light tone was hard to maintain, but to shout about good offers being rarer than handsome, eligible dukes guaranteed some sibling or servant would take notice of this discussion.

The medical calls were taking a toll on Nita, and on the entire family, in fact. Nita had been plump as a younger woman, sturdy and rounded. She was nearly gaunt now, and her mouth was grim far more often than it was merry.

Addy Chalmers had an unfortunate fondness for gin. Had Nita acquired an unfortunate fondness for misery?

"I am trying not to make a mistake, Kirsten. I have made mistakes in the past. Mr. St. Michael is a good man, he'd provide well, and he's said we could bide here in Haddondale."

St. Michael was also a shrewd man, then. Nita would look much more favorably on the suit of a gentleman who'd offer her proximity to her family—and her patients.

"And yet you hesitate," Kirsten said, "and claim you are being sensible. Why can't you be sensible about sick babies? Leave them to those professionally trained to deal with them, Nita, or to those who conceive them. Nicholas will be in a much better humor if you do."

Kirsten would be in a better humor too, because then no one would have to worry that Nita's next sniffle could turn into her last.

"If you should fall ill, Kirsten, shall we summon Dr. Horton?"

Nita might as well have offered Kirsten a plate of boiled cabbage. "I will die before I let that old man near my sickroom."

"*Many do.*"

And there, in three syllables, Nita presented an argument Nicholas himself could not entirely gainsay. Horton was old-fashioned and regarded suffering, particularly the suffering of women, children, and the poor, as either God's will or penance for past or future wickedness.

Convenient theology indeed, when a physician was incapable of rendering aid.

"What does Mr. St. Michael say about your disappearing at all hours to treat the unwell and infirm?" Kirsten asked.

Nita set her bag in her lap. "He has come with me more than once on a call to the Chalmers family, and when I told him how to deal with his ailing sheep, he listened to me—and he thanked me."

Shrewd, indeed, but diagnosing sheep or dandling a newborn

presented far less risk than entering a household in the grip of influenza, which Nita had often done.

Kirsten would thrash St. Michael if he abetted Nita's folly to that degree.

"Most self-respecting men would expect you to stay home and look after your own family, Nita. Most worthy men would consider themselves failing in their duty to protect you if they allowed you to deal with sickness outside of your own household. Nicholas berates himself for this very shortcoming constantly."

Nita's calm expression faltered. "Mr. St. Michael is not most men. Did you know he's a French *comte*?"

A dodge, a good dodge. Had Mr. St. Michael in fact given Nita assurances that his wife was welcome to traffic in lung fevers and wasting diseases, or had Nita simply leaped to this conclusion? Shame on any man who professed to care for Nita if he encouraged her to risk her well-being on behalf of ungrateful strangers.

"I had heard there was a French title," Kirsten said, rather than further antagonize her sister. "Della says he's called the Sheep Count." A play on words for those who knew their rural lore.

"I had not foreseen marriage," Nita said, bewilderment creeping into her tone. "Then here *he* is, quite sure of his objectives, among whom I apparently number. I rather like being one of Tremaine St. Michael's objectives."

Nita was arse over teakettle for the man, and about time. Based on her smile, her shepherd-boy-turned-nabob had done a bit more than cheat at cards and recite Scottish poetry.

"I would ask you for a long engagement," Kirsten said, rising. "Once you're Sheep Countess-ing, Nicholas will try to march me up the church aisle again, and I do not fancy reminding the local eligibles that I am indifferent to their charms."

Nita rose as well and linked arms with Kirsten. "I haven't made up my mind about Mr. St. Michael, but it's Susannah I fear for. Edward Nash is not the great bargain he thinks he is. I trust you will agree with me on this?"

"I'm considering a plan," Kirsten said, glad for somebody to share it with. "I'll get myself compromised with Edward at the assembly, and he'll have to offer for me if he wants those sheep. I'll refuse him, and Suze will surely see he's not worth her affections."

The plan was half-serious. With the least provocation, Kirsten would set it in motion, though the idea of permitting Edward Nash liberties was distasteful in the extreme. He smoked a pipe, for pity's sake, and was overly fond of pomade.

"I really do not fancy hearing those same old Shakespeare sonnets at every family gathering," Nita said. "Compromising yourself seems a bit drastic though."

Nita spoke so evenly, Kirsten took a moment to realize she was teasing—mostly. They were still giggling and plotting when they reached the house, and Kirsten realized something else.

Nita had left her medicinals out in the snowy garden, where, as far as Kirsten was concerned, they could jolly well stay.

Tremaine wanted to arrange for delivery of his letter when various nosy Haddonfields would not have a chance to inspect the address. He also wanted to assure himself that Lady Nita had no regrets about their shared intimacies.

And that she'd not contracted any dread diseases in lieu of breaking her fast.

"Mr. Haddonfield," Tremaine said, finding his quarry in the breakfast parlor. "Will you escort me to the village?"

His Handsomeness paused with a toast point half-way to his mouth. "Now?"

Lady Susannah looked up from her book. "Of course he means now. Go, George. Be hospitable and pick me up more peppermints at the apothecary."

George rose and set his toast on his sister's plate. "I am your slave in all things, dearest Susannah. Don't suppose you've a ton of books I'm to drop off at the lending library?"

"Half a dozen or so, on the sideboard in the front hall," the lady said, taking a bite of the toast. "You might also ask if they have the new edition of—"

"You ask the next time you raid the library," George said, kissing her cheek. "Your literary raptures with Mr. Dalrymple might as well be in a foreign tongue, and I'm sure Mr. St. Michael would like to be back from the village before spring."

The exchange was cozy, good-natured, and loving in a way Tremaine didn't understand. He and his brother hadn't had that sort of repartee. René had suffered a spare's envy and restlessness, compounded by absent and then dead parents and a grandfather's stubborn notions.

George bowed to the countess and took Tremaine by the arm. "If we hurry, we can stop by the lending library before Dalrymple's at his post. The man could have talked Caesar back across the Rubicon."

"Who is this 'we,' Haddonfield? I'm off to arrange for the delivery of some letters." Also to ambush Lady Nita. Lady Kirsten could join the outing or not, but George was a necessary chaperone.

Now.

Now that Tremaine had fixed on a marital objective, his intended deserved every public appearance of propriety, because that way—as every courting couple knew—the improprieties could be more easily undertaken in private.

Tremaine was donning gloves in the back hallway—the scene of a memorable kiss—when the ladies came in from the garden on a gust of frosty air.

"I vow it's getting colder by the hour," Lady Kirsten said, stomping snow from her boots and shaking the same from the hem of her habit. "You gentlemen are daft if you're riding out."

Lady Nita was unfastening her bonnet on the far side of a hanging ham. She either would not or could not meet Tremaine's eye.

"Mr. Haddonfield and I are off to the village for a few errands, and then I thought we'd look in on the new lambs," Tremaine said.

"There are more?" Lady Nita asked from her side of the ham.

"The Christ Child could reappear in that sheep byre," Lady Kirsten said, "and I'd be more interested in a hot cup of chocolate. I bid you all good day."

The lady had a way with blaspheming, and she winked at Tremaine as she marched past him.

"Will you join us, Lady Nita?" Tremaine asked, shifting so he needn't put his question to her around a joint of pork.

"Do come, Nita," George said. "You can listen to Dalrymple complain of his mother's chilblains, while St. Michael and I have a toddy at the inn."

"Is Dalrymple a follower of Lady Susannah's?" Tremaine asked. If so, then Nash had competition or could be made to believe he had competition.

"Alas, no," George said, whipping a green scarf around his neck. "Dalrymple is old enough to be Susannah's papa, and his mother accurately recounts life before the Flood. The man can talk books though. Shall we be off?"

George bustled out the door, leaving Tremaine alone with Lady Nita, despite a kitchen full of chattering servants a few yards away.

"My lady, how are you?" Tremaine could see that she was tired—also in want of kissing.

"Addy's baby had a touch of croup. She should be well enough in a day or two."

He kissed Nita's cheek. "The child will thrive a while longer, thanks to you. Will you come with us? I've missed you." Spoken like a callow swain, God help him. A sincere, smitten callow swain.

"Atlas has already been unsaddled," she said, tucking Tremaine's hair back over his ear and letting her hand rest on his shoulder.

"Take another mount, then." He kissed her other cheek, a charming Continental custom insufficiently appreciated in Britain.

"I should change."

Because she wore the same dowdy, cabbage-scented habit she'd worn on their other outings to the Chalmers residence. In the warmth of the hallway, that scent blended with smoked meat and wet wool, and dragged Tremaine back to his childhood.

"You should come just as you are. I'm sending a letter by messenger, George is returning books for Lady Susannah, and something was mentioned about stopping by the apothecary for peppermint drops."

Nita's expression changed, and her hand disappeared from Tremaine's shoulder. "I left my bag."

"I beg your pardon?" Tremaine dropped a kiss on her mouth and something inside him settled agreeably lower.

"My bag of medicinals," Nita said. "I forgot it in the garden, on a bench in the gazebo. If we go to the apothecary, I can stock up on some of the depleted stores. I left all of my peppermint oil with Addy, because if one child falls ill, the others could easily follow."

Nita retied her bonnet ribbons, her movements brisk.

"You'll accompany us, then?"

She shot a look over Tremaine's shoulder, longing in her gaze. "I shall."

"Grab something to eat," Tremaine said, because she'd missed breakfast and food was hardly abundant in the Chalmers household. "I'll fetch your medicinals and let the stable know you need a mount."

"My thanks." She strode off in the direction of the kitchen, damp hems swishing.

Tremaine admired the view, though his joy in the day dimmed.

He'd made passionate love to the lady not twelve hours earlier, but this morning, she showed more enthusiasm for a hot cup of tea than for his kisses. Was her reticence a result of fatigue, preoccupation with the ailing child, or disappointment in his amatory overtures?

∽

Nita would forever associate the scent of damp wool with Tremaine St. Michael's kisses. She gulped her tea at a kitchen window so she could watch him retrieve her medical bag from the gazebo, then stride off to the stables.

He should wear a hat in this cold. If she were his wife, she could scold him—remind him—to wear a hat.

If she were his wife, she would have kissed him back too.

"Bread and cheese, your ladyship," Cook said, passing Nita a thick sandwich. "Would you like more tea?"

"No, thank you." Nita would like time to change into a more fashionable habit, to tidy her hair, to use her tooth powder again, and have a long, fragrant soak in hot water and scorching memories.

She instead took a bite of bread, cheese, and butter, and headed back out to the stables.

"My lady, your gloves." Cook hurried after her and passed her the neglected items.

"I have grown forgetful lately," Nita said. "Thank you."

Nita stuffed the gloves into her pocket and crossed the garden at a decorous pace, munching her makeshift breakfast. Was this love, this tongue-tied, breathless stupidity? She didn't care for it, though she cared for Tremaine St. Michael.

Him, she could tell about Addy's baby and know he'd grasp the situation in all its precariousness. She could wear her old habit around him and not worry that he judged her for looking unfashionable.

Surely that acceptance and caring—and the sweet, stolen kisses—were love too?

"There you are," George said as his chestnut gelding was led out. "One despaired of seeing you before spring. How is Addy's baby? It was the baby, wasn't it? Elsie Nash's boy has a bad sniffle and children seem to catch everything."

George was a good brother, though he would not have asked after the baby at the breakfast table.

"The infant should soon be fine, though croup can sound terrify-ingly awful. What have you stuffed in those saddlebags?"

"Susannah's latest haul of books. She's getting worse, Nita, and I didn't think she could be any worse."

A placid bay mare came next, the horse nominally Susannah's, though the beast was seldom put to use. Mr. St. Michael led her out, the wind whipping at his dark hair.

"Up you go, my lady." He didn't position the horse near the ladies' mounting block, but rather, stood at the mare's shoulder. When he'd boosted Nita into the saddle, he twitched her skirts over her boots, muddy hems and all.

"I hope you took the time to break your fast?"

He was concerned, as a husband might be concerned. Nita liked that enough to run her fingers over his hair before she donned her gloves.

"I ate. Mount up, Mr. St. Michael, before my poor brother freezes to the saddle."

Mr. St. Michael didn't smile, but a hint of mischief danced in his eyes as he patted Nita's knee.

Abruptly, she grasped exactly what thoughts filled his male mind: *If you don't start calling me by my name, I'll spend before I've so much as kissed you.*

Nita repeated that quick stroke over his hair, but this time she sneaked in a light pinch to his earlobe. She would soon be as bad as Nicholas.

Lovely thought, and until she was officially betrothed, *Mr. St. Michael* would have to tolerate proper address from her in public.

George set a brisk pace, which made conversation difficult, and when they arrived at the village, Mr. St. Michael volunteered to return Susannah's books before he stopped at the inn.

"Shall I accompany you?" Nita asked as George took the horses to the livery.

"You shall join George at the apothecary," Mr. St. Michael said, "where for you, I am sure, hours feel like minutes, as if you were in the land of fairies. When we return to Belle Maison, you will take that soaking bath, won't you?"

He'd kissed Nita with that question, though nobody's lips had touched anybody else's.

"I shall, and take a nap as well. While my dreams were pleasant last night, I could have wished for more time spent in my warm, cozy bed."

Nita had verbally kissed Mr. St. Michael back, though his smile was mostly in his eyes. "You shall have that time, my lady. All the time you desire."

He bowed and marched off, full of energy and purpose, and cutting a fine figure in his riding attire.

"Stop gawking," George said, coming out of the livery and taking Nita by the arm. "Though I admit he's worth a second look."

George was the brother closest to Nita in age, and his unconventional attractions had never been a secret to her, nor had they been anything but natural to him.

"Hush," Nita said. "Nicholas worries that I'll contract some dread disease, but he worries gossip will see you swinging from a gibbet."

"The difference being," George said as they crossed the frozen green, "you can choose to stop dealing with sick babies and consumptive grandmamas, while I can't help but notice your Mr. St. Michael."

"Do you never notice the ladies, George? Mr. St. Michael has proposed to me, and I would hate to think my husband—"

"St. Michael doesn't *see* me, Nita. I'm not sure I'd respect him if he did, not when my regard is that of a rutting colt and flatters nobody. I do notice the ladies—I happen to like any number of them —and I notice the women too. Have you accepted his offer?"

George had a touch of Kirsten's directness, at least with Nita. Maybe that was why she'd confided the news of Mr. St. Michael's offer to George and Kirsten first.

"I have not. The more impetuous I want to be, the more deliberate I must be. I hardly know him, George."

"Good for you," George said as he held the door to the apothe-cary for her. "You are a treasure, and any man who can't see that is a fool. Make St. Michael beg. It will do him good."

Gracious, George could be fierce. "Thank you, George."

He ambled off in the direction of the sweets, while Nita took a moment to inhale the fragrance of the shop. She loved this little estab-lishment, where each shelf held glass or ceramic jars, tidily labeled, clear up to the rafters. Behind the counter, Mrs. Grainger read a newspaper, her glasses halfway down her nose, her gray bun listing to the side.

"Lady Nita, welcome!" she said, putting the paper aside and pushing her glasses up. "Always a pleasure. What can I help you with today?" Nita was probably Mrs. Grainger's best customer, but Edna Grainger was also an ally, keeping Nita apprised of who was coming down with an ague, whose cold was improving.

They were deep in a discussion of the best method for distilling peppermint oil when Tremaine St. Michael joined them at the counter.

"Your errand is accomplished, Mr. St. Michael?" Nita asked, resisting the urge to rearrange his scarf—purple wool this time, an unusual color.

"Books delivered, and a lecture on the novels of Mrs. Radcliffe received. Are your purchases here complete?"

"They are. Mrs. Grainger, you'll send the lot to Belle Maison?"

"This very day, my lady, assuming the snow holds off."

Nita did unwrap Mr. St. Michael's scarf, because the ends dangled unevenly. "Susannah would have tarried at the library until nightfall," Nita said, rewrapping the scarf, "reading just one more chapter before deciding whether to borrow a book. She ought to reside above the library and save herself a lot of time and hauling about of books. This is lovely wool."

Mrs. Grainger had bustled off to her scale, and George was prob-ably snitching lemon drops. Nita snitched a kiss. A brief, stolen peck on the lips, disproportionately satisfying for the surprise and pleasure it lit in Mr. St. Michael's eyes.

"You are bold this morning," he said softly.

"I am in charity with the world, apparently."

He stood a hair too close, which was lovely. "As am I. Does your brother George fancy that woman?" Nita left off patting Mr. St. Michael's lapel to see George deep in conversation with Elsie Nash. "George and Elsie are friendly, I'm sure."

Elsie stood with her head cocked, as if hanging on George's every word—or as if hiding her bruises.

"That's Nash's sister-in-law?"

"Elsie Nash," Nita said, wondering if Elsie was purchasing cosmetics to hide future bruises. "She's lived with Edward nearly two years, along with her son."

"The next baronet, until Nash can find a woman willing to marry him. Why doesn't Mrs. Nash remarry? She's a pretty little thing, and I can't imagine keeping house for Edward results in any compensation."

Nita's first instinct was to deliver a retort about a woman's options being limited and no husband being better than the wrong husband, but Mr. St. Michael had a point. Elsie was comely, cheerful, and hardworking.

And Edward bullied and abused her. He was probably no better with Digby. Edward was, however, Digby's guardian, and thus Elsie was trapped.

"Nita," George said, escorting Elsie to the front of the shop. "Young Digby has apparently acquired a prodigious sniffle. What should Elsie do for the boy?"

Irritation with George warred with concern for little Digby, because this too was a legacy from Nita's mother. In the middle of the churchyard, in the middle of shopping, or in the middle of a lovely little flirtation with Mr. St. Michael, *anybody* might accost Nita for a medical consultation.

She loathed discussing personal business in public places, and yet, no matter the location, she would be expected to focus all of her attention on the self-appointed patient, and diagnose and prescribe—accurately—on the spot.

What Elsie ought to do was send Digby to public school, where he'd be given hot broth and three days in bed with *Robinson Crusoe* to entertain him.

"Tell me Digby's symptoms," Nita said, drawing Elsie over to the window and away from the menfolk. Elsie was deep in a mother's recounting of her son's every woe and feebleness when from behind them, Nita heard Mr. St. Michael murmur to George.

"Mr. Haddonfield, shall we fetch the horses? I do believe it's beginning to snow and I would like to look in on the herd's new arrivals on our way home."

CHAPTER TWELVE

As a very young man, Tremaine's fascination with, and devotion to, the gratification of his breeding organs had bordered on an obsession. Life had been a procession of frustrated urges, fantasies, frequent occasions of self-gratification, and the rare, much-anticipated interlude with a willing female who knew what she was about.

Such females became more readily available as Tremaine's circumstances improved, while his preoccupation with erotic gratification had curiously ebbed. And thus the first of many adult insights had befallen him: he excelled at wanting what he could not have, and the roots of that dubious talent twisted around childhood memories best left unexamined.

Those roots yet held life, apparently, because as Tremaine assisted Nita to dismount outside the sheep byre, he wanted to swive her all over again, but more than that, he wanted her formal acceptance of his marriage proposal.

"We shouldn't linger," she said, her hands remaining on his shoulders. "We're apparently in for some weather."

Nita was lovely, with the snow dusting her scarf and lashes, when by rights she should be chin deep in a hot, scented bath. Instead, she was paying a call with Tremaine on a flock of woolly beldames.

I love you. The words sounded in his mind—only in his mind, thank God—as startling as they were heartfelt. "Let me take the horses around back," he said, "out of the wind. Go inside. You'll be warmer."

He kissed her on the lips, George having had the great good sense to look in on Kinser. A capital fellow, George, if somewhat given to scolds. Tremaine tied the horses to the rowan growing at the back of the byre and sent a prayer skyward that the damned snow let up.

So he and his lady could *linger*.

"How do you tell the sheep apart?" Nita asked when Tremaine joined her inside the byre. While not cozy, the little stone structure was appreciably warmer than the out-of-doors and full of fat, milling sheep. Some reclined on the straw, chewing their cud, some sniffed at Nita's hems, two were nursing lambs, and one napped with a lamb—Tremaine's little ram—curled at her side.

"'You tell them apart the same way you do people,'" Tremaine said. "By their facial expressions, their general appearance, their voices, the way they move. Shall we look in on our young friend?"

As they approached the sleeping pair, the ewe awoke but remained curled in the straw.

"I'm glad I wore my old habit now," Nita said, drawing off her gloves and kneeling. "He's painfully dear."

She meant that, meant that the sight of the lamb cuddled against his mama made her heart ache. Tremaine's damned heart ached too, at the sight of Nita petting the little fellow and blinking hard.

"Will wee Annie be well?" he asked.

Nita used her gloves to swipe at her eyes. "She should be. Croup is common and needn't be serious. Shall we give him a name? Something gallant and brave?"

How brave did a fellow have to be to curl up against a warm female and drift into dreams?

"Call him anything you like, my lady. He'll be honored among all the other rams of the herd to have been given a name."

Marry me. Let me give you my name.

The ewe was a tolerant sort, or perhaps she recalled the scent of the humans intruding on her afternoon slumbers. She sniffed at Nita's hand, then gave her baby a few licks around his ears.

"Don't wake him," Nita told the ewe. "Little ones need their rest."

Tremaine drew Nita to her feet and straight into his arms. She went willingly and the simple feel of her against him, even through layers of winter clothes, settled his nerves a sorely needed degree.

"Have you considered my proposal?'"

Nita nodded against his shoulder and remained right where she was. Not well done of him, to raise the topic here, among the beasts, with the scents of straw and livestock thick in the air. And yet the location was appropriate too. Tremaine had first noticed Nita—truly noticed *her*—when she'd been so concerned with a newborn lamb shivering on the frozen earth.

"I want to be sensible," she said.

"'You've been sensible until you're sick with it," Tremaine said, though ironically, Nita's selfless, tireless, pragmatic medical skills made others well.

He could spare her that paradox and would, gladly.

'Not sick with it," Nita said, "but lonely, certainly. With you, I need not pretend to be someone I'm not."

"I do not contort myself for the sake of social niceties," Tremaine said, stroking a hand over Nita's hair. "And I protect those entrusted to my care. My wife will not be allowed to scamper off to a war-torn country while I have breath in my body, Nita Haddonfield. Consider yourself warned."

Nita could do with protecting. Her family had given up that cause years ago, and Tremaine looked forward to remedying their lapse. He'd even entertained the notion that Nita was marrying him in part to allow her to withdraw from her medical folly gracefully.

When Nita drew back, Tremaine let her go, though it pained him.

"Such dramatics. I have no intention of frequenting any battle-fields, Mr. St. Michael. The sheep seem healthy," she said, holding her glove out for another lamb to sniff. "They all seem wonderfully healthy despite the wretched weather. This makes me happy."

There was that smile, the one Tremaine was learning to watch for. "Good health makes them happy too, to the extent sheep trouble themselves over finer sentiments. Will you make *me* happy, Bernita Haddonfield?"

It was a day for unintended questions, apparently. Nita studied Tremaine for an interminable moment, her smile hovering shy of full bloom. Outside the byre, some old ewe bleated, suggesting George Haddonfield might be heading in their direction.

"One cannot *make* another person happy, Mr. St. Michael, any more than one can make another healthy."

Tremaine could not fathom where Nita's hesitance came from, though she was imbued with more natural caution and intellectual thoroughness than many ladies of her station.

"Last night you made me something," Tremaine said. "If not happy, then very close to it. I hope the sentiments were shared, and I hope we can share them again, soon and often."

Last night, for all his caution, he might have made them both parents. The notion alarmed him, and pleased him, both.

"Last night was... lovely," Nita said. "I *felt* lovely. I should feel naughty and upset with myself, and guilty of course, but I cannot. I've tried, and all I can feel is... lovely."

For a time in Tremaine's arms, Nita had esteemed herself, to use George's word, and some of that sense lingered in her bearing, in her pleased, private smile. Victory whispered to Tremaine from the shad-owy, aromatic depths of the sheep byre.

"Nita Haddonfield, if you don't know by now that you are lovely" —also dear, kind, smart, brave, *and well worth protecting*—"I will consider it my greatest honor to spend the rest of my life convincing you of it."

Flowery speeches did not impress her, though neither did they chase away that naughty smile.

She pulled on her gloves. "You are lovely too, Mr. St. Michael."

He was besotted. "Tremaine, if we're to be lovely together." A gravid ewe butted him gently above the knees, another warning that George approached.

"You allowed that we could bide in Haddondale?" Lady Nita asked.

Just like that, in the dead of winter, spring arrived to Tremaine St. Michael's heart, to his entire life.

"We assuredly can. My business interests require that I travel, but I have good stewards and factors, and you'll want to be near family." Particularly as the babies arrived, which Tremaine had every confidence they would.

"At the assembly then," she said, whipping the tail of her scarf over her shoulder—no fluttering for his Lady Nita. "Nicholas can make the announcement, but let's save discussion of the details for later, Mr. St. Michael. The weather is worsening, and I've yet to have my soaking bath."

Nita swept out of the sheep byre before Tremaine could even kiss her. In her wake, two of the lambs went dancing across the straw, leaping and bouncing for no reason and inspiring the third lamb to totter to his feet.

"Your name is Lucky," Tremaine said, picking up the tup and kissing his wee woolly head. "Your name is Lucky, and you're for the breeding herd, my friend. Lucky St. Michael, that's you."

He set the lamb down to play with its fellows and marched out into the winter weather, which was, indeed, worsening by the moment.

~

Back in the sheep byre, Nita had stifled the urge to tackle Tremaine St. Michael, smother him with kisses, and announce to the livestock that she'd become engaged to a man she could esteem very greatly indeed.

Her intended had been by turns abrupt, bashful, endearing, and confident, but he'd given her two assurances she'd needed.

First, they could dwell in Haddondale, where her family and her patients were, and second, she need not become some indolent domestic ornament to please anybody's sense of the appearances—no contorting herself to appease "social niceties."

What a splendid man Tremaine St. Michael was.

Also passionate. Nita particularly liked that about him, and if she had lingering misgivings about undertaking holy matrimony with a man she'd only recently met, well, that was to be expected. They'd have a lifetime to get to know each other better.

"I do believe our youngest sisters are in the stable yard," George said as the horses trudged up the increasingly snowy lane. "Perhaps the Second Coming is imminent."

Susannah and Della sat side by side on the ladies' mounting block, apparently waiting for horses to be brought out.

"They're going for a hack in this weather?" Mr. St. Michael asked.

Nita didn't dare think of him as Tremaine, lest she slip before her siblings, but he was Tremaine. *Her Tremaine.*

"Looks like they're headed somewhere," George said, "though I suspect their errand is in the direction of Stonebridge. Nothing less compelling could tear Susannah from her books, but I refuse to provide an escort. My arse is frozen."

Brothers. Nita trotted ahead. "Halloo! Shall you take your mare, Suze? She was a perfect lady for the duration, and I've warmed the saddle."

"I'll take her if Susannah won't," Della said.

"My saddle won't fit you," Susannah rejoined. "Though it fits Nita well enough. Was the library open?"

Mr. St. Michael drew rein and swung off his horse. "It was, though I must warn your ladyships, the lanes are snowy, the temperature is dropping, and I doubt the earl would approve of a protracted outing in such weather."

"We can have this argument in the barn," George said, handing his horse off to a groom. "I can't forbid you from going, ladies, but I can advise against it, as Mr. St. Michael has."

"Susannah needs to bring old Edward up to scratch before the assembly," Della said, hopping off the mounting block. "If he doesn't get the proposing done soon, she'll start back in on the Old Testament, and all will be wars, slayings, and begats until Beltane."

A wintry silence greeted that announcement, then George laid an arm across Della's shoulders.

"Come with me now, Della. Nobody's riding anywhere, and somebody needs to wash your face with snow before Susannah throttles you."

He marched Della off toward the house while Susannah remained sitting on the mounting block, looking pale and chilly.

"Della's simply being honest," she said. "Mr. St. Michael ought to know by now the Haddonfields aren't overly burdened with decorum."

Before the grooms led Mr. St. Michael's horse away, he extracted something from his saddlebags.

"If you're not to pay a call on Stonebridge, perhaps this will enliven your afternoon. My ladies, I bid you good day."

He passed Susannah two books, kissed Nita's cheek, and strode off after George and Della. Nita wanted to follow him, but he'd guessed correctly. Susannah was in a state, clutching the books to her middle as if she'd hold in a great upset, or perhaps a bout of cursing.

Susannah had not been heard to curse since she'd been seventeen and vexed beyond bearing with certain other young ladies whose company she endured at tea dances.

Nita took a seat beside Susannah as the last of the horses was led into the barn.

"Della saw Mr. St. Michael last night," Susannah said dully. "He was coming from your room at a late hour. I like him, but be careful, Nita." Suze offered a warning rather than a reproach, which was not like her.

Susannah hadn't even looked at the books. "I will be careful and so will he. Were you truly haring off to Stonebridge in this weather?"

"I was honestly hoping to be stranded there for a day or two." Her gaze was flat, her cheeks pale, and on her head was a perfectly impractical toque garnished with pheasant feathers.

Nita wrapped her scarf around Susannah's neck. From the direction of the garden, somebody shrieked, suggesting George had administered cold, wet fraternal retribution for Della's thoughtless words.

A snowflake landed directly in Nita's right eye, bringing with it a frigid stab of sororal intuition. "Has Edward Nash taken liberties with your person, Suze?"

"Don't scold me, Nita. While Papa was alive, I didn't feel so ancient, but now Nicholas is the earl, and soon even Della will have made her come-out. I long to be married and have a family. That's all I want, and all I've been raised to want."

All any of them had been raised to want.

"Here is what you need to know," Nita said in the same brisk tone she'd summarize a treatment regimen for a cranky patient. "I love you, and Edward is not good enough for you. He has problems, Susannah, financial and otherwise, that make him a poor candidate for your affections. Elsie does not speak well of his disposition or his temperance. If he has taken liberties, then you will tell me, and I'll provide you what aid I can, including tisanes that will bring on your menses."

Susannah straightened. "There are such tisanes?"

I will kill Edward Nash. "Every midwife and herbalist knows of them, and Mama certainly did too. They are by no means foolproof, but the sooner you take them, the safer and more effective they are. Have you missed your monthly yet?"

"No, not yet."

Thank God. "If it's any comfort, I know exactly how you feel."

Susannah leaned against Nita's shoulder, a gesture of defeated affection Suze hadn't offered her older sister in a decade.

"You couldn't possibly know how I feel, Neets. I have been an idiot. Three times, and Edward has yet to propose, because of those stupid perishing sheep."

When had Nita allowed the Bard to so thoroughly kidnap her sister?

"I could too know," Nita said. "I'll describe the symptoms, with which I have firsthand acquaintance: bewilderment, self-castigation, and a towering fear that one's fall from propriety will become glaringly evident. After a day or two, you admit to disappointment, in the fellow, in yourself, and in the experience. Most of all, in the experience. Then it happens again, and you can see no improvement, and that's even more disappointing."

Susannah wiped at her cheek with the end of Nita's scarf. "Disappointment, by God. The first time, Edward was in a hurry, and I was quite honestly surprised. The last time, I let him ambush me in the saddle room. Do you know how itchy a horse blanket can be against one's fundament?"

As itchy as self-doubt, as itchy as regret against a woman's heart.

"Probably as itchy as a worn wool rug in the servants' parlor," Nita replied. "Did Edward force you?"

Susannah kicked her boot heels against the solid wood of the mounting block. "No, he did not. He persuaded, and I thought I was being shrewd, creating an obligation to offer for me, which is an awful thing to admit. I was an idiot. Edward did not have to force me, not the first time."

Which meant something less than charm had resulted in the subsequent occasions. Damn Edward.

"Norton was much the same," Nita said as somebody pulled the barn door all but closed against the worsening weather. "He insisted I'd like it, that the business improved with repetition. Norton lied, if he meant repetition with him."

"Norton?" Susannah sat up. "Norton Nash? Nita, he was sent down from university any number of times. You poor thing, he had a *cowlick*."

"Mama was ill, I was lonely, and he was charming." How simple it sounded now—and how pathetic. How desperate.

"Maybe loneliness qualifies as an illness in young women, then, because I'm not sure I even like Edward. I thought I did. I like Shakespeare, mostly." Susannah sounded so cast down, so betrayed.

"When it's the right man, you'll know it. Your hindsight will be stunningly clear, then. Edward's not the right man, Suze."

"Are your tisanes effective?"

"Very little about medicine is guaranteed." While Nita's determination to help her sister was unrelenting, and certain parts of her were becoming *quite* chilled. "I should have paid more attention to you and less to Addy Chalmers and Harrison Goodenough."

Nita would never admit that to Nicholas though, any more than she'd admit sick babies terrified her.

"When a man shoots himself in the foot, his situation is hard to ignore, Neets."

"True enough." Old Mr. Goodenough had been drunk at the time, trying to fire from the saddle at some varmint and unable to get his gun from its scabbard. "What will you do, Suze?"

Around them, the stable yard was filling up with snow, while from inside the barn, the comforting scents of livestock and hay wafted on a chilly breeze. Concern for Susannah weighed down Nita's happiness at being engaged and leavened her joy with gratitude.

Tremaine St. Michael was so much more worthy than all the Norton Nashes in the world, *and he was hers.*

"I will read"—Susannah peered at the books—"Mr. Burns's poetry and some essay by a Mrs. Wollstonecraft. Looks interesting. I like Mr. St. Michael, Nita. He isn't silly, and yet he can laugh."

Odd that Susannah, a sober soul if ever there was one, should make that observation.

"Mr. St. Michael respects my medical knowledge and is a marvelous kisser." Odder still that Nita should offer that.

Susannah stood, books in hand, and whipped off the fetching, impractical little hat. "Best of all, Mr. St. Michael hasn't a cowlick."

They returned to the house on that cheering observation, then commended each other to the comforts of a long, hot soaking bath.

The snow let up after dumping a foot of cold inconvenience on all in the shire, though as Tremaine's visit to Kent stretched on, he enjoyed a sunny sense of a negotiation coming to a profitable conclusion. He'd tendered his offer to Lady Nita; she'd investigated his prospects and found them to her liking.

Several days after Tremaine had become engaged, all that remained was to agree on settlements with the Earl of Bellefonte.

Who was nowhere to be found. Tremaine prowled the library, the parlors, the estate office, even the corridors of the family wing. He came upon Lady Della, nose down in Mrs. Wollstonecraft's eloquence, in a cozy parlor graced with a hearth and two braziers.

"I beg your pardon for disturbing you, my lady, but I can't seem to locate any of your siblings."

Nor would Tremaine ask the servants for the whereabouts of his prospective in-laws, lest talk ensue. Lady Nita had said an announcement at the assembly was in order, and until then, Tremaine would observe utmost discretion.

"We've been abandoned," Lady Della said. "Do come in lest you let out all the warmth I hoard so jealously."

They were to be family, so Tremaine closed the door. Lady Della was at a dangerous age, when young ladies could get themselves into trouble with what felt like daring but was in truth foolishness, and yet Tremaine liked what he knew of her.

"Nita and Kirsten have saddled up in the interests of enjoying fresh air, though I suspect they'll visit the Chalmers household,"

Lady Della said, putting her reading aside. "Susannah went with them, intent no doubt on the lending library, and George rode as escort to ensure no riots ensued when all of my sisters rode out at once."

From her cozy parlor, the junior sibling somehow knew the whereabouts of four adults, none of whom Tremaine had been able to track down. A farewell visit to the Chalmers family was understandable, or perhaps Lady Nita would entrust their welfare to Lady Kirsten.

"Why didn't you go with them?" Tremaine asked. The snow had kept everybody on the Belle Maison premises for several days, though Bellefonte himself had worn a path to and from the stable. His countess occasionally went with him, though nobody rode out.

"I have a sniffle." Lady Della sniffed delicately, mocking Tremaine, herself, or polite fictions in general. "I like your Mrs. Wollstonecraft, and I like better that you'd wave her at Susannah."

An ally among the in-laws was never to be taken for granted. "Everybody needs a break from Shakespeare."

"Also from *Debrett's*. My come-out was delayed thanks to Papa's passing, but Nicholas's grandmother would have me recite from *Debrett's* as if it were Scripture."

"I've found it useful," Tremaine said, taking a place near the fire. In cold weather, even a cozy room had chilly floors, a situation Lady Della managed by keeping her slippered feet up on a hassock.

"Will you and Nita make an announcement at the assembly?" She fired that salvo while casually draping a brown and red wool afghan over her knees. As the only dark-haired Haddonfield, the colors flattered her.

"An announcement?"

"Coyness is not your greatest talent, sir. Nita has been different lately. She smiles inwardly and isn't so brisk outwardly. I saw you coming from her room the other night, and I saw her the next day. She wore ear bobs to dinner."

Little sapphire and gold drops that went marvelously with

Nita's eyes and with her smiles. The countess had mercifully seated Tremaine next to his intended, so he could torment himself with sidelong glances and the occasional brush of hands under the table.

Nita was owed a bit of wooing, though the sooner they were wed, the better.

"Perhaps the lady and I were merely having a late-night chat about a medical condition."

"You weren't suffering from a medical condition," Lady Della said, "though it apparently afflicts some men worse than an ague. If Susannah and Mr. Nash make no announcement, then I'd beg you and Nita to keep your news quiet as well."

"I haven't said we have news." Though Lady Della had a point. If Susannah were not engaged, kindness suggested an announcement should wait.

"I am the youngest," Lady Della replied, sounding not very young at all. "I am the smallest, and sooner or later you will hear that I'm an indiscretion for which the old earl forgave my mother. Susannah needs to wed, Mr. St. Michael. I know you want those sheep, and I mean no insult to your regard for Nita, but Susannah needs those sheep more than you do."

Tremaine took a seat beside Lady Della uninvited. "You should not confide the circumstances of your birth to even me, my lady. While your situation is common enough among titled families, the information could be used to your detriment."

She held out a plate of biscuits, not ginger. Lemon, maybe. Tremaine took one to be polite.

"Nita said you were kind." Lady Della set the plate down beside Mrs. Wollstonecraft. "I don't like Mr. Nash, but I can tell you Susannah has *need* of him, and that means she needs those dratted sheep."

Lady Della's expression was disconcertingly determined, and she was regarded by her siblings as adept at gathering information. She appeared to be a darling little aristocratic confection, but something—

or someone—had roused her protective instincts where Lady Susannah was concerned.

Tremaine took a bite of biscuit and yielded to the prodding of instinct.

"Do you make a habit of catching your sisters in their rare improprieties?" Lady Della had seen something, caught a glimpse of liberties permitted or even vows anticipated. Did Nita know Susannah had mis-stepped? Did Susannah know her lapse had been observed?

No wonder Bellefonte often wore a harried expression.

"I make a habit out of looking after my siblings," Lady Della said, that cool, adult thread more evident in her voice than ever. "They look after me. I'm simply returning the favor. That goes for George too."

Whatever His Handsomeness had to do with the topic at hand.

"I've already decided I can't ask for the sheep to be included in Lady Nita's dowry," Tremaine said, finishing a scrumptious lavender-flavored biscuit. Why he should share his decision with Lady Della was a mystery. Perhaps one spoke thus with siblings, even when they were acquired by marriage.

"So you'll buy them in a separate transaction six months hence," she retorted, "and Nicholas will be the soul of accommodation in this scheme because he's another dunderheaded male. I'm telling you, Susannah needs those sheep."

"If I could find the earl," Tremaine said, "I'd cheerfully negotiate settlements with him that will preclude me from ever owning those damned sheep, but he's eluding my notice. Given his size, this suggests he doesn't want to be found."

Given the earl's besottedness with his countess, it suggested his lordship was elsewhere in the family wing, perhaps using a snowy morning to further secure the succession.

"Nicholas makes birdhouses when he's wrestling with a problem." Lady Della offered the biscuits again. "Leah sometimes helps him or joins him in his workshop simply to bear him company and get away from the rest of us."

Her comment brought a memory to light, of Beckman Haddonfield hanging a fantastical birdhouse in the lower branches of an oak at Three Springs. The miniature chalet, complete with a tiny carved goat on the roof—a bearded, horned male—had been a wedding present from the earl.

"Bellefonte *makes* those birdhouses?" The workmanship had been exquisite, far too fine to hang in a tree. "Those birdhouses could fetch a pretty penny as parlor ornaments."

Tremaine betrayed his mercantile soul with that comment, and the look Lady Della sent him—eyes dancing, lips threatening to turn up—said she knew it. He stuffed half another biscuit in his mouth before he could utter more ridiculousness.

"Nicholas will be cheered to hear that his woodworking passes muster," Lady Della said. "He's also quite skilled with a muck fork, which I'm sure his countess took into consideration when he asked for her hand. His workshop is at the back of the stable. Go into the saddle room and you'll find a small door on the back wall. Nobody ever thinks to look for Nicholas behind a small door."

Nor would they think to find a small sister guarding his welfare.

"My thanks," Tremaine said, rising. "Shall I have a footman bring more coals for your brazier?"

"And have the staff know I've been closeted with you? No, thank you."

She dismissed Tremaine by the simple expedient of resuming her study of *A Vindication of the Rights of Woman*.

Like all the Haddonfields, Lady Della was clever, but she wasn't restless with it the way Nita and Kirsten were, nor did she enjoy Susannah's domestic inclinations.

Lady Della was lonely though, Tremaine would have bet William on that. That's what her announcement of her age, size, and bastard status had been about. She was lonely and expecting to be overlooked by her newest sibling-by-marriage.

Tremaine would not overlook her—or underestimate her. By supper at the latest, she'd figure out that an agreement preventing him from owning the sheep would pose no bar to his *leasing* the same animals.

Which left Tremaine to puzzle over why Nita had neither told him she was paying one last call on the Chalmers family nor invited him to escort her.

CHAPTER THIRTEEN

Susannah's birdhouse had been easy. Nick had devised a structure that looked like a set of shelves holding various volumes—Fordyce's *Sermons*, Shakespeare's plays and sonnets, Wordsworth's latest poems. These, Nick fashioned into a home for birds, two stories of books high, the finished product fooling the eye from only a few feet away.

"Nita took me by surprise," Nick informed a fat, white tomcat tending to its ablutions on the work bench. "One hardly knows what to give her, she's so damned independent."

The sketchbook in front of Nick was open to a blank page, the same blank page he'd been staring at for an hour.

"Sheep, maybe, because she's attached the affections of the Sheep Count, but what if she disdains his suit?"

Nick drew the pencil from behind his ear and tried a few lines in the direction of a woolly merino.

"Sheep don't typically hang about in trees." Neither did books, come to that. "Cats do." Kirsten might like a cat-shaped birdhouse if ever she found a man she couldn't demolish with feminine indifference.

Fifteen minutes later, Nick tossed down his pencil, disgusted. His birdhouse sheep all looked like clouds with cloven hooves.

"Nita might have cornered St. Michael in some cozy parlor and made him recite more poetry to her, might have dragged him into the village to get the gossips excited, might have gone off to count lambs with him, but no. She must deal with some colicky infant or worse."

The cat stropped its head on Nick's chin and left a trail of brown paw prints on the white page.

A tap on the door interrupted Nick's musings, while the cat switched directions and made another pass beneath Nick's chin. Nick's countess had doubtless come to rescue him at last from his doleful musings.

"Come in, lovey," Nick said without turning. "I've missed you sorely and need some kisses to cheer me up."

"I'd be happy to indulge you, Bellefonte," said an accented male voice, "but your brother George might become jealous, to say nothing of your countess's consternation."

Well, hell. Nick closed the sketchbook and pivoted on his stool. "St. Michael, good morning. I was expecting my countess." And what had George done now to provoke such a comment?

"You make your birdhouses here?" St. Michael stood inside the door, studying Nick's workshop. He wore riding attire, his greatcoat was open rather than buttoned, and his hands were bare.

"I do, and I come here to think." The cat put two paws on Nick's shoulder, as if contemplating assuming a perch there.

"Lady Nita has accepted my suit," St. Michael said, reaching for a "book" then drawing his hand back. "A *trompe l'oeil*. Very clever. I didn't think old Fordyce would be to your taste."

"I have sisters, and thus Fordyce graces our library. They read him when they're in want of merriment. I suppose you've come to talk about the damned sheep?"

In other circumstances, St. Michael might have been a friend. He was shrewd, did not stand on ceremony, and enjoyed the pragmatic outlook of those born to a former generation of Continental aristos, and yet he wasn't at all who and what Nick had envisioned for Nita.

"I've come to talk about Lady Nita's settlements, assuming you'll bless our union."

St. Michael left off inspecting the birdhouse and moved on to the tools Nick had hung along one wall. Some Nick had made himself, the grips smoothed to exactly fit his grasp.

"You aren't like any earl I've met before," St. Michael murmured, "and I've met plenty."

"You aren't like any sheep farmer I've met before. With respect to the settlements, my father set aside funds for each of my sisters, but his means were modest."

"I am not marrying your sister because I need more coin," St. Michael said gently. He lifted a hammer off the wall. "This could do some damage."

The handle was oak, the weight one Nick had forged as a younger man.

"Stop playing with my toys, St. Michael. The purpose of the settlements is not to entice you to offer for the lady. *She* is your prize, and woe to you if you don't realize that. The settlements are for Nita, so she knows we value her and will see her provided for should she be widowed."

Though Papa hadn't managed to set aside enough to guarantee that outcome, unless Nita was widowed in great old age. Nick had explained these circumstances to his sisters and had yet to find a remedy for it. The cat commenced kneading Nick's shoulder, needle-like claws digging through the fabric of his shirt and waistcoat.

St. Michael set the hammer back in its bracket and plucked the cat away just as Nick would have set the beast on the floor. The dratted pest commenced purring as St. Michael scratched it under the chin.

"How can I have a serious negotiation, Bellefonte, when you allow even the beasts to do as they please with your person? What is your position on the sheep?"

"Leave the sheep out of this. I've had other offers." St. Michael's fingers paused, and the cat commenced switching its tail.

"Other offers? Plural? Does Lady Kirsten have a suitor perhaps?"

"None of your damned business, but if she did, her suitor would doubtless want those sheep too."

St. Michael resumed studying the birdhouse, as if the books were truly titles on a library shelf. "If you are thinking of the sheep, I am their best option. I take excellent care of my livestock."

"I'm thinking of my sisters. Edward Nash knows Susannah's portion is modest, and he's willing to accept valuable consideration in place of coin."

St. Michael made a face, like a cat who'd chanced upon a cream pot undefended in the pantry and had taken a lick only to find the contents soured.

"Lady Nita does not favor a match between Mr. Nash and Lady Susannah," St. Michael said as the cat purred in his arms. "Please ask her why."

"Lady Nita has reasons of her own to take the Nash menfolk into dislike. I cannot allow her fancies to cheat Susannah out of a decent match." Though Nick didn't care much for Edward. The man dressed his widowed sister-in-law like a farm wife, took no interest in his nephew, and leered at tavern maids despite paying his addresses to Susannah. "Nash is the first man Susannah has looked upon with favor, and thus I am bound to encourage such a match."

"Lady Nita's objections to her sister's choice are specific to Mr. Edward Nash. I strongly urge you, for the sake of Lady Susannah's well-being, to speak with your sister."

"Do you think I haven't tried?" Nick asked, rising from his stool. "Nita Haddonfield could teach stubbornness to mules. If she's disinclined to broach a topic, it remains unbroached."

St. Michael deposited the cat on the workbench. It sat upon Nick's closed sketchbook, tail wrapped around its paws in perfect, insolent contentment. Nita's suitor took the vacated stool, lounging back to prop his elbows on the workbench.

"You'll be glad to give your sister into my keeping?" he asked.

Sisters were not livestock, to be surrendered in the marketplace for a sum certain. "In the churchyard," Nick said, "I will present a vapid smile for all the biddies, and I'll accept good wishes on Nita's account with my usual faultless good cheer. To all save my wife, I will pretend to be vastly pleased that Nita will be your *comtesse*, but, St. Michael, I'd hoped every one of my sisters would be treated to something of a proper courtship."

"If I've found favor in Lady Nita's eyes, isn't that courtship enough?"

Apparently more than enough, if Della's mutterings were to be believed. "I am angry at my father," Nick said, dragging a second stool up beside St. Michael's. "I'm frequently angry at the late earl, which he likely considers repayment of consideration long overdue."

The cat's scratchy tongue swiped across the top of Nick's ear. The little beast had remarkably foul breath.

"My rage at my parents lasted years after their deaths," St. Michael said. "My father's willingness to die amid his wealth, I could understand—France was his home—but my mother had a choice. She could have remained in Scotland and raised her sons or returned to the greater comfort of my father's holdings in France. She chose the luxury, despite the peril, and my grandfather, who might have stopped her, deferred to her husband's authority. Lady Nita would choose her children. She's a reliable partner, and she and I will get on well enough."

Kirsten, George, and Della had each assured Nick that Mr. St. Michael was getting on with Nita *famously*.

At all hours, and in the privacy of her ladyship's bedroom.

"You underestimate my sister," Nick said, sitting forward, out of range of cat kisses. Let St. Michael deal with overly affectionate felines.

"Most men underestimate most women, and perhaps the ladies like it that way," St. Michael said, dragging the cat off Nick's sketchbook and holding the creature up like a feline rag doll. "Have you no respect, cat? Bellefonte is not one of your pantry strumpets to endure your overtures."

The cat was still purring, even dangling at St. Michael's eye level.

"He can't hear you," Nick said. "Poor blighter's deaf as a dowager duchess. I've a physician friend who pointed it out to me."

"You're sure he's deaf?"

"David, Viscount Fairly, trained as a doctor in Scotland and is canny as hell. He demonstrated the cat's disability in various ways. Poor creature can't hear a thing, though he senses vibrations, has excellent eyesight, and does not lack for female companionship."

"Interesting." St. Michael set the cat back down on the workbench. "If you don't do something with those sheep soon, they'll develop all manner of ailments. You've a few smaller specimens among them already."

To hell with the damned sheep. "You're not getting those sheep, St. Michael. I'm sorry to disappoint you." Now the cat perched, one paw on Nick's shoulder, one on St. Michael's.

"Will Nash get them?" St. Michael asked.

Persistent, the both of them, though it was some consolation that the cat liked St. Michael. Nick put the presuming feline out in the saddle room, while St. Michael remained at ease on his stool.

"I'm upset with the late earl," Nick said, "not because his circumstances precluded lavish dowries for my sisters. Rents do not provide the income they once did, taxes climb yearly, and launching more than a half-dozen children is expensive. Papa did the best he could."

"And yet, you'd read dear Papa the Riot Act now if you had the chance," St. Michael said. "Why? He did not abandon you in a strange country where you knew little of the languages and nothing of the customs. He did not parade around his chateau, while you subsisted on tough mutton and endless church services."

Beneath St. Michael's curiosity lay hard memories. Nick hoped Nita, with her tender, lonely heart, was not marrying a hard man.

"Papa knew he was dying," Nick said, though the words were difficult. "He sent us all away. Beckman was to take the Three

Springs estate in hand. I was to find a bride. George lingered in the vicinity of Cambridge, mostly to keep an eye on Adolphus, and the girls were banished to relatives and house parties. My brother Ethan, from whom Papa had been estranged, was invited to make a final call, and Nita was allowed to remain at Belle Maison."

"Because of her medical knowledge?" St. Michael suggested.

"Nita is very knowledgeable, but she's still unmarried, for all she's had her Seasons. I am angry with my father for taking advantage of Nita. She ran this place while my brothers and I were sowing wild oats, while her mother fell ill, while the old earl faded."

Nick's recitation was drifting from an explanation to a confession, and maybe that was appropriate.

"Lady Nita did a fine job," St. Michael said. "Many women find ways to be useful despite spinsterhood."

Nita would have her hands full with this one, but so too would St. Michael have his hands full. "Nita did not graduate from the schoolroom to spinsterhood, you dolt. She graduated from the schoolroom to *widowhood*, without any of the intervening years of laughter and happiness, without any babies or grandbabies to love, without even the preservation of a spinster's unworldliness. Her mother was something of a healer, but Nita has far eclipsed her mother's example, and trespasses now on all manner of miseries with impunity."

St. Michael's features shuttered, suggesting Nick's point eluded his grasp.

"I thank you for passing along your fraternal sentiments, Bellefonte, but we've yet to resolve the settlements."

Leah had counseled Nick to patience where St. Michael was concerned, and as ever, the countess had seen clearly.

"Listen to me, St. Michael, or there will be no need to discuss settlements. Women like Nita need to feel needed. Papa took advantage of that, until Nita forgot she could say no, until she thought all the burdens she shouldered, the babies she could deliver, were the sum of her value. Leah has relieved Nita of the weight of running

Belle Maison, and Nita has gone halfway into a decline over that kindness."

Nick picked up his hammer, and as it had for years, it fit his hand perfectly. "I'm guilty of colluding in this sad tale," he went on, "but I'm charging you with setting matters to rights. Let Nita attend the lying-ins if you must, but no more sickrooms for my sister, no more tending gunshot wounds, no more putrid sore throats or gangrenous toes, no more—"

At the door, the cat scratched to be let in. Nick's woodworking shop was the warmest place in the barn by virtue of braziers full of hot coals, in addition to the proximity of large, shaggy horses.

"You allowed her to deal with... that?" St. Michael said, abruptly appropriating a very French portion of dismay.

"Makes me bilious to think of it," Nick said, using a hasp to stir the coals in one of the braziers. "The allowing started before my father fell ill, so yes. Nita knows her herbs, but she's also a competent surgeon and physician. Dr. Horton is behind the times in his science, and most people around here know it and take advantage of Nita accordingly."

"Then Horton should find a younger assistant."

St. Michael was a dab hand at solving other people's problems. Children would cure him of that arrogance if Nita didn't see to it.

"I've told Horton that," Nick said, "and he scoffs at the very notion. Vicar agrees with him and says the problem is that Nita lacks a proper sense of her place in the world. I cannot say the man is wrong."

Though neither was Nita to blame for allowing others to need her.

The cat on the far side of the door was aggravatingly persistent.

"Your vicar may not be wrong," St. Michael said, "but he's not very Christian either. If he did more to inspire his flock's charitable impulses, Lady Nita wouldn't be scouring your larder for the parish poor."

The Scots were of necessity a practical people, also fiercely loyal to family. St. Michael would not criticize Nita for her generosity or caring, and that was some relief.

"The old vicar was a kinder soul," Nick said, feeling abruptly chilly. "We miss him." Nick missed his father too. Sorely, every day. For the first time, it occurred to Nick that Nita must miss her papa every bit as much if not more.

And her mama and her other married brothers, for whom she'd made Belle Maison a well-organized, comfortable home.

"You are worried for your sister's happiness," St. Michael said, taking the hammer from Nick's grasp and hanging it again in its assigned location. "That speaks well of you. Whatever funds you have set aside for Lady Nita, I will triple them upon our marriage and you can manage them as you see fit. I want six rams, one tup, and twelve ewes, of my choosing, including the tup's mama."

"Agreed," Nick said, "but only because you will give Nita those happy years, those children and grandchildren. Choose the best of the herd, and convince her that she need not accept every obligation put before her, that she's dear and precious in herself."

The hammer would not hang straight for St. Michael, and the damned cat would not cease scratching at the door, so Nick took pity on the beast.

"I have promised your sister we can bide near her family for much of the year, though the matter of children is in the Almighty's hands." St. Michael paused in the open doorway. "As for that other— the sore throats and whatnot—she's done with it, particularly with the infections and diseases. As my countess, she'll have many agreeable tasks to keep her busy, and her health will no longer be put at risk for others. I've warned her that I take seriously the welfare of my dependents, and Lady Nita is done waging war on illness and death."

Nick would have been more reassured by this pronouncement had Nita been present to confirm it. St. Michael at least had the right objective.

Nick offered his hand. "Best of luck, St. Michael, and welcome to the family."

St. Michael shook firmly, then departed, leaving Nick once again in the cat's company, with no earthly idea what manner of wedding gift to make for his oldest sister.

~

"That is ten pounds," Kirsten said.

"Not my ten pounds," Nita replied, stuffing the money back into the pocket of her cloak. "Mr. St. Michael asked me to pass it along to Addy, but one hesitates."

"You think she'll drink it?"

Kirsten rode a flighty, elegant mare with a fine opinion of herself, though this morning, Hecate was content to plod along at Atlas's side.

"I often wonder how I'd fare, were I in Addy's place," Nita said, turning down the lane that led to the Chalmers cottage. "If a young man wheedled my virtue from me, got me with child, then abandoned me, opening the door for his family and mine to turn their backs on me as well, how would I manage?"

"You're thinking of Norton? Any one of our brothers would have brought him up to scratch, Nita."

Atlas stumbled, an occasional bad step in snowy footing common for even the most surefooted horse.

"I'm thinking of myself, of whether I could have borne to become Norton's wife. I wanted to be in love with him, but—" Compared to what Nita felt for Tremaine St. Michael, her attraction to Norton Nash had been more curiosity and boredom than affection.

And loneliness. Heaps and years of loneliness. "Norton was more fun-loving and less vain than Edward," Kirsten said, "but Elsie got the pick of that litter."

While Susannah had made a play for the runt.

"I'm encouraged whenever I see smoke coming from Addy's chimney," Nita said, drawing Atlas to a halt before the rickety porch. "Smoke means Addy hasn't left her children to freeze to death."

Kirsten unhooked her knee from the horn and slid to the ground, her mare taking a sidewise step to enliven the maneuver.

"Is that why you didn't call upon your fiancé's escort for this outing?" Kirsten asked, running her stirrup up its leather. "You worry that someday, you'll come up this lane and find another dead baby?"

Nita got off her horse, for once finding Kirsten's blunt speech appropriate. "Nobody talks about it, but I delivered that child and I do fear for her siblings." Babies died with appalling frequency, but a baby stood no chance when the mother resumed drinking shortly after her lying-in.

"I've always wondered how the men of this parish engage Addy's services," Kirsten said, passing Nita one of the two sacks they'd brought. "Many of those fellows grew up with her, saw her at services, and knew her parents. How can they undertake *dealings* with a woman whom they knew was once respectable, when they might instead offer her gainful employment?"

"Lady Nita!" Evan stood in the doorway, his little face wreathed in smiles, the blue scarf about his neck and the ends dangling nearly to his knees. "And Lady Kirsten! The baby's awake, and I'm learning the letters for my name."

"Letters are a fine thing," Nita said, entering the cottage. Addy sat before the hearth in the rocking chair, Annie cradled in her lap. "Addy, good day."

"My ladies." She rose, bobbing a curtsy with the child in her arms. "Evan, close that door or we'll all freeze. Mary, wipe your brother's nose."

"How is Annie," Kirsten asked, "and how are you, Addy?"

"Annie is better, and we're managing." Managing did not mean the cottage offered any hospitality. Even a cup of tea was an extravagance beyond Addy's means.

"Managing is the best many of us can do," Nita said, peering at the baby. "Her color's good and she's breathing well."

Addy kissed the child's brow, the gesture both defensive and protective. "I'll not lose this one. Not this one too."

Kirsten took the sack Nita had been clutching. "Children, I'll slice you some bread, and there's butter and jam in these sacks somewhere. Perhaps you'll help me find them?"

The household afforded no more privacy than it did hospitality, though Kirsten would hardly gossip and the children were absorbed with the prospect of good food.

"I do not judge you, Addy," Nita said, taking off one glove and running a finger over the child's cheek. "I certainly do not judge wee Annie."

The baby rooted against her mother's shoulder, a normal, healthy infant indication of interest in nutrition, the same interest shared by the other children.

"Come sit with me," Addy said, moving toward the sleeping alcove.

Nita followed her behind the curtain to a pathetically tidy square of bedding, an extra blanket—one Nita had brought when she'd first learned Addy was carrying—folded at the foot of the bed.

Addy passed over the baby and loosened her jumps in anticipation of nursing her child. When her clothing had been rearranged, Addy put the baby to her breast with the detached efficiency of an experienced mother.

"I want to tell you something, my lady."

Dread swept up from Nita's middle, like a cold gust tearing into a cozy parlor from a window slammed open by a winter gale.

"You're not surrendering this child to the parish," Nita said. "I'll not take her to the foundling hospital either."

The baby latched on greedily, her mother wincing. The late countess, a mother of seven herself, had said afterpains were often as painful as the birth pangs, and yet Nita envied Addy her discomfort.

"I'll not surrender the child to the parish," Addy said, "though I understand why you'd think that of me. I need paper, Lady Nita, and pencil. I've a letter to write. I hate to ask, when you've done so much for me, but I have a cousin in Shropshire who last I heard had longed for children and been unable to have them. Her husband's a kind man, and she wrote to me even after Mary came."

That would have been as much as ten years ago, and yet Addy still clung to hope regarding this cousin.

"You'd send the baby to her?" Nita hated that notion. A newborn needed her mother.

"And Evan. Jacob and Esau are good, sturdy boys, but Evan needs a trade. I won't want to, and certainly not until the baby is weaned, but I cannot—"

A combination of emotions chased across Addy's once-pretty features. Determination, resignation, anger, and despair were all made more passionate by the mother-love nature intended every child to know from the moment of birth.

"You cannot what, Addy?" Nita asked. Beyond the curtain, the cottage had grown quiet as the older children consumed the bounty of bread, jam, and butter.

"I cannot continue as I've been doing. I can't go back to it, Lady Nita. You might think I've grown accustomed to the shame, to the men, but I haven't. I want better for my Annie, and for Mary too."

Did anybody ever grow accustomed to shame? To guilt? "What about their fathers? Might they at least help the children?" Did they feel any shame?

"The only one I know for sure is Mary's father, and he's gone. His family won't help, and Mary's growing too pretty."

Nicholas might allow Mary to join the kitchen staff at Belle Maison, but then what of the younger children?

"Mr. St. Michael asked me to give this to you," Nita said, drawing the ten pounds from her cloak. "It won't solve any greater problems, but it will give you time to heal from Annie's birth, to write to your cousin, and consider your options."

Addy used one finger to break the suction between the infant and the nipple, and switched the child to the second breast.

"That's from Mr. St. Michael?" Addy asked, looking anywhere but at the money.

"He will not expect anything in return. He and I are to be married, and he once lived as a poor lad would, Addy. This is for the children."

Nita tucked the money under the single thin pillow at the head of the bed. The pillowcase still had a border of fine white work, suggesting it was a relic of Addy's trousseau.

"We'll miss you here, Lady Nita, but he's a good sort, your Mr. St. Michael."

Beyond the curtain, Evan quietly asked for more bread and jam. His siblings remained silent in the face of that bold request, but Kirsten must have obliged, for soon a chorus of, "Please, Lady Kirsten, me too!" followed.

"You needn't miss me," Nita said. "Mr. St. Michael has said he'll find us a property in the neighborhood."

The idea was satisfying, like fresh bread, butter, and jam for a lady's soul. In that single magnanimous gesture, Tremaine had assured Nita that she could still contribute to her community, still uphold the tradition passed down to her by her own mother.

"I don't attend services, my lady. Vicar made it clear I was not welcome."

"I didn't mean you'd see me only at—"

The baby made a noise suggesting her nappies were in immediate need of attention.

"One end fed, the other end clean," Addy said with good-humored patience. She passed Nita the baby, did up her bodice, and took Annie back. "I didn't kill my baby, Lady Nita."

The stink one infant could create was prodigious. "I would never accuse you of that."

"Because you're too kind. When I know I'm carrying, I try to stay away from the gin and have only the small pints most women drink from time to time. Spirits are dear, and my children need to eat. I drink so I can earn money."

So Addy could tolerate the attentions of her customers in other words. Nita rose from the bed.

"You needn't explain this to me, Addy. Many other women would have put their children on the parish and gone to London by now." Though the parish might not accept these children, notwithstanding that they'd lived their entire lives in Haddondale.

"Nothing but disease awaits me in London, I know that," Addy said, laying the child in the middle of the bed. "I also know many would rather I leave, but I can't do that to my children. I try not to drink, and when the babies come, as long as I can, I stay with them."

"But they must eat, so you resume your activities in the village."

Addy drew the curtain back, revealing the four older children gathered around the hearth, all eagerly demonstrating their letters for Kirsten.

"And to do that, I drink. I also drank when the last baby died, though God knows, heaven must be an improvement over what I can offer here."

That sentiment was so miserable, so honest, Nita could not accept it. "Look at your children," she said. "They're warm enough, they have food in their bellies. You have more means to care for them now than you've had for years, Addy Chalmers. You will write to your cousin; I will speak to Nicholas. Surely Belle Maison can use a scullery maid or a shepherd boy."

On the bed behind them, the baby fussed, waving small fists in the air.

"You should burp her," Nita said, "when her nappy has been tended to."

"I smell a stinky," Evan chirped from the hearth.

"I'll change her," Mary said, springing up and snatching a clean cloth from a stack on the table.

"They're good children," Nita said, "and you're right to want something better for them. I will be back, Addy, with pencil and paper, at least."

Jacob, Esau, and Evan were apparently smitten with Lady Kirsten. When she stood, their little faces fell.

"Time to go?" Kirsten asked a bit too cheerfully.

"If you're done with your scholars," Nita replied.

Addy rolled her eyes, but she was smiling too.

Nita mentally added some simple books to the list of provisions she'd bring when next she visited, and soon she and Kirsten were back in their respective saddles, though they rode into the wind on their homeward journey.

"How do you stand it?" Kirsten asked before they'd reached the end of the lane.

"Stand the smell?"

"The smell, the dirt, the hopelessness. Addy isn't much older than you, and she'll likely die soon of the pox, cold, starvation, or sheer melancholia. I don't want to go back there, Nita. I should be kinder, I should be braver, but I don't want to go back there. Addy is fallen, and those children are doomed."

Atlas plodded along, head down. The weather seemed to have subdued even Kirsten's mare.

"I don't want to go back either." Nita never wanted to go back, not to a home where babies had died, not to see that infection would soon take a man's life if he were unwilling to part with his foot, not to offer useless tisanes to an aching old woman who longed for heaven.

"Then why do you do it?" Kirsten wailed, swiping at her cheek with the back of her glove. "Why do you make yourself stare at that mean, smelly cottage, those pinched faces, that dear little baby?"

Kirsten had barely glanced at the baby.

"I thought Addy's drinking was what had taken the last child from her," Nita said. "I couldn't bear for that to happen to wee Annie."

Kirsten sniffed. "Everybody knows Addy's drinking cost that child her life."

"Everybody's wrong," Nita said. "I was wrong too. The child's death sent Addy back to the gin. Babies sometimes die for no reason, and this was apparently one of those times. I want Annie to live. Her mother wants that too."

Like any normal mother would want her child to live, thrive, and have a chance in life.

"While her father wanted to dip his wick," Kirsten spat, "and then likely stand up with you or me at the assembly. I accompanied you to that household because I was curious, Nita, not because I'm prone to Christian charity. I wanted to see how low Addy Chalmers had fallen, wanted to see what became of a woman without virtue. I'm sorry."

Nita steered her horse around a frozen puddle rather than observe that Kirsten had seen all of that on her first visit to the cottage.

"Frightening, isn't it?" Nita said. Frightening and exhausting. "I've committed the same lapses in judgment Addy has, and so apparently has Suze. Suze and I suffer no consequences, while Addy has lost all."

"Not all. She has those children, and—like half the ailing people in this shire—she has you."

Nita urged Atlas to a trot, anxious to return to her intended. Kirsten was right though. The ailing people in the shire did have Nita, so rather than ride straight for home, first she'd pay brief calls on Alton Horst and Mary Eckhardt.

CHAPTER FOURTEEN

Tremaine liked Nita very much; he did not like having a fiancée. Old feelings, of hope and anxiety, pleasure and resentment, came with being engaged.

Also a little madness: What if Nita changed her mind? What if she went to the Chalmers cottage and never came back? What if she rode away, fluttering her handkerchief in farewell, and he never saw her again?

Fortunately, after Tremaine had spent a morning staring at correspondence, Lady Nita came striding across the snowy garden, Lady Kirsten beside her. The noon meal featured servings of good cheer along with the ham and mashed potatoes.

At table, Lady Nita had shown to excellent advantage in a gown of green velvet with a lavender fichu and matching shawl. The smiles she'd aimed at Tremaine had been soft and precious.

The hand she'd stroked over his thigh beneath the table had been pure devilment.

Dinner had been more of the same, the time spent with the ladies afterward even worse, until Tremaine had pled the beginnings of a genuine headache. He'd undressed, washed, and then repaired to bed with a treatise on foot rot that did nothing to soothe his tattered nerves.

When somebody tapped on his door, he snarled his response. "Come in."

"Tremaine?" Nita slipped around the door, her hair in that single golden braid over her shoulder, her attire again a blue brocade dressing gown and gray wool stockings.

He rose off the bed. "I was expecting a footman with a bucket of coal." Or perhaps George Haddonfield come to flirt.

Nita locked the door, a snick of metal on metal that might have been a pistol shot, so loudly did Tremaine hear it.

"I've missed you, Tremaine St. Michael."

She tossed that admission at his figurative, betrothed feet, a challenge and a concession all in one. The demented part of Tremaine that waited for her to abandon him was reassured by her words. The male part of him nearly pounced on her in reply.

"We shared two congenial meals today," he said, prowling closer, "and sang a recognizable duet after dinner." He stopped immediately before her. "You can't possibly be missing me."

Nita went up on her toes to kiss him, bringing Tremaine a whiff of lavender, lemons, and a different sort of madness altogether. With one hand, she cupped his jaw.

With the other, she gently squeezed his cock. "Tell me you missed me too, Tremaine. We're engaged. Sentimental talk between us is permitted."

This woman was not bent on talk. "You should not be here, my dear." *Stay. Please stay.*

Another squeeze, marvelously firm. "I agree. I should not be here. You should have come to my room. The corridors are chilly, and my feet are cold."

As Tremaine's mouth descended over Nita's, his instincts tossed out a theory: Nita was also plagued by the fear that their vows would never be spoken, that Tremaine would abandon her to putrid sore throats and cursing Quakers, never to have babies or a family of her own.

When he might have plundered, his kiss instead cherished. "Will you allow us to be married by special license, my lady?"

"Stop negotiating, Tremaine. Nicholas told me he acceded to your terms, now you will accede to mine."

Nita's list of terms began with another prodigiously thorough kiss and a few sanity-robbing squeezes.

"*That*," she said against his mouth, "is for spending the afternoon with your correspondence."

Tremaine kissed her back, then scooped her off her cold feet and deposited her on the bed.

"*That* is for imperiling my limited skill with dinner conversation, Lady Nita. When we're married, we will sit at opposite ends of a proper table."

She hauled him closer by virtue of two fists snatching him by the lapels of his night robe. "Not at breakfast we won't. Not when we're dining in private. Not when we're picnicking by the river."

Tremaine loved her. Loved her courage and boldness, loved her compassion for those less fortunate, loved her ferocious desire for him.

"You will marry me by special license," Tremaine said, untying the sash of her night robe, "or you will take pity on a poor, defenseless fiancé and leave my bed."

The sad, lonely, disappointed part of him still expected her to do just that—to tease him to within an inch of his sanity, then flounce off into the night. The rest of him was glad she'd had the presence of mind to lock the door five minutes ago.

"Make love with me, Tremaine. I told Nicholas I'm insisting on a special license so as not to overshadow Della's come-out this spring."

Tremaine paused between untying bow number 884 and yanking open bow number 885. "Do you have another reason for a special license, my lady?"

Nita ran her hand over his hair, the tenor of her caress shifting their discussion from the verbal battledore of mating adults to an exchange between lovers.

"I'm afraid when I wake up tomorrow, I'll find that I dreamed you," she said. "You never visited Belle Maison, or if you did, you rode on your way, having bargained Nicholas's sheep away from him. I'm nobody's fiancée, I'll be nobody's wife. I'm plain, dependable Lady Nita, and always will be."

Tremaine curled down to press his cheek against Nita's, and when he should have confided in her about a small boy with a huge heartache, his orphaned courage dodged behind the prudence of a self-sufficient adult male.

"I'm here, Nita. I'm real, and I'm your fiancé. We will marry whenever you please. The license should be delivered on Monday."

Words were in short supply after that. They undressed each other slowly, between kisses, caresses, smiles, and whispers. Threats alternated with promises until Tremaine was poised over his intended, skin to skin beneath the covers.

"Do you still fear I'm a figment of your dreams, my lady?"

"Part of me will likely always fear that," she said, her fingers laced with his on the pillow. "Somewhere along the way, between my parents' funerals and my brothers' weddings, I lost a part of myself, Tremaine, and you've found it for me."

Nita had lost the courage to hope, and how well Tremaine knew that poverty. Life became a matter of tackling challenges, of focusing always ahead, never behind.

And never inward.

"When shall we be married?" he asked, as he began their intimate joining. "We haven't chosen a property for our own, and that might take some time."

In Nita's arms, Tremaine had chosen all the home he'd ever need, and yet he held off the completion of their union.

"I don't care where we live, Tremaine, provided the place is free of creeping damp and drafts. *Stop negotiating.*" Nita lunged up with her hips and took the initiative from him.

"Tuesday," he rasped as he set up a deliberate rhythm despite the desire rioting through him. "Tuesday morning."

"Early," she whispered, locking her ankles at the small of his back. "Maybe even Monday evening."

They were to be wed within the week, and this was not their first anticipation of those vows. Tremaine should have treated his lady to a leisurely coupling, letting anticipation build, exploring her responses and his own.

Urgency rode him mercilessly, robbed him of finesse, and left him desperate. Nita came apart beneath him, keening softly against his shoulder, shuddering through her pleasure. When her grip on Tremaine's hands slackened and he was sure she was sated, Tremaine gave himself permission to follow her into satisfaction. Pleasures stormed through him, dissolving plans, thoughts, and even most of Tremaine's fears.

But not all. Though it contradicted Tremaine's most passionate desire, at the last instant he lunged back and spilled his seed between their bodies.

∾

"Are you nervous?" Della asked.

"Not about another assembly," Nita replied, slipping a simple gold bracelet that had been her mother's around the wrist of her right evening glove. Tremaine had told her the previous night that a ring would arrive with the special license. "Are *you* nervous?"

Della admired herself in the cheval mirror, though she had to tilt it first, because it had been angled for Nita's height.

"Nervous about another interminable evening country-dancing with the same fellows I've been dancing with since I put up my hair? Swilling the same tepid punch, nibbling the same stale sandwiches?"

Older sister's instinct told Nita that Della was nervous, though not about the assembly.

"London is no different, Della. A lot of boredom punctuated by the occasional passable dancer or clever verbal exchange. You look over the fellows, they look you over. The only differences between a London ballroom and the Haddondale assembly rooms are the quality of the tailoring and the fact that, at some point, you'll be permitted to waltz."

"The only difference," Della said, tossing herself onto Nita's bed, "is that I'll come home this summer more disenchanted than I am now. I understand why you look after all the sick babies and doughty elders, besides the fact that it keeps Mama's memory closer for you."

Nita tugged at her glove beneath the bracelet, because the jewelry had bunched up the leather below her wrist.

"Honor Mama's memory?" she muttered. "By sending Mr. Clackengeld his headache powders and thumping Dora Angelsey's chest?" Mama had never set bones, never courted the vicar's ire with her charity, never read Paracelsus or Galen.

Never tried to revive a baby who'd departed the earthly realm, felt the very heat leaving the infant's body while the mother sobbed uselessly across a cold, barren cottage.

The dratted bracelet had been a bad idea, and now the clasp was caught on the glove.

"You use Mama's recipe for your headache powder," Della said. "Her very recipe in her handwriting. You now ride the horse who used to pull Mama's gig. That's a step in the direction of eccentricity, you know. Atlas is a fine fellow, but he's not saddle stock for a lady."

Atlas was a fine mount for a tall rider. Mama had doted on him and Mama had loved this stupid gold—

"Get this blasted thing off me," Nita said, shoving her wrist under Della's nose. "Atlas was going to waste, and this bracelet is too small for my wrist. You should have it."

Della scrambled to the edge of the bed and took Nita's wrist in her hands. "You're giving me Mama's bracelet? This was her great-grandmama's, Nita. Are you sure?"

Great-Grandmama had been the original healer in Nita's family, a formidable German lady who'd famously advised the present King's governors on his health many decades ago.

The King had fallen quite ill in later years, nonetheless. "The bracelet is yours," Nita said as Della worked the clasp open. "I tend to those Dr. Horton either cannot or will not treat properly. Mama has been gone for years now, and her memory has nothing to do with anything. If you remain lounging on my bed, you'll wrinkle that dress, Della."

Della held up the bracelet like a prize pelt. "I've loved this bracelet," she said, draping the length of gold around her wrist. "It's simple and graceful, and even a debutante can wear it in the evening. Thank you, Nita."

Nita fastened the clasp for Della, on whom the bracelet was elegantly loose. Della remained sitting on the bed, holding up her arm so the bracelet caught the light of a dozen candles.

"I shouldn't wrinkle my dress, my brow, my gloves... You tend to babies so you don't go mad worrying over—heaven spare us!—wrinkles. Silk and velvet will wrinkle, but we wear them because they feel divine, light and warm even when wrinkled. You heal people because it warms your heart in a way having a dress free of wrinkles never will."

Sometimes, caring for the sick warmed Nita's heart, more often it broke her heart.

George stuck his head into Nita's room, rapping his knuckles on her door. "Fifteen minutes, you two. Nicholas says he'll open the dancing with Leah, and he's already pacing the library. Kirsten and Suze are down there tormenting him while Leah makes a final stop in the nursery."

"And Mr. St. Michael?" Nita asked, stealing a glance at her image in the mirror. Even saying his name pleased her and banished some of the upset Della's comment had caused. Nita would soon be Mrs. St. Michael.

Very soon.

"St. Michael's my next stop," George said, "though may I say, you both look delicious and will be the envy of all, save our sisters, who are also very nicely turned out."

George withdrew, and Della bounced off the bed. "George should be married. He's too dear to wander around the Continent pretending he's debauched."

Excellent point. "George is not debauched," Nita said, "but his more unconventional tastes are problematic."

"Byron has the same tastes," Della retorted, "and he didn't depart for the Continent until his creditors took exception to his debts. He married."

"Byron married miserably by all accounts and he is titled." Though Byron was also a father at least twice over. "Shouldn't you be fetching your boots, Della?"

"I'll fetch my boots," Della said, "but you needn't feel guilty just because you and Mr. St. Michael are besotted while George remains lonely."

Della was formidable when hurling insights. Nita folded a shawl over her arm and gave Della a one-armed, possibly even dress-wrinkling, hug.

"You'll make new friends in London," Nita said, recalling all too well the same false platitudes flung at her as she prepared for her come-out. "And you will always be welcome in my home. Mr. St. Michael is in want of family. I think that's one reason he's attracted to me, because I bring a large and loving family to the union."

"A large and loud family," Della said, smiling. "You look lovely, Neets. Mr. St. Michael's regard has brought a sparkle to your eye. I'm envious."

Della was also sweet, as George was sweet. Della's envy was a cheerful gift, laughingly tossed into Nita's lap. "I love you, Della Haddonfield, and I will miss you when I leave this household."

Della hugged her back, the embrace leaving Nita unaccountably melancholy. Della skipped off in search of her boots, and Nita grabbed a beaded reticule from the vanity. She was to be married, the plainest, oldest, least romantic of the Haddonfield sisters, and married to a dear, handsome man of means.

Nita could hardly believe her good fortune, despite Tremaine's assurance that their vows would soon be spoken. He was Nita's lover already, her friend, and her fiancé. That he'd denied himself the pleasure of spending his seed in the conjugal act was an indication of his regard for her, surely.

So why did Nita feel as if Tremaine withheld from his prospective wife not the risk of conception, but rather, a piece of his heart?

She took one last look at herself in the mirror, but Della had tilted it, so Nita's reflection was from the shoulders down. Now that she had the privacy to study her image, she was vaguely disturbed by what she saw.

"I look like Mama." The realization brought no joy. From the neck down Nita looked very much like a gaunt, pale, even spectral version of her departed mother. She turned from the mirror, blew out the candles one by one, and prepared to smile and dance her way through yet another local assembly.

Two violins in close harmony and a wheezy little spinet were small competition for dozens of pairs of dancing feet. The thump and slide of those feet echoed a thumping in Tremaine's temples. Nita, however, was luminous in her blue velvet finery, a smiling, sparkling testament to gracious cheer and graceful movement.

And she was soon to be his.

"The winter assemblies always have a desperate quality to them," Edward Nash observed from Tremaine's side. "One certainly wishes the rooms had more open windows."

Alas, one might be tempted to jump from such a window, though

Tremaine could identify no specific reason for his irritability other than present company.

"Mr. Nash, greetings. Your sister-in-law is a lovely addition to the gathering." Lovely, but when greeting Elsie Nash, Tremaine had sensed that the woman also suffered anxiety over more than her attire, which was several years out of fashion.

No blackened eyes, though. Tremaine had been relieved to note that Elsie Nash was free of injuries. Nita would likely have called Mr. Nash out otherwise.

"Have you and Bellefonte come to an agreement regarding the merinos?" Nash took a gulp of punch that Tremaine had set aside after one cautious sip.

"Business at a social function, Mr. Nash?" Tremaine countered softly. "Surely we should focus on which lovely lady we'll lead out next rather than on a herd of sheep?"

Tremaine had been at pains to ensure the sheep were as good as in Nash's grasping, gloved hands—if that's where Bellefonte wanted them—despite Nita's loathing for Edward Nash. Let him take up bargaining with the earl—or with Lady Susannah.

"Bleating sheep, bleating women," Nash said. "The topics are related. Susannah will see that I have those sheep, I'm sure."

Lady Susannah, for pity's sake. "You're that confident of your suit?"

"The Haddonfield sisters are *de trop*," Nash replied. He probably thought himself sophisticated, but his tone marked him as a petty man. "Bellefonte has an heir in his nursery, and aging aunties are an expense the earl doesn't need. Susannah knows this."

No doubt because Nash subtly reminded her of it. The set was ending, not a moment too soon. Nita curtsied to her partner, some old fellow who'd nearly shot off his own foot the previous summer, if George Haddonfield was to be believed.

"Lady Nita is apparently free for the next dance," Tremaine said. "You'll excuse me if I avail myself of her hand."

"Do I take it you've offered for Nita Haddonfield?"

Nash had spoken loudly enough that in the absence of the sawing fiddles and pounding feet, his question caused heads to turn. His complexion was flushed, and the glass in his hand trembled slightly.

Foxed, and in public, no less. This was what came of socializing with the neighbors.

"If I have offered for Lady Nita," Tremaine said, "and if she has done me the honor of accepting, then Bellefonte will surely announce our engagement soon, won't he? Perhaps the earl's reticence is intended to allow others time to contribute their own good news to the general gaiety."

Tremaine would have strode away on that observation—Lady Susannah was to be pitied her choice of swain—except Nash put a hand on Tremaine's arm.

"You'll not have those sheep, St. Michael. Take to wife whomever you please, but I've made my position on the sheep quite clear."

Tremaine spared a moment's pity for the sheep, who had no choice in the matter. "Best of luck then, in all your ventures."

"You're the one who'll need the luck." Nash's jollity was forced, and every person in the assembly room would have heard him. "If you marry Lady Nita, she'll soon bring every foul disease and noxious ailment to your doorstep. Or will you curtail her nonsense, as Bellefonte should have done when he inherited the title?"

Bellefonte was busily studying his drink four yards away, the countess's hand tucked around his arm rather like a manacle.

Tremaine spoke loudly enough that nobody would mistake his words. No wife of his would suffer the judgment of her inferiors, much less become an object of gossip for having overindulged her charitable impulses.

"Nash, surely you comprehend that if a new husband is conscientious in the prosecution of his duties, the new wife will have no thought for colicky babies or consumptive uncles? Any lady who becomes my *countess* will have many duties, all of them as pleasurable for her as I can make them, and none of them imperiling her welfare."

Tremaine shook free of Nash's clutches and winked at his intended. She no longer needed to tolerate the meddling of such a disgrace, because Tremaine's words were sincere. A husband was entitled to pamper his wife and to be pampered by her.

Also to protect her. He'd made damned sure Nita understood that very point. Nita smiled slightly, then turned to address her brother George. Lady Kirsten appeared at Tremaine's side and aimed a feral smile at him.

"Ask me to dance, Mr. St. Michael. Ask me to dance now."

Apparently, Lady Kirsten wanted a piece of Nash's hide as well. Tremaine bowed over her hand. "My lady, may I have the honor?"

She curtsied, the movement having something about it of a duelist's opening salute. Lady Kirsten danced with an effortless grace few women shared, and yet she wasn't Nita, whom Tremaine would rather be partnering.

"Don't look for her," Lady Kirsten hissed. "Don't smile that indulgent, besotted smile at her. Don't frown at me, or I'll tramp on your idiot foot."

Her expression bore a cordial regard, her eyes promised murder.

The poor dear was probably jealous. In all modesty, Nita was marrying quite well—Tremaine would resume use of his French title if Nita preferred—and Lady Susannah was at least marrying. Lady Kirsten was doubtless suffering the pangs of impending spinsterhood.

"Have I offended, my lady?"

They turned down the room, the floor being considerably less crowded as a result of the choice of dance. Nita twirled by with her brother George, her smile serene.

"You have offended me, indeed," Lady Kirsten murmured. "I wish you the joy of your damned sheep."

A dramatist, then. Every family had one. "Nash is half-seas over, and some banter between the fellows will only cause a little talk. I suggest you aim your criticisms at the good squire, and in Lady Susannah's hearing. Nash is really not worthy of her."

Lady Kirsten's foot came down on Tremaine's, and though she was wearing slippers, she was no delicate flower.

"Nash is a presuming idiot," she said. "We'll find some way to deal with him that doesn't reflect poorly on Susannah. You, however, are a fool."

Tremaine executed the figures of the dance with the skill of any man born with both French and Scottish antecedents, while his mind considered Lady Kirsten's apparent upset. As Nita sashayed around the dance floor, she appeared as gracious and poised as always, chatting with her brother, smiling, and in full possession of her good humor.

Her poise should have reassured Tremaine.

When the music finally came to a close, Tremaine bowed, Lady Kirsten curtsied low, and he led her back to the side of the room. George and Nita joined them as lines formed for another country-dance.

The room was both warm and fragranced with the exertions of the assemblage, despite some merciful soul having cracked open a window.

"Lady Nita, you dance quite well," Tremaine said. The three siblings exchanged a glance, suggesting Tremaine had accused his beloved of having horns and a tail.

"As do you, Mr. St. Michael," Nita replied. "George, perhaps you and Kirsten would be good enough to fetch us a glass of punch?"

George hustled off, dragging Kirsten with him.

"Lady Kirsten took exception to my earlier remarks to Nash," Tremaine said quietly, because wallflowers, dowagers, and gouty old squires were scattered around the room. "I apologize for engaging the fool in repartee, but he was being an idiot."

"I understand."

Uncertainty blended with the single sip of cheap punch in Tremaine's belly. "What do you understand, my lady?"

Her smile was benevolent, her countenance composed. "Edward has visited the punch bowl frequently this evening, and Susannah has ignored him. Some gentlemen deal poorly with having their wishes thwarted."

"Good for Lady Susannah." Tremaine assayed a smile in the direction of his fiancée, but her gaze had returned to the dance floor. His uncertainty acquired a hint of irritation as it occurred to him that Nita had the knack of appearing more composed as she became more distraught.

That recollection cheered him not at all.

How could you?

Nita tapped her toe more or less at random, smiled at whoever glanced her way, and filled her mind with the memory of Annie's dirty nappies, the scent of boiled cabbage, Fordyce's sermons, *anything* to keep from crying.

Tremaine St. Michael expected his wife to sit at home and darn his stockings while children suffered and mothers worried helplessly. The betrayal of his public declaration, the sheer presumption of it, hurt like a dislocated joint.

Worse was the sense of having missed the most important symptoms as she'd examined the patient. Nita had noted Tremaine's pragmatism, his honor, his generosity, and, yes, his gloriously healthy manly physique. She'd been fascinated with his kisses and his passion.

She had utterly ignored what defined him, though: a protective instinct that stretched to distant herds of sheep, his horse, families of hungry children, and cousins in the far-off Highlands.

Such a man was not prepared to tolerate the risks Nita took as a healer.

"Punch," George said, bearing two cups and a brilliant smile. Kirsten had taken herself off, thank goodness, though pity the fellow with whom she next danced.

"Lady Nita." Tremaine passed Nita a glass, though the last thing

Nita wanted was to add tepid, sickly sweet punch to the upset roiling in her belly.

"My thanks." She touched the cup to her lips without imbibing, and Tremaine appeared to do the same. Just as he'd appeared to be everything her heart desired.

"Elsie Nash was asking for you, Nita," George said softly. "She's frantic about something, unless I miss my guess."

Tremaine winged his arm, Nita pretended not to see it.

"I won't be long." She passed George her cup and hurried away, grateful for an excuse to leave Tremaine's side. He did not comprehend the hurt he'd done her, and that only made the situation worse.

"Lady Nita, good evening." Elsie's smile was brittle, though she was prettily attired in a gown of emerald green. "Are you enjoying the gathering?"

No, Nita was not, and she'd probably never enjoy an assembly again. "Elsie, what's wrong?"

"Edward would not let me send for you, but Digby is quite ill. Horton will bleed him, and even Penny didn't favor bleeding a child. I thought if you could stop by—"

Elsie paused to smile at the vicar, who tottered past with his missus, dancing being a sure cure for gout, of course.

"You want me to leave the assembly?" Nita was in no mood to deal with an ailing child, but she was happy to leave the gathering, even to once again sneak up the back stairs at Stonebridge. Anything to get free of this place.

"You can return before anybody knows you've left." Elsie waggled her fingers at Della, who looked far too sophisticated as she turned through the figures of the dance. "Edward insists the boy make the trek to the vicarage daily, despite the weather, despite Digby's cough growing worse. I fear for my son, or I wouldn't ask."

Behind Elsie's fine manners lurked a mother at the breaking point, the same breaking point Addy Chalmers had danced along for years.

Damn Edward Nash, damn all the hale, healthy men who thought their needs trumped anybody else's.

"Avoid the punch," Nita said, "and if somebody asks, I sought a moment of fresh air to clear my head. Tell Kirsten to dance with Edward, and then let Della and Leah have a go at him."

"Thank you, my lady. If there's ever anything I can do to repay you, you have only to ask."

Nita returned to George's side, and that meant once again facing Tremaine. He was painfully attractive in his evening attire, and he danced beautifully. His smile was indulgent and sweet.

Nita longed to be Mrs. Tremaine St. Michael, but did Tremaine honestly believe choosing wallpaper for his formal parlor was more important than a small boy's life?

"George, I need a moment of your time," Nita said.

"Mr. St. Michael, you'll excuse us?"

The special, just-for-you smile faltered. "Are you well, my lady?"

"I enjoy excellent health, thank you." Despite tired feet, an aching heart, a throbbing head, and a crushing bewilderment, Nita yet enjoyed excellent health.

Offer to come with me. Please, offer to come with me, and I'll hold out hope that we can reconcile our differences. Except that since becoming engaged to her, Tremaine's public behavior had been punctiliously proper.

"I'll await your return, then." He bowed smartly and Nita had no choice but to lead George from the room.

"What in the hell are you doing, Nita Haddonfield?" George asked as he held her cloak for her. "Your absence will be remarked, and Elsie Nash was near tears when she accosted me."

"I'm near tears too, George, but nobody will remark my absence as long as Mr. St. Michael is standing up with the wallflowers. Take me to Stonebridge, please."

George cursed colorfully—he was a Haddonfield, through and through—then shrugged into his greatcoat.

"It's the boy, isn't it? He's worsened, and Nash has denied him medical care."

Nita wrapped a scarf around her neck. "If Edward has denied Digby the tender ministrations of Dr. Horton, then we may hold out hope of the child's eventual recovery."

If only Nita could be as sanguine about her own marital prospects.

CHAPTER FIFTEEN

"Dance with me, Mrs. Nash?" George held out a hand to Elsie, willing her to accept his invitation. Before dropping George back at the assembly rooms, Nita had tasked him to convey news to a worried mother, and George would not fail either woman.

Elsie didn't immediately take his hand, though George did not withdraw his offer. "You don't want to be seen dancing with me, Elsie. Dance with me anyway. I promise I'll not inflict any unwanted kisses on you."

He'd surprised her—also himself. She placed the tips of her gloved fingers on his palm.

"I'd be honored, Mr. Haddonfield." Then, as George led her out onto the dance floor, she added softly, "It isn't what you think."

The orchestra lumbered through the triple meter introduction to the evening's second and final waltz.

"What do I think?" George *thought* Elsie was too sweet to live in fear of Edward Nash's next bout of temper, too good to endure the situation she'd been thrust into.

"You think a few wild oats on your part would give me a permanent dislike of a man I've known to be nothing but honorable," Elsie said softly. "You're very wrong. Edward's petty tyranny is all that limits my association with you."

The music began and George moved off with Elsie in his arms. She was smaller than his sisters, more easily led, and entirely feminine.

His goddamned idiot cock took note of that last, his personal sexual weather vane, cheerfully aligning itself with any available breeze. He'd sowed acres of wild oats in places both predictable and unlikely, and had little harvest to show for it.

"Digby is flirting with lung fever," George said. "Nita isn't worried, but she mixed up mustard plasters for his chest, ordered willow bark tea to keep the fever down, and beef tea to ease his throat. I've had a word with Vicar. Edward will receive a note tomorrow canceling Digby's lessons for the week because of Vicar's gout."

The choir fund was five pounds richer for Digby's holiday, affirming once again that Vicar's view of Christian charity did not match George's.

"Thank you," Elsie said. "Please thank Lady Nita for me as well. If I lose Digby, you should fear for Edward's life."

They twirled around the room, not with the vigorous pace of the London ballrooms, but in a slower, more lilting tempo suited to ending an evening. George resisted the urge to tuck his partner closer, because Edward was regarding them owlishly from his post by the men's punch bowl.

"I know what desperation feels like, Elsie, and you cannot give in to despair. You are all Digby has, all that stands between him and Edward's worst impulses. Digby needs you, and you aren't without friends. Call on me before you do anything rash, and I'll not fail you."

Those words were rash. George had some personal wealth, but where Elsie and Digby were concerned, he had no authority.

"You must not involve yourself," Elsie said. "Edward would take it amiss. I thank you for the dance, Mr. Haddonfield."

The music came to a final cadence. George bowed, Elsie curtsied, and he had no damned choice but to escort the lady to Edward Nash's side. Nicholas rescued George from having to make small talk with a man who deserved to be horsewhipped.

"George, our ladies are pleading fatigue," Nicholas said. "Unless you want to walk home, I suggest you accompany me to the livery. Nash, your sister-in-law looks somewhat fatigued as well."

Nicholas beamed at Elsie. Charming the ladies came as easily to Nick as dancing did to George.

"Perhaps we might offer Mrs. Nash a ride home," George said. "We brought both the carriage and the sleigh, didn't we?"

George had brought the sleigh, there being no room in the carriage, and by now the sleigh had returned from taking Nita home to Belle Maison.

"We do have two conveyances," Nicholas replied. "Come along, Mrs. Nash. My countess has missed your company, and your brother-in-law is likely joining the gentlemen removing to the common for a final pint or two."

Well done, Nicholas.

Nash's scowl vanished like hoarfrost before the rising sun. "A pint or two? Don't mind if I do," he said. "Dancing works up a man's thirst. Elsie, you'll accept his lordship's hospitality. Bellefonte, Mr. Haddonfield, I bid you good evening."

Nash sauntered off a bit unsteadily, while George offered his arm to Elsie. "Come along, madam. I'll take you home in the sleigh, and you'll be spared his lordship's dubious attempts at flirtation."

"I take offense at that," Nick said. "Holy matrimony has only honed a natural talent where my flirtations are concerned. Ask my countess, if you don't believe me."

Nick was on his good behavior because the ladies were present. Doubtless George would get a verbal birching for abetting Nita's early departure.

"Where did Mr. St. Michael get off to?" Elsie asked.

"He declared a need to walk back to Belle Maison," Nick said.

"Something about inferior spirits and a salubrious dose of fresh air. I'd expect a former Scottish shepherd boy to have a harder head, though I well understand an appreciation for fresh air."

"Mrs. Nash and I are away to the livery," George said, parting from Nicholas at the cloakroom, where various Haddonfield females were sorting capes, scarves, boots, and muffs. Susannah in particular looked ready to leave.

When George reached the street, Elsie walked along beside him, not hurrying him as a sister might have, but as if she genuinely enjoyed his company.

"Will you soon be traveling again, Mr. Haddonfield?"

"Might you call me George?" And, yes, he was soon to depart for Germany, of all the cold and distant places, and from thence to Poland and possibly Russia.

"If I call you George now, I might slip when Edward's underfoot. He claims you're an unwholesome fellow who ought not to be allowed onto the Stonebridge premises."

"Unless, of course, my escort will free Edward for additional pints of grog. I may be unwholesome on occasion, but I'd never strike a woman. How do you stand him, Elsie?"

A light snow fell, muffling the merriment coming from above the inn and lending the fading ring of sleigh bells and coach harnesses a fairy-tale quality.

"I hate Edward, if you must know," Elsie said. "He has squandered Penny's funds. He's Digby's guardian though, so I've nowhere else to go. I was honestly hoping Lady Susannah's settlements would put Edward's finances to rights, even if that will do nothing to restore Digby's funds."

Elsie was hanging on then, out of sheer determination, and that realization tore at George.

"I could kill him for you," George said. "I'm heading off to the Continent this spring. I could simply depart ahead of schedule."

He was only half joking.

"I've considered poisoning him," Elsie said, and she wasn't even one-quarter joking. They rounded the corner of the livery, and abruptly the noise and bustle of the assembly's end was behind them. "Sometimes, I think I'm in a nightmare that will have no end. I have a little money I've hidden from Edward, and I think about running away with Digby, taking ship even, but Edward has the law on his side. At least now, I share a roof with my son."

George didn't think, he simply took Elsie in his arms. "You are a good mother, Elsie Nash, and I have funds enough to see you safely to Italy or even America. No child should grow up in fear for his health, his future squandered by an uncle with too few scruples and too much pride."

Worse yet, the varlet was too free with his fists, which also boded ill for Digby's future.

Elsie leaned against George, as if for one moment she let him have all of her weariness and fear, all of her anger and despair. To hold her felt good, though holding her wasn't nearly as much comfort as she deserved.

And then she kissed him.

George's mind manufactured a single thought—kissing Elsie felt good too—before he began kissing her back.

When last Tremaine had been intimate with his intended, she'd chided him for not pursuing her to her room, for inflicting on her an occasion of *cold feet*. Tremaine's feet were cold, his nose was an icicle affixed to the front of his face, his ears were no warmer, and his toes were nodding cordially to frostbite.

He trudged on, as he'd trudged through many early Highland storms, past the sagging fences of Stonebridge, past Belle Maison's sheep pastures. In another mile, he'd warm up, and the temptation to walk right past the Belle Maison drive dogged his steps.

Nita had disappeared on George's arm and not returned, suggesting she'd gone off on one of her medical calls. Elsie Nash's boy, most likely.

Something contagious, because winter was contagion's social season.

The Haddonfield carriage team trotted past, though Tremaine doubted the inhabitants had seen him. They'd be tucked up in their cloaks and mufflers, dissecting who had made sheep's eyes at whom, and whether certain couples were quarreling.

Tremaine considered the matter for a frigid half mile and concluded that, just perhaps, he and Nita were quarreling. Something he'd said in his exchange with Nash hadn't set well with her ladyship.

Perhaps he ought to have officially acknowledged their engagement rather than danced around it? Surely an announcement was Bellefonte's to make?

Perhaps Nash deserved a more pointed scolding? Tremaine had certainly wanted to scold Nash more soundly. Thirty paces at dawn would convey Tremaine's sentiments handily.

He was still debating what he would have or should have done differently when he let himself into Lady Nita's room. They were to be married in a very few days, and knocking seemed a bit silly.

Also perilous, because a fellow who knocked was a fellow who could be told to go away.

"Good evening, my lady." God help him, Nita's hair was unbound, a shimmering river of golden fire streaming over her shoulders as she sat before the hearth, one bare foot up on a hassock, the other tucked beneath her.

"Greetings. You didn't think to take off your coat?" Nita wore her blue brocade night robe while Tremaine—foolish of him—still wore his greatcoat, scarf, and gloves.

"I needed assurances that you are well," Tremaine said, unraveling the scarf from his neck. "You left with George, and he returned without you. I was concerned."

Worried, angry, sick with an orphaned boy's unreasonable fear for her welfare.

"I'm sorry. As you can see, I'm yet in excellent health."

Excellent health. Tremaine loathed that phrase. Unless he missed his guess, Nita was in an excellent temper—or something. He stuffed his gloves into his pocket and hung his greatcoat on one of the bedposts.

"What are you reading?" he asked, taking the poker to the fire, then adding more coals.

"Paracelsus in the original Latin."

Tremaine had hated Latin, though it had made learning Italian and Spanish easier. After grafting Scots and Gaelic, then English onto his French, Latin had been the outside of too much.

"What does Paracelsus have to say?" As long as Nita wasn't telling Tremaine to leave, he'd continue to cast lures. A cheering thought befell him: perhaps her monthly had arrived midway through the assembly. That would explain much, despite protestations of excellent health.

"He says that washing surgical instruments between each use results in fewer cases of infection and fewer deaths from infection. He said this hundreds of years ago, and yet English medicine still fails to heed his wisdom."

The sooner Nita gave up her medical pastime, the happier their pillow talk would be.

"Somebody should tell that to the army surgeons," Tremaine said, taking a seat on Nita's hassock. "Those who die on the battlefields are often envied by those who are wounded."

"I have written to Wellington's personal surgeon," Nita said, drawing her second foot under her. "He did not favor me with a reply."

Smart fellow, or Nita would have bombarded him with learned correspondence. Of course, if the smart fellow had paid attention to Nita, fewer lives would be lost in the hospital tents.

That thought did not sit at all well. "How's the lad?" Tremaine asked, gently untucking a slender female foot from under the lady's fundament.

"Digby? How did you guess?"

"I was once a lad too, and winter was not my favorite season to mind the sheep. Your feet are not cold tonight."

Tremaine needed to touch some part of Nita, because despite her dishabille, she was once again the remote, polite woman he'd first met in a chilly stable at this same hour days ago.

"Digby's circumstances are poor," Nita said. "Edward might wish the boy dead."

While half the shire probably wished Edward would find his eternal reward. "Nash is an idiot, but surely even Nash wouldn't wish harm to a mere boy?"

Tremaine's mother had turned her back on two mere boys, though for the first time, he admitted that in so doing, she'd assured those boys physical safety and a childhood in the care of a loving, if gruff, relative.

"Edward would not admit even to himself a wish to harm Digby," Nita said, "but the Nash men have always been competitive with each other. Penny Nash married and produced a son while his brothers did not or have not. Why are you here, Tremaine?"

He was there to make love with his intended, to assure himself that all was well between them. He kissed Nita's ankle, which bore a slight scent of honeysuckle.

"I wanted to waltz with you this evening, but your sister dissuaded me. Did you want our engagement announced after all?"

"No. Shall you come to bed, Tremaine?"

Nita regarded her foot, cradled in his hands. Her brows were knitted, her expression puzzled, as if symptoms would not add up to a diagnosis.

Being married to Nita Haddonfield would involve work, though unraveling the mysteries of her moods and mental processes was work Tremaine would enjoy. She was a challenge—his challenge.

"Let's to bed," he said, rising and extending his hand to her. "We must talk about the ideal home in which to raise our family."

Tremaine was no expert on women, but such a topic ought to catch Nita's interest. She rose from her perch and went to the vanity, then sat and began plaiting her hair.

"I gather you anticipate getting many offspring with me?" she asked, whipping her hair into three skeins.

Tremaine unknotted his cravat and undid his sleeve buttons. "God willing, it shall be my privilege to give you babies, my lady. I'm not particular about the gender either. A French title is a business convenience, not who I am, so don't you dare think our daughters will matter less than our sons."

Nita winced, as if she'd found a knot among her tresses. "Very democratic of you."

Tremaine sat on the bed to get after his boots, which by rights ought to have been left in the kitchen for a good oiling.

"Very paternal of me. I'm also of the Continental opinion a woman ought to nurse her own children, though I'll accede to your wishes in this regard."

Nita turned on her dressing stool. "Did you know the Duchess of Kent refused to use a wet nurse for her little Princess Alexandrina?"

Finally, a spark of interest.

"And you approve, suggesting we've found an area of parental agreement even before we're wed. Did you enjoy the assembly?"

Nita turned back to face her vanity. "One endures the assemblies, for the most part."

Such was Nita Haddonfield's lack of guile that she hadn't accounted for Tremaine being able to read her expression in the vanity's mirror. Something or someone had upset her badly.

Tremaine pulled his shirt over his head, peeled out of his breeches, and stalked up behind her.

He took the ribbon from her fingers and lashed it around the tail of her braid. "You are tired, and in need of cosseting, my lady. Come to bed and pick out names with me. I'm told people in our situation are entitled to silly behavior."

Also lusty behavior, which, according to every shepherd Tremaine had shared a fire with, could cure all manner of megrims and melancholia.

Nita rose when Tremaine would have begun that cosseting with a gentle hug.

"I'll get the candles if you'll bank the fire," she said, starting with a branch on her mantel. One by one she blew out each flame, the shadows in the room gradually converging into darkness.

Tremaine locked the door, scooped coals into the warmer, banked the fire, and ran the warmer over the sheets. He hoped—a dangerous undertaking, hoping—this was the start of a routine they'd share for the next five decades, but Nita's mood was off, and he still had no idea why.

Maybe that was also part of married life?

Nita unbelted her robe, then drew her nightgown over her head. For a procession of instants, Tremaine beheld his intended by the flickering light of the fading fire. Long, graceful limbs, pale skin, rosy breasts, full hips gently curving into a feminine waist, a thatch of reddish gold curls at the juncture of her thighs.

"I am marrying a beautiful woman." Inside and out, beautiful in her heart, in her body, in her restless, vigorous mind.

"While you are handsome," Nita said, climbing onto the mattress, "and deserving of some cosseting yourself. Have your tups continued to recover?"

Tremaine joined her under the covers and she cuddled up along his side, a quietly perfect moment.

"I heard from my man today, and, yes, every one of them is up and about, swilling water like a sailor at his grog and gobbling up all the grass hay we leave out for them." This time next year, those lads would all be anticipating their first lambs, and perhaps Tremaine would be too. "Kiss me, Nita Haddonfield. Will you like becoming Nita St. Michael?"

Nita kissed him, a slow, nearly reverent tasting that fueled the desire simmering whenever Tremaine thought of his lady.

"We'll not get much cuddling done if you keep that up," he muttered, arranging himself over her and kissing her back. "Though I suppose we can always cuddle later."

We cannot always cuddle later.

Nita ran her hands over the elegant musculature of Tremaine's shoulders and back, smoothed her fingers over his fundament, and tried not to cry.

She refused to marry a man who dismissed her ability to heal others. Tremaine of all people ought to understand that a meaningful life involved doing what needed to be done, not simply what one was pleased to do.

He was protective of others. Nita admired that about him, admired so much about him, but he would not allow her to be protective too.

"Make love with me, Tremaine."

He'd once granted her a boon, to be redeemed at the time and place of her choosing. Nita seized this moment, knowing Tremaine might despise her for her selfishness come morning. She was being greedy and probably stupid, but she'd have decades to regret this impulse and to treasure the memory of her foolishness.

Tremaine was a gifted kisser, but at Nita's words, he moved lower, applying his mouth to her breast.

"I can't think when you do that," she whispered, cradling him closer. "I can't—"

He desisted, and she would have yanked him back to his post, but the sensation of his tongue tracing her ribs skittered along paths already illuminated by desire. His next destination exceeded even what Nita had imagined a man could do with his mouth.

"Do you like this?" he asked, nuzzling her low on her belly. "You taste of flowers even here, you know. Meadow flowers"—he took a wet, slow swipe at her sex—"and lavender"—another swipe, while Nita clutched at the pillows with both fists—"and a hint of honeysuckle."

A hint of madness, as if Tremaine were trying to change Nita's mind with pleasures dark and dear.

"Tremaine, you needn't—"

"Hush, love." His mouth affixed to a part of her person Nita could name only in Italian. God in heaven, no wonder Nicholas and Leah were stupid with desire and affection for each other.

That was Nita's last coherent thought before Tremaine drove her through ecstasies undreamed of even in her anatomically enlightened imagination. Fireworks of pleasure lit her up from within, sensation upon sensation followed by emotions without names in any language she knew.

When Tremaine had finished working his mischief, he pillowed his cheek on Nita's breast.

"Have I pleased you, my lady?"

He'd shocked her with the intimacy and generosity of his attentions. "You've undone me, in so many ways. I hadn't known... One overhears one's brothers being crude, but—"

Tremaine traced a finger over Nita's lips. "There's more, you know. You can put your mouth on me, use your hands on me. You can ride me, we can mate like sheep, on our knees. I expect this is the purpose of the wedding journey, to see all the sights and wonders lurking between the sheets while the great capitals and royal courts are thoroughly ignored."

Oh, Nita would miss him. Miss his dry humor, his lusty male body, his everything.

"Will you make love with me now, Tremaine? As a man makes love with a woman?" As a husband makes love with his wife?

"You need not ask, you know," he said. "The two shall become as one flesh, and that means I'm yours for the having. I grow aroused simply watching you braid your hair."

He was aroused now. Nita could feel him, hard, warm, and unapologetic against her hip. More than physical pleasure, more than an erotic education, what he gave Nita now was a form of marital trust she did not deserve.

"I'm asking, Tremaine. Make love with me."

The wrongness of what Nita demanded blended with the arousal simmering through her to create a combustible mixture of longing and heartbreak. When Tremaine joined their bodies with one slow, deep thrust, Nita came apart again, more intensely than before.

"You just missed Copenhagen," he teased, subsiding to a slow, rocking rhythm. "Next, we can love our way through Paris and on to Bonn. I do love you, you know. Very much."

Nita would miss him for the rest of her life. "Enough chatter or we'll miss Berlin."

"Can't miss Berlin, Geneva, or Rome..."

Tremaine loved Nita until she'd lost every part of her heart, and most of her wits, until she was sore and aching and an entirely different woman from the lady who'd thought to snatch a memory from a soon-to- be-former lover.

"Tremaine, please. Now."

He understood. He hitched himself over Nita as she pressed her face to his shoulder and endured pleasure that had acquired an edge of hurt exactly fitted to the emotions wracking her.

"Hold me," Tremaine rasped. "Never let go, not ever."

He spoke not only as a lover, but also as a man who'd trusted Nita with his heart. When he spent his seed this time, Nita felt the warmth of it deep inside, and she held him as if she'd never let him go.

Dawn came late in winter, but hunger could wake a man when sunshine was in short supply. Tremaine remained curled around his beloved, sated in ways that had nothing to do with food and everything to do with a special license.

"You're awake," Nita murmured, rolling over. "Shall you go?"

Did she want him to go? The door was locked, the maids and footmen not yet stirring.

Tremaine rearranged himself, so his arm was around Nita's shoulders and the glorious warm length of her tucked against his side.

"We never did decide what sort of house we're to raise all those children in, my lady. Or shall I call you *comtesse?*" After the night they'd shared, Tremaine was at risk for referring to his intended as lovey, lambie, and even lambie-love. "While you ponder your answer, I'll tend to the fire."

The room was chilly, but nothing like the shepherd's huts Tremaine had known as a boy. Glorified windbreaks with a chimney, most of them, the better to lose the fire's warmth to the howling night air.

Nita watched him stir the ashes, toss on some kindling and then a few coals. Despite the chill, Tremaine hadn't bothered with clothing, it being a wife's privilege to admire her spouse's unclad form as much as she pleased.

And a husband's privilege to be admired, though Nita's gaze held anxiety.

"Shall I love you again?" Tremaine asked, rejoining her under the covers. "Whisk you past the pleasures of Athens?"

Nita bundled up next to him. "You shall not. I'm in need of at least three soaking baths. I doubt you're in much better condition."

Tremaine was in excellent condition, though a bit sore. "I can be a gentle lover, you know."

Nita turned her face to his shoulder, as if he'd offered not a tease but a taunt.

"Nita, was I too rough? Be honest."

She bit him gently. "You were nearly perfect. You even taste good."

Tremaine heard the *nearly*, and unease prowled past a morning's normal complement of desire.

"We never did talk about a house, my lady." Again, that lure did not seem to catch Nita's fancy.

She tucked a leg across Tremaine's thighs and brushed a thumb over his nipple.

"Very well, we shall talk about this house you're so fascinated with."

Nita should be fascinated with the dwelling she'd make her own, any woman should be. Tremaine caught her hand in his and kissed her knuckles.

"I prefer comfort to fashion," he said, "though the two can be found together. I have an extensive collection of art and sculpture, which can go in a gallery rather than a family wing. I also favor spotless kitchens and a comfortable servants' parlor. As hard as they work, the staff should at least have a cozy place to take their tea."

Nita twitched, a peculiar hitch of her shoulders. "All fine priorities in a family home, but for me, the herbal is the most important room. I like the herbal near the laundry, so I have fresh water. An herbal must also be ventilated and have excellent light. I need enough space that I can have visitors there too, and I need shelves to store recipes and references. I'm very particular about my herbal."

Unease grew inside Tremaine, because his prospective wife hadn't mentioned her nursery or her private parlor.

"Why would you need room for people to visit you in your herbal, Nita? You'll have formal parlors, informal parlors, and very likely your own personal sitting room."

Not to be confused with the sitting room they'd share, adjacent to their bedroom.

She rolled to her back, her gaze on the blank expanse of ceiling above them. "Tremaine, when people seek my healing abilities, they are seldom comfortable doing so in a parlor. Particularly if I'm to examine them, the herbal serves better."

"What are you saying?" An old-fashioned lady of the manor

might tend her own family, even her own servants, but not friends or strangers from outside the household. Even servants were more properly the responsibility of the housekeeper than the lady.

"I danced with Harrison Goodenough at last night's assembly, Tremaine."

"The name means nothing." Panic started flinging fears at Tremaine's composure: Did Nita's intended mean nothing to her?

"He's getting on, but last summer, he had a mishap with his gun and shot himself in the foot."

That one. "Then he's a fool, and a lucky fool."

"He was nearly a dead fool. Dr. Horton wanted to amputate the foot, though the bullet had only grazed the side of it. A great mess and a nasty wound, but no damage to the bones. I saved that foot. I saved a man's ability to walk unassisted across his own acres, to dance with a woman less than half his age. I very likely saved his life."

Tremaine's imagination saw fluttering handkerchiefs, but he kept his tone agreeable.

"You're proud of that, rightly so, my lady. What does that bit of poulticing and stitching have to do with our household?"

Nita sat up, taking away her warmth and about half of Tremaine's patience. They'd had a wonderful night, and now she was off on some female flight that made no sense.

"Croup can kill a newborn," she said. "They're not even supposed to have croup, but Addy Chalmers lives in straitened circumstances, and Evan has ever been sickly. Had I not responded when Mary sought my aid, wee Annie could be dead."

Inside Tremaine, something did die. He didn't give it a name, but it was a close relative of hope and healing, the very gifts Nita spread before any who sought them from her.

"You are telling me that even when we marry, even when our own children fill our nursery, you will continue to tend any and all who have need of you." Tremaine had called upon negotiating skills to offer that summary, upon the ability to restate in the clearest terms an opponent's position, usually before he annihilated that position.

Nita left off studying the small blaze lighting the hearth and turned to regard Tremaine. Her braid was ratty, her shoulders bare, and her eyes shadowed with sleep.

"I have a gift, Tremaine St. Michael. I can save lives. I can reduce and eliminate suffering. I've worked hard to acquire these skills, and planning your dinner parties or picking out wallpaper for your nursery is not more important than wee Annie's life. Addy is at the end of her tether. Losing one more child will see the others on the parish and Addy in a pauper's grave. I can't have that on my conscience."

Tremaine climbed out of the bed, barely keeping his voice below a shout. "Has it occurred to you that *you* are perhaps the reason Evan remains in poor health?"

His question was desperate, but Nita's life was arguably in the balance along with Tremaine's sanity and most of his honor.

How had he not seen this? How had he not realized that Nita's sense of responsibility had defined her for too long to be eclipsed by a recent attraction to a mere husband?

"I haven't treated Evan," she said, drawing the covers up under her arms.

"You treated Digby Nash, and he's ill. Then you lark into the Chalmers household, dispensing sweetness, light, and very likely contagion."

Tremaine's reasoning was cruel, *also entirely valid.*

"I take precautions," Nita said, reaching for the blue robe draped across the foot of the bed. She couldn't grab that robe and keep the covers under her chin, so Tremaine tossed it to her.

"You cannot take precautions in a cottage that lacks washing water and strong soap," he said, yanking his shirt over his head. "You cannot take precautions against the foul miasmas you breathe in. You cannot ever take precautions that will render you as safe as you'd be if you resigned your post as ministering angel to all in need."

"I cannot and will not let children die when I can help, Tremaine. I cannot allow women to suffer a complaint of the privy parts because they're too ashamed to seek Horton's dubious counsel. Where is your Christian charity?"

Tremaine jerked on his breeches. "Where is your sense? I don't begrudge any woman the assistance of a midwife, and I don't object to your brewing tisanes or mixing powders to ease suffering, but is wee Evan's runny nose more important than the lives of your own children? I warned you I would not willingly allow my wife to risk her safety, and every sickroom you visit is a battleground, Nita Haddonfield."

Why hadn't he seen this issue for the tragedy it was? Nita Haddonfield would likely go on for years saving the lives of neighbors who neither paid her nor respected her for her skill, until one of them afflicted her with an illness even her formidable constitution couldn't survive.

"I have no children of my own," she said, "and it appears that will always be the case."

"That is largely your decision." Tremaine wanted to snatch up his boots and stomp out of the room, but Nita's stubbornness was only a small part on her own behalf. "I don't fault your kindness, my lady, but I cannot abide the notion that you repeatedly put yourself and your loved ones at risk merely for the asking. *You risk your life*, Nita, for anybody who asks it of you. I offer you happiness and a husband's rightful protection, and you disdain my suit."

This was the real tragedy. That Nita Haddonfield would die unnecessarily soon of consumption, lung fever, or putrid sore throat. The world—and Tremaine and any children she might have—needed her alive.

"I never foresaw that I might marry," Nita wailed softly. "Matrimony wasn't in my plans."

Tremaine took a seat beside her on the bed, heart breaking, pride in tatters. "Nor in mine. Who will tend you when you fall ill? Dr. Horton?"

Nita apparently hadn't foreseen this eventuality either, and Tremaine nearly howled with frustration. A heart this pure and determined was a danger to itself, and yet Nita would not allow him to protect her.

"My sisters will look after me." A desperate hope, based on her uncertain tone.

"They'll have husbands and children of their own," Tremaine said, looping an arm around Nita's shoulders. "I cannot change your mind, can I?"

Because to change Nita's mind would mean he'd changed her heart, and behind all the poise and practicality, Nita Haddonfield was cursed with a tender, generous heart.

Which Tremaine treasured. A man who seized opportunities when more cautious souls hesitated was also a fellow who occasionally blundered badly.

"Can you provide my neighbors with good health?" Nita asked, her head on his shoulder. "Can you make Horton wash his instruments when he doesn't even bother to wash his hands? We do not know exactly what causes disease, but Horton cheerfully attributes illness to moral lapses, and suffering to moral atonement. He's a medical barbarian, and all they have."

Truly, Nita faced a formidable enemy, as did Tremaine. "Are you rejecting my offer of marriage, Nita Haddonfield?"

"Are you rejecting my calling as a healer, Tremaine St. Michael?"

Was he? Tremaine stroked a hand down the frayed golden rope of her braid and tried to find an answer that was at least honest.

"I am in want of courage, Nita Haddonfield. As a small boy, I watched the lady who meant everything to me sail away, never to return. Every time you visit a patient suffering from contagious illness, you take that same risk. I lack the fortitude to send you on such voyages at any hour of the day or night, particularly when I know your journeys might bring death home to your own children."

Or to her husband, though Tremaine wasn't worried about that fool.

Nita leaned against him more heavily. "You ask an impossible choice of me."

"The situation we face is not impossible," Tremaine said, "but simply sad." Very sad, and while a part of him wanted to argue and rail and do violence to the breakables, another part of him noticed what the small boy had not wanted to admit:

The lady was in tears as she made her choice— bitter, heartrending tears.

CHAPTER SIXTEEN

Nick regarded his guest, soon to be his brother-in-law. "You're up early considering half the unmarried women in the shire were chasing you about the dance floor last night."

"May we take our meal to the library?" St. Michael asked, though his breakfast consisted of two pieces of buttered toast.

Nick picked up a plate of eggs, toast, and ham. "By all means. My sisters will soon wander in, and no battle has ever been dissected as thoroughly as they can dissect a country assembly over their morning tea."

St. Michael was a handsome rascal, but he was a tired handsome rascal. Some of the starch had been danced out of him, or perhaps the rotten punch had served him ill. They trundled along quiet corridors into the warmth of the library, putting Nick in mind of their first meeting, only days ago.

St. Michael took a seat opposite Nick's desk while Nick occupied the same chair his late father had used behind the desk.

"Do we have a reason for hiding from the women, other than sheer male cowardice?" Nick asked around a mouthful of eggs.

"Well, no, actually. I'll be leaving later today, assuming the weather cooperates. Lady Nita has declined my offer of marriage."

St. Michael munched at his toast as if he'd reported a slight dip in the value of some shares he held on the Exchange.

"You are related to me by marriage, St. Michael, and I mostly like you," Nick said. "If you've broken my sister's heart, you had nonetheless best have your affairs in order. Nita's besotted with you—my own countess has confirmed my opinion on the matter."

Leah usually confirmed Nick's opinions, except when he was dead wrong on an issue of importance, and Nita's engagement was of utmost importance.

"I am besotted with her as well," St. Michael said in that same pass-the-butter tone of voice, "though you do the lady no favors if you bring that up in her hearing. She has stated terms I cannot accept, so I'm leaving the field. You will not chastise her, you will not bully her, you will barely notice my absence, Bellefonte, or *your* affairs had best be in order."

The earldom was seven kinds of a mess, but Nick's marriage was in order and that was what mattered most. St. Michael stared at his toast as if he'd no idea how it had arrived in his hand.

Nita truly had turned down the poor sod, and St. Michael hadn't seen that coming.

"Nita adores you, St. Michael, and she is not a woman prone to adoration. What happened?"

A simple question shifted the discussion from a tense negotiation to a session of shared male bewilderment. St. Michael returned his toast to its plate and helped himself to a ginger biscuit from the crock on the desk.

"I didn't pay attention to what matters," he said. "I know better. I paid attention to Nita's sweet smiles, brandished my own version of same, made a few ringing pronouncements about guarding my wife's welfare, and congratulated myself on being a shrewd, bold, lucky fellow. But the devil's in the details, right? Except a woman's passion is not a detail."

Nick nudged the biscuit crock closer to his guest. "I am Oxford educated and a belted earl. If you speak slowly and use small words, this time you might make sense." A biscuit went down to defeat at the hands of St. Michael's limited vocabulary.

"Lady Nita's passion is healing," he said, dusting his palms. "I thought I was her passion, or marriage to me and a family of her own. I was wrong."

Those last three words were painful to hear.

Nick crunched a strip of bacon into oblivion. "I'm frequently wrong. One survives the indignity somehow. Have another biscuit."

St. Michael took the lid off the crock and peered at the contents. "I thought it reasonable to expect that a mother would keep her children safe from illness—and herself too, of course."

Nick quite agreed, but he was Nita's older brother and the head of her family. Nita had scoffed at his pretensions to authority for years.

"Maybe a marriage needs to be built on more than reason?" Nick pushed his plate away and took a biscuit.

"Duty, certainly, should play a role," St. Michael replied. "I tend to my business because I'll not follow in my father's footsteps, living off my ancestors' wealth and a rank I did nothing to gain. A man must guard his honor as he sees fit, and for me that means commercial industry."

Nick silently admitted to having been wrong himself: Tremaine St. Michael was not greedy, not amassing coin for the power it afforded him. He worked because it was all he knew to do, just as Nita needed her bilious spinsters and teething babies to give her life meaning.

"I'm sorry, St. Michael. My door will always be open to you. Women have been known to change their minds."

Though not Nita Haddonfield. She was a female monument to dearly held convictions, and her stubbornness alone had probably routed death more than once.

"I don't know how to convey this without inspiring you to

violence," St. Michael said, "but your sister might find herself forced to wed me."

No wonder the miserable blighter looked as if he'd had too much punch.

"Nita is a Haddonfield, and allowances must be made," Nick said. "I have reason to believe—"

"If you say I was not her first, I shall kill you, Bellefonte. Nita's decisions are not subject to your judgment." St. Michael broke a biscuit in half and offered Nick the larger portion, which, being a prudent older brother and a belted earl—also a man who'd known heartbreak—Nick accepted.

"I have reason to believe," Nick went on, "Nita has tisanes and potions that will prevent any untoward consequences of your visit here."

St. Michael's expression went from fierce to stricken, and his half of the biscuit hit the desk, leaving crumbs all about.

"Am I to thank you for that disclosure, Bellefonte?"

Nick swept the crumbs into his palm and deposited them in the dustbin. "I suppose not. What will you do?"

What was Nick to do with the sheep he'd intended to provide St. Michael as a wedding gift? Bloody beasts were eating a prodigious amount of good hay, and old Difty Kinser said a record crop of lambs was on the way.

"I will travel on," St. Michael said, getting to his feet. "George passed along some useful information regarding German hostelries, and I've connections with most of the Pumpernickel Courts." St. Michael spoke as if he were planning the funeral of a loved one.

"Shall I send George with you?" Though the weather was again threatening a reprise of winter when spring really ought to be nudging winter aside.

St. Michael put the lid back on the biscuit crock. "No, you shall not. Mr. George Haddonfield has all the earmarks of a fine shepherd and man of business. You will transfer the sheep to Mr. Edward Nash in anticipation of his offer for Lady Susannah. First, however, you will put the fear of a sound thrashing in Nash should his temper threaten to turn violent."

Nick took a bite of cold, buttered toast. "Are you daft? I don't want Susannah marrying that buffoon. If I had any doubt of it, the way he went swimming in the punch bowl last night confirms that he's not a suitable *parti*. I cannot stop Susannah from accepting his suit, but if I withhold the sheep, I won't hasten her doom either."

St. Michael ran a hand through neatly combed dark hair.

"Bellefonte, please attend me. I will be leaving shortly and I'm in no mood to humor earls with poor hearing. You will transfer the sheep to Nash, today if possible, whether Lady Susannah marries the fool or not, because Elsie Nash and her boy are trapped in that household."

Trapped. On the way home from the assembly, Leah had described Elsie's situation with the same word.

"My men of business made Nash a delicately worded, conditional, and lucrative offer for those sheep through the post yesterday afternoon," St. Michael said. "A paragraph buried in the convoluted text requires that Nash turn over guardianship of the boy, Digby, to you or the guardian of your choice. Nash will sell me the sheep at a significant profit to him. I'll transfer them to your brother George in exchange for his willingness to serve as my factor in France from time to time. If you need funds for the boy, I'll provide them."

The toast went down reluctantly. "Why will you provide Nash the funds he needs to put Stonebridge to rights?"

"Lady Susannah is Nita's sister. If Susannah is not happy, Nita cannot be happy, and many men drink to excess only when their fortunes sink. With Lady Susannah's help, coin in hand, and you and George to keep an eye on matters, Nash's worst tendencies can be curbed, particularly if the boy and his mother are not a financial drain. It's a compromise, my lord, as many bargains must be. Lady Susannah deserves better, but a gentleman does not argue with a lady."

Did Nita realize the caliber of man she was rejecting? "That is a significant investment based on hope, St. Michael."

"On prediction, your lordship. I'm no longer in the business of hoping."

St. Michael's scheme bore a hint of intrigue, and yet Nick couldn't find a flaw with it. "You'll be out considerable coin, and George might not want the sheep."

"You underestimate your brother, my lord. He's nobody's fool, not afraid of hard work, and he listens more than he talks. He also loves his sisters as dearly as you do, and his good qualities are far more numerous than his few trivial shortcomings. Rent him pasture if you must, but if he has sense, he'll soon have his own establishment."

Nick took a swallow of tea to ease the lump in his throat caused by cold toast, but the tea had grown cold too.

"I underestimated you, St. Michael," Nick said. "Nita will regret refusing your suit, and when she does, I hope your affections are not otherwise engaged. One question, though. You have land in France and probably relatives there too. Why hire George to oversee those holdings?"

St. Michael stalked off in the direction of the door. "Because I am sick to death of travel, and the time has come to put my memories of France behind me. You will offer my farewells to your countess and your siblings."

Then he was gone, leaving Nick with a sister to console—and lecture.

~

"I have means," George said. "A great-aunt on my mother's side decided that because I was neither heir nor spare, nor handsome by-blow, I ought to have a start in life. I also have some luck with investments. You and Digby would want for nothing."

The Stonebridge kitchen was warm because the morning's bread had just come out of the oven. The fresh-baked fragrance competed with the stink of tallow though, a scent George associated with student lodgings and cheap inns. If he didn't propose to Elsie here, though, sitting with her at the kitchen table, he'd likely never have another opportunity.

"Digby was resting quietly when you brought me home," Elsie said, "and if it weren't for him..."

Some of George's proposal was because of the boy, but not all. By no means all.

"Elsie, I'm the son of an earl. Nicholas will support my request to become Digby's guardian if we're married. Edward will not quibble at allowing me to assume the boy's expenses, and in a few years, Digby will be off to public school in any case."

The weak light filtering through the windows showed the fatigue around Elsie's eyes, but also the beauty of her features. She was small and weary, and yet she had lovely eyes, an elegant profile, and a mouth—

That mouth had the power to wake a man up, to reveal to him choices he could make, paths he could choose.

"You pity me," Elsie said, "and yet I'm tempted anyway, George Haddonfield. Digby likes you, and you'd be a wonderful father."

George took her hand, a hand that shouldn't have calluses. "I will make you a wonderful husband, Elsie, or give it my best try."

"I should not have kissed you."

That's all they'd done—kiss, albeit with startling passion—and on the short drive to Stonebridge, they'd snuggled under the lap robes necessary when traveling by sleigh, as any couple might have snuggled.

"Why shouldn't you have kissed me?"

Her expression said his question surprised her, but George was in earnest, and a Haddonfield bent on an objective was not deterred by a little resistance.

"You will think me wanton," she said, "and then Edward's low opinion of me will be justified."

"You are no more wanton than I am." George kept his voice

down, because the Stonebridge household was not yet awake. He'd ridden over before first light and was intent on bringing good news home with him.

"You're a man—" Elsie began, as if the entire species need not fret over anybody's good opinion.

"I am a man, one who has found himself occasionally attracted to members of his own gender. I probably will in the future as well, but here's what matters, Elsie Nash: I like you exceedingly and I'm attracted to you. You're tolerant, kind, fair-minded, and a devoted mother. My regard for a passing handsome or even pretty face is eclipsed by the loyalty those characteristics inspire."

He hoped.

George's hope was based on several solid realities. First, his involvement with men had never gone beyond the casual or the physical. Men were a lot of bother, in George's experience, full of strut and blather, every bit as capable of drama as the blushing debutantes filling any ballroom.

Second, his regard for Elsie included a fat dose of physical attraction, and finer emotions as well. He respected her, he enjoyed her company, he *liked* her.

He liked her a lot, always had.

Third, there was the boy. Digby needed a father, somebody to stand between him and Edward Nash. George could hardly be that father if he spent his evenings larking about London, bored, randy, and causing his family worry.

Elsie got up and used the bunched fabric of her apron to protect her hands as she turned the cooling loaves of bread out of their pans. Steam rose from the turned loaves, one, two, three. She watched the steam as if it held the mystery of eternal happiness.

"I'll want more children, George. If you can't—that is—Digby needs brothers and sisters. When I'm gone, I don't want him to be alone. So if you seek a white marriage, then, much as it pains me, I'll have to decline."

George was on his feet, arms around her, before she got out

another word.

"Hush. I'm as able to give you children as the next man, Elsie Nash. You're dear and desirable, and provided you find some similar attributes about my humble self, we'll manage splendidly."

She felt right in his arms, sweet, good, and precious.

"I won't be demanding. I won't nag, George. I promise.

The daft woman was giving him permission to stray. "I'll be demanding," George said. "I'll demand of myself the same faithfulness and loyalty I expect from you, Elsie. I'll demand that my vows are spoken in earnest, not empty words. I'll demand that you and Digby never want for anything and never fear for your well-being. Should anything happen to me, my family will provide a home for you both."

Of that, George was certain. By the end of the day, Nicholas and their sisters would be certain of it too.

Elsie laid her head on his shoulder. "Then yes, a thousand times yes. I will gladly marry you, George Haddonfield. The sooner the better."

George imprinted the moment on his memory: Elsie in his arms, the kitchen quiet and fragrant with fresh bread, weak winter light coming through the window, and peace and joy flooding his soul.

"When does Edward rise?" George asked. "I'll speak to him today, unless you'd rather I wait." As a widow, Elsie could remarry where she pleased, though George would observe the courtesies for her sake, provided those courtesies didn't take too long.

"Edward didn't come home last night," Elsie said. "He occasionally over-imbibes and spends the night at the inn. He comes home in a foul temper the next morning, having drunk too much and gambled too deeply."

"He'll not trouble you with his moods once he knows we're engaged," George said. "I'll retrieve him from the inn and improve his mood before he arrives home."

Elsie eased from George's embrace. "Be careful, George. Edward's foul moods can turn violent."

"I know how to be careful, Elsie. Start packing. We'll be married within a fortnight."

When she ought to have beamed a smile at George worthy of a prospective bride, Elsie walked him to the back hallway and took down his greatcoat.

"We're not married yet, George. Don't turn your back on Edward. My heart would break if he hurt you."

"Edward Nash has indulged his last violent mood." George whipped his scarf around his neck and kissed his intended once more for luck.

Before Elsie allowed George to make good on his pronounce-ment, she grasped the ends of his scarf and kissed him right back.

"I wanted to take my leave of you in private," Nita said, though most of her didn't want to take any leave of Tremaine at all.

She could no longer read his expressions, or perhaps she no longer merited much emotion from him. He cut an elegant figure in his riding attire, though riding boots were next to no protection from the elements.

"I hadn't thought to trouble you with farewells," he said, crossing his bedroom to close the door behind her.

"You didn't sleep well."

And Tremaine hadn't locked the door. He could still read Nita, apparently, because he drew her into his arms. His generosity was more than Nita could endure.

"Tremaine, I'm sorry. I never meant to mislead you." Tears welled, when Nita had been certain she'd never cry again. Her head throbbed, her eyes were scratchy, and her voice sounded as if she'd overindulged at the men's punch bowl.

"I wanted to be misled," he said. "Maybe you did too."

Badly, badly, Nita had wanted to be misled, also loved and accepted. "I should not have—"

"Made love with me last night? Perhaps not. I'll have a lifetime to puzzle out your motivations, won't I?"

The small sting of his words was nearly welcome, because Nita's motivations had been foolish and selfish. Desperate. Would she ever stop feeling desperate?

"Maybe we wouldn't have children," Nita said miserably, though no method of preventing conception was foolproof, except the one she'd failed to use.

"We'd have children, God willing. Many children, and even if we weren't so blessed, there's you, my dear. I will pray nightly for your continued good health."

Tremaine's hand on Nita's hair was a benediction and a torment, a final tender caress and reminder of all Nita was casting aside. She'd wracked her brain for a compromise, for a way through their dilemma.

Wee Annie, gasping for every breath, choked the life out of Nita's hope. Mr. Horst, his cough finally quiet, closed the lid of its coffin. Mary Eckhardt, coming through another winter of successive ailments, put flowers on the grave.

Tremaine's mother, choosing death instead of watching her sons grow to manhood, sang the final dirge.

"I'll keep you in my prayers as well," Nita said, though she couldn't step back, couldn't move away from the warmth and comfort of Tremaine's arms. Even when a knock sounded on the door, she stayed in his embrace.

"Nita, I'd give you my handkerchief," Nicholas said, hovering by the doorway, "but I'll need it myself. Lovey, please stay with Nita while I see St. Michael on his way."

Still, Tremaine made no move to step back, and Nita realized he was leaving the final instant of their parting up to her. Not exactly a kindness, maybe more of a closing argument.

They belonged together, and wee Annie deserved a chance in life too. Both were true.

Nita stepped back, snatching at the handkerchief Tremaine held out to her, a white flag of surrender that bore his initials and his scent.

"Fare well, my lady," he said, making the words both a parting and an admonition. "If you ever have need of me—"

"Good-bye," Nita said, kissing him, though Nick and Leah were both in the room.

She stayed where she was, back to the door as Tremaine walked out of her life. When his footsteps had faded, she crossed to his bed, unbelted her dressing gown, and climbed under covers that still bore his scent.

"I shall cry now," Nita said, because Leah had offered not a single word. "I shall go completely to pieces, and sob and scream, and wail, and carry on. I will put Mrs. Siddons to shame with my self-indulgent dramatics. You'd best leave. I've just sent away the only man I'll ever love, and he is too g-good to hate me for it."

Leah settled at the head of the bed. "I'll leave if you want me to, but as for that other, all the tears and self-indulgence, I say you're past due. You've soldiered on long enough, Nita Haddonfield, and heartbreak is one tragedy a lady should not have to deal with alone."

Leah wrapped her arms around Nita, which only made the tears come faster.

"I was hoping to have a word with George before I left." Tremaine had also been hoping for a miracle, a brilliant insight that would allow him to renew his offer of marriage to the only woman he'd ever love.

For Nita's very stubbornness and selflessness, Tremaine loved her, even as he wanted to pen her into a luxuriously appointed stone keep, where disease and a charitable heart couldn't lay her low.

"I was hoping you'd marry my sister," Bellefonte said as they crossed the chilly garden. "George is probably still sleeping off the effects of truly bad punch. Looks like we'll get more snow this afternoon."

The sky was indeed adding its melancholic contribution to a day Tremaine wanted behind him.

"I'll be in London by midafternoon, then the weather can do whatever it pleases."

Except bad weather meant Digby Nash's lung fever might get worse, and Nita would be at greater risk of illness herself.

"Are we in a footrace, St. Michael?"

"I'm trying to outrun a broken heart." Where in the bloody hell had that come from?

"You'll lose," Bellefonte said with the merciless certainty of experience. "You can't outrun a broken heart, can't out-think it, can't out-drink it, or out-swive it. If it's any consolation, I don't blame you for putting Nita's welfare above that of the parish poor. Nita never visits the nursery at Belle Maison. That arrangement works for an auntie, but not for a mother."

Nita avoided the nursery in part because she would not expose the Bellefonte heir to contagion, but also because she'd thought never to have children of her own.

"God damn you and your attempts to cheer me up, Bellefonte."

"Anger doesn't work either," Bellefonte said pleasantly, "not for long. George's horse is gone."

They'd reached the relative warmth of the stables, and indeed, George's handsome gelding was not in its stall.

"Perhaps your brother has gone to check on the sheep," Tremaine suggested, though nothing about this day would go as planned. "Mr. Kinser was nipping from a sizable flask at last night's assembly."

"We were all nipping from sizable flasks once we'd got a taste of that devil's brew in the punch bowl."

Edward Nash had been nearly facedown in the punch bowl, like a hog at his slops, while Nita had been risking her health, tending to a boy whom Nash—

"Promise me you'll keep Nash on a short rein," Tremaine said. "Make him beg Lady Susannah for her hand, preferably in public, on his knees. Make him promise her that he'll fill the library with the books of her choosing."

"Excellent idea," Bellefonte said as William was led out. Two sacks were draped over his withers, probably Nita's doing. "I wish you weren't leaving, St. Michael. I could learn from you. That bit with the sheep was brilliant—also generous."

"One-third of the proceeds of the sale of the sheep funds are to be deposited in a trust for the boy. You and George are the trustees." Tremaine hadn't intended to disclose that either. "Nash might be under the mistaken impression the offer he received for the sheep was from his great-uncle, the newly remarried baronet, whose title Digby is unlikely to inherit."

"*Newly remarried?*"

Bellefonte was entirely too trusting, but then, many good men were. "To the lovely Miss Pamela Sandeen," Tremaine said, "late of Hagerton Crossing, Derbyshire. Her father's in trade, her mother's people are bankers, and one hears things."

Bellefonte eyed the lowering sky. "Let me guess: She made her bow only last year and comes from a family legendarily prone to producing male offspring?"

"The baronet's bride is from a family of fourteen, twelve of them boys. Her come-out was two years ago," Tremaine said, repeating the contents of the report delivered to the Queen's Harebell by messenger. "Nash's prospects linger mostly in his mind. The present baronet allowed his lady a year's engagement, though by all accounts the couple is shamelessly affectionate."

"Maybe I'm not so reluctant to see you get on your horse," Bellefonte said slowly. "I assume you researched my situation thoroughly before enjoying my hospitality."

Yes, Tremaine had, and Lady Della's come-out weighed heavily on the earl's mind. "Not thoroughly enough, my lord."

When Tremaine extended a hand to Bellefonte, he was yanked into a sturdy male embrace, thumped stoutly between his shoulder blades, then shoved in the direction of the mounting block.

"Godspeed, St. Michael."

Tremaine climbed into a bloody cold saddle, saluted with his crop, and turned his horse in the direction of Town. As he trotted past the sheep pastures, he noted two places where the stone walls were giving way to the heave of ground alternately frozen and thawed. The sheep would spot those weaknesses any day, and then Lucky's mother and her friends would go on a grass-drunk tour of the neighborhood.

A drunk of any kind had pathetic appeal. Tremaine reached the village on that thought, and saw George Haddonfield's horse tied outside the inn. The familiar call of business sounded in the part of Tremaine's mind that hadn't the decency to be felled by grief.

He prided himself on snatching commercial opportunity where it arose, no matter how inconvenient or awkward, and George Haddonfield would make an excellent factor both in England and abroad.

Though look where snatching opportunity had landed Tremaine with Nita.

Business be damned. Tremaine could solicit George's assistance by letter. He urged William on past the green, but the horse balked.

"If you tarry here in Haddondale, you'll only have that much more foul weather to deal with later in the day," Tremaine informed his horse.

William moved forward at a grudging shuffle.

"You want a go at the horse trough," Tremaine reasoned. Particularly in winter, watering a horse frequently was part of good care, and William was owed excellent care. Tremaine turned the gelding toward the Queen's Harebell, a crackling in the pocket of his greatcoat catching his attention.

"Bother this entire day," he said, swinging down before the inn.

A responsible man did not neglect his horse. Then too, Tremaine and George should talk, no matter how badly Tremaine wanted to put distance between himself and a certain dear, stubborn former fiancée.

CHAPTER SEVENTEEN

George surveyed the inn's common, disappointment blighting his good spirits. He wanted to buy somebody—anybody, everybody—a celebratory drink, but the only creature stirring was a bleary-eyed maid.

"Is Bartlow about?" George asked her.

"In the back, making coffee," she said, bobbing a curtsy. "He'll have a sore head though, so you'd best not shout." She scurried off toward the kitchen, while George hung his greatcoat on a peg and stepped around behind the bar.

"Mornin', Master George," Bartlow said, emerging from the kitchen with a towel over his shoulder. "What can I do for ye?"

He was a good-sized wheat-blond fellow with a full complement of the publican's good cheer, usually, but this morning Bartlow was moving slowly and speaking softly.

"I'm in search of Edward Nash," George said. "Where do you keep your cinnamon, Bartlow? I mean to stand Mr. Nash to a toddy or two."

The fixings were at hand, all but for the spices.

Bartlow took up a stool while George stirred together enough spirits for two drinks.

"You don't want to be disturbin' Mr. Nash, Master George. He'll have a powerful head, and him not so kindly when in such a state."

"Shall I make you a toddy as well?" George asked, because he was in charity with the world, which was surely a harbinger of a happy marriage.

"Aye. That'd be a mercy."

Tremaine St. Michael strode into the common, his expression suggesting sore heads were in ample supply throughout the shire.

"Mr. Haddonfield, have you found employment at this fine establishment?" St. Michael asked.

St. Michael was soon to be family, so George poured more spirits. "I'm here to fetch Edward Nash back to the comfort of his own hearth. Bartlow, get him down here and tell him I'm brewing his breakfast. St. Michael, you'll join us?"

St. Michael had a rather grand beak of a nose, which he wrinkled. "I'd like a word with you first, though if Nash bestirs himself, I suppose my manners are up to the challenge."

George's sentiments toward Nash were of the same variety, though because Nash would also be family, George kept mixing.

"What brings you out on this fine and frosty morning?" George asked St. Michael.

"Business, you might say. You need spices, if you're attempting to brew a toddy, and before I forget, tell Kinser he'll want to mend his pasture walls sooner rather than later."

"You tell him," George said. "Unless I miss my guess, you'll be underfoot for the next fifty years or so." George bellowed for the maid to bring him the spices, and to hell with anybody trying to sleep off their excesses upstairs.

St. Michael slouched onto the bench in the snug. "Your guess regarding my future whereabouts would be in error, Mr. Haddonfield."

"Forty years then, because Nita will wear you out." The maid brought the spices, then disappeared back into the kitchen. Elsie probably had the same ability to move silently, for which Edward Nash ought to answer.

George heated his mixture over the coals in the common's enormous hearth, poured two drinks, and joined St. Michael in the snug.

"Congratulate me, St. Michael. I'm to be married."

St. Michael put two documents on the table. One was foolscap with a list of some sort written upon it, the other was an official document, complete with a dangling seal.

"Felicitations on your impending nuptials, Mr. Haddonfield. Condole me, however, for I'm *not* to be married. You see before you a special license that, alas, Lady Nita has declined to put to its intended use. I'll keep that one, as a memento. This other paper is a list of properties in the area I thought might suit your sister. Perhaps you and your bride will take up residence in one of them."

"Bloody benighted perdition," George said, sliding a drink before his companion. "I'm sorry. Did Nita cry off?"

St. Michael took a dainty sniff of his toddy, as if it were whisky. "We would not have suited. You and Mrs. Nash have my best wishes, and I would like to discuss a business matter with you when you're recovered from your nuptial joy."

"Are you truly that coldhearted? We would not suit, best wishes?" And how did St. Michael know to whom George had proposed?

St. Michael had yet to sip his drink when Edward Nash came thumping down the stairs in the middle of a silence just about to turn awkward.

"What in the sodding hell requires that I rise at an indecent hour at your request, Mr. Haddonfield? And what's *he* doing here?" Nash asked, blinking at St. Michael.

St. Michael rose. "I'm leaving. Mr. Haddonfield, you may expect further correspondence from me on the subject of serving as my factor in France. Mr. Nash, good day."

"It ain't a good day," Nash said, swiping the drink George had intended for St. Michael. He drank about half the toddy before pausing. "Nita sent you packing, then?"

"Lady Nita, to you," George said, in unison with St. Michael.

"She's not anything to you though, is she, St. Michael?" Nash asked with nasty glee.

George could smell the man's breath from two yards away—rot and ruin blended with poor personal hygiene—which meant St. Michael was getting a blast as well.

"Her ladyship will always have my utmost esteem," St. Michael said, abruptly sounding significantly more Scottish. "I suggest you guard your tongue, Mr. Nash."

George had heard that cordial, nearly pleasant tone before, in various gentleman's clubs, when the hour had grown late and masculine honor was fueled by an excess of spirits.

"Don't mourn Lady Nita's rejection too deeply," Nash said. "My brother Norton said her virginal passions compared unfavorably with Addy Chalmers's fledgling sorties into sin."

Before George could act, St. Michael had snatched the drink from Nash and dashed the contents in the idiot's face.

"Take back those words, sir, on behalf of both women."

"I must agree, Nash," George said, rising. "Though your ungentlemanly observation explains why the oldest Chalmers girl looks so familiar."

A muscle leaped along St. Michael's jaw.

Bartlow stood halfway down the stairs, and the scullery maid scuttled out from the kitchen, turned around, and scuttled right back the way she'd come. On the stairs, four bleary-eyed fellows held perfectly still.

"It's the damned truth," Nash said, swiping at his dripping chin with a wrinkled handkerchief. "Nita Haddonfield is a cold fish, poking her nose where it doesn't belong, basket of medicinals over her arm, while she puts on airs like some angel of mercy when she's spread her legs—"

St. Michael clipped Nash on the jaw, a mere tap compared to

what he could probably do, and compared to what George wanted to do.

"Apologize for that intemperate speech," St. Michael said. "Admit the mistake of your words, the lingering influence of last night's drink, and apologize. When your own household has benefitted from Lady Nita's generosity and expertise, you are the last who should be allowed to malign her. The lady has rejected my suit, but I have not abdicated the honor of protecting her good name. Apologize, Nash. *Now.*"

Nash cocked back his fist with all the finesse of a first former and swung at St. Michael's jaw, then further impugned his gentlemanly credentials by shaking his limp fingers as if he'd plowed them into a stone wall.

"I'll meet you," Nash cried, "you jumped-up excuse for a Scottish sheep farmer. I'll meet you and we'll see whose apology is in order. Nita Haddonfield has long been a plague on this shire. She has no care for a woman's proper place, hasn't an inkling of proper medical science, and the sooner she's—"

St. Michael set aside the tankard from which Nash had been drinking. "As you wish, Nash. Lady Nita has borne the censure and indifferent thanks of her neighbors for too long. *Your disrespect of her ends now.* Name your seconds."

Bartlow lowered himself to sit on the steps. The other guests silently exchanged money.

While George tucked the list of properties into his pocket and passed St. Michael the special license.

Nita's throat hurt, her head hurt, her eyes hurt. She sat at the kitchen table sipping a posset that helped with those various pains, but nothing would assuage the ache in her heart.

"I should be drinking pennyroyal tea," Nita informed a marmalade pantry mouser. "The idea makes me bilious."

She took another sip of her posset, then another. This was why men got drunk, because it hurt too much to remain sober. Nita would never chastise Mr. Clackengeld for his excesses again.

She was about to drain the contents of her mug when a gust of cold air heralded a commotion at the back door. The cat leaped onto the table and glowered in the direction of the noise.

"Don't touch my drink," Nita said, rising—a bit unsteadily. The boot boy had opened the door, though he apparently didn't know what to make of Addy Chalmers.

"Addy, is Annie well?" Maybe the drink was to blame, but Nita could not find the resolve to don her gloves and cape and slog through a chilly morning to tend the child.

Please, not today. Though she would. Of course she would.

"Annie is fine, but, Lady Nita, I was at the livery, mucking stalls because Mr. Clackengeld is the worse for drink this morning. I knew he would be, and yet the horses must be tended, mustn't they? The lads were talking, and they'd heard it from Bartlow's scullery maid when she brought in the eggs."

Addy was agitated. A mother with a child at the breast shouldn't be agitated.

"What did she hear?" Nita asked.

"Your Mr. St. Michael has been called out by Edward Nash. They're to fight a duel, pistols, and George is Mr. St. Michael's second."

Nita sagged against the wall between her sisters' everyday cloaks, hung in age order on pegs. A hanging ham dangled by her shoulder, and her posset abruptly provided anything but comfort.

"A duel?" Nita whispered. "Why, in the name of all that's sensible—?"

That Tremaine St. Michael—shrewd, calculating, brilliant, and dear—would go off to face death, and over what? Some rash words? A stupid exchange between stubborn men?

Nita would have been enraged, but the idea that Tremaine could *die* kept her pinned to the wall, knees abruptly threatening to refuse their usual office. Death had no honor. A man who woke up hale and hearty could repose in a coffin by nightfall. Tremaine was daft if he thought he alone could cheat death.

Daft and endlessly, hopelessly dear.

"Men can be stupidity itself when they get to flinging their honor about," Addy said. "You should sit down, Lady Nita. You look a mite peaked."

"Excellent suggestion, but I cannot seem to move." Or breathe, or think. *Tremaine could die.* A quick end if he took a shot to the heart. A terrible, lingering death if the wound festered in a limb, and the worst death of all if the bullet hit his belly.

Nita had not absorbed the grief of Tremaine leaving her future, and now this most awful, non- negotiable, permanent...and he'd apparently chosen this path *willingly*.

"You!" Addy snapped at the boot boy. "Fetch the countess, or my lady's sisters, and be quick about it. Mind the earl doesn't see you."

"A duel." A funeral, more like. Nita could adjust to a world without Edward Nash in it, but she could not fathom that Tremaine might have Edward's blood on his hands. Far better to let intemperance end Edward Nash some months hence, or bad fish— anything that posed no risk to Tremaine St. Michael's continued well-being.

"Come, my lady," Addy said, taking Nita by the arm. They steered around hams, cloaks, boots, braided onions, and the marmalade cat to return Nita to the worktable.

"Why pistols?" Nita wailed softly. "Gunshot wounds bleed like the devil and can so easily kill a man. They get infected, they disfig- ure. I hate gunshot wounds." Nita hated all wounds, come to that, wounds to the heart most of all. "I believe I'm tipsy."

"I'm the last who'd judge you for that," Addy said. "Norton Nash told me that guns are preferred to swords so the duel is more quickly over, and because guns allow the duelists to delope. Everybody fires into the air, honor's avenged, and the gentlemen can get back to their clubs and cards."

"Norton Nash told you that?" The scoundrel with the cowlick, may he rest in peace, whom Nita was relieved not to have married.

Addy swung the teakettle over the coals. "Norton liked to talk almost as much as he liked to engage in other activities. We were to be married, but because he'd bought his colors, he said we should keep our engagement quiet. You'll not tell anybody?"

Nothing made any sense. "Why wouldn't I tell Nicholas, who will hold Edward accountable for Norton's bad behavior? Nicholas cannot engage in duels because Leah would kill him and he's the magistrate. Mary is a Nash, isn't she?"

With the same bright red hair Norton had been so vain about—no cowlick, though.

"Would you turn your bastard daughter over to Edward Nash's tender mercy? I considered approaching Penny Nash, but didn't because he might well have left the matter in Edward's hands. I'm sorry—I know you were sweet on Norton too."

Half the shire had apparently been *sweet on Norton*, though what did that matter when Tremaine was facing death?

"Addy, good day." The countess came down the kitchen stairs, followed by Susannah, Kirsten, and Della. Leah's greeting held a question, because Addy would no more presume on Belle Maison's hospitality than she'd open the dancing at an assembly.

"Edward has called Tremaine out," Nita said. "Tremaine could die in the next hour, and I'm about to be sick."

"No wind," George said. "That's a good thing."

The lack of wind was a matter of indifference to Tremaine. "What's *he* doing here?"

Here was a clearing in the Belle Maison home wood, one apparently denuded of deadfall and brush by the enterprising Chalmers lads. Patches of snow alternated with bracken and bare, frozen ground.

"Horton is the only physician in the neighborhood," George said, "and you've agreed to face a fellow over a pair of loaded pistols. When you're through dispatching Nash, you might consider shooting me. Nicholas is the magistrate and takes a dim view of ritual murder because it upsets his countess."

Other people had woes and worries. Tremaine recalled that as he passed his coat to George. The cold air would wake Nash up, which struck Tremaine as fair, if loaded pistols were involved.

"What would the lovely Mrs. Nash have to say about your demise?" Tremaine asked, passing George two gold sleeve buttons and rolling back a cuff.

"As long as you kill Edward first, Digby will inherit Stonebridge, so Elsie would manage. I'd like to survive until my wedding night though."

"I thought as much," Tremaine said. "Will Bellefonte truly be upset with you?"

George draped Tremaine's coat over William's saddle. "He'll be upset that he couldn't be here and must instead bide at home with the womenfolk, pretending he's not worried to death about you. Nash is not accounted any kind of shot."

"He's no kind of man," Tremaine said, "though I won't be his executioner. Did you know his youngest brother had taken liberties with your sister?"

A man facing death lost his tenuous grip on the niceties of polite conversation. Then too, George was apparently a friend willing to waive those niceties. Across the clearing, Nash was bouncing around as if boxing with an imaginary sparring partner.

"Norton Nash was a handsome charmer," George said, "but he's a dead handsome charmer. Nita never said a word, though Addy Chalmers's situation bears consideration. Addy was a decent girl until she turned up with child shortly after Norton joined up."

"And we're told life in the country is boring," Tremaine said.

He was not afraid to die. Every shepherd stranded in the high pastures in the midst of an early winter storm came to terms with death. A businessman impersonating a Frenchman on a Continent wracked by war attended to the same reconciliation.

But Tremaine St. Michael did not want to die. He did not want Nita burdened with his death, and he did not want to give up hope that somehow, he and Nita might come to terms.

"I'll see if your opponent is done impersonating Gentleman Jackson after a few pints too many," George said, clapping Tremaine on the shoulder and crossing the clearing.

Tremaine had no patience with the aristocratic lunacy of "the field of honor." Life was precious, and he'd no more blow Edward Nash's brains out over a few stupid words than he'd drive his sheep into the sea.

And yet, Lady Nita Haddonfield's good name could not go undefended any longer. Her brothers were bewildered by her, her sisters fretted for her, but none of them defended the honor of the only woman Tremaine knew who battled death with no thought for herself. Horton's criticisms, the vicar's snide sermons, Nash's sneering condescension were unacceptable.

Ingrates, the lot of them.

Nash's heir might be dying of lung fever but for Nita Haddonfield, her courage, her generosity, and her command of medical science.

As George conferred with Nash's seconds—he had two who apparently knew little about the entire undertaking, because they'd had to consult Dr. Horton frequently—Tremaine was smacked by an insight.

He was risking death because of a stupid slur to Nita's good name. When Nita risked death, *she at least did so in the name of restoring some helpless soul to good health.*

Though Nash would delope. The bad shots always deloped rather than expose their lack of skill.

"Gentlemen, take your places," George said.

Tremaine went to the middle of the clearing and turned his back to his opponent. When Nash took his place, Tremaine could smell rank sweat and ranker spirits, and the entire undertaking acquired a pathetic quality.

Tremaine might want to shoot the scoundrel, but Nita wouldn't appreciate that.

As the count slowly progressed, Tremaine paced along, sorrow and sweetness walking with him. He might never kiss Nita Haddon-field again—"five"—never hold her again—"seven"—never argue with her again—"ten"—never see her smile again.

Sorrows, all of them.

But he had kissed her—"twelve"—held her—"fourteen"—argued with her, and beheld her many smiles—"sixteen." God willing—

On the count of eighteen, a pistol shot rang through the clearing, and a burning pain cut through Tremaine's right calf.

Incredulity leaped along with physical agony. Nash—bedamned, idiot scoundrel and general disgrace—had ruined an excellent riding boot.

And fired early.

"Foul!" George cried. "Mr. Nash, you've fired before the end of the count. Mr. St. Michael, you may take your shot."

Fire, Tremaine would, though turning around was a rubbishing uncomfortable undertaking with a boot full of hot coals. He raised his arm, straightened it—the gun shook not at all, while Nash was wetting himself—then cocked an elbow and fired aloft.

As the second shot rang out, George dashed to Tremaine's side and got an arm around his waist.

"I've never seen such poor marksmanship or such bad form. We can have Nash arrested, you know. Nicholas will oblige."

"Why is Horton coming over here?"

"Because you've been shot, old boy," George said gently as he helped Tremaine to the edge of the clearing. "You're leaving a bril-liant little trail of blood in the snow, and that can't be an encouraging sign."

Horton bustled up, a black bag clutched in his hand. "Cut that boot off him, Mr. Haddonfield. My scalpel will do the job."

He produced a thin knife from his bag, a rusty stain along its blade.

"And then you'll use that knife on me?" Tremaine asked.

"The blade is sharp," Horton retorted, "and you're not in a position to be choosy, sir. Damned lot of nonsense, if you ask me."

Nita Haddonfield's good name was not a damned lot of nonsense. Blood created a sticky warmth inside Tremaine's boot, his calf was on fire, and George Haddonfield was all that held him up.

"Doctor, your services will not be needed," Tremaine said. "My thanks for your time."

"St. Michael, don't be an idiot," George hissed. "You're losing blood. A bullet could be poisoning your leg as we speak. I can't carry you back to Belle Maison."

"William can carry me," Tremaine said, though his own voice sounded far away and very like his grandfather's. "The question is, will Lady Nita treat me if I survive the journey?"

~

"Two shots," Leah murmured as she paced her private parlor. "They couldn't even take their stupidity out of hearing of the house?"

"Sounds travel in cold air," Kirsten said. "Nita, are you feeling better?"

"I'm not as queasy." Nita was not *better*. Those pistol shots only confirmed that two grown men with far better things to do had aimed deadly weapons at each other.

"If Edward survives, I will cut him directly in the churchyard," Susannah said. *Titus Andronicus* lay open on her lap. "I'll be sure the entire village is watching, and Vicar too."

"Vicar has already taken me into dislike," Nita said. "No need for you to get into his bad graces too."

"We can start our own congregation," Addy suggested. "Women who refuse to let Vicar's opinion of them rob them entirely of faith."

"Hear, hear." Della raised the teapot as if it were her personal drinking horn. "At least the duel is over. Those shots came from the direction of the home wood. Shall we send Nicholas to investigate?"

"I'll go," Nita said, rising. "If a duel has been fought over me, then I have no more good name to protect, do I?" For her sisters' sake, that notion really should bother her, but all that mattered was that Tremaine be alive and stay that way.

"You certainly do," Addy retorted, "but I'll go with you."

The other women were on their feet in an instant. "I'll give Edward the benefit of my opinion regarding dueling," Susannah said, tossing poor *Titus* in the direction of the sofa.

"I'll bribe George," Kirsten added. "He was present when Edward issued his challenge. Men never tell us the parts that matter, and Della says she saw George in a compromising situation with a certain comely widow."

"Nicholas can't go," Leah said, "but he'll want specifics. Who was the widow, Kirsten?"

Nita was fairly certain who the widow was. She did not, however, recognize this band of angels intent on protecting her from the very bad news that might have resulted from the duel.

"You needn't accompany me," she said. "If I'm to be ruined, the less you're seen in my company, the better."

"You're not ruined," Addy said fiercely.

"I agree with Addy." Leah, as the countess and highest title in the shire, could speak with authority. "Nicholas will dissuade anybody from discussing today's events. Men must be allowed their silly crotchets, after all. Ladies, we'll need our boots and cloaks."

"Nita should bring her medical bag," Della said. "Duels can get messy."

"Surely not—" Nita began, because that bag was an item of loathing among her family members and had figuratively cost her a future with Tremaine.

"Horton will be there," Kirsten added. "And Edward thinks of himself as a great rural sportsman. I don't doubt Mr. St. Michael is an excellent shot."

Good God, Horton, with his dirty instruments and complete disregard for the patient's pain. Terror for Tremaine threatened to choke Nita where she stood.

"Fetch your bag," Susannah said.

"Get your cloak," Leah said, "and I'll fetch the medical bag for you."

George Haddonfield was apparently a connoisseur of good whisky. Tremaine had nearly drained that worthy fellow's flask before William shuffled to a halt. The horse stood placidly outside the Belle Maison kitchen door while Tremaine enjoyed another dram. Excellent stuff. Slowed down the cold creeping over a man from within.

"I'll find a footman," George said, swinging off his gelding. "Don't, for God's sake, fall out of your saddle. Nicholas might even be about, and if he can help, that's one less source of gossip—"

The kitchen door opened and a half-dozen women in cloaks and scarves emerged.

"The jury has assembled," Tremaine murmured. "Ladies, I apologize for my condition. Bit messy, you see. Mourning the end of a fine boot and a finer engagement."

"He's tipsy," George muttered. "Nash fired early and St. Michael got the worst of it, but you lot aren't to know any of that."

"Stone sober," Tremaine retorted cheerily. "But, alas, not in any condition to dismount unaided."

"I'll lead the horses to the stable," Susannah said. "Leah, let Nicholas know Mr. St. Michael has survived his ordeal. If I'm not back by noon, I've gone to kill Edward Nash."

"You can't kill him," Addy Chalmers said—what was *she* doing among the assemblage? "He's Mary's uncle. I'll go with you."

"Get Mr. St. Michael into the kitchen." Nita spoke with the crisp dispatch of a field marshal confident of victory. Pain hadn't robbed

Tremaine of consciousness, but the relief of knowing Nita would tend him nearly put him into a swoon.

"I'm sorry to bother you, my lady," Tremaine said as George more or less pulled him off his horse. "Hadn't meant to impose, but Horton was there with his dirty knife. Paracelsus would disapprove."

"I would disapprove," Nita said. The damned woman was smiling, also crying, as she slipped an arm around Tremaine's waist. "Slowly, George, and once we get Mr. St. Michael out of the cold, his bleeding might become profuse."

Tremaine's heartache was already profuse. "You may remove my leg if you like," he said as he was half carried into the kitchen. "You are already in possession of my heart."

"A tipsy shepherd poet," George murmured. "Where do you want him?"

"On the table. I'll need blankets, more whisky, quantities of sugar, bandages, and as much prayer as you can muster."

"What about my heart?" Tremaine asked as he was propped against the kitchen worktable. "Do you need that as well?"

Nita held a flask up to his mouth, more of George Haddonfield's lovely brew. Tremaine dutifully gulped but fought off a growing mental fog, because he needed an answer to his question.

"Shall you hold on to my heart, Lady Nita?"

"You're tipsy, Mr. St. Michael, and weak from loss of blood. Right now, I'll hold on to your leg while George cuts your boot off."

Tremaine might have importuned Lady Nita further, but she kissed him, a sweet, nighty-night kiss that boded well for his heart. She'd also called him Mr. St. Michael in the brisk tones that had ever been a cause for good cheer. When George started peeling off the abused boot, an agony of fire shot through Tremaine that did not bode at all well for his leg.

He let the darkness take him, because if anybody could restore him to adequate health, it was Nita Haddonfield. Though—alas for true love—that admission rather shot the other boot off of Tremaine's objections to her medical calling.

Tremaine St. Michael had been lucky. Edward's shot had apparently hit a rock and scraped a deep furrow in the victim's flesh, though the bullet had spent most of its force before striking Tremaine.

The scar would be substantial, and the blood loss had been as well, but if infection didn't set in, the patient would recover.

Nita was a ferocious opponent of infection. No ammunition, not Cook's hoard of white sugar, not her stores of honey, not George's last bottle of what he called "winter whisky," was too precious to spare in the fight against infection.

"I've seen an infected toenail carry a man off," Nita said, speaking around a lump of fear that was her constant affliction of late. "It wasn't a peaceful death either. Not for the patient, not for his family."

"And not for you," Nicholas replied. He'd accosted Nita outside Tremaine's room, and all Nita wanted was to get back to her patient's side.

"Nicholas, if you lecture me now on the inappropriateness of my medical endeavors, I will kick you where it hurts." Though Nita was too tired and heartsick to kick anybody very hard, and in fairness, Nicholas himself had shown her that maneuver when she'd turned twelve.

"What if we have a civil discussion?" Nick countered, taking the tea tray from Nita and setting it on the sideboard across the corridor. "What if you allow the head of your family and your dearest, sweetest brother a moment of your time? St. Michael won't be dancing down the lane anytime soon, Nita, and you haven't shown up at a meal for three days."

"You are my nosiest and most bothersome brother." Nick was also the largest, strongest Haddonfield, and when he settled his arms around Nita, she could do nothing but accept his embrace.

"How is the patient?" he asked.

Nicholas always smelled good, though since his marriage, his scent bore an undernote of lily of the valley. Leah's influence, no doubt.

"Resting quietly." Nita gave Nick the medical euphemism for "as well as can be expected," but it was also the truth. Tremaine seemed to realize that rest was an ally, or perhaps years of racketing about in pursuit of trade had worn him out in ways that didn't show.

Nick steered Nita to a window seat at the end of the corridor. The chill of a winter afternoon rolled off the glass at her back, while Nick wedged his warmth against her side.

"What does resting quietly mean, Nita?"

"It means, so far, infection hasn't set in, though a bullet wound can fester slowly, depending on its depth and where it strikes. If the bone is shattered, then significant damage is done to the surrounding tissue, and—"

Nick kissed her forehead. "Have a care for my luncheon, Sister. Will St. Michael come right?"

"I don't know." The fear was in Nita's belly too, like a wasting disease. Mostly, the fear was in her heart. "I *never* know. I think the patient is fading, and then for no reason, they're up and about, begging for a strong cup of tea and wishing me to perdition. I think surely, surely, another patient is mending well, and they slip away in the middle of a morning."

Nick's arm settled around Nita's shoulders, a comforting weight. "Shall I ask Fairly to have a look at him?"

Nick was asking, not ordering, demanding, fussing, or complaining. He'd charged into the kitchen as Nita had examined the wound to Tremaine's leg, turned white as new-fallen snow, and abruptly quit the room. Since then, he'd been quiet, his expression considering rather than put-upon.

And Nick had made an excellent suggestion.

David, Viscount Fairly, was a neighbor who lived two hours' ride across the shire. Fairly was also a physician trained in Scotland, where the best and most forward-thinking practices were taught. Nobody had dared suggest consulting with Horton—Nita would soundly kick any who mentioned *that* name—but Fairly was a different resource entirely.

"A fine notion," Nita said, the fear easing marginally. "Please have the viscount pay a call. I know he doesn't practice, but we've had a few discussions, and he doesn't reject my ideas simply because of my gender."

"A man of sense, is our David. I am a man of sense too."

Nick was a man of heart. "Whatever you're about to say, Nicholas, just say it. I'm too tired to shout at you and too worried to indulge in verbal fisticuffs."

"Glad to know it, because my countess has gone several rounds with me lately, and I did not emerge victorious. Here is what I need to say: I am proud of you, Nita Haddonfield, for the convictions you put ahead of your own comfort and convenience, for your courage, for your ferocious appetite for knowledge. St. Michael will soon be back on his mettle, hatching schemes regarding my sheep and speaking in that execrable poetic dialect for the amusement of all. His good health is exclusively your accomplishment."

"The good Lord alone—" Nita said, trying to rise. Nick gently pulled her back to his side. "The good Lord and my dear sister. You think I strut about here, dandling my heir and plaguing my sisters, but I've also done some listening and some nosing about the village. Horton is a disgrace, and nobody uses him if they can help it. They all turn to you, the wealthy, the poor, the hopeless, and you never turn them down. Do you know what we call this behavior?"

"Stupid," Nita said. "You've called it dangerous, mutton-headed, headstrong—"

Nick had shouted those words and more at her, and while Nita needed to return to Tremaine's side, Nick would not let her go until he'd said his fraternal piece.

"All very true," Nick said, "but it's also *honorable*, Bernita mine. To look after those who can't look after themselves, to attend to duty rather than convenience. You have reminded me of what honor requires, and I'm grateful."

That last word—*grateful*—wasn't one Nita heard very often. "Is that an apology?"

Nick removed his arm. "Not quite, and this is where my countess and I differ. Shall we look in on your patient?"

Nita shot to her feet, then grasped Nick's arm to steady herself.

"You need to eat something," Nick groused. "Something more than tea and ginger biscuits."

"I do, but about this apology?"

"I'm not apologizing for worrying over your safety and health, Nita. I can't help myself. I worry about those whom I love, and you are among that number. You always will be. If that's a kicking offense, then have at me. Where I *do* apologize is for failing to respect your abilities and the passion with which you share them. For that, I apologize heartily."

This conversation—a conversation, not an argument—was important. The part of Nita that loved Nicholas knew that. The rest of her dreaded what she'd find when they entered Tremaine's room. He had been resting quietly when she'd left him only moments earlier, and yet he might be fevered or worse upon her return.

She worried for Tremaine, despite all sense to the contrary, as Nick worried about her—*as her entire family had worried about her for years*.

"I worry," Nita said, hand on the latch. "God knows I worry. I cannot blame you for the same trait." Nita could, rather, commiserate with Nick for the helplessness and anxiety that caring produced.

"He'll be fine," Nick said, opening the door. "Bothersome, scheming, and he talks funny, but St. Michael will be fine."

CHAPTER EIGHTEEN

Nita had brought reinforcements in the form of her brother the earl, though she was thankfully without the damned tea tray. A man who needed assistance getting to the chamber pot had reason to view the tea tray askance.

"St. Michael, you're awake."

"Astute as always, Bellefonte."

"If you want to continue to make free with my nightshirts, you'd best wake up your manners," the earl retorted, taking a seat on the bed. The jostling produced only discomfort, not the agony it might have a few days ago.

"I forgot the tea tray," Nita said.

Bother the damned tray. "I wouldn't mind a ginger biscuit or two," Bellefonte commented, apparently getting comfortable on Tremaine's bed.

Nita scurried out, though to Tremaine, she looked increasingly worn and worried. Also dear. Inexpressibly dear.

"I sent Nash off to his uncle," Bellefonte said, the pretense of genial bonhomie disappearing as Nita left the room. "I'm the magistrate, and I've become creative when the need to lay information is upon me—public drunkenness, attempted manslaughter, slander, assault...care to add any more?"

A weight lifted from Tremaine's mind. Nita should not have to tolerate a weasel living in the same neighborhood. Then too, Nash's own safety probably required that he bide a distance from Lady Susannah.

"Elsie Nash might have some useful thoughts about the handling of her son's inheritance," Tremaine said.

"My thanks, and Nash ought to thank you as well. Susannah's sentiments regarding her former suitor defy genteel description, thank the Deity. Nita, Elsie Nash, and Addy Chalmers are also out of charity with him."

As was Tremaine. A decent pair of boots cost a pretty penny, but Nita Haddonfield's good name was worth more than all the sheep in Britain.

"Nita cares for *you*," Bellefonte said, scratching his back against the bedpost the way a horse might use a stout tree. "I care for Nita, therefore I'm having a competent physician come around to look you over."

"Not Horton," Tremaine said, visions of a dirty scalpel rising from his nightmares. "Nita won't stand for the insult."

"I'm not sure what to do about Horton, but he'll not set a chubby foot on my property, lest Nita fillet me. You're managing?" Bellefonte inquired with carefully casual commiseration.

"I'm planning my apology," Tremaine said. "Lady Nita saved my leg, if not my life."

"Never easy, planning an apology. I'll leave you to it." Bellefonte patted Tremaine on the knee and rose.

"I could use a footman if you find one free." Or Tremaine could hobble behind the privacy screen on his own, bashing about like a drunken bullock along the way.

"Nita spikes the tea with laudanum," Bellefonte said. "That's why you're a bit unsteady. The leg will be fine or Nita would have relieved you of it."

"Good to know." Also awful to know, because Bellefonte was no longer teasing. Tremaine sank against the pillows, awaiting torture by ginger biscuit and spiked tea. He went back to work planning his apology but was distracted by the disturbing fact that Nita might well have taken a saw to him—a clean, sharp saw—had his injury been of a different nature.

She would have hated the entire ordeal but tended to Tremaine to the best of her ability anyway. When it was Tremaine's life in jeopardy, he'd relied on Nita to use the very skills he'd expected her to deny others. A lifetime of apologies might not suffice, though he'd start with one good one and hope for a miracle.

The fourth day of Tremaine's convalescence saw a change in Nita's patient.

"What are you doing out of bed?" she asked.

"Hobbling slowly," Tremaine retorted. "Impersonating my grandfather when his rheumatism acts up. No wonder wounded soldiers are eager to have at their enemies once more. Marching about is tedious, but a bullet wound is a damned inconvenience."

A recovering patient was a damned inconvenience too, because as soon as he was hale, Tremaine might well be on his way.

"Please sit," Nita said, when what she wanted to do was put an arm around Tremaine's waist and wrestle him back to bed.

"I shall sit on the sofa," he replied, wobbling off in that direction. George or some other traitorous brother had provided a pair of crutches. Tremaine's skill with them suggested this treason had been committed at least a day ago.

"You may sit where you please, sir, but you'll prop up your leg."

Tremaine looked like he wanted to argue, a sure sign of recovery. His hair was combed, and his dressing gown neatly belted, though his feet were bare.

"I hate being invalided," he growled, "and hate more that I've prevailed on you to tend me."

As if Nita would allow anybody else near him. "I won't be tending you much longer. Lord Fairly says your wound is healing beautifully."

"Nonsense. An unsightly rip in a man's flesh cannot be beautiful. Would you please sit beside me?"

A rip in a man's flesh could be gorgeous, when little heat or swelling accompanied it, the scent lacked any hint of putrefaction, and the edges were already beginning to knit.

Nita set a hassock before Tremaine and took a seat beside him rather than argue.

"Nicholas let Edward Nash escape to his uncle's," she said. "I wanted to shoot Edward in the leg and leave him to Horton's tender mercies."

That sentiment was hardly to her credit as a healer, though Nita's sisters, Leah, and Addy shared it with her. Susannah's quotations were recently all drawn from the Bard's bloodiest tragedies.

Tremaine took Nita's hand. "I saw the knife Horton intended to use on me. George was to cut off my muddy boot with it, then pass it over to Horton."

"I'm surprised you remember that." Did Tremaine also recall telling Nita that his heart was already in her keeping? Nita would never forget those words.

A silence took up residence where Nita's heartfelt confession should be. She held on to Tremaine's hand and tried to recall how to begin her well-rehearsed speech.

"I was wrong."

They'd spoken the exact same words at the exact same moment. Tremaine kissed Nita's knuckles, though he was also trying to hide a puzzled smile.

"Any woman who rescues me from certain butchery or worse when I've castigated her for rescuing others can be as wrong as she pleases," he said. "Nita, can you forgive me?"

She leaned into Tremaine's solid warmth—she was on his good side, not that it mattered.

"There's nothing to forgive, Tremaine. Nothing."

Tremaine's arm came around her shoulders. "I said I would not marry you if you persisted with your medical activities, then I expected you to save my life. How is this not gross arrogance, selfishness, bullheadedness, and a reason to hate a man?"

How was it not entirely understandable—now? But where to start? "My family loves me."

"I love you too, lass." A grumpy disclosure, not a declaration.

Nita waited, because the fingers stroking her cheek were as gentle as Tremaine's tone was gruff.

"Dueling is a stupid, reckless, violent exercise in lunacy," he said, "but it can sort out a man's priorities. As I marched off the steps in that clearing, I did not think about commerce. I did not consider how to market merino wool most profitably. I did not wish I'd written one last letter to my factors in the Midlands."

Nita slid her hand inside Tremaine's dressing gown, needing to feel the beat of his heart beneath her palm. "I hope you paid attention to the counting, sir."

"More than Nash did, apparently, but that's irrelevant. What's relevant is that memories of you and hope for a future with you filled my heart and my mind as I paced toward my fate. You, Nita Haddonfield. You matter more to me than my fears that you'll be carried off by some dread disease. If I could have five years with you, or five minutes with you, *why would I deny myself that joy?*"

"Because you're not a fool," she said, kissing his wrist. "I've had a change in perspective, Tremaine."

"As long as you remain in my arms, you may explain this change in perspective."

"Addy Chalmers brought us word of the duel. Ladies aren't supposed to know of such things, but we often do. I had my bag in hand and was on my way to the woods when George brought you home."

"I recall a *posse comitatus* of your sisters, the countess, and Addy. They wouldn't have let you go alone."

"I understand that now," Nita said. "They want to protect me. My siblings aren't angry at me for tending others; they are *frightened* for me. When Addy told us you were to face Nash over a pair of pistols, I was terrified. I could not think; I could not move. I could not even pray, Tremaine. *You could have died.*"

Nita had been terrified, paralyzed, mute, and horrified, even as she'd silently bargained with the Almighty. *Please, keep the man I love safe.* How did soldiers' families deal with that terror day after day, year after year?

How had Nita's family dealt with it?

"What could possibly daunt your bottomless courage?" Tremaine asked. Was he growing tired?

"I haven't much courage," Nita said. "Nicholas says I'm honorable because I help where I can, but I'm not brave, Tremaine. Much about medicine scares me or disgusts me. I can admit that now."

To him.

"You never appear scared or disgusted. You appear determined and capable. You're also very pretty."

He truly was on the mend, thank heavens. "Have you been drinking your tea?"

"No, love. Not after your brother told me you spike it. Tell me more about being afraid, Nita."

Yes, tell him. Tell him that too, because it made all the difference. "When I snatch up my bag and march off to a sickroom, you are *terrified* for me. I see that now. Not annoyed, not affronted. I grab my medicinals the way you fellows take up your dueling pistols, and I march off against an opponent who doesn't wait for the count, who observes no protocol, who kills entire families without even alluding to concepts of honor or reason. You are not being pigheaded or backward or narrow-minded when you ask me to give up seeing patients; you are as frightened as I am."

As frightened as Nita had been for years.

Tremaine passed Nita a handkerchief. She'd soon have a collection with his initials embroidered on them.

"I love you," he said, kissing her ear. "I love your kisses and your passion, your polite reserve, your humor, stubbornness, and courage. I want very much to marry you, Nita Haddonfield. If that means I send you off to do battle with the plague itself, I still want to marry you."

"I *don't* want to do battle with the plague," Nita wailed softly. "I want to marry you, to have great, fat, healthy babies with you, to scold you for letting our children spoil their supper with ginger biscuits.

"But people know I'll help," she went on, "or try to help, and Mama told them all I have a gift. So they call upon me when there's illness or injury in the house, and if I don't go, who will? Horton is backward and bumbling, and even he senses that his knowledge is badly out-of-date. I can't leave people to suffer or die when I might help, but I won't lose you, Tremaine. I cannot."

Nita fell silent when she wanted to rant. She could have lost him to Edward Nash's pride, stubbornness, and shortsightedness. She could not bear it if she lost him to her own.

Nita was a sweet, warm, tired—and *upset* weight against Tremaine's side. Every time he'd surfaced from his laudanum dreams, she'd been by his bed. Often he'd found her hand in his, and sometimes she'd fallen asleep like that—curled over in her chair by his bed, her hand wrapped around his.

"I quizzed Lord Fairly as he thumped and poked at me." Tremaine had had commercial dealings with Fairly several years back without ever learning of the man's medical abilities.

"About sheep?"

"Not about sheep. No titled Englishman knows more about sheep than I do." Tremaine had amused her. God willing, he'd amuse Nita often in the coming years.

"Go on, Tremaine. Would you like a ginger biscuit?"

"Please God, not another ginger biscuit. Fairly is something of an expert on the export of medical treatises and instruments."

"He's quite knowledgeable," Nita said. "Also kind. When I can't find a reference in English to a disease or herbal remedy, he often has something in his library."

Fortunately, the estimable Lord Fairly was happily married, else Tremaine might have questioned his generous literary motives.

"Fairly spent his early childhood in Scotland and returned there for some of his medical training. He's skilled as both a surgeon and a physician, unlike your Dr. Horton."

Nita shifted, so she straddled Tremaine's lap. "Can you be comfortable like this?"

No, he could *not.* "Cuddle up, love. My leg is fine and I've missed you."

She settled closer, and Tremaine forgot what he'd been bleating about—ah, the ever-helpful Lord Fairly. "I asked Fairly to find us a pair of physicians to open up a practice here in Haddondale. At least one of them must be young and recently educated. The other can be older, provided his training exceeds the theoretical foundation given to most English physicians. Will you interview these fellows, put them through their paces?"

Nita kissed him. "I love you. We need a good midwife too."

Apology accepted, apparently—proposal as well—and she'd antic-ipated Tremaine's very next point.

"Consider it done, madam. You will interview her too."

Nita tucked herself agreeably closer, such that Tremaine endured a throbbing of the blood in a location other than his wound.

"If only you could find a replacement for Vicar. He delights in carping about a woman's pain being her just deserts for leading Adam astray. Makes me wonder about the gout he complains of at such length."

Tremaine saved puzzling over the theology of gout for some other day. "Your brother mentioned Vicar's increasing age to Fairly, and I heard them discussing an in-law of Fairly's as a possible replacement. Nita, you do know that under this dressing gown, I'm wearing nothing but a nightshirt?"

She sat up. "You're injured, Tremaine. You mustn't overdo."

At least she was crestfallen to deliver that opinion. "I must contradict you. Lord Fairly was clear that I should resume normal activities as soon as possible, allowing pain to inform my choices. I'm in pain, Nita. Will you, please, relieve my distress yet again?"

"We'll marry, won't we, Tremaine?" She unbelted his robe as she put the question to him. "I've been a touch queasy in the last day or two, which makes no sense, but I do want to marry you. I'm done battling contagion, Tremaine. Let your physicians duel with that reprobate. I'll attend the occasional lying-in, I'm sure, and I can always be counted on to deal with injuries—my goodness."

A part of Tremaine was showing off its exuberant good health and high spirits.

"I've missed you," he said again. "Might I hope you've missed me?"

"Desperately," Nita said, rising and locking the door. "Do you still have that special license?"

"I assuredly do," Tremaine said as Nita resumed her place on his lap, and he got to work on the drawstring of her bodice. "We'll find a property nearby, and—"

Nita kissed him to silence and then to bliss upon bliss and then to a lovely, sleepy embrace, during which Tremaine considered names for their firstborn, when in the past, he might have counted sheep.

EPILOGUE

"The greatest plague ever to bedevil mortal man," Tremaine said, "the greatest threat to his peace, the most fiendish source of undeserved humility is *his brother-in-law,* and titled brothers-in-law are the worst of a bad lot."

Tremaine's boots thumped across the carpet of Belle Maison's library, his pace, to Nita's ear, solid and even, though only weeks ago he'd been brought to bed with a bullet wound.

"Nicholas frets," she said. "It's his nature. He can't help it, and marriage and fatherhood have made him worse."

Impending fatherhood had made Tremaine worse too—also better, at least in terms of tenderness, quiet kisses, caresses, and the pace with which he pursued his commercial activities.

"But why did Bellefonte muster the entire regiment to see us off?" Tremaine sounded Scottish all the time now. "One likes a bit of dignity about one's leave-takings."

He marched to a halt before a tall window and held out a hand to Nita. "Finally, the last of the recruits arrives."

"The Holland bulbs along the south-facing garden wall are sprouting" Nita said. A woman in anticipation of motherhood appreciated new life in all its brave splendor. She leaned into her husband, wondering how she'd ever managed, how she'd endured, without his love to sustain her.

"Are you certain you want to take this journey with me?" he asked, tucking her against his side. "I've wondered how my households ever functioned, how I managed, without you to take matters in hand."

This happened frequently—their thoughts ran in tandem, much as Tremaine slept in tandem with her.

"We will make a wedding journey of it," Nita said. "Nicholas has assured me the house we've chosen will be entirely refurbished by the time we return. George will steward your acres, and Digby will aid him. I want to meet your grandfather, Tremaine, and he apparently has demanded to meet me."

Demanding family no longer bothered Nita as it had prior to her marriage, though she'd been happily busy establishing her household with Tremaine. Nicholas had insisted on a family gathering prior to Tremaine and Nita's departure for Scotland and points distant, even summoning Beckman and Ethan and all their family.

The last time they'd been together had been the old earl's funeral, and Nita agreed with Nicholas—better to gather for joy than sorrow. Better to assure Tremaine he'd married not only a loving wife, but also an entire clan of loving, if bothersome, in-laws.

George and Elsie had come over from Stonebridge, which George had purchased from Edward for the sum of Edward's debts. Edward was rumored to be the elderly baronet's whipping boy, though even the post of charity relation hadn't lessened Edward's fondness for gin.

"You're thinking about him again," Tremaine said, kissing Nita's temple. "You'll upset my son with such unworthy ruminations."

Nita was carrying a girl. She knew this through some instinct foreign to modern medicine. The Doctors Macallan—a pair of brothers from Aberdeen—laughed at her prediction, but their sister—an experienced midwife—pointed out Nita had as much chance of being right as wrong.

The village had no sooner stopped gossiping about Dr. Horton's retirement than Vicar had announced his decision to join households with a brother living outside Bath. Lord Fairly's brother-in-law, a fellow named Daniel Banks, was to assume the Haddondale pulpit within the month.

"George and Elsie live the closest and yet they are the last to arrive," Nita said as George escorted his wife past a flower bed where daffodils still slumbered beneath cold earth. "Why do you suppose that is?"

"Mrs. George Haddonfield has developed delicate digestion of a morning," Tremaine said. "One is burdened by such confidences in the middle of an otherwise unremarkable game of cards for no earthly reason I can fathom."

In other words, Tremaine was overjoyed for George and Elsie, as Nita was.

"Mind your enthusiasm for the topic, Tremaine, or they might name the baby after you."

As Nita crossed the garden on her husband's arm, Tremaine peered down at her. "Do you think George might name a boy after me? Bellefonte will be jealous. I rather like the idea, though 'Tremaine' might be an awkward name for a girl."

He was enthralled with the notion, clearly, and when Nita gave birth to a daughter on a lovely autumn morning, Tremaine suggested the child be named Nicolette St. Michael.

The girl's siblings—of which there was eventually an entire herd —in fact called her Dr. Bo Peep. Nicky St. Michael, much to her parents' pride, became highly skilled in treating any and all ailments and injuries commonly suffered by sheep.

TO MY DEAR READERS

I so enjoyed reading through Tremaine and Nita's story again, and re-acquainting myself with the denizens of Haddondale and Belle Maison. I hope you like the revised cover too, though I've set myself a challenge finding art for Daniel and Will that I will like as much.

In addition to buffing up my backlist titles, I'm also adding to the front list.

Look for **Yuletide Gems** in your local library's ebook collection on or around September 27. This is a Regency novella duet written with writin' buddy Christi Caldwell, wherein we celebrate the joys of the holiday season—and the joys of libraries! If you cannot find this title at the library, you can buy it from our author **web stores**, (and international readers can find it on Kobo). We do not plan a retail release for these stories until the 2024 holiday season, (and yes, we will have a print version for 2023).

November will see the launch of **Miss Dauntless**, Mischief in Mayfair Book Five. Marcus, Earl of Tremont, and Mrs. Matilda Merridew take a fancy to each other, but then Matilda's long-buried past rises up to complicate matters. I had such fun with this one!

If you've been following my Lady Violet Mysteries, look for

Lady Violet Says I Do in January 2023. And if you're an audio book fan, please know that the whole Lady Violet series is being released on audio, and **Lady Violet Investigates** is already available.

Wheee!

I mean... Happy reading!

Grace Burrowes